Veteran Avenue

Veteran Avenue

MARK PEPPER

URBANE
Publications

urbanepublications.com

First published in Great Britain in 2017
by Urbane Publications Ltd
Suite 3, Brown Europe House, 33/34 Gleaming Wood Drive,
Chatham, Kent ME5 8RZ
Copyright © Mark Pepper, 2017

A CIP catalogue record for this book is available
from the British Library.

ISBN 978-1-911583-31-8
MOBI 978-1-911583-33-2
EPUB 978-1-911583-32-5

Design and Typeset by Michelle Morgan

Cover by The Invisible Man

Printed and bound by CPI Group (UK) Ltd, Croydon, CR0 4YY

urbanepublications.com

For my daughter, Jade.
Since you, I know why I'm here.

Acknowledgements

Firstly, and for obvious reasons, I would like to sincerely thank Matthew Smith of Urbane Publications. He is a rarity among publishers; someone who treats authors with respect and as sentient human beings.

I also owe a huge debt of gratitude to my old RADA classmate and fellow Urbane author, Mark Mayes, for tracking me down online and then pointing me in Matthew's direction with an optimism that verged on psychic.

Lastly, as ever, thanks to my wife, Jeannifer, and my family, for their love and support.

Chapter 1

1978

He watched the ball of dust caused by his father's abrupt stop roll along the bumpy track and slowly disappear into the perfect August blue. Listening to the burbling engine of their rented Ford sedan, little John Frears let his eyes wander over their accidental location.

They were near the path of the Oregon Trail, the route west of the early settlers. They had stumbled across an abandoned goldmining town, set in a clearing in a great forest that spread for miles, carpeting the mountains. The undulating earth was covered by scrub, with clusters of silver fir soaring here and there. Ahead was a row of stores and a saloon, their longevity assured by the searing, arid climate. Had the Magnificent Seven galloped into view, guns blazing, John would not have been at all surprised. Further on he could see other buildings, the heart of this deep-shaft mining venture. The largest was three stories of sun-bleached grey wood, dotted with empty black windows. Suffering gentle subsidence, it rose out of a hollow in the ground, topped by a smaller structure that from a distance looked as though it was made of matchsticks. Brightly-rusted iron arms thrust out from its sides, then down into the earth, rigid steel cables taking the strain.

Behind the wheel, Vincent Frears was still scanning left and right.

'Which one's the Holiday Inn?' he said.

His wife Gwen huffed. 'You are such an idiot. I told you not to get off the highway. I knew we'd get lost. God, I can't even see this place on the map.'

'Listen, those timber lorries were a damn menace. What if a log had fallen onto the car? You read about things like that – *couple killed in holiday crush horror.*'

John frowned. In this theoretical tragedy, were his parents assuming his survival or ignoring his existence? No doubt the latter.

'And this is better, is it?' Gwen asked. 'Stuck in the wilderness. No idea how to get back.'

'We drove uphill, so we drive downhill. It's not difficult. We're not lost.'

'So where are all the other sightseers?'

'At all the boring places that everybody else visits. I've brought us on an adventure, my love.'

'You really are an idiot.'

John watched his mother take a swig of warm Coke from her bottle, while his father lit a cigarette and belatedly thought to switch off the ignition. After hours of perpetual engine noise there was now nothing but ticks and pinks, and an almost subliminal rasp of cicadas.

Ten minutes later his parents had shifted, backs to each other, doors open, feet in the dust. With the temperature outside nudging ninety, and the car's interior even hotter, John wanted to get back to the highway and its blissfully speed-cooled air, but until the parental sulk had run its course he knew that wouldn't happen.

He was getting bored and decided a joke was in order.

'Muuuuuuum …'

Had she shown even the slightest acknowledgement of his existence he might not have said it.

'Is that a rattlesnake by your foot?'

His mother shrieked, stepped back on the sill and jumped up inside the car. Unfortunately for her, Vincent had not paid extra to rent a convertible. John had to laugh. His mother half-concussed, it was his father who reacted – a rare show of marital solidarity.

'Stupid bugger!' he said, getting out and yanking his son into the sunshine to deliver a slap that made John's eyes well up and his chin go twitchy. Vincent ducked his head back in the car to see his wife rubbing the crown of her head, and John watched him almost give in to a sympathetic sentiment. Instead, he reached in and grabbed the map off the dash, then marched away to study it under a nearby mountain hemlock, raising puffs of dust as he went.

John hated sulking; adults sulked, and he would be nine next March. With his ear still ringing, he mustered a smile for his sour-faced mother.

'Sorry, Mum.'

She didn't bother to meet his eyes, only managing a grunt.

'Can I go exploring?'

She nodded once and John was dismissed. He had heard it said that if you gave a person enough rope they'd hang themselves. If that were true, then he had already used up more lives than a dead cat and often wondered if he could ever roam far enough to feel the line go taut. Today, he mused whether that might be down a mine shaft or into the belly of a Grizzly. He snatched his Action Man from the rear seat.

'Back in a bit,' he told his mother, to maintain his private illusion that someone cared.

He got out of sight as quickly as possible. The terrain and wild scrub gave him good cover. Under the baking sun he dashed between ancient mining machinery, through juniper and sagebrush, from one doorway to another. He was itching to explore, to perhaps find a forgotten nugget of gold, but he didn't dare set foot across a threshold. This was a ghost town and he was frightened. He could feel a rotten quality about the place, as though it still had some dying left to do.

On the far perimeter of the clearing, where the forest rose up and claimed the land back from transient mankind, John discovered some log cabins stretching away into the cool murk of the trees. Clutching his Action Man, he ran in circles and figures of eight, whooping like a native Nez Perce Indian working up to scalp a few cheeky settlers from the east who had come to plunder his birthright. Weaving complex shapes among the live trunks and dead lumber, he skirted closer to the obstacles until the wood began to graze his bare arms, raising wheals that began to speck with blood.

Then he hurtled around a cabin and collided with something that hadn't been there on his previous circuit. Dazed, he stepped back and stared up at a grinning face.

The man was rake thin, with fine, greying hair, which was in need of a trim. John thought he looked about the same age as his grandad back in England. He was wearing jeans and a blue check shirt with the sleeves rolled up. And at the end of his sinewy right arm, dangling by his side, twig-like fingers were curled around the butt of a black pistol.

'Whoa there, son,' said the man with a gentleness John rarely heard from his parents.

'Sorry,' John said, transfixed by the gun.

'No problem. Are you hurt? Didn't mean you to run into me.'

'I'm okay,' John said, his face dripping sweat onto the bed of old fir cones and pine needles at his feet.

'How 'bout your arms?'

John inspected the bloody scratch marks on his skin.

'Sting a bit,' he admitted, panting.

'I bet.' The man tucked the gun down his waist. 'Where're your folks?'

'Are you a ghost?'

'No, son,' the man said with a smile. 'Not yet. So ... you're English. Didn't expect that. Got a name?'

'John.'

'John,' the man repeated, and savored it for a moment. 'I like that. Strong, no nonsense. And how old are you, John?'

'I'll be nine next March.'

The man nodded. 'That's good,' he said, and extended his right hand. 'Well, John, I'm Chuck, and I'm real glad to make your acquaintance.'

They shook hands, and John's eyes kept going back to the gun.

'Does this scare you?' Chuck asked, tapping the butt of the pistol.

'No.' Although this looked like a worst-case-scenario stranger-encounter, John sensed no danger. Indeed, of the three adults in the vicinity at that moment he felt that Chuck offered by far the greatest wealth of love.

'Should do, John. Ain't a toy.'

John shrugged; he was too young to enter the firearms debate.

'Your GI Joe own a gun?'

'My what?'

'Your doll.'

'He's not a doll, he's an Action Man,' John said, holding the plastic figure to his chest.

'Okay, no offense,' Chuck said with a laugh. 'We call them GI Joes over here.'

'Oh. I left his gun in the car.'

Chuck gave a mock scowl. 'Gun in the car, you say? That ain't much use. Soldier's gotta keep his weapon with him. First rule of combat.'

'Are you a soldier then?'

The smile faded. 'No, son. Not a soldier, not a ghost.'

'Then why do you have a gun?'

Chuck's eyes seemed to mist briefly, as though a poignant image had blown across them. He looked pained as he searched for an explanation and appeared no more satisfied when he finally gave one.

'It's a keepsake, I guess.'

'A what?'

'Uh … a souvenir,' Chuck said, and was clearly even more disturbed by this description. He stared off into the forest but his focus was a world away.

'Can I hold it?' John asked, breaking the man's reverie.

'The gun?' Chuck shook his head. 'Like I said: ain't a toy.'

'Please. I promise I won't shoot anything.'

Chuck sighed. 'Well, I guess if I make it safe …'

He pulled the gun from his jeans and pressed a button just rear of the trigger, making the magazine click out a half inch from the butt, which he then removed completely. He worked the slide and ejected the round still in the chamber, pushed it back into the top of the clip, popped the clip safely in his shirt pocket, de-cocked the empty gun and offered it to John.

Awed, John took the weight of it in his small hands.

'Wow,' he said. 'Will it kill someone?'

'Stone dead.'

'What sort is it?' he asked, turning the pistol over in his hands.

'Smith and Wesson, Mark Twenty-Two, Model 0, self-loading nine millimeter.'

'Wow.' He pointed it around the forest and made shooting noises at the trees.

After a few seconds Chuck said, 'That's enough,' and beckoned for the gun to be returned. 'And if that's the first and last time you touch one of these things, it'll still be one time too many.' He didn't bother to reinsert the clip, merely tucked the unloaded weapon down the small of his back and lowered himself to his haunches. 'Now, you gotta return the favor,' he said, raising a finger to point at John's toy.

Ordinarily, no one got to hold his precious Action Man. Other people tended to angle his limbs into rather unmilitary positions and twist his head so it faced backwards. But in this instance John willingly presented it for inspection and Chuck gratefully accepted. He cradled the Action Man upright in two open palms, leaving the arms and legs at attention and the head face forward. Head bowed, Chuck lightly brushed a thumb over the scaled-down crew-cut.

'Did you have one once?' John asked.

After a moment, Chuck replied with the slightest nod, and a strand of his fine hair fell across his forehead. John waited patiently for his toy to be returned but Chuck didn't move. Another long strand of hair swished down, then a dark spot appeared on the miniature battle jacket. John checked the tip of Chuck's nose for a trickle of sweat but it was dry. Another drop of moisture splashed on the tunic and soaked in, then a third, followed by a steady succession of drips. John bent at the knees and dipped his head so he could see Chuck's face. He watched as the tears fell from his eyes, now squeezed tight shut, and sensed he should let whatever was happening run its course. The uniform was soon a shade darker.

Eventually, Chuck sniffed and began chortling quietly – staccato bursts of breath through his nostrils. He took a swatch of his shirt front and wiped his eyes, and, when he looked up, both the laughter and the tears were gone. His eyes were blank and bloodshot.

'Why are you sad?' John asked.

Chuck managed a glimmer of a smile, and handed John his Action Man.

'You look after him. He's a fine soldier.'

John regarded the small figure. In the intense heat, the material was already lightening to its true color.

Chuck raised himself from squatting and adopted a more serious attitude. 'John, I need you to come some place with me. Take about a half hour.'

John nodded eagerly.

'How 'bout your folks. They expecting you back soon?'

'They don't care,' John said, unconsciously rubbing his recently-slapped ear.

'Sure they do.'

'They smack me.'

'Ah, that don't mean they don't love you.'

'They smack me a lot,' John said, brimming.

Chuck responded by hunkering down again and pulling John into a hug. John shut his eyes and wrapped his arms tightly around Chuck's shoulders, one hand scrunching a handful of lumberjack shirt, the other letting his Action Man dangle on the man's back. The feel of an adult embrace had freed the tears.

'*John!*' A frantic scream from his mother.

John opened his eyes to see his parents standing frozen between two log cabins twenty feet away, and realized they must have seen the pistol tucked down Chuck's waistband next to his spine. Noting their panicked expressions, a cruel part of his brain was glad to see them so agitated. Perhaps Chuck was right – perhaps they really did care.

Breaking the hug, Chuck glanced over his shoulder, straightened up and turned to face them.

'John, come here,' Vincent ordered, his voice both even and fearful.

He stayed where he was.

'*Now.*'

John shook his head.

'Don't be afraid, just walk quickly towards me.'

'I'm not afraid, Dad; you are.'

'Please let him come to me,' Vincent appealed to his son's apparent captor.

John inclined his head to ask permission from his friend.

'Remember we have to go someplace?' Chuck said in response. 'Still happy to come along?'

John nodded. 'We have to go someplace, Dad.' Then he added in his best American accent: 'Take about a half hour.'

Chuck smiled, which Vincent took as a cue to start slowly towards them. But Chuck darted a hand behind his back and produced the gun, holding it by his side, muzzle to the ground. Gwen let out a startled squeal while her husband stopped in his tracks.

'Folks, you must believe me: as God is my witness, I wish no harm on your son. I'd sooner shoot myself.'

Vincent began edging forward again but quickly halted when Chuck raised the Smith & Wesson.

'That said, you try and stop me concluding my business with him, I will consider it open season on you.'

'*Business?*' Vincent echoed. 'What business?'

'I need to borrow your son for a while. Now I appreciate how that must sound, but I will fetch him straight back to you, happy and healthy.'

John was looking up at the gap on the underside of the pistol where the bullets went. It wasn't loaded; he knew that, and he could have let his father know, but he kept it to himself.

'Please don't take him away,' Gwen pleaded.

'It's okay, Mum, I want to go. Don't worry, I'll be all right.'

Chuck offered a reassuring smile. 'If you want to wait here, we'll be back soon. Don't try and follow. That rental of yours ain't got four-wheel drive; can't believe you made it this far.'

'Don't hurt him,' Gwen begged.

'I won't.'

'If you don't bring him back to us ...' Vincent said, his words laced with impotent threat.

'Don't fret none, I will.'

Chuck began retreating through the firs, and John did not need a physical tug or any verbal encouragement to go after him.

Chapter 2

The ten-minute climb passed in silence. The track weaved narrowly along the edge of a deep gorge. John gazed down at the sheer drop to his right, but he wasn't scared. He was simply thrilled to be riding in a genuine American pick-up truck, listening to the V8 grumble under the hood as it powered them up the bumpiest path he had ever traveled. He held onto the door handle with one hand, his Action Man with the other, and he didn't once think to feel sorry for his parents. Perhaps this might teach them a lesson.

Eventually, Chuck turned off into the forest, picking a familiar route through the firs until they shortly arrived at a small log cabin. John noticed to his right a circle of tree stumps and a large pile of dead and withered branches. Chuck turned off the engine.

'Welcome to my home, son. Something on your mind?'

'Why don't you want to live near people?'

'No point. Most people got nothing to say worth a rat's ass – forgive my French.'

'Don't you get lonely? I would, I'd hate it.'

Chuck shrugged. 'You get used to it.' He climbed down from the truck and slammed the door, then went round to the passenger side and opened it. John hopped out and surveyed the cabin.

Compared to the ones in the ghost town, it looked almost brand new. The lumber was fresh, the structure sturdy, the angles sharp and the window glassed in. He glanced at the nearby tree stumps and realized how it had come about.

'Built it myself,' Chuck said, seemingly reading his thoughts. 'When I knew it was God's will I be up here.'

'Gosh,' was all John could say.

Chuck gently snatched him off the ground and sat him on the built-in tool box behind the cab.

'Now, son, in a moment I want you to go inside. On your own.'

John nodded from his high perch.

'When you do, I need you to take a good look around. Understand?'

'Why?'

'Never you mind. You take a real good look around, then you come out and tell me if you seen anything made you feel ... kinda strange. Can you do that?'

'Yes, why?'

Chuck held a finger to John's lips. 'No answers today. Not today. If I'm right, you'll find out in due time.'

'Right about what?' John persisted as Chuck took his finger away.

'No good me telling you, John; don't understand it myself. And maybe I'm mistaken, maybe nothing in it. Might be I'm just an old fool.' But from his expression he didn't appear to think so. He lifted John down to the ground and affectionately ruffled his hair. 'Door's open. Go on in.'

The cabin was one space with a single window in a side wall. The interior timber had been left in its natural state. John thought some white paint would have lifted the gloom and perhaps made Chuck feel a little more cheerful. He made a mental note to suggest it and began to inspect the place, as instructed.

To the left was a kitchen and bathroom area – a round metal hand basin set on two stacked empty crates. On the plank floor beside it were several large plastic containers of various size and color, which he took to be Chuck's water supply. Next to them were a couple of cardboard boxes filled with canned foods and provisions. Chuck did his cooking on a camping stove, hooked up to a gas cylinder. In the middle of the room was a table and chair. On the table was a plate, a cup, a set of cutlery, and an old mining lantern, which appeared to be the only light source when the sun went down. To the right was a camp bed, an alarm clock on an upturned crate, and a box of books. There was no wardrobe, only a suitcase pushed under the bed. It all seemed highly impermanent, as though Chuck had not believed he would be there for very long.

And none of it gave John any untoward emotion, except he couldn't understand how anyone could live so simply. Poor Chuck had nobody to talk to and nothing to do except read. What did he do out here? Did he have a job? John had seen park rangers on his travels but they all wore uniforms and drove official vehicles with fancy crests on the doors. Besides, this was no park, this was a wilderness; you had to get lost just to find the place.

The planks creaked underfoot as he walked the confined space.

'Something kinda strange,' he said to himself, eyes flicking from one spot to another. He stopped and studied several items hanging on the log wall at the foot of the bed: a calendar and three framed photographs.

The August scene on the calendar was one John had viewed first-hand: Crater Lake in the Cascade Mountains. The dates beneath were crossed off up to the thirteenth. Today was the fourteenth. He unhooked the calendar and laid it on the bed, wanting to see how many places he could recognize out of the twelve months. He turned to the front cover, to a river scene and a flowery pronouncement: *Beautiful Oregon - 1978*. He then flipped to January and a snowy Deschutes National Forest.

'Been there,' he said, and noticed the dates below the picture. All of them from the first onwards had been crossed off, the same as August. John quickly checked the months in between. Every day of every month had a line through it, like a countdown. He wondered what on earth Chuck had been waiting for all this time, and how many more days he would need to cross off before it arrived. He checked September, October, November and December to see if Chuck had circled a date he was working towards, like Christmas Day on an advent calendar, but they were unmarked. It didn't make him feel strange, though, only puzzled. He returned the calendar to the month of August and reached it back onto its hook, then began poring over the three photographs.

The first was a black-and-white picture of Chuck as a younger man, arm in arm with a pretty woman in front of a church. John took their clothes and grins as confirmation that they had just been married.

The second was a color shot of a soldier in camouflage uniform, standing against a helicopter with his machine gun. John guessed he was about twenty years old.

The third photograph was also color. A girl about John's age. She was posing on a beach with the ocean behind her. A toothy smile and dark, mischievous eyes, her face framed by an abundance of fiery red curls. The shutter had frozen the flapping of her dress in the breeze, its white material patterned with a repeating motif of Mickey Mouse and Minnie Mouse inside a large love heart.

John would have liked to feel strongly about all this if only for Chuck's sake, but he didn't. He made a final slow scan of the interior, coming full circle to again face the girl in the Disney dress. Nothing affected him in any way he could describe as strange.

'Sorry, Chuck,' he said to the monochrome newlywed on the wall.

'Nothing?'

John jumped and spun around.

'You don't feel nothing?' Chuck said from the doorway, a weary desperation in his voice.

'What am I looking for?'

Chuck didn't answer, simply entered the cabin and sat heavily at the table. He shook his head.

'Jesus H Christ,' he growled.

John frowned. He blamed his parents. If they'd bothered taking him to Sunday School he might have known Jesus had a middle name, and what it was. He quietly approached. Chuck was lost in his thoughts and didn't know he was there, or didn't bother to register the fact. He sat his Action Man on the edge of the table, angling his joints so he balanced on his own, all the time thinking of names that began with H. He could only think of one.

'Is it Harry?' he asked.

Chuck's head flew round, his face shining with delight.

'What's that, son? Is it *Harry*?'

Confused by this sudden mood swing, John felt he needed to take a step back.

'I don't know,' he said carefully. 'Is it?'

Having looked ripe for a screaming *hallelujah*, Chuck now checked himself as he clocked John's complete absence of understanding.

'Is it ... what, son?'

'Is it Jesus Christ's middle name?'

'Is what?'

'Harry.'

'Huh?'

'Jesus *aitch* Christ.'

Chuck closed his eyes and wilted on his seat.

'Oh ... I see. No, son, I don't believe it is.'

'No,' John said, 'I didn't think it could be.'

The cabin felt dry and airless and John's energy was sapped by it. He took his Action Man and went to sit on the camp bed. For five minutes he looked around the room, uselessly hoping that he might see something *kinda strange* so he could announce as much and restore a smile to Chuck's face. He certainly needed one. He hadn't moved. His elbows were planted on the table, his fingers clasped beneath his stubbly chin. Every thirty seconds or so he would turn his head slightly and fix John with a troubled, squinting stare, before shifting his gaze a few feet to the wall – the calendar and the three photographs.

John decided he had to say something; it was getting late and he was beginning to feel concerned for his parents' state of mind.

'Why have you been crossing all those days off the calendar?'

Either Chuck didn't hear or ignored him.

John tried again: 'Who are those people in the pictures?'

Chuck straightened up on his chair, allowing him to remove the Smith & Wesson from his waist. He took the clip from his shirt pocket, stared at the uppermost bullet in the stack for a moment, then inserted it into the gun until it clicked home. He pulled the slide back, exposing a portion of the barrel, and let it spring forward, taking a round into the chamber. The weapon ready to fire, he de-cocked and placed it on the table.

'Chuck ...?' For the first time, John was afraid.

'You did nothing wrong, son, don't think you did. I'm the one to blame, not you. I reckon I've been a fool. I thought the good Lord had smiled on me, showed me a sign, led me into this wilderness for a reason, but it seems I'm just a lonely old man with a head full of stupid ideas.' He stood up, walked over to the foot of the bed and unhooked the picture of the girl in the Disney dress. 'Listen, John, I appreciate you coming up here; you were very brave. And be sure to tell your folks I sincerely regret any distress I may have caused them.' He sat down beside John, creaking and sagging the bed, and began to open the back of the frame.

John watched in silence and gathered this was the item he should have picked out. The photograph was removed and placed in his lap. The flame-haired girl grinned up at him, but still he was unmoved. All he felt was a child's natural curiosity.

'Who is she?' he asked.

'My granddaughter.'

John continued looking at her image as he suspected he was meant to until Chuck spoke again.

'Son, when you go, take this picture with you. Will it fit in your pocket?'

'I'd have to fold it.'

There was no reply, so John glanced sideways and saw Chuck was visibly loath to damage such a treasured possession, regarding the girl's face with great fondness and equal sadness.

'I can keep it in my hand,' John suggested.

'No, I don't want your folks seeing it. They'd take it off you and throw it away. No, you're gonna have to fold it, just … don't put the crease through her face.'

John nodded, folded it carefully and tucked it in the front pocket of his shorts.

'Thank you,' he said politely, although he had no idea why he should want the gift he had just received.

'Like I say, John, I reckon I'm mistaken. But might be you just don't know things yet. Time … time may tell. All I ask is that you keep the picture safe. Don't ever lose it. Keep her safe, John. Promise me.'

'Okay.'

'Say you promise.'

'I promise.'

'Then I believe you,' Chuck said, rising to his feet. 'Now you'd best be getting back. I've kept you way too long as it is.'

John stood up and could feel the shape of the photo against his thigh. He knew he had to go but he was worried about leaving Chuck on his own, so when Chuck crossed the room to shove the gun down his waist again, he quickly slipped his favorite toy beneath the top blanket; a little friend to keep his big friend company.

At the door, Chuck produced the keys from his jeans and hooked a finger at John to follow. He didn't notice the missing Action Man. Together they walked out to the pick-up under the canopy of firs and climbed into the cab.

'Know what?' Chuck said, the key poised at the ignition. 'If I was your pop, I'd have sent your mom back down to the highway, see if she couldn't flag down a state trooper. Which case, I'm apt to get shot if I take you all the way, and that's not something you should see. Think you can find your way through the trees if I stop short? I'll point you in the right direction, you just keep walking.'

'Okay,' John said.

'Got your picture?'

John slapped his pocket. 'Safe and sound.'

Chuck cut the grumbling V8 as soon as they joined the mountain track. It was steep enough to allow them a coasting ride down, so John thought he was just trying to conserve gas. He imagined these big engines fairly guzzled fuel. Then he noticed how Chuck's body was canted to the left, his head half out of the window.

'Chuck –'

'Ssshhh.'

John shifted to high kneeling and thrust his head out his side. He listened for sirens, thinking Chuck was doing the same. What he heard a few minutes later was his parents, screaming and shouting in the forest below for their offspring to answer them. John instinctively drew a breath to respond, but clamped his mouth shut, recalling that Chuck did not want a confrontation.

The stealthily-rolling truck was already slowing. When they came to a halt, Chuck yanked on the handbrake and turned to face his young passenger on the padded bench seat.

'Well, son, this is where we go our separate ways. Remember your promise to me: keep my granddaughter's picture safe. If you are the one, you'll need it. I've done all I'm willing to do. I'm tired. Right or wrong, I ain't gonna wait another day.'

Hearing this abject surrender, John began to panic. He shuffled on his knees across the seat.

'But what are you going to do?'

Chuck shook his head, and John saw in his eyes that the gesture did not indicate he was undecided – quite the opposite: he had made a firm decision; he just wasn't about to share it.

'Where are you going to go?' John asked, ridiculously concerned for this relative stranger.

'I hope some place good.'

'Come with us. We're going home soon.'

Chuck laughed, but not unkindly. 'Reckon your folks might have something to say about that, don't you? No, John, it's too late to start over. See, this ghost town and me, we got something in common: we're still here, but just the shell; the heart died out of us years ago.'

'Your heart's good, I know it is,' John protested, trying not to cry and failing.

Chuck smiled gratefully. 'Son, I want you to give me a big hug, then you're getting out.'

John sniffed and blinked to control his sorrow, wrapped his arms around Chuck's shoulders and squeezed with all his might. Chuck patted his back to soothe him, and John could have stayed like that for hours. Very quickly the driver's door was released and he was hoisted past the steering wheel and lowered to the ground. The door slammed shut and the engine roared into life, making him jump back, then Chuck reversed into the forest to turn round. In the second before he shifted into first, he grinned at John, raised his left arm and gave a loose salute – a swift flick of his fingers off his eyebrow. John did not have time to respond in kind; Chuck had looked away and was already skidding back onto the track, the huge tires spewing clouds of dirt as they sought traction on the incline.

Chapter 3

Love, absent for years, now overwhelmed him. His parents had heard the truck roar off and had come tearing out of the forest to find their son standing alone. Airborne dust had turned the wet tracks on his cheeks brown.

Never mind Chuck and his gun, Gwen nearly killed John with her bare hands, so forcefully did she hug him. Plucked off the ground and held to her bosom, his shoulder became sopping wet with her laughing tears of relief. Vincent threw his arms around them both, a tire iron in one hand. Words soon emerged from their moans.

'Are you all right?'

'What did he do to you?'

'Why are you crying?'

'Are you hurt?'

'Where is he?'

The questions kept pouring into his ears from mouths pressed tight against his head.

'Yes ... nothing ... don't know ... no ... gone ...'

Then his father was off and running towards the track, makeshift bludgeon in his fist. The dust disturbed by Chuck's hasty retreat was still settling. The sound of the V8 was fading into the mountainside.

'Come back down here, you fucking *arsehole!*' Vincent yelled into the sweltering blue yonder, shaking the tire iron.

Still hugging John, Gwen screeched over his shoulder, almost deafening him.

'*Vinny!* Stop it, you bloody idiot! The man's got a gun!'

It had the desired effect. Having made his point – which had not impressed his son one little bit – Vincent returned to his family but did not re-join the clinch.

'Right,' he said, breathing heavily. 'First thing, get the police up here. John, where did he take you? Could you show them? Gwen, put him down for a minute.'

She did so, but kept hold of John's hand and began dragging him towards the forest.

'We can talk about this later, Vincent,' she said, not waiting for him to follow. 'I want to get away from this place.'

Jogging to keep up, Vincent continued the interrogation.

'Where did he take you, John? Can you remember?'

'Not really.'

'Did he take you anywhere special?'

John stuttered, and silenced himself. He wanted to protect Chuck. Apart from making his parents sick with worry, the man had done no harm to anyone.

'No, we just drove around the mountain.'

The forest swallowed them in shadow. Further on, John could see the group of cabins where he had first run into Chuck. Vincent overtook his wife and son and blocked their path, forcing them to stop.

'You drove around? For a fucking *hour?*'

'*Don't* swear at him!' Gwen said, glowering. She side-stepped, barged past and carried on running.

John was glad of his mother's defense and fleet footwork; he was a terrible liar when pinned by a disbelieving stare. His father fell in behind them again, panting hard as he caught up. They ran past the cabins and out into the sunshine of the ghost town. To John, it felt as though he had been gone for years, as though a lifetime had passed since Chuck had enticed him away.

They raced in silence across the clearing. Ten yards from the car, Vincent tripped and went his length – a *whump* and an '*Oof!*' behind them – but Gwen never broke her stride and John was not allowed to. She jumped onto the back seat with him, curling an arm around his shoulders. John could smell her perfume, pungently reactivated by her sweat. She bellowed unsympathetically at her husband to pick himself up. Grimacing, Vincent gained his feet and limped towards them covered in dust. He reached the car, chucked the tire iron on the passenger seat and set his right foot on the sill to inspect the worst of his injuries. A pale globule enlarged on his knee until the meniscus broke, releasing a dark stream down his leg.

'*Vinny!* Get in the bloody car!'

'Keys!' he said, slipping in behind the wheel. 'Shit, where are the keys?'

Gwen cursed under her breath, let go of John and leaned forward between the seats – better to scream at her fool husband.

'*You* were driving! *You* had them! *Find* them!'

'Shit!' Vincent rubbed his palms over his pockets but they were flat and empty.

Had his parents been quiet for just two seconds, John could have told them not to panic – Chuck was long gone. But they continued ranting at each other so he sought another way to help. His perfect eyesight scanned the earth where his father had fallen and spotted the circular red fob the rental company had attached to the keys. He decided it would save time if he simply retrieved them himself.

His mother made a grab for him, missed and squeaked in horror. As she became instantly hysterical, Vincent gave his lungs another good workout. Clearly, their son was fleeing back to his abductor, their weird affinity too strong to break.

John stopped running, although not in response to his parents. He bent and snatched the keys off the ground and turned to jangle them aloft.

But it was not this that silenced their protestations.

A noise: a single crack, carried to them from the distance on the telegraphical mountain air.

The gunshot lingered in John's ears long after its brief resonance had truly vanished. It had not sounded like the guns he heard on *Starsky and Hutch* every week. When they went off, they were bigger, fuller, more significant – explosions more than cracks. Before that day, he had never heard the real thing; nevertheless he knew it had just happened. A petty noise, belying its effect. And he knew in his heart what it meant for his friend with the V8 pick-up.

He felt the presence of his parents a couple of paces to his rear, having vaguely heard them climb from the car and wander over, their argument abruptly spent.

'Son ...?' his father said in a whisper.

John realized by his absence of shock that this moment had been inevitable. He didn't feel like crying. He had shed his tears in the truck, hearing the life ebb from Chuck's voice, a precursor to the bodily death that had been marked by the gunshot. Some place deep inside him seemed to understand all this; a level he couldn't contact, but which spoke to him in the language of intuition, unaffected by age or experience.

'It's okay, Dad. You don't have to call the police now.'

Chapter 4

2013

It had been twenty-two years since John Frears had seen Donnie Chester. During that period both men had barely kept in contact, often going two or three years without saying hello, but they had never lost touch and both had made repeated promises to visit. If John couldn't get to Los Angeles, Donnie would fly to London. However it happened, one day they would find a little time and get together.

Now that time had finally arrived, it was John who had crossed the Atlantic and he still couldn't see Donnie because Donnie had been buried in a closed casket.

The cemetery was small and quietly idyllic; Beverly Glen in the eastern reaches of the Santa Monica Mountains between Los Angeles and the San Fernando Valley.

The service at an end, Donnie's father grabbed a handful of dirt and chucked it in the hole. It spattered on the lid of the lowered metal casket. He stepped back and wiped one gritty palm roughly against the other. His face was unreadable, but that indelicate movement of his hands betrayed an emotion more complex than mere grief. His duty done, he broke from the circle of mourners and marched off towards the cemetery road.

John watched Dodge Chester go, and understood his impatience to be away. The turnout had been poor, the whole occasion a sham. Those who had shown up had seemed more embarrassed than upset. The circumstances of Donnie's death had evidently caused more distress than his actual passing. The email John had received from Donnie's sister had frankly explained the situation. Virginia had sent the same message to every name in her brother's address book, with the rider that she did not expect a favorable response. Had John not been at such a loose end, his would have been another polite refusal.

Wearing dark glasses to mask her pain, Virginia took a handful of earth off the mound and dropped it in the grave. Behind his own shades, John watched her intently. She was deeply beautiful, mixed race. She turned and began slowly towards the cars, and, after adding their own dirt to the lid, the other mourners followed suit.

All except John. He loosened his black tie to let a bit of air down his collar – December and the mercury was touching seventy – and, staring into the darkness at the silver box, his thoughts became memories.

The minister, still standing at the head of the grave, instantly brought him back to the present.

'Terrible business,' he said dourly.

John glanced up but let the facile observation remain rhetorical.

'Have you come far?' the minister asked.

'London.'

'Really? Long way. You must have been very close.'

'I hardly knew the guy.'

The minister frowned.

'Nice service,' John said, dropped some dirt in the hole and returned to his rental car.

A few miles away in Westwood, Hayley Roth parked her old white Beetle Karmann convertible on Veteran Avenue and stepped into the Los Angeles National Cemetery. It was the antithesis of the one in Beverly Glen: a hundred and fourteen acres; traffic hum twenty-four hours a day, courtesy of the Interstate 405, the San Diego Freeway, which delineated the cemetery's western perimeter.

She stopped and scanned the depressing vista. The northern half of the cemetery contained upright markers, meticulously-aligned white tablets. The southern half, beyond the trees and the central columbarium, contained the ground-flush markers. Beyond those, Sepulveda Boulevard and the 405, was the Veterans Administration Medical Center.

Hayley started walking, the stem of a single white rose pinched between thumb and forefinger. Years of tracing the same route through the headstones allowed her to find the one she wanted without searching. At its base, the petals of her last token of remembrance had turned brown and crispy. Beside it was a large spray of fading red roses, a sign that her mother had recently been there. Hayley wished they could have knelt together, but theirs was not the happiest of relationships.

She lowered herself and placed her rose, then turned her eyes to the sky. The vast blue was marred only by the crossing contrails of two high-altitude airliners, and Hayley smiled faintly. It looked like a crucifix, a sign from her father that he was listening. She had always believed only the bones were beneath ground. What mattered, the spirit, was free somewhere far above.

'Lot to tell you today, Dad. Some bad, some good. Bad first …'

This one-way chat was a monthly ritual. Her husband Larry saw it as an obsession but she didn't care. It refreshed her soul. She could offload her anxieties, share her hopes, speak her deepest thoughts out loud. It was cheaper than the shrink – just the gas to get there.

Absently pulling blades of grass from the turf, Hayley rambled on for several minutes. She was worried about Larry. His work partner had recently keeled over from a fatal coronary, which had set him soul-searching. At forty-two years old, Larry's mid-life crisis had pounced and Hayley was bearing the brunt. He wasn't violent, but she could sense something nasty threatening, like thunderheads on the horizon.

She was quiet after that. By admitting her fears they had somehow been validated. Now, she was more concerned than ever. When she passed on her good news it didn't greatly lift her mood.

'I'm through to the second interview for *Malibu Mischief*. This afternoon. It's a soap. Daytime, but Amanda says viewing figures are good and it might find an evening slot soon. I'm being seen for a main character. It could be the break I've been waiting for.' She rolled some blades of grass gently between her fingertips and thought back to her graduation from UCLA. 'Twenty-three years. My God … that's an eternity when you want something so badly.' She managed a wan smile, slightly ashamed. 'Dad, if you could get someone up there to pull a few strings ...'

There didn't seem much more to say. She knelt in silence for a few minutes, her thoughts diffuse but shot through with apprehension. Her marriage was her whole life, and what if it really was beginning to fall apart? Where would she find a meaning to her existence? Her acting career was going nowhere, never had done. Except on these rare interview days, it was hardly more than a figment of her imagination.

She closed her eyes and whispered to the heavens.

'I love you, Dad. Please help me today.'

She collected the month-old rose, stood up and set off back to her car. Along the way she dropped the brittle bloom in a trash can full of them.

Seated again in the Beetle, she checked her reflection in the rear-view mirror. In accordance with the casting director's advice, she had applied make-up sparingly and had pulled her long russet curls back through an elasticized cinch into a pony tail. Her face looked fine, but the decorative ribbon over the cinch had worked a little loose so she bowed it again. This was the first time she had worn it to an interview, although she had several the same, all cut from a favorite childhood dress. Perhaps it would bring her luck.

Food and drink awaited the mourners at the Chester residence. Having formed part of the cortège to the church, John easily remembered the short route back. He drove his rented Chrysler through salubrious Beverly Glen, past detached homes and luxury cars.

When he arrived outside the house on Angelo Drive, Virginia was on the sidewalk looking agitated. He parked and got out.

'Is everything okay?' he asked, removing his sunglasses.

She stopped checking up and down the road. 'Uh, you're ...'

'John.'

'John, yes. No, my father's gone. We came back together in the limo, then he drove off in his Jeep. I should have listened; I knew he didn't want anyone back here. It was me. I insisted we do this right.'

'You only get one chance to say goodbye,' John said, trying to reassure.

'I know. I wish my father did.'

'He will – given time.'

Virginia was glancing up and down the road again, impatiently jangling a set of car keys in her hand.

'You've no idea where he went?' John asked.

'I think I know *exactly* where he went, that's the problem. The mood he's in, he shouldn't be anywhere near a gun.'

John gently touched her forearm. 'Hey, calm down. Explain. Where's he gone?'

She collected herself. 'My father owns a gun range in the Valley.'

'I see. I think Donnie mentioned it once. And are you worried about your father or other people?'

'I'd just prefer he wasn't around guns right now. He's had problems for years. Ever since I was a kid. I'm scared this might push him over the edge.'

'Problems … in what way?'

'His was the generation that went to Vietnam.'

'Oh. Enough said. Are you going to look for him?'

'I have to.'

Virginia pressed a transmitter on her key fob. In front of them, the indicators of a red Audi TT winked twice, and from under the hood a remarkably lifelike voice announced, '*Dis-armed!*'

She slipped in behind the wheel, then debated for a moment before asking: 'John, would you come with me? You might help.'

'How?'

'You told me earlier you knew Donnie in the Persian Gulf. Maybe you can remind my dad of a time when he was proud of his son.'

Chapter 5

'This is Six Adam Nine at Tamarind. Code Four on that domestic.'
Officer Larry Roth released the button on his shoulder
mike. No charges pressed, no arrest papers served. A peaceful
conclusion, but his heart was hammering and his blood felt like
pure adrenaline in his veins. He reckoned the job would kill him
in the end. Nothing newsworthy like a terminal gun battle. Stress.
Plain and simple. The residue of fear. In time it clogged the arteries
as sure as a diet of bourbon and burgers. Each time the dispatcher
called, the body responded, all systems to red alert. This could be
the day someone starts shooting. Ninety-nine to one against, but
it's the thought that counts. The brain could stand down pretty
quickly from combat-ready; not the body. The body stayed wired
for hours. At the end of the shift, relaxation came out of a bottle
or not at all, but it never flushed away the stress, which built and
built and built until …

He stopped the silent strobing of lights on the roof of the black-
and-white Dodge Charger, swung a U-turn in the street and
cruised away.

'Larry, can you believe that guy?'

'If I wanted a conversation I'd start one.'

The rookie was really beginning to irritate. Joey DeCecco wasn't a kid, but he'd replaced an officer of thirty-five years' experience. A month ago, Officer Frank Dista had suffered a massive heart attack in the station locker room. Nothing theatrical; he had made a startled face, seized his chest and dropped dead. Larry had watched it happen, had smelt the stench as Frank's bowels let go, and the shock had been extraordinary. Twenty years policing the streets of Hollywood had shown Larry a lot of hurt, but nothing had struck home like this. A profound sense of futility had swamped him then, and he had been wading deeper every day since.

He turned the car onto Sunset Boulevard. He could feel DeCecco's eyes boring into him and guessed an apology was in order, but his guts were balled too tight. It was DeCecco who spoke.

'Officer Roth, I'm sure you'll tell me if I'm speaking out of turn, but why don't you put in for some stress leave?'

Larry clenched his teeth – a dam against a torrent of expletives. He pulled the Charger into the curb and turned to his new partner.

'When you've been in the job more than five minutes, DeCecco, *then* I might listen to your opinion on my state of mind. Until then, keep your eyes open and your mouth shut.'

DeCecco didn't reply.

'Good,' Larry said. 'Now you're learning.'

An awkward silence reigned for ten minutes. The tension in the vehicle was palpable. Larry knew he was perhaps treating DeCecco unfairly but he was too screwed up to make amends. Frank's death had got him thinking. What was the point risking his life for these people? Was he really making a difference? Even the slightest? He didn't think so. If he defused a domestic one day, it might go off fatally the next. His was a finger in the dyke when the hole was fist-sized.

The dispatcher's voice came over the radio.

'Six Adam Nine, see the man at the corner of Van Ness and Lemon Grove.'

Van Ness and Lemon Grove was at the south-east corner of the Hollywood Forever Cemetery, where it bordered the back-lots of Paramount Studios.

Larry left the car on Van Ness and entered the cemetery via the Lemon Grove Gate. Eddie wanted to see him. Eddie always asked to meet at the same intersection, but he meant inside the cemetery, specifically behind the tomb of Douglas Fairbanks Senior. DeCecco obediently followed, asking no questions, and Larry kept several steps ahead as though he didn't *have* a partner.

Set in the Fairbanks Gardens at one end of a long rectangular pond, Douglas Fairbanks' resting place was an ostentatious affair in white marble. The tomb itself was raised on a platform of three steps, and a three-sided pillared monument had been erected behind it, straight from a Roman B-movie, featuring Fairbanks' profile inside a laurel wreath above his name and dates: 1883-1939. It was encircled to the rear by conifers and a low stone wall, and it was here that Eddie liked to meet – in the shadow of greatness. Unfortunately, his information didn't always match his sense of the melodramatic.

'Hey, Officer Roth,' Eddie greeted him, then pointed to a nearby mausoleum, an awed look on his ratty face. 'You know who's in there?'

'Rudolph Valentino.'

'Oh, I told you already.'

'Every time, Eddie. You tell me every fucking time.'

'Who's he?' Eddie nodded at DeCecco, who was holding back a few paces.

'New partner. What have you got for me, Eddie?'

'Oh, yeah, Jeez, sorry about Officer Dista – I liked him.'

'What have you got for me?'

'Hey, new guy,' Eddie said. 'Come over here.'

DeCecco approached. 'What?'

'You know all these people in here? They're *dead* famous.' He convulsed with laughter.

'*Eddie!*' Larry kept his hands to himself but walked his informant back against the monument until they were practically touching noses. 'If I wanted jokes I'd be in the Comedy Store, not here talking to you.'

As Larry's number one snitch, Eddie wasn't used to being coerced.

'Hey, come on. Officer Roth, it's me. I make you laugh, remember? Since when d'you lose your sense of humor?'

Larry's sharp intake of breath was enough for Eddie to work out the probable timing for himself.

'Oh, okay. Sorry. I know you and Officer Dista was tight.'

'Yeah yeah,' Larry said, stepping out of Eddie's halitosis. 'Can we get down to business or am I wasting my time?'

'Don't worry,' Eddie said, grinning. 'You ain't gonna regret being here today. But you gotta promise: you make detective on the back of this, you don't forget who made it happen.'

Larry groaned at Eddie's typically delusional *braggadocio*. 'Sure. You'll forgive me if I don't run off and get measured for a suit.'

'No bullshit, Officer Roth. What I got for you – it's big.'

'It'd better be, Eddie, because I give you fair warning: *Job* is not my middle name today.'

After Eddie had finished his spiel, Larry was quiet for a moment. If it was true and he made the arrests himself, it would be something to be proud of. Something Frank could have been proud of. It was something to aim for, a reason to keep on wearing the uniform. But only if he took down the perps himself. No suits or SWAT teams calling the shots.

Shit. DeCecco. Frank would have gone along with it. But a rookie? Would he risk a dangerous, maverick bust in his first month on the street?

'So, Officer Roth ... you got something for me now?'

Larry knew what he meant but narrowed his eyes at him. 'Like what?'

'I was thinking a C-note,' Eddie said hopefully.

'A hundred? You owe me fifty. That last tip you gave me? Fucking no-show. Captain thought I was an asshole.'

Eddie shrugged and smiled. 'Hey, I don't got no crystal ball.'

Despair swooped down on Larry like a bird of prey. Its shadow filled his head. He was sick of bartering with scumbags.

'We're done here, DeCecco,' he said tersely. He turned and hopped the low wall, brushed through some shrubbery and walked away across the lawn. DeCecco followed.

'What about my money?' Eddie complained.

'Kiss my ass,' Larry said over his shoulder. 'Cash on delivery.'

Three seconds elapsed before Eddie could formulate a response. 'Officer Roth! You want I should talk to Internal Affairs?'

Larry halted like he'd bumped into an invisible brick wall. He could feel DeCecco's scrutiny, a sidelong look of suspicion.

'You're on the take,' Eddie said too loudly. 'You think I don't know? Oh, yeah, you've been on the pad for years, you and Dista both.'

After pausing to let a couple of civilians pass on a nearby pathway, Larry unsnapped the hammer restraint on his holster, swivelled and raced back towards his snitch, leaping the shrubs and wall in one. Eddie scrambled back but only as far as a conifer that got in his way. Larry stared at him for a moment, checked again for witnesses, and drew his .40 caliber Glock 22 sidearm.

'You wanna drop a dime on me, Eddie – what the fuck, I don't care any more.' He put the Glock's muzzle against his informant's top lip.

'Larry, it's not worth it,' DeCecco said, joining them. 'Let's go.'

'Stay out of it! But you muddy Frank's name, Eddie, I swear I'll kill you. No one's gonna ask where's Rudolph buried. They're gonna ask where did that rat-faced motherfucker Eddie get his face blown off. See, I pull this trigger, your teeth turn to shrapnel. The lower half of your face exits through your brain stem. So how you gonna talk to IA then, huh? You piece of shit. Frank Dista was the best cop I ever knew.'

Terrified, Eddie stammered, 'I wouldn't screw with you, Officer Roth, I wouldn't. It's just talk, crapola. You know me.'

DeCecco spoke calmly: 'Officer Roth … lower your weapon.'

Larry eyed Eddie uncertainly, then slowly retreated and slipped his gun back in its holster, clipping over the restraint.

Eddie was still wide-eyed, but his fear was rapidly changing to furious indignation.

'I can't believe you did that. I can't believe it! After all I done for you. I only wanted what was mine. What? You think the service I provide is *free*? If you don't wanna pay, *officer*, then fuck *you*. I don't need this shit. I could get killed talking to you.'

'Yeah, you could,' Larry said pointedly. 'And if someone was to put the word out, you would. Now … this information – the Armenians. How solid is it?'

'It's a rock,' Eddie said through gritted teeth, accepting he had the most to lose.

Larry produced a roll of bills from his pocket, peeled off two ten-spots and dropped them on the grass.

'That's for you. And our little arrangement stands. You don't cancel it – I do. At a time of my choosing. Yes?'

Eddie's head was micro-nodding already from the adrenaline, but he said 'Yes' anyway, just to confirm.

'Good. And if you ever mention Frank's name again – to anyone – I *will* send you to meet him.'

Chapter 6

The name of the gun range brought a smile to John's face: DODGE CITY. Blue neon, lettered Western-style. It was located in Reseda, in the sprawl of the San Fernando Valley.

They hadn't spoken much on the journey down. John assumed Virginia had a lot on her mind and allowed her the peace to mull it over. He had gleaned only her job: a costume designer for the movies. The rest of the time the silence between them was strangely comfortable.

Virginia parked the Audi beside her father's blue Jeep Grand Cherokee. It was the only other vehicle in the small lot, since Dodge had temporarily closed his business. As John stepped out of the air-conditioned interior he noted the temperature had risen with their descent from the hills. The heat felt good, reminding him of his years spent abroad. He would have preferred it even warmer but he wasn't complaining. He had left England in its usual miserable state: cold and wet and grey. A balmy December was a luxury these days.

Virginia pressed the key fob transmitter and the car replied, '*Armed!*'

The building stood alone. As security was paramount, there were no windows, but a lapse had occurred today. The metal shutter over the entrance had been rolled up on its tracks and not pulled down again. Virginia cupped her hands to the glass to cut the reflection.

'Yeah, he's in there,' she said.

She needn't have told him; John could hear the muffled shots. Peering in, he could see a store to the front. It was dark inside, but he could make out shelving and display counters, and, beyond a viewing window at the back, the range itself. The range lights were on but Dodge was not firing from any of the visible booths. Virginia tried pushing the door, which didn't budge.

'Well, at least this is locked,' she said, opening her bag to produce a set of keys.

As she did so, John saw she was packing a stun-gun.

'How many volts?' he asked casually as she let them in.

'A mill. Why?' She winked at him. 'Thinking of trying it on?'

John grimaced. 'A million volts? Think I'll wait for a written invitation.'

She laughed. 'You do that.'

She pulled down the outer shutter so it locked automatically, and closed the interior door behind them. Inside the building, John got his familiar tingle of excitement. Ever since that day in Oregon as a boy, his most abiding passion had been for firearms.

A brief lull in the gunshots, then they resumed. Virginia led him through the store, its goods dully illuminated by the spill-through of light from the range. Holsters, books, reloading equipment, calendars, body-armour, gun safes, laser sights, T-shirts and baseball caps with insulting logos regarding the anti-gun lobby. The counter section to the left was stocked with handguns for sale, prices tagged to the trigger guards. Against the wall was a locked rack of rifles, shotguns, semi-automatic assault weapons. Beneath them, stacked cartons of ammunition. Under the furthest glass counter was another array of handguns and ammo. Lying between a Ruger .357 and a 9mm Beretta was a sign: *For Rent*.

John wandered back to the wall displaying the assault weapons and stared at them. A part of him wanted to shun his fascination, but it was the smaller part and it couldn't override their allure. Ginny joined him.

'There may be some empty gaps here soon,' she said. 'State pols are after a total ban on assault weapons.'

'Way too late,' he said. 'You can legislate but you can't uninvent.'

'True. You like all this, don't you.'

'I shouldn't but I do. You?'

'It's been our livelihood for years. I can't bite the hand that feeds.'

'But in an ideal world ...' he probed.

She smiled faintly. 'Donnie would be alive and my Dad wouldn't have gone to Vietnam. Why even think about it? It's a fairy tale.'

The viewing window was made of double-sheet acrylic glass. They both nosed up and saw Dodge in the far right booth, white shirt, collar open, tie discarded. He was in a combat stance, ear-defenders over the shaved dome of his skull.

The door to the range was on the far left and Virginia moved towards it. Had she made to enter at that moment John would have grabbed her. It didn't do to spook an armed man who thought he was alone, especially one with *problems* whose son had just died. But she stopped and waited for the next lull before opening the door to poke her head in. John could see through the window that Dodge had slipped the ear-defenders onto his shoulders.

'Daddy!' she called, and ducked her head back.

He spun around and John understood her continuing reluctance to simply walk in. Dodge had his hand on the butt of his back-up weapon, a hip-holstered Walther P99 – a sensible precaution for the owner of a hood's paradise.

'Ginny?'

'I've got someone with me. Okay to come in?'

Dodge answered with an apathetic shrug and turned back to the booth.

John was several inches taller than Dodge Chester but he didn't feel it. He had met such men before – authority beyond the physical. The shaved head made it hard to tell his exact age, but, given his military service, John put him at around sixty-five. They both stood behind him as he carried on pressing bullets into the top of a clip, loading from a carton of fifty. There were two more empty clips on the loading table, and the floor was littered with over a hundred and fifty brasses and three discarded boxes.

Virginia gave John an encouraging nod, but he was stumped. What was he meant to say? He was a complete stranger to Dodge, and had only known Donnie for a matter of days, over two decades earlier.

'Daddy, you remember John? He came all the way from England.'

'Uh-huh.' Dodge inserted the clip into a Colt .45 and clicked it home, then released the open slide to chamber the first round. He settled the ear-defenders over his head, thrust the gun towards the target and squeezed off seven shots.

John watched the slide of the Colt ram back and forth, ejecting and loading until the last round left the muzzle and the slide locked open, releasing the final brass and a wisp of smoke. He couldn't tell where any of the slugs had hit because the silhouette was already so riddled its paper guts were entirely missing.

'*Daddy!*' Virginia shouted.

There was no reaction for a moment, then Dodge hung his head. He set the Colt down, removed his ear-defenders and turned round. John could detect the sting of recent tears in his eyes.

Dodge made no attempt to disguise the weariness in his voice.

'What do you want, Ginny? You want me to thank this gentleman for making the effort? Fine. Thank you, son, but you should have put the airfare to better use.'

'I wanted to pay my respects.'

'You think my son deserved respect?'

'I think any man who fights for his country when he's not conscripted to do so deserves respect – yes, sir.'

'Respect lasts as long as a man values it; no longer.'

'Fair enough. I didn't come here to argue with you.'

'Then why did you come?'

'John knew Donnie in the old days,' Virginia answered, nudging John in the arm.

Dodge huffed. 'We all knew Donnie in the old days, Ginny. The old days are gone. They're not some currency you can use to pay off today's debts.'

'But the past matters,' she said. 'You *know* it does.'

With fiery eyes, Dodge stared her into a cowering silence before softening his gaze and looking at John.

'How exactly did you know my son?'

'We met during the First Gulf War.'

'So my daughter brought you here to talk nostalgia, did she? Well, I know my son was a good soldier once, I don't need to be told.'

John shot Virginia a hopeless glance; her father's defenses were too well-established.

'Daddy, John actually fought alongside Donnie.'

'Bullshit. Either you're clutching at straws or he's lied to you. The British Army did not fight with the US Eighteenth Airborne on the western flank – the French did.'

'Designated the *Daguet* Division,' John said. '*Deuxième Régiment Étranger d'Infanterie*, subordinate to *Sixième Division Légère Blindé, Force Action Rapide.*'

'Talk English, son.'

'I was a Legionnaire. We were probing Iraqi territory long before any British or American forces.'

'You were in the French Foreign Legion?'

'For seven years. I left as a sergeant.'

'Based where?' Dodge quizzed, still skeptical.

'*Quartier Vallongue*, Nîmes.'

'What was wrong with the British Army?' Virginia wanted to know.

'I preferred the Legion; they discourage contact with the family.'

'A regular *Beau Geste*,' Dodge said without humor.

'Something like that. Listen, for what it's worth, Mr Chester, I liked your son, and I don't make friends easily.'

'Thank you, but it's not worth the breath it took to say it.'

'I understand.'

'Do you? I don't think you do. If you came all the way from England you must be badly in the dark over this. My son was buried in a closed casket because his face had been *shot off*. Did you know that? Did my daughter tell you that in the email I asked her *not to send*?' These last words were directed at Virginia, but his focus quickly swung back to John.

'Not that detail, no, sir.'

'I'm just glad his mother never lived to see this day. So what did she tell you that made you fly all this way? Tell me, what? Donnie died in a car wreck?'

Virginia drew a harsh breath to object but John held up his hand. He spoke to Dodge in a level, cautious voice.

'She said Donnie had hired himself out to the Urabeños in Colombia. She said he was killed in a shoot-out with DEA agents in Mexico whilst protecting a narcotics consignment bound for the United States.'

Dodge looked winded, as though he was receiving this information for the first time. Perhaps he had not heard it put that succinctly, like a headline on the TV news. He glowered at his daughter.

'*That's* what you put in the email?'

'I didn't want anyone showing up under false pretenses.'

'I didn't want anyone showing up *period*,' Dodge said, then looked at John. 'So what's your excuse? How come you thought the sun shone out of my son's ass?'

'*Dad!*'

John felt the need to extricate himself and decided to come clean. 'I didn't,' he said. 'I knew your son as a good soldier and we liked each other. But I'm only here because I fancied a holiday. I have no family and I got your daughter's email between work contracts and I thought, what the hell, I've never been to California; Oregon when I was a kid but never California. My being here is simple expedience, sir, nothing more than that.'

Virginia was looking at him with disappointment in her eyes.

'Sorry,' he said to her. 'It's the truth.'

She gave a feeble smile. 'My fault. I shouldn't have brought you here.'

'I'll get a cab back; you stay with your father. Sir, I apologize for intruding on your grief. I wish we could have met under happier circumstances.'

Dodge didn't answer and Virginia didn't prompt him. John walked to the door at the end of the acrylic glass. As he grabbed the handle, a voice stopped him. It was oddly humble, from the mouth of a subdued Dodge.

'You could have taken your vacation anywhere in the world. You didn't need to be here today.' He paused. 'Thank you.'

'You're welcome,' John said with a smile. 'By the way, you need a new B twenty-seven.'

Dodge looked at the bullet-riddled B27-type silhouette.

'Yep, forty-five makes a real mess. Army should have never dropped it.'

'It's a fine weapon. Could do with a few basic modifications, though.'

'How's that, son?'

John let go of the door handle and walked back. Dodge couldn't see but Virginia was smiling; her father had been side-tracked – far better than any nostalgia trip.

'May I?' John asked, indicating the pistol.

Dodge moved away from the loading table. 'Be my guest.'

John picked up the gun. Its weight felt good. He had missed handling such firepower. He didn't have to read the barrel markings to identify the exact make.

'Colt Government, mark four, series seventy,' he said. 'Well, to start with, I'd polish the feed ramp, throat and polish the barrel, adjust the extractor, check the recoil spring against the load, fit combat sights and give it a decent four-pound trigger pull. Also lower the ejection port, open up the magazine well and fit a full-length guide rod.'

'You could do that?' Dodge asked.

'No,' John said perversely. 'When I left the Legion at the back-end of ninety-five I was all set to embark upon a career as a pistolsmith. But I didn't get any further than reading up on it.' He dropped the mag out of the Colt. 'Mind if I squeeze off a few?'

'Sure,' Dodge said, and touched a button on the booth wall. An electric pulley whirred overhead, reeling in the old target, while John began loading from the carton.

'So why didn't things work out?' Virginia asked. 'What happened?'

'Dunblane. March ninety-six.'

She winced. 'God, of course; those kids in Scotland.'

'Gun ownership in Britain was always a house of cards. Dunblane brought it down. The right to bear arms isn't a very British concept. We don't have the history like you do.' He pressed in the last round, slotted the magazine in the butt and worked the slide. The riddled target arrived and Dodge exchanged it for a fresh one, then sent it back out.

'You want these?' Dodge asked, pointing to the ear-defenders.

'Nah. I like it when my ears ring.'

'Why didn't you move someplace else?' Virginia asked. 'Learn your new trade where guns are allowed?'

John shrugged. 'Dunblane was certainly sobering, but it wasn't that. It wasn't a moral choice. I suppose it just gave me the chance to reassess. Maybe I should move on. Maybe I'd been around guns for long enough. Problem is, I can't settle. I've been globe-trotting for nearly twenty years, taking one job after another.'

'Doing what?' she asked.

'Security Consultant, mostly. And that's not a euphemism for anything more dangerous; it's just advice. If you get the right client, it pays well. Lots of paranoid rich people out there. I advise and I move on. Leave the briefcased Uzis to other people.'

Dodge had stopped the silhouette twenty-five yards downrange. John waited for it to hang still, adopted a two-handed point, aimed and squeezed the trigger. He proceeded to empty the clip, then placed the Colt on the table and brought the target in. As it approached, he realized his mistake. He had gone for head shots, putting a tight bunch of holes through the silhouette's black face.

It stopped in front of them. They all stared at it. They stared for no more than five seconds but it seemed to John like an hour.

'French Foreign Legion, you say?' Dodge said severely.

It sounded like the sort of question you weren't meant to answer. 'You're sure not DEA?'

Gallows humor: a soldier's last line of defense. John looked on as Dodge began tittering like a child, making hysterical squeaks that became roars of bass laughter. John knew it was okay to join in. In truth, he couldn't help himself. Dodge might break down in a few moments, but they could all howl until then. Life was demonstrating one of its more quirky truisms: the worse the tragedy, the sicker the joke.

Spluttering his amusement, John glanced at Virginia who was trying to maintain some decorum, scowling at both men. He turned his back fully on Dodge and indicated with his eyes that she should join in; however unseemly, this was a necessary release for her father, perhaps the only one he would allow himself. She got the message and started smiling. It seemed an effort and John understood why. Dodge's laughter was maniacal, somehow ugly. Virginia couldn't look at her father, but John saw her listening, using the sound of his laughter to spur her own.

In defiance of death she came alive, and John could not take his eyes off her.

Chapter 7

At the end of their shift, Officer Larry Roth took his rookie partner for a beer. Joey DeCecco didn't want to go but that was irrelevant to the final outcome. Larry chose a bar some distance away from their station. He reckoned a heated discussion was on the cards and he didn't want any other off-duty cops being a party to it.

Larry led the way in his silver 1980 Corvette Stingray. Aside from Hayley, it was his only true passion. Unlike Hayley, it didn't suffer his moods. The 5.7 liter V8 happily took all his anger and turned it into speed, whereas his wife simply absorbed it. She had no release. She shopped, kept house, and waited interminably for Hollywood to throw her a crumb from its table, which she would scrap over with a dozen other failed actresses. Her monthly visits to the cemetery seemed to have a cathartic effect, but he didn't approve. Ultimately, such morbid fixations had to be unhealthy. As her husband, he was aware that his love should have been easing her burden, but since Frank's death it had been buried deep inside him under an avalanche of fear and confusion. He had lost touch with his finer emotions.

Behind the 'Vette, DeCecco followed on his black Harley Low Rider. Watching in his rear-view mirror, Larry had to admit he looked cool.

His eyes returned to the road, his thoughts to Hayley. They were a world apart. Her job was fiction, in more ways than one. His was hard fact. Once, that difference had provided an essential counterpoise. Her enthusiasm could lift him; his pragmatism could ground her. Now ...

Larry shook his head to dispel a growing sense of futility. They were approaching the bar. He had to think clearly. He parked the Corvette on the street and got out. DeCecco pulled in behind, removed his open-face helmet and ran a hand through his black crew-cut. Larry offered a counterfeit grin, then held open the bar door.

There were fewer than ten patrons. The place was small with redwood cladding on the walls. A collection of neon beer signs – dazzling palettes of color in the gloom, glinting off the line of chrome beer taps.

'Joey, what are you drinking?' Larry said amiably, settling on a stool.

'I'm gonna call my wife. I don't want her getting worried.'

Larry offered what he thought was a winning smile. 'Sure. Coors?'

'Just a soda.' He set his helmet on the bar and went back outside onto the street to make the call in private.

Larry's jovial façade vanished. 'Asshole,' he muttered. He ordered the drinks and waited. Two minutes later, DeCecco ambled back and sat down.

'You tell your wife you're with me?' Larry asked.

'Yeah.'

'What did you say? You're having a brew with a psycho cop and if you're not home in a couple of hours to call the station?'

DeCecco shook his head. 'I told her an hour, then call.'

Larry forced a laugh. 'Joey, Joey. You're concerned about Eddie? Don't be. File and forget. It didn't happen.'

'So how often should I expect these things not to happen?'

Larry barely maintained his smile. 'Don't take this the wrong way, but the only reason you got a problem with what I did today is you're a rookie. You don't know shit. But that's okay. I can make allowances for that. Get it off your chest, and then I'll explain how it is.'

'Okay. You pulled your piece, stuck it in a man's face and threatened to blow him away. Because you're a cop that makes it okay? That stinks. You ever notice what's written on the door of the black-and-white?'

'Police?' Larry said facetiously.

'*To protect and to serve.*'

'Oh, that.' Larry calmly took a draught of his Coors. 'You'll learn,' he said.

'Meaning?'

'One day soon you'll walk into a situation, play it by the book and wind up real sorry.'

DeCecco smiled crookedly. 'Why? Because I don't get off on playing Dirty Harry?'

'It's the principle. You take control. If criminals can't respect the law, they gotta be made to fear it.'

'Oh, my mistake. I thought Eddie was some shitbird CI you were meant to look after. I didn't realize he was El Chapo in disguise.'

Larry couldn't think of a fast enough retort, so he supped his glass dry, burped, and ordered another.

'Listen, Larry, I appreciate your partner died recently, but that's no excuse. If you're hurting, get help; don't take it out on some innocent.'

Larry leaned in so they were almost butting heads.

'Did I hit the little fucker? Did I even touch him? No. I do not have a hand problem, Joey. Never have.'

'Well, you sure as hell got a head problem,' DeCecco said, and took his first taste of soda.

'Oh, fuck you. Tell me: why did you become a cop? It's pretty fucking obvious you don't have the stomach for police work.'

Looking straight ahead at the spirit shelf, DeCecco reacted calmly with a strange smile. 'I got the guts for more than police work, pal.'

Studying his partner's expression, Larry noticed something he'd never seen before. Despite the smile, a cold glint in his eyes that made him seem more self-assured. Larry's bristling attitude suddenly flattened. Instead of arguing, he decided to take DeCecco at his word and use it for his own ends.

'That's good, Joey. Maybe I underestimated you. So maybe you won't find my next proposition too shocking.'

DeCecco looked sideways at him.

'Remember what Eddie said?' Larry asked.

'Yeah. You tell Captain Gilchrist yet?'

'No, we're gonna deal with this one ourselves.'

'Say again.'

'Another beer!' Larry called to the bartender.

'Jesus, you are one soup sandwich,' Joey said.

'I thought you had the balls.'

'I do. What I don't have is any inclination to play Russian roulette.'

'Aw, don't fucking exaggerate.'

'I see, we're back to cursing at the rookie.' DeCecco stood up. 'Forget it. I'll talk to Gilchrist myself.'

At their apartment in Sawtelle, Hayley was torturing herself as she always did. It didn't help. She never clarified anything in her mind. The truth was, she could never tell. Sometimes she could read well and fail, other times think she'd screwed up and still get the part. But that didn't stop her mentally replaying every interview on a continuous loop, searching for some hook to hang her hope on.

Today it was worse. The stakes were higher: fame and fortune. Opportunities like this for female bit-part players of her age were increasingly rare. She was on the cusp of perpetual oblivion.

The burning incense sticks had not soothed her. Layers of smoke hung thickly in the living room, making her eyes smart. Her books on PMA were useless this evening. A major disappointment might be looming, and it was hard to maintain a Positive Mental Attitude alongside the thought of what might have been.

She viewed *Malibu Mischief* as a panacea. It would cure her career, heal her husband, mend her marriage. With the boost to their joint income, Larry could get out of law enforcement, perhaps open a business, maybe even retire. They could live happily ever after like people did in the movies.

A headache was pounding in her skull; she had to get some air. She went outside onto the walkway that overlooked a communal pool in need of a clean. She unbowed the ribbon in her hair, pulled off the cinch and let her curls fall free. The patterned material in her hand bore the repeating motif of Mickey and Minnie Mouse inside a love heart. Recently, her childhood seemed to belong to another person; it felt like she'd been a failing actress all her life. Yet she was still naïve enough to believe a childhood memento might bring her luck.

She wanted to scream. The yearning to succeed was unbearable. Her mood had degenerated over the day into one of unprecedented foulness. She could feel this despite the lack of anyone to bounce it off. When Larry came home, she would have to be extremely careful.

An hour later and her headache was as bad as her mood. The physical pain fuelled the mental agony and vice-versa. Hayley was still on the walkway outside her front door, the ribbon from her old dress weaved between her fingers. TVs were on in surrounding apartments, an assortment of muted sounds from the various channels. Across the way, the couple in number thirteen were having one of their regular disagreements, which Hayley reckoned would one night end with a gunshot.

Down on the street, Larry arrived home, the Corvette's V8 announcing his presence. A couple of roars as he revved the engine, then silence. He was late. She hadn't noticed the time, but now she did it annoyed her. Before he entered the courtyard she retreated into the apartment and quietly closed the door, then dumped herself on the sofa and zapped the TV into life. If Larry was not in a vastly better frame of mind she would feign interest in a movie. A clash on this particular evening might prove too volatile.

He came in and shut the door behind him.

'Jesus, Hayley, it's like a fucking opium den in here.'

He was bombed; she could tell without turning round.

'Why d'you burn that shit?'

The past month, such comments had become standard. Any other day she would have ignored it. Tonight, despite her best intentions, she switched off the TV and challenged him with a look.

'Now I gotta open all the fucking windows – *Jesus*.'

'I can't believe you drove home like that.'

'Believe it,' Larry said, his eyes all bloodshot and defiant.

'In case you'd forgotten, you're a cop.'

He paused at the curtains. 'And now I'm a shit-faced cop. Hayley, no more fucking incense.'

'Do you think you could talk to me without cursing?'

'Yeah, but I ain't fucking about to.' He drew the drapes apart and threw open the window.

'You've changed,' she said sadly.

'Frank died.'

She rolled her eyes. 'Don't I know it.'

'No, you don't. You only think you do. I was there. I watched it happen. One second he was standing there, the next ...'

'And I suppose you're the only person in the history of the world to have lost someone you cared about.'

With utter contempt, Larry said, 'What? You mean your old man? You didn't even know the guy.'

'So I shouldn't feel any loss, is that it?'

'Loss maybe, but you're fucking obsessed.'

'Stop cursing at me!' She got up and went into the kitchen, purely to escape the other room.

'You are!' he shouted, and tailed her in. 'You go to his grave every fucking month.'

She stood at the sink, showing him her back. 'I like to remember,' she said. 'What's wrong with that?'

Larry howled a laugh. Hayley heard the fridge door open and guessed he was after a six-pack. He returned to the living room and she followed to see him tear off a tin of Budweiser.

'*I like to remember* ...' he mocked. 'Jesus.' He cracked the tin and guzzled some beer. 'Remember what, Hayley? You never even met the guy. Exactly what memories are you referring to?'

She was livid. He had often questioned the frequency of her visits, but he had never maliciously undermined her devotion in this way. She should have gone to bed at that point. She knew how obtuse he could be after drink. She knew there was no point reasoning. But he had prised the scab off her most vulnerable wound on a day when her head ached like pity and her career hung in the balance. She was about to start yelling, but a surge of sadness stole much of her intended volume.

'Maybe that's the whole point. I don't know anything. All I have is that gravestone with his name on it. If being there makes me feel close to him, is that so wrong?'

'And how about being close to me?' he said pathetically.

Hurt and amazed, it was Hayley's turn to howl a laugh. She might have gone on to spell out the irony had her head not emptied of all thought as her vision filled with bright jags and shards, then did a quick-fade to black-out.

Chapter 8

In the end, John didn't get a cab back to Beverly Glen. The three of them perforated over a dozen targets, and Virginia was a match for them both. Emptying firearms was perhaps a strange thing to do on such a day but it passed the time and united their focus elsewhere. Virginia seemed grateful. When her father whooped at a perfect heart shot, she gave John a little smile. Dodge was engrossed in their friendly competition, spending difficult hours in relative relaxation. After a tense start, the two men had gelled. There was a generation between them, they had fought different wars, but they were both old soldiers.

And they could both drink. After locking up at DODGE CITY, Virginia drove them to a nearby bar. The two-seater Audi being somewhat impractical, she took her father's Jeep, and while she stayed sober they held a private wake for Donnie. They sunk beers, shot pool and talked about old times, but it was clear that certain topics were taboo and no amount of alcohol would change that. Donnie's recent history was off limits, likewise any mention of the problems Dodge had been suffering for years. But, even without Virginia's warning, John would have known not to probe. As he recounted tales of his years with the Legion, Dodge had ample opportunity to offer military anecdotes of his own. He didn't, and John had never been more curious about another man's past. Finally, when Dodge began looking seriously morose and neither man could sink a ball except by accident, Virginia suggested it was time to leave.

Dodge fell asleep on the way back, a disturbed doze full of nonsensical mutterings. Virginia took no notice and John gathered she had heard it before – her father's demons loosing their insidious poison.

'Where are you staying, John?'

'Best Western on Sepulveda.'

These were the first words between them and they were already on Mulholland Drive, nearing Beverly Glen. As before, John had felt no need to force conversation. Some odd intuition told him they would have all the time in the world to talk. He only hoped she felt the same.

After a moment, she said, 'Well, you can't drive.'

'I'll get a cab.'

'If you like. Or you can stay at my dad's.'

John nodded. 'What about you?'

'I'm staying. He might need me tonight.'

They put Dodge to bed then came back downstairs. The buffet was still there on the kitchen counter. The foil had been peeled back on several of the platters but the mourners had made little impression on the food beneath. Most of the glasses were unused, the bottles undisturbed. John wondered how long they had stuck with it, awkwardly swapping condolences when the closest bereaved were not even there to hear them. What was a respectable amount of time? Fifteen minutes? Half an hour? Did three or four sidle off before they all got the message and filtered out to their cars? Or was there an honest spokesperson among them? *Dodge and Virginia aren't here and Donnie was an asshole. Let's go.*

'Help yourself,' Virginia said to him.

John shook his head. 'I'll have bad dreams if I eat now.'

'Bad like my father?' she asked.

'I doubt it.'

'Don't you dream about being back in combat?'

'Sometimes. I suppose like any soldier who's seen active service.'

'Where were you apart from the Persian Gulf?' she asked as she started putting the food away in an enormous fridge.

'Bosnia in ninety-three as part of UNPROFOR; Rwanda in ninety-four; Bosnia again – Sarajevo – in ninety-five after the Dayton Peace Agreement as part of IFOR.'

'Oh, John ...' She shook her head. 'Those places. You must have seen some terrible things.'

Though it wasn't a subject he had ever talked about, with Virginia he felt ready. What stopped him was just how much there was to come out, and how depressing it would be for a person already in deep mourning. So he shrugged it off.

'There's a lot of wickedness out there. Listen, Virginia, you must be shattered, don't stay up on my account.'

'I am tired,' she said. 'But if I don't have a strong drink I won't sleep.'

From the sideboard she selected a bottle of Canadian Club and a can of Seven-Up, and mixed them together in two long glasses. John looked around the room as she did so. Light and airy, stools at a breakfast counter, recessed spots in the ceiling. It reminded him of kitchens in every American sitcom. Virginia handed him his drink.

'To Donnie,' he said, raising his glass.

She smiled. 'My big brother. May he find peace at last.'

They both drank, then she led him through to a spacious living room. On the floor was the thickest carpet John had ever sunk his feet into. Virginia flopped into a white leather sofa and patted the cushion beside her. He sat down and scanned some photographs on a high mantelpiece above a marble fireplace. There were several of Donnie and Virginia growing up; two of an attractive brunette who John assumed to be the late Mrs Chester; a shot of Virginia with Robert De Niro; one of Donnie in uniform; but none of Dodge, not even as a civilian. John's desire to learn about the man grew tenfold.

'So, John, what are your plans? Are you visiting with anyone else?'

'No, you're it.'

'Oh. When's your return flight?'

'It's open. My visa allows up to three months. Then you'll have to marry me or I'll be deported and blacklisted, never to return again.'

She gave a wry smile. 'You're a little blasted, aren't you.'

'That's rude, considering you hardly know me.'

'*Blasted.*'

'Oh, that, yes.' He grinned and took a sip of his drink.

'Do you like the States?' she asked.

'What I've seen of it. Actually, I feel very odd being here.'

'How so?'

'I don't know. I've spent time in a lot of countries but I've never felt I wanted to stay for very long. I noticed it the moment I stepped off the plane. I felt very calm yet somehow full of energy. I'm buzzing and relaxed at the same time, but they're not at odds. It's weird but it feels great, like the atmosphere really suits me. There's an odd quality to it.'

'That's the air pollution.'

'You're not taking me seriously.'

She replaced her smile with mock chagrin. 'I'm sorry. Go on.'

'No, you're right, it sounds stupid. I just feel ... at home.' He thought about it, and nodded to affirm the accuracy of his assessment. He looked at her and gave another nod. 'Mmm, that's exactly what I feel.'

She offered a beautiful smile. 'That's nice.'

Some mutual thought made them clink glasses, and, as they drank, their eyes met and locked – long enough for John to believe a connection had been confirmed. Virginia kicked off her shoes and pulled her legs onto the sofa, curling them beneath her.

'Tell me about England,' she said, her softer tones indicating he had not been mistaken.

'Not much to say. I feel nothing special for the place. I don't even have a British passport any more. After five years Legionnaires are offered French citizenship. It seemed rude not to accept.'

'So why did you join the Legion? What was the problem with your family?'

John stopped smiling and gazed down into his glass.

'Sorry,' she said. 'None of my business.'

'No, it's all right,' he said. 'I was an only child. For my parents that was one too many. I am a walking abortion.'

She gasped at his terminology.

'True. I know because my father told me one night when he was too drunk not to lie. I'd asked why they'd never shown me any love. He didn't try to deny it, just said they'd been all set to get divorced, then my mother got pregnant with me. Amazing how people can still screw when they hate each other's guts. Anyway, they talked a lot about a termination, but she couldn't do it. After I was born they stayed together for my sake, which was daft considering they never forgave me for it. There's only one time I remember seeing any genuine concern from them. Nineteen seventy-eight. The infamous Oregon vacation.'

'What happened?'

John smiled queerly at the memory. 'Maybe some other time. It's late and it's a long story.'

'Okay. So you grew up and decided you wanted a career in the military.'

He nodded. 'My parents kicked up a fuss, said I was stupid, I'd only wind up getting killed in Northern Ireland. Really gave me a hard time, almost as if they cared. So I compromised. I chose a unit that doesn't go anywhere near Northern Ireland. Eighteen years old, I traveled to the recruiting office at Fort Nugent in Paris. They sent me down to the Legion depot at Aubagne where I survived a fortnight of selection tests, then on to Castelnaudary for the toughest fifteen weeks of my life. Never seen my parents since, never wanted to. For all I know, they could be dead.'

'They have no idea what happened to you?' Virginia asked, equally shocked and fascinated.

'No. They finally got what they wanted: I simply disappeared.'

John knew there wasn't much a person could say to that, so he quickly changed the subject.

'What about you? Your life?' he asked.

'Dull by comparison.'

'Well, I see De Niro on the mantelpiece so it can't be that boring.'

'Bob,' she said. 'I call him Bob.'

'Naturally. Anything coming up?'

'Yeah, I've already drafted some sketches for a new movie I'm working on.'

'So you'll be at the Oscars next year – can I come?'

She smiled and patted his thigh. 'We'll see.'

'Any skeletons in the closet?' he asked, and instantly cringed.

'It's okay,' she said. 'Not really. A failed marriage eight years back, that's all. I stupidly fell in love with an actor. He was already in love – with himself. Totally self-obsessed. He's got nowhere.'

'What about your mum? Do you mind me asking?'

'No. She was a lovely woman. A pediatrician. She died six years ago of a brain tumor. My dad was devastated. He puts on a brave face but he's not much better about it now.' She sighed. 'But … he copes. It's just one more thing to add to all the crap that's been going on in his head since the war.'

John debated whether or not to pry, but his curiosity was immense. 'What happened to your dad in Vietnam? Or is it just that he was there?'

'I don't know. He won't say and I stopped asking a long time ago.'

'Was he regular Army?'

'I really don't know.' She finished her drink. 'Refill?'

John gave Virginia his glass, which she took through to the kitchen.

'I'm in love,' he muttered to himself, and couldn't recall feeling quite this way before.

She returned a minute later with more booze and sat down. Her expression had changed. She looked troubled.

'What's up?' John asked, taking his drink.

'I was just thinking about Donnie.'

John could only nod in sympathy.

'We had no idea he was in South America. And to be mixed up with the drugs trade ...' She shook her head, lost for words.

'He wanted excitement,' John said. 'It's not easy going back to Civvy Street after the Army, especially when you've seen action.'

'But it's not like he went to work in a car wash or a burger joint.

He did close protection for some major Hollywood players. I know because I got him in. That's got to be interesting, moving in those circles.'

'Yes, but after being in combat, for some people *interesting* doesn't cut it, only *dangerous*. The closest would have been if some stalker had come out of the crowd shooting at a film première, and after six months he'd obviously decided it wasn't going to happen. He needed to be where guns were used for more than self-defense.'

Virginia looked confused, and John returned her frown.

'What?' he said.

'What do you mean *after six months*? My brother was a bodyguard for a lot longer than six months.'

John must have cringed.

'Wasn't he?' Virginia asked.

John felt decidedly uncomfortable. He clearly possessed more of the facts than Donnie's own flesh and blood.

'That's what he told us,' Virginia said. 'He was working security jobs abroad. London, Paris, Rome. He was with an international agency that got him contracts all over the world. Are you saying that's not true?'

'Damn,' John said awkwardly. 'I wish someone else could be telling you this.'

'What? Telling me what exactly?'

'Please remember I'm only the messenger.'

'John ...?'

'Donnie being In Colombia was something of a natural progression. He'd been working as a mercenary for years. He was in the former Yugoslavia a year before I first got there, training the Bosnians and then fighting with them. Ninety-five he was in Sierra Leone fighting the rebels. Zaire in ninety-six.'

'Zaire? Doing what, for Christ's sake?'

'Nothing, as it happens. President Mobutu had organized a huge mercenary force to regain some billion-pound gold mine lost to the Tutsi rebels. By early ninety-seven there'd still been no counter-offensive so Donnie left the region. We sent each other the odd email after that, but it was just *hi, how are you doing, let's meet up again one day.*'

'You didn't know he was in South America?'

'No, he became very scant on detail after Zaire. Now it's obvious why.'

Virginia absorbed the numbing truth of her brother's last years.

'This goes no further. My father can't know any of this.'

John nodded. 'I understand.'

'I'm going to bed. This day needs to end.'

'Sorry about the revelations.'

'Not your fault.'

They finished their drinks and went upstairs. Virginia poked her head into her father's room to check on him.

'He's sound,' she whispered to John.

'Will he dream?' John asked.

She shrugged, then pointed across the landing. 'You're in there. Bed's made up. Bathroom's next door along.' She pecked his cheek. 'Sweet dreams, *sergent*. Thanks for being there.'

John felt his heart flutter and his face redden, and the tough Legionnaire was nowhere inside him.

Chapter 9

He had done a terrible thing last night. By physically assaulting his wife he had overstepped an invisible boundary. He could backtrack and never again venture across, but his mark was indelible, like the handprints of the stars forever set in concrete outside Grauman's Chinese Theater. Larry had entered the dark world of spousal battery. In his job he had always despised violent husbands, now he was one.

He was alone in the bedroom, sprawled fully-clothed on top of the duvet with a pounding headache. For all he knew, Hayley was still lying on the living-room floor. When the tin of beer had struck her forehead she had collapsed like a rag doll, and he had been reminded of Frank. For a long while he had simply stared at her, his sense of horror dulled by the alcohol. Later he had gingerly checked her pulse, half-expecting to find it absent – another domestic fatality – but she was alive. He had considered trying to wake her after that but was too frightened and in no mood for further upset – to see the pain of betrayal in her eyes. As it was, he had pulled his personal handgun from its concealed belt holster and perched back on the sofa with it. He had fondled the chromed Tanfoglio .45 for ten minutes, his mind filled with despair. Eventually he had stepped over his unconscious wife and gone to bed. Any less drunk, any less tired, he might have put the muzzle in his mouth and pulled the trigger.

As he rolled off the bed, something ground hard against his ankle. He extracted the offending article from down his sock. Last night he had forgotten to remove it or simply hadn't cared. He looked at the Tactical One-Hander in his palm, then thumbed the seven-inch blade from its housing. The steel flashed in the morning sun. He put the knife on his pillow and strained his ears for any sound in the apartment. It was silent. Perhaps Hayley *had* died during the night. Damage from head trauma did not always manifest itself at the time of the injury, and he had certainly delivered one hell of a missile with that tin; he had only taken a couple of mouthfuls from it.

He hurried into the living room but she wasn't there. She had picked herself up and skipped out. His Budweiser was on the carpet, its contents spilled into a stain. He angrily kicked it across the floor.

He had to find her, patch things up. The problem was, he still didn't feel in a very loving mood. Although he was desperately sorry, deeply ashamed, nothing fundamental had changed. He might apologize and mean it, but he knew he could easily react the same way again at the very slightest provocation. The old Larry was still locked away and no nearer to breaking out. He went through to the kitchen and made a pot of coffee, sat down with a large mug and sipped until the caffeine ordered his senses.

Concluding his wife had fled to a friend's house, he returned to the living room, opened their address book and began ringing the likely candidates. After years on the street he was attuned to distinguishing fact from fiction. The average person was a terrible liar. Intonation, body language, skin coloration – there was a host of unconscious tells. Over the phone he would have to rely on voice only.

He rang around, but none of those who answered made him at all suspicious.

Perhaps Hayley was at the cemetery, crying at her father's grave, bemoaning her husband. It made him seethe to think so. The guy had been bones for over forty years. How did it help? He couldn't imagine kneeling at Frank Dista's headstone, blubbing his heart out. For one split second it crossed his mind that he might recover more quickly if he did, but he was a cop not an actress.

Still holding the phone, he laid it gently back on the hook, a fresh thought dragging his movement. His eyes narrowed. There was one other person he might try. He lifted the handset, set it down again. What was the point? Hayley never spoke to her mother. Some disagreement thirty-odd years back had queered their relationship. Would she really have run home to Mommy?

As a cop, he had learned not to discount anything. Humans were capable of amazing behavior at both ends of the moral spectrum. He found the number, picked up and punched the buttons.

'Hello?' said a female voice at the other end.

'Mrs Olsen, this is Larry.'

'Who?'

'Hayley's husband. Is she there?'

'Hayley got married?'

Already he knew the call was wasted; there was no recognition in her voice. Dementia? The stress of the estrangement?

'Yes, you were there,' Larry said, referring to the one extremely strained and ultimately short-lived *rapprochement* between mother and daughter.

'Was I?' said Mrs Olsen. 'Oh, yes, I remember. How are you, Gary?'

'Larry. My name's Larry.'

'Oh. You mean she and Gary got divorced?'

He made a face at the phone. 'No, Mrs Olsen, she married Larry not Gary.'

'Oh, that is a shame. I liked Gary. He was a police officer, you know.'

'I know. I'm that police officer. My name's Larry. Is Hayley there?'

'No, she's at the UCLA.'

'Jesus,' he muttered. 'No, she's not, Mrs Olsen, she graduated years ago.'

'Theater Studies. She studies Theater Studies.'

Larry gave up. 'Yeah, right, gotta go, Elvis Presley's at the door.'

There was a pause, then, 'Don't be ridiculous, the King's dead. August sixteen, nineteen seventy-seven. I remember I was baking cookies when I heard the news.'

'My mistake, it's James Dean,' he said, and hung up.

So, Hayley had to be at the cemetery. There was nowhere else she could be. He would have to drop by there before his shift. Find her, make up with her, swear he'd never lay another finger on her, promise to get counselling. In fact, lie all he had to, just so long as his wife was back in their bed tonight, where she belonged.

That morning, Hayley's first view of the world transported her back to childhood. She was thoroughly disorientated. She awoke to a familiar room, but one that belonged to the past. Then a more bizarre thought: she was still a kid and had dreamt of a future yet to unfold. A scary time in which her hope had died and love did not exist.

Gradually the truth overcame. She was an adult and that future was now.

Her old posters were still tacked up. Dustin Hoffman as *The Graduate*; Charlie's Angels; David Soul. She was filled with nostalgia and missed the naïve optimism of her youth, believing a future generation would be pinning Hayley Olsen to their walls. Her childhood had been far from happy, but at least her faith had been intact – one day she would be famous.

She touched her injured forehead. The skin was not broken and the swelling had gone down overnight. Where the tin had hit there was now just a hard knot. She imagined the mirror would show her a nasty bruise.

Her mother had been wonderful. There had been no sense of rebuke, no cold front; the difficult years had melted away. The small bungalow seemed like the home it once had been. Hayley got up and dressed and went into the kitchen.

Sitting at the table with a cup of her favorite Lipton's tea, Marie Olsen smiled with love and sympathy as her daughter entered the room.

'Morning, sweetheart, how did you sleep?'

'Pretty good, considering,' Hayley said, sitting opposite. In the daylight, her opinion of last night was confirmed: her mother had lost a lot of weight.

'How's your head? It looks sore.'

'It is. Are you all right, Mom? You look a little gaunt.'

'I'm fine. How about you? Do you want to see a doctor?'

Hayley declined. 'Any bagels?'

'Of course. Tea or coffee?'

'Tea, please. I can do it.'

'You sit down.' Marie rose unsteadily to her feet.

'Sure you're all right, Mom? Your color's not so good.'

'Getting old, dear.'

Marie popped two bagels in the toaster and poured some tea

from the pot. She looked back at her daughter with troubled eyes.

'Larry called,' she said quietly.

The name made Hayley freeze.

'Don't worry, darling, he doesn't know you're here. I employed a few old acting skills. He thinks I'm a crazy old broad. I kept calling him Gary.'

Hayley smiled. 'Thanks, Mom.'

Cheerily, Marie said, 'I thought this morning we might pop along to the Boardwalk.'

Up to the age of nine, it had been a weekly treat for Hayley. Venice Beach was only a ten-minute stroll from the bungalow. They would roam among the tie-dyed street traders, snigger at the bodybuilders in their enclosure, paddle in the ocean whilst eating ice cream. Just mother and daughter. Until things had changed.

'I'd love to,' Hayley said.

'You can drive us. Put the top down.'

'Deal.' But Hayley wondered why her mother didn't want to walk the short distance. She had always been sprightly enough.

The bagels jumped up in the toaster. Marie snatched them onto a plate, whistling as they burnt her fingers. She buttered them, set the plate in front of her daughter and sat down.

'Thanks, Mom,' Hayley said, and began to eat. After two bites she realized she wasn't hungry; the emptiness inside was nothing to do with food. She drank some tea instead.

'What will you do?' asked her mother.

'About Larry? Go back, I guess. He was drunk, he reacted. It's just a bruise.'

'But he could have killed you.' Marie reached a hand across the table. 'Don't make excuses for him, sweetheart.'

Hayley shot an acid stare, then immediately squeezed her mother's hand by way of an apology. A lot of years had passed; it was time to forget.

'Sorry, Mom.'

'Don't be. I understand your anger. While you were under this roof you hated me.'

Hayley shook her head but knew it lacked conviction.

'It's okay,' Marie said. 'When you finally left home, like you, I breathed the biggest sigh of relief.'

'I know.'

'You don't, my love. Not why. With you gone, I wasn't constantly reminded of the selfish bitch I'd been. It's the reason I gave up my acting career. I loved acting but I didn't want to make it any more. I didn't want anyone looking up to me, thinking I was something special when the reality was so different. On those few occasions we've got together since, I've purposely engineered our arguments so you wouldn't want to see me again.'

Hayley found a long-held belief beginning to crumble, and it was wonderful.

'Because of guilt?' she asked.

'Of course because of guilt.'

'But I always thought you hated me for speaking out like I did.'

'No, darling.' Marie's eyes filled up. 'God, no. Not for one second.'

Larry was sitting on the hood of his Corvette in the parking lot of the LAPD's Hollywood Station. He had taken an end space on one the rows, so he could spot when DeCecco arrived. He knew the Harley, but didn't want to risk DeCecco slipping past unnoticed in a car. Colleagues waved at him as they came and went, starting or ending their shifts. He returned their greetings, occasionally being forced into some lightly insulting banter. The sun was trying to lift his spirits, blazing down on him, but it warmed his skin and nothing else. His heart was cold. He had failed to locate his missing wife. Hayley was not at her father's grave, which was gratifying in one respect, but also annoying for the simple reason that he didn't know where else to look.

The grumble of the Harley Low Rider could be heard before it was seen, and Larry stiffened at the sound. He hated DeCecco. Ordinarily he might have quite liked the guy, but events had dropped certain people several slots down his league table. If he could attack Hayley, whom he loved, he reckoned he was capable of killing his new partner.

He watched as DeCecco waited for the security gate to roll back. Under the peak of his crash helmet, the rookie's eyes were shielded by impenetrable Wayfarers, but Larry knew he'd been spotted. When the gate had retracted sufficiently, DeCecco opened the throttle and surged past the Corvette and a row of black-and-whites towards a space at the far end of the lot. Larry hurried over. He didn't want to appear panicked but he had to catch DeCecco before he got inside.

DeCecco dismounted, removed his helmet and started towards the entrance.

'Wait up!' Larry called. 'We need to talk.'

Joey carried on walking. 'You said it all last night.'

'No, I didn't.' Larry dodged in front and stopped his progress. 'You wouldn't let me.'

'Put it this way: I heard all I wanted to hear.'

'But not all you *needed* to hear.'

DeCecco sighed impatiently but did not attempt to barge Larry aside.

'Okay, talk.'

'Not here. In my car.'

The Corvette's red leather seats were warm. The morning sun had direct access through the open roof. Larry faced his partner and hung his left hand over the central T-bar above his head, trying to appear casual to any onlookers. He got straight to the point. DeCecco had made his objections known already so there was no use skirting.

'Joey, you are going to do this thing with me so you better get with the program. If you go upstairs with this I will wreck your life, and I ain't talking no Serpico shit here, trying to get you ostracized. I mean I will fucking destroy you. Are you getting this?'

Staring straight ahead through the windshield, his face set like stone, DeCecco said nothing, which Larry took as a cue to continue.

'Come on, think about it; it's going down on our turf a half hour before our shift ends on the last of our three twelves this week. Okay? I mean that's fucking ordained.'

'No, that's happenstance, Larry. Shit goes down all the time in this town. You know that.'

'You're not listening. Again, you're not listening. Fuck, Joey, I need this bust. I need it. And *you* need it. This could make your career. You don't want to make detective?'

Joey faced him. 'What I want, you lamebrain, is to stay alive. I want to be a father. My wife is pregnant with our first child, eight months along. You didn't know that, did you? You never bothered to ask about me – am I married, do I have kids.'

'Are you married, do you have kids?'

DeCecco gave a withering sneer. 'What an asshole.'

'You seriously want me to talk about diapers and white picket fences?'

'You mean in preference to you telling me yet again how you

saw your partner die? Yes, that would make a pleasant change. For your information, I do know what a cadaver looks like.'

'Saw one on the TV, huh?'

'Whatever. Listen, Larry, if you have a death wish, that's your problem, but don't wish it on me. Either you make an appointment with psych services today, or I won't just tell Gilchrist what Eddie said, I'll tell him what you did, and what you're asking me to do right now.'

'You wanna trade threats, Joey? Fine by me. You heard of CIW out at Chino?'

'The women's prison, what of it?'

'You fuck with me, you'll be taking Junior there to visit with Mommy.'

The color drained from DeCecco's face and Larry guessed that was a bad sign – the blood heading elsewhere, into Joey's biceps. But Larry had to say more or the threat would be empty.

'I'll make sure she's found with a shitload of narcotics in the trunk of her car.'

Larry hadn't thought through his use of such shock tactics. What he was suggesting could certainly be arranged. The question was whether he'd sink so low as to make the necessary phone calls.

DeCecco was motionless for several seconds. Then the magnitude of the threat seemed to register and he erupted. Growling a curse, he leapt across the center console and grabbed his partner by the throat. In the confined space, Larry flailed to fend him off, but DeCecco's grip was torqued up to lethal, that steely glint in his eyes again like the previous night at the bar. Only colder – killer's eyes.

Larry thought he was going to die. While he still had the physical strength and mental spark, he ceased his ineffectual struggle and snatched the Tanfoglio from its holster and thrust the muzzle under DeCecco's chin. The .45 was kept cocked and locked and Larry now thumbed off the safety. Two seconds later he would have pulled the trigger, but DeCecco heard the click and came partly to his senses. He didn't release the stranglehold but it loosened sufficiently for the greyness to depart Larry's brain.

'Get the fuck off of me!' Larry wheezed. '*I mean it!*'

DeCecco instantly let go and sat back in his seat. He fumed for a moment then got out of the car. After slamming the door, he took his crash helmet off the Corvette's hood and swiped it at the wing mirror, smashing it to the ground. Instead of walking away, he stood there defiantly, looking in through the open roof. Larry quickly holstered his weapon and got out, eyes belatedly darting here and there, checking for witnesses to what had just occurred, and what still might. Thankfully, no one in the lot appeared to be staring, but time would tell; no senior officer could ignore such a serious falling-out.

'You broke the glass, Joey,' Larry said hoarsely. 'That's seven years' bad luck.'

'I'm not superstitious.'

'That's irrelevant. You cross me, I'll cram all your bad luck into sixty seconds.'

DeCecco smirked. 'Anytime, Larry. You and me. Hand to hand.'

'*Mano à mano*,' Larry mocked. 'You got me real scared.'

'I should do. But you obviously didn't read my résumé.'

Mother and daughter shared the most pleasant half hour. Despite her worries, Hayley couldn't remember a time in recent memory when she had felt more relaxed. A vital connection had been re-established, and she considered it had been worth the physical hurt to bring it about. A bump on the head to cure a lifetime of anguish seemed a more than fair exchange.

One thing had been niggling: why her mother had not employed the same strategy she had professed to using before? Namely, manufacturing an argument to put some distance between them. She finally had to ask.

'Mom, what's changed since the last time we met?'

Marie flinched almost imperceptibly. 'How do you mean?'

But Hayley had noticed that split second's discomfiture. 'I think you know.'

Marie gave a little shrug, stood up and guiltily turned her back, busying herself at the sink.

Hayley felt an immense flood of sadness. Something was very wrong. She looked at her mother's hair, bunned at the nape of her neck. Once dark and lustrous, now predominantly grey and flyaway, it seemed somehow to encapsulate the tragedy of their lost years.

'Mom ...'

'I have cancer.'

Hayley felt her eyes go wide, her empty stomach churn. The lump on her forehead began to throb crazily. If she hadn't been seated, she would have collapsed.

'Is it ... serious?'

Marie turned round, smiled faintly. Hayley shook her head, horrified by her crass remark; when was cancer ever playful?

'I mean –'

'I know what you mean, dear,' Marie said gently. 'Yes, it's serious. It's terminal.'

As the prognosis sunk in, Hayley felt her strength ebb away. 'It can't be,' she said, 'there must be some treatment.'

'I take something for the pain, but no ... not a cure. Not at this stage. It's everywhere.'

'Surely they could have caught it earlier. Weren't there any signs?'

Marie nodded slowly and resumed her seat. She smiled as one who had made her peace.

'I left it too late. Not a mistake; a conscious decision. I felt no desire to halt its progress.'

Hayley was incredulous. '*Why?*'

'I'm tired. For years, when I've closed my eyes at night I've wished they wouldn't open on another morning. I've been living in limbo, sweetheart. When your father died, my life ended. I guess, if you love someone, it always feels that way for a while. But for me it never got any better. I did try. Well, you know how that worked out; things just got worse. Which only confirmed how futile it all was. Some people get two chances in this life, sweetheart, some don't. I didn't. So I don't regard this illness as anything bad. On the contrary: I wish it could have happened sooner.'

Sorrow gave way to anger. Hayley's brimming tears subsided. She shot to her feet, knocking the chair over.

'I'm not listening to this. I've only just found you; I am not letting you die. Pack a case, we're going to the hospital.'

She righted the chair and looked expectantly at her mother, but she didn't honestly believe her words would have any effect. Smiling benignly, Marie stood up.

'Come on, daughter-of-mine; let's go down to the Boardwalk.'

'Hey, Lar, how's Joey shaping up?'

Fortunately, Larry was hidden from the questioner by his locker door; the mention of DeCecco had transformed his expression into pure disgust. He could recognize the voice. Only one person called him Lar, and he hated the abbreviation. Kevin Mallory, a beat cop with five years on the force. He was by-the-book, as straight as they came. With some difficulty, Larry produced a smile and stepped back to show it to Mallory. He continued buttoning his black shirt as he answered with a lie that pained him.

'Oh, pretty good.'

'Yeah,' Mallory said, 'he should be with his background.'

It was just the two of them in the room. DeCecco was upstairs getting a coffee. Mallory sat down on the central bench to tie his bootlaces.

Larry frowned. 'Background?'

Mallory laughed. 'Yeah, *right* …'

'What background, Kevin?'

Mallory looked up from his boots. 'You don't know?' he asked, astonished. 'You haven't talked to him yet? Lar, you've been partners a month.'

'Kevin, what are you talking about?'

'He's ex-MARSOC.'

'What?'

'Marines Special Operations Command. The élite. Like the Army's Green Berets or the Navy SEALs. You didn't know that?'

Larry felt his skin goosebump. He'd been tangling with a genuine hard-ass and hadn't known.

'No,' he said, feigning nonchalance. 'How come you know?'

'He told me. We got talking.' Mallory stood up and began combing his hair in the locker mirror. 'He's a cool guy.'

Larry was computing the information. DeCecco's comments now made sense – about having seen a corpse, having the guts for more than just police work, his résumé. But he didn't want to believe it.

'That's bullshit,' he said. 'Why leave an organisation like that to join the LAPD?'

'Hey, we're not so shabby.'

'Kevin, we're the fucking boy scouts compared. No … it's bullshit. He's lying.'

'I saw his armed forces card: USMC Retired.'

Larry felt sick. He knew it was true. Which meant DeCecco could have killed him earlier, snapped his neck like a dry twig. The choke-hold had been nothing but a warning, a statement of intent.

'Yeah, Lar, you got yourself one hell of a partner.'

Larry slammed his locker door and glowered.

'Do me a favor: stop fucking calling me Lar. My name's Larry.'

Mallory held up his hands in defense. 'Hey, no problem.'

'And I *had* one hell of a partner. Frank was the best. I don't give a fuck what the Marines taught Joey DeCecco. The streets are different. He knows dick about being a cop.'

Still with his hands in surrender mode, Mallory said nothing. Larry buckled on his utility belt and headed out of the room to find his errant partner.

On the upstairs landing he stopped dead. DeCecco was just leaving Captain Gilchrist's office.

Chapter 10

Jet-lag kept John in bed until past two p.m. He knew nothing of the day until Virginia brought him an extremely late breakfast. Bacon, scrambled eggs, beans and hash browns, orange juice and coffee. All sleepy-eyed and shock-haired, he sat up in bed to take the tray on his lap. Exposed from the waist up, his body was still tautly-muscled from his military years.

'You should be in the movies,' Virginia said.

He smiled at the compliment. 'Thanks for breakfast.'

'I'm serious. I can talk to someone if you like. I've made some good contacts.'

'You don't know if I can act.'

'Hey, this is Hollywood – who cares?'

He laughed. 'You old cynic.'

'Eat,' she said, and sat at the foot of the bed.

John tucked in, and although she seemed happy enough just to watch him, he soon began to feel uncomfortable. He felt like an interloper in the Chester household. His motive for traveling all this way was not entirely pure, a fact he had admitted at the range yesterday. He wasn't sure he deserved all this attention from Donnie's sister.

'I did like your brother,' he said.

'I know.'

'I wouldn't have come otherwise, holiday or no holiday.'

'I believe you. Don't feel guilty.'

Virginia had him figured, which came as a relief.

'I just don't want you to think I'm freeloading,' he said.

'I don't think that at all; I like having you here.'

John grinned. 'If you pass me my wallet, I'll show you something,' he said. 'Jacket, inside pocket.'

Virginia retrieved it, sat down again and offered it, but John shook his head.

'Open it,' he told her.

She did, and a smile blossomed and John knew why. In the small photo-window was a shot of two soldiers in different desert-pattern uniforms. They were leaning against a sand-colored personnel carrier, laughing, strong arms around broad shoulders. They had taken their helmets off for the picture, but their assault rifles were slung on the chest. Donnie with his M16, John with his FA MAS.

'That was gee minus two,' he said. 'Feb twenty-second, two days before the Ground War.'

'You've kept this with you since nineteen ninety-one?'

'It means a lot to me. I liked Donnie. We got on. Clicked straightaway, almost like we were brothers.'

She took the photo out and regarded it fondly, then gave John a long smile.

'I'm glad you met Donnie,' she said.

'So am I,' he said.

Virginia picked up his wallet, and John continued eating. After a few moments he realized she had not reinserted the picture, but was instead staring again at the small plastic window in the brown leather. He finished his mouthful.

'Before you ask,' he said, 'I have absolutely no idea who that is.'

She gave him an odd look. 'I beg your pardon?'

He gently took the wallet off her and looked at the other photo he always kept with him. Since the Gulf, it had been out of sight beneath his wartime memory, but it had been with him a lot longer.

'Souvenir of Oregon,' he explained, but knew it explained nothing to either of them. He handed back the wallet and finished his coffee.

'Oregon? You mentioned that last night. What happened?'

'Well, long story short: I bumped into some fellah who ended up giving me this picture; insisted I take it.'

'Pretty girl,' Virginia commented, then looked up. 'You really don't know who she is?'

'He said it was his granddaughter.'

'Why did he want you to have it?'

'He thought I might be –' John made a spooky face '– *the one.*'

'Like in *Highlander*.'

'Like … I have no idea. It was a very strange day.'

'Sounds it. So why keep it with you all these years?'

John gave the only reason he could: 'He made me promise.'

Virginia didn't understand, but knew he didn't either so didn't push it. She looked again at the photo – the grinning girl with the fiery red curls, standing on a beach in a distinctive dress. With her gaze elsewhere, John took the opportunity to eye his hostess. In the sober light of day, he stood by his drunken assessment of the previous evening: he was hopelessly in love. Suddenly an outrageous suggestion came to mind and was out before he knew it.

'Fancy coming away with me?'

'Where?' she said, unfazed.

'Oregon?'

Her enthusiasm shone through. That they liked each other was obvious; he was glad she had tacitly agreed not to play games.

'Yeah, I'm up for a road trip,' she said, then checked herself. 'Oh. My dad.'

'Of course. Sorry, I got carried away. He needs you here.'

She nodded but seemed uncertain, clearly finding it hard to pass up.

'What the hell!' she announced like it was the most momentous decision of her life. 'Dad's coped with worse. And it's not like Donnie died yesterday. It's been two months, it's just the Mexican authorities wouldn't release his body until now.'

It was clear she was trying to convince herself. Shamefully perhaps, John let her.

'Yeah, let's go,' she said. 'I'll see if I can borrow the Jeep; swap it for the Audi. We'll need four-wheel drive. The roads can be pretty tricky this time of year. So is this simple nostalgia or are we on a mission?'

He considered with a smile. 'Nostalgia. Retrace the childhood route.'

'Can you remember it?'

'I know we did all the touristy bits.'

'And what about the photograph? Think you could find the guy who gave it you? Ask him why? Or is that a long shot?' She answered her own question: 'Yeah, I guess it is.'

A ghostly pistol report rang in John's head, an echo from the past that made him shiver, but John skirted the pertinent fact.

'No, we could look, but where we met was miles off the beaten track. We were lost when we found the place; could be anywhere.'

'Okay, so it's a vacation. When do we leave?'

John was startled again by her open excitement. It made him

laugh. The connection he had found with Donnie seemed to be tenfold with his sister.

'I just need to check out of my hotel and we can be on the road by this evening. Unless that's too soon.'

'No, tonight's good. I'll drive down to the range, exchange vehicles, and we'll meet back here at six o'clock.'

She turned to leave the room but John stopped her.

'Virginia ... are you sure about this? Apart from leaving your father on his own, you hardly know me.'

'What better way to get acquainted.'

Relieved that this own doubt had not triggered any in her, John renewed his smile, although it felt rather imbecilic on his face now.

'Saddle up, soldier,' Virginia said. 'Wagons roll at eighteen hundred hours.'

Apart from a few words of necessary official communication, the occupants of Six Adam Nine had been utterly quiet. Larry was deep in thought, deeply puzzled. Why was he still being allowed to cruise the streets, passing himself off as guardian of the good and true? Following DeCecco's visit to Gilchrist's office that morning, he had not believed he would make it down the station steps; a summons had seemed inevitable. Yet here he was, their shift nearly at an end, and everything seemed hunky-dory. His shield was on his chest, his weapon on his hip. He couldn't figure it out. How come they weren't on the captain's desk, surrendered by a cop in disgrace?

Had he challenged DeCecco he might have established the facts, but one thing had stopped him, a consideration he was loath to admit but could not deny because an old adage kept repeating in his head: all bullies are cowards. He was scared of DeCecco. He couldn't look on him as a simple rookie any more. DeCecco was ex-Special Forces. Beneath that mild exterior lurked one of Uncle Sam's killing machines, and it didn't seem policy to rile him.

But the hours of uncertainty had taken their toll. His head was a mess. To at least salvage his marriage he needed to establish if his career was over, because not knowing was driving him crazy, which only made him liable to further violence. That he was still on the streets didn't mean a whole lot. It was early days. Maybe IA had been busy tracing Eddie, and were now in the process of investigating certain not-entirely-unfounded allegations of corruption.

When the dam eventually broke, Larry forced himself to speak pleasantly.

'Joey, you talked to Gilchrist earlier. Anything I should know about?'

'Did I?'

Larry stopped the Charger on a residential street and cut the ignition.

'Yeah, I saw you leaving his office,' Larry said.

'You're right,' DeCecco said. 'But before we get started, I need to give you my best advice on something.'

'What's that?'

'Don't go for your weapon like you did this morning.'

Although his brain told him to mutely accept the warning, Larry's mouth was in cahoots with his pride. 'Or what?' he said.

'Or the medical examiner who deals with your body's gonna find fifteen outshoots from no visible entry wound. If you get my drift.'

Larry decided it probably wasn't a threat he should mock; DeCecco's eyes had lost their humanity again. This time his mouth did the sensible thing and swallowed his pride.

'So what's the deal, Joey? Should I be expecting a welcoming committee when we get back?'

'If you mean will I be taking any more of your crap, the answer is no.'

'*Shit*, you fucking blabbed! I knew you would!'

'I put in for a transfer. Highway Patrol. Motorcycle unit. Captain knows I ride a bike. Okay? Nothing about you, nothing about Eddie.'

Larry considered, and reckoned DeCecco was telling the truth.

'Oh. Good. Thanks.'

He started the engine and moved off down the street.

Smug. Larry was the epitome of smug. He couldn't remember ever feeling so smug. His threats had worked, after all. DeCecco was smart and wasn't willing to put his pregnant wife at risk.

'So what about this bust tomorrow night?' Larry asked, pushing his luck.

'It's not up for discussion.'

'But you didn't blow the whistle on it. I think that means something. I think that means we got us a green light. I reckon a guy like you must be itching for some real action. Huh? Am I right, Joey?'

'Officer Roth, if I wanted a conversation I'd start one.'

Larry laughed. 'Hey, *touché*. But I know what I'm talking about. I heard about you from Mallory. MARSOC, right? Impressive. What unit? Where were you based?'

There was a deliberate pause before DeCecco indulged the question.

'First Marine Raider Battalion, Camp Pendleton.'

'Uh-huh, just along the coast, I've driven by it many a time. You with them a while?'

'Five years. Regular Marines for five years before that.'

'Okay. You, uh ... get into any scrapes?'

'It's a wicked world, Larry. We were put to good use.'

'Yeah, I bet. So … what's different now with this bust? It's just more bad guys who need taking down. It's the same thing, you just got a change of uniform.'

'Protocol,' DeCecco said. 'Correct procedure. That's what's different. Good intel, planning, preparation, having the right equipment for the job, the right people for the job – which category you do *not* fit into. You stray from those principles, everything gets FUBAR.'

The Charger halted at a stop sign and Larry faced his passenger.

'Joey, we can do this, smooth as silk. We'll work out a plan. Listen, if you're worried about the bim back home, just don't tell her.'

'*Bim*? You mean my *wife*?'

'Turn of phrase,' Larry said, shrugging. 'No offense.'

'Roth, be warned: talk about my wife is off limits to you. And if she gets so much as a parking ticket I will be coming to you personally for an explanation. *Capice?* Now shut the fuck up.'

Larry couldn't believe how his respect quotient had plummeted just recently. Simmering, he moved the Charger through the intersection and proceeded to stare at DeCecco as he drove, only briefly checking ahead every few seconds. A response was formulating in his head.

'Eyes on the road, asshole,' DeCecco said.

'Yeah, but I'll be driving tomorrow night, Joey, and I'm gonna take us right by the address Eddie gave us at the exact same time he gave us, and if I see anything that don't look completely kosher I'm stopping to take a look, and if you don't come with me you're the bad cop, not me. You don't back up your partner, *rookie*, forget it, you'll make *yourself* an outcast. So that's how it's gonna be, Joey, just you and me. You got that? *Capeesh*, you fucking wop?'

'Wow, an asshole *and* a racist,' Joey said, his response perfectly mellow. 'Sure, I hear you. Of course, between now and then some concerned citizen might just make an anonymous call to the captain's office.'

Larry sneered. 'What happened to *mano à mano*, Joey? You think you can't take out a few *rabiz* on your own? You need SWAT to help?'

'The only help I need right now is psychiatric, for you. Someone draws down on me, that's their funeral. You're the liability. I am not walking into a potential firefight with a fucking loon like you for back-up. No way.'

'Yes you are. Let's get a coffee, talk about it. Work out a plan of attack. You want a coffee, Joey? I need a coffee.'

'Pal, you need fucking IV Valium.'

Larry slowed the Charger and turned at an intersection, heading for a quiet coffee shop he knew. The maneuver brought the winter sun directly in through his window; a symbolic ray of hope.

Chapter 11

The answering machine showed a continuous red light: no messages. It took a moment for Hayley to realize that meant her husband hadn't called either; she had been more eager to hear from her agent. She needed this job more than ever now. *Malibu Mischief* would use up her time, absorb her thoughts. With a dying mom and a marriage in the balance, she did not want hour upon empty hour to bleakly muse. The money and fame would be pleasant by-products; the occupation was everything.

She left the phone on answer mode, sat in the darkened living room and stared intently at the tiny red light until all around it blackened and disappeared. After a while she began to blink at one second intervals and made believe it was the machine with a message for her. She closed her eyes and imagined hitting the replay button and hearing her agent's voice speak those magic words. Then she pictured her subsequent trip to the cemetery to relay the good news and thank her dad for his unseen hand in events.

A key in the latch. Hayley snapped her eyes open. The red light was constant. The fantasy shattered. Larry was home and her heart began to thud. She became suddenly aware of the time; his shift had ended two hours ago. Where had he been since then? That was easy. The real question was how much had he drunk? The knot on her forehead was now throbbing in time with her pulse.

He stepped off the walkway and closed the door behind him. When he clicked the wall switch, Hayley heard a little gasp escape his mouth. Shocked or relieved or both, the faintest of smiles appeared on his face.

'Hey,' he said quietly.

Hayley couldn't be sure, but he seemed sober. Her mouth flickered hopefully at the corners.

'Jesus, did I do that?' he asked.

She tipped her head forward; both a nod and a way to tumble hair across the bruise.

'I am such a prick,' Larry said. 'I never meant to hurt you. I just lashed out.'

'Where have you been since work?'

'Just driving. I had to think.' He came over and towered above her.

'Sit down,' she said.

He did so, but left a cushion between them. Hayley was glad – she had not asked him to sit so they could be close; she had felt intimidated by his fists level with her face. She didn't know what to say but she guessed her presence in the apartment spoke for itself. She had come back, and Larry had a second chance.

'Hayley ... darling ... I want you to know that I will never, ever, do anything like that again. I am so ashamed. I allowed my problems at work to become your problems. I didn't talk them through with you, I took them out on you. I need help, I know that now. I made an appointment today with a counsellor. I also want to apologize for my cruel remarks regarding your father. You should feel at liberty to visit his grave whenever you wish, without fear of ridicule from your own husband. In future, you will have my total support. Okay?'

Hayley looked down at her lap, unable to respond, and her curls swished forward like theater curtains to hide her face. She still had doubts, and plenty of them. Larry's words sounded too much like the final draft of a prepared speech, not a spontaneous gushing from the heart. That would account for his two hours' driving around.

'Come on, Hayley, please talk to me. I appreciate you might want to cut loose from me, and if that's your decision I won't try and stop you. But please don't. Please. I was a good husband once, I can be again. I'm not asking you to forget, just … forgive. One time only.'

Crazily, Hayley wanted to snigger. His last line had made him sound like a desperate door-to-door salesman. She had to say something or risk laughing. She steeled her expression and shot it towards him, and was surprised by how much venom was instantly on tap.

'Fine, but you pull shit like that again, I am so fucking gone.'

With eyebrows raised high, Larry could only nod.

'Have you eaten?' she asked, standing up.

He shook his head.

'Omelette?' she asked.

He nodded. 'Thank you.'

Listening to his wife crack eggs in the kitchen, Larry seethed. Hayley made two people that day who had slapped him down. His pride was stuck in his gullet like he'd swallowed a Ninja throwing star.

He remotely switched on the TV, then instantly pressed *mute*. Something else was bothering him.

'Where did you stay last night?' he called as conversationally as possible.

'My mom's.'

Her *mom's*? 'Hayley, come in here.'

She appeared in the doorway.

'You made up?' he asked.

'It was long overdue,' she said, her expression incongruously somber.

'And is she ... okay?'

'She's great,' Hayley said curtly, and returned to the kitchen.

'She's, uh ... fully *compus mentis*, then?'

A puzzled Hayley came back into the doorway, then a slight smirk showed she understood his question.

'Oh, yeah,' she said. 'Mom mentioned she gave you the run-around. Did you forget she used to be an actress?'

Larry faked a self-deprecating smile. 'Stupid me.'

Hayley returned to the cooking and Larry cursed under his breath. Make that three people denying him his due respect. He could just picture them, laughing away in that little Venice bungalow, pitying the dumb duped cop who didn't know twenty-four carat bullshit when he heard it.

Once upon a time, life had been very simple. Special Forces made things that way. You followed orders. A soldier's loyalty to the unit, and the unit's allegiance to the flag – those things were unequivocal. Questions of morality rarely entered into it, much less issues of right or wrong with regard to the law.

Now, even though Joey DeCecco was The Law, everything was shades of grey. The only black and white was the car he rode around in. His partner had given him a real headache. Joey knew he had gotten Roth pretty shaken up, but his own fears had not been allayed. He had been put on notice that his wife was fair game. If he did talk to Gilchrist and Roth did follow up on his threat, breaking the bastard's neck would serve only as revenge.

Joey twisted the faucet and stopped the jets. He could hear Laura in their bedroom, humming some jolly tune. He stayed in the shower for several minutes, a steady succession of drips tapping his flattened crew-cut. Eventually he swivelled the leaky head off to one side. His skin had turned to gooseflesh. Laura DeCecco was still making happy noises in the bedroom, excitedly sifting through a huge pile of baby clothes donated by her sister. Every so often, the humming would give way to coos of delight.

He climbed out of the shower and began towelling himself. His head kept making involuntary little shakes, though it didn't negate the impending choice. How could he endanger his wife? If he said no to Roth, he was taking a mighty gamble on the man's state of mind. Was he really on the ragged edge? Joey thought so, and if he tipped over, why would he not take someone with him?

He shook his head – a conscious movement this time. He couldn't do it, he couldn't take the risk. The stakes were too high: Laura and their unborn child. The scan indicated a boy – his son. They were too defenseless. He at least had a fighting chance.

'Honey, come in here!' Laura called.

Joey wrapped the towel round his middle and went through to see the tiny clothes neatly arranged across the bed. Laura beamed at him, the same beautiful smile that had first captured his heart, but more radiant these days, aglow with the inner fire of motherhood. Then her gaze fell to the bed again, hypnotically drawn.

'God, Joey, just look at these things. Can you believe it?'

Joey approached, stood behind his wife and circled his arms around her.

'They're cute, Babe,' he said over her shoulder. 'Real cute.'

'Aren't they?'

He gathered up her night-shirt with his fingers until it lay across the top of her warm, swollen belly, and placed his palms over his son. He nudged his nose through Laura's long dark hair into the nape of her neck and he closed his eyes.

'Feel those kicks,' he whispered. 'He's strong.'

'Just like his dad.'

Joey wasn't so sure any more.

'I love you, Laura,' he said. 'I love you both. Very, very much.'

She laid her hands over his, squeezed them, turned her head and kissed him.

'Make love to me, Joey.'

Joey hadn't thought he was in the mood, but found himself overruled; beneath his towel, something stirred. Its ascent was stopped by his wife's bare ass. Laura took his hands and raised them under the high-bunched hem to her breasts, voluptuously enlarged by her hormones. He caressed and she moaned, feeling behind to undo his towel, which fell to the carpet. Joey bent at the knees, allowing his penis to rise horizontal between her legs, hard against her vagina. Then he gasped as she delved a hand and touched what was poking through.

Later, Joey helped Laura put the baby clothes away in the nursery. Characters from *Toy Story* ran around the walls, and a cot had been installed, caging an army of plush animals.

Joey's preoccupation with work was etched into his face again. He could feel it there, narrowing his eyes, pinching his lips. The decision had been made. Now he was bulling himself up. If it had to be done, he was undoubtedly best-qualified for the job. The danger would be in letting Roth take control – and lose it.

Hopefully, Roth wasn't as dumb as he was crazy; maybe he was relying on his partner's expertise to get them through. But Joey couldn't help thinking how bloody things might get, and how some of it might escape from his own veins.

Laura pushed a drawer to and peered at him.

'Hon, you okay?' she asked.

'Sure.'

'Really? It's not that whacko partner of yours, is it?'

He shrugged. 'Kinda. No problem.'

'Honestly?' she said, pressuring him with her eyes.

Joey wanted to open up, even more than he'd wanted to spew his guts to Gilchrist that morning, even more than he'd wanted to sever Roth's spinal cord every second since he *hadn't* spewed his guts. He shared everything with his wife. It was the most complete relationship he knew.

The words would not come out. At eight months pregnant, Laura required *beaucoup* R & R. She didn't need her milk soured by his troubles. He couldn't even tell her about his transfer request; on the heels of her last query, she would have no doubt something was wrong.

'Yeah, don't worry,' he said with a reassuring smile.

'You can talk to me, Joey. You know?'

Laura was a teacher by profession, and Joey thought she sounded like she was speaking to one of her kids. It didn't bother him. She had taught him love, plucked a real softie from inside this macho Marine, and he would be eternally grateful.

'Nothing to say,' he lied. 'Listen, d'you mind if I hit the sack? I know it's early, but I'm tired.'

'Sure, you go. I'll stay up awhile.' She kissed his lips.

'Goodnight, Babe,' he said to her, then stroked her belly. 'Goodnight, son.'

Laura grinned. 'Sweet dreams, Daddy.'

He left the nursery, crossed the landing and entered their bedroom, only to stand there as in the shower, paralyzed by his thoughts. His eyes idly wandered the walls, not really seeing anything. His focus had pulled back into his head to view a waking nightmare on the inside of his skull. Laura and their newborn, the boy swaddled in white, crying lustily as babies do; the mother in black, streaming the silent tears of a widow.

Suddenly his awareness came back to the room, something on the wall demanding its return. Moving towards it, Joey squinted like he'd never seen it before. He took it off the wall. The frame was specially made, slightly deeper than standard to accommodate the enclosed items.

His Marine insignia were mounted behind the glass. Three gold-colored metal badges. Naval Parachutist, Combatant Diver, and Distinguished Marksman. He remembered the day the first of those, the "gold wings", had been officially pinned to his blue dress uniform – the proudest day of his life. Only surpassed by the occasion of his marriage to Laura, and every day since the creation of that new life inside her.

He sank onto the bed, rested the frame on his lap and stared at it.

'What aren't you telling me, Joey?'

He didn't jump. He had somehow sensed Laura's presence in the room a split second before she spoke.

'I can't hide from you, can I?' he said.

'Not even with all your camo-cream and special training.'

She waddled over to the bed and sat heavily beside him. She took the frame off him and put it to one side, then held his hands. He sighed but didn't speak.

'Hey, I can handle it,' she said. 'I let you go off with the military to God-knows-where in the world, didn't I? How much worse could this be?'

'You weren't pregnant then.'

'Come on ...' she glanced down at her belly '... you're saying this mini-Marine can't take it?'

His eyes moistened as he laughed.

'Tell me, Joey. You know I won't let up until you do.'

He nodded and gave in – a willing surrender.

Joey told his wife everything. Everything save one piece of information. He couldn't allow Laura to know she was a potential target of any revenge Roth might choose to exact should Joey not be completely obedient to his demands. She was nearing full term. It would do immeasurable harm to her last idyllic days of pregnancy. The magic would vanish, and he had never seen someone so suited to the prospect of motherhood as his wife. She was in her element, loving every moment. How could he ruin that, even to maintain the perfect honesty their marriage had been built on?

So Joey told her only what Larry had planned, and not what might happen should he welch on what Larry wrongly perceived to be the obligations of a decent partner.

'So that's the choice,' Joey summed up. 'Either I rat him out or I go along with it. Either way spells trouble.'

'Hmmm,' Laura went, then took his framed badges off the bed and hooked them back in place.

Joey thought she didn't seem particularly perturbed and decided not to stress again the seriousness of the situation. If she had chosen to ignore the severity of his plight, maybe he should let it be. As an expectant mother, perhaps she possessed some inbuilt defense, a block against life's woes, a natural safeguard for the baby.

Laura came back and sat on the bed. 'I think,' she said, 'that you need to avoid pissing this guy off at all costs.'

'Yeah, you're right,' he said. 'Thanks.'

Laura gave him a wry look. 'Did you think that was my advice?' she asked. 'And you were ready to accept it?'

'Well ...'

'Honey, I'm pregnant, not retarded. It's my hormones have gone crazy, not my head.'

'So what is your advice, Babe? Go to the captain and risk becoming an outcast for ratting on a colleague who I know is highly regarded, or go to war with a bunch of heavily-armed Armenian drug dealers? Because, either way, I am screwed.'

She did not echo his despair even faintly. In fact, she smiled.

'Oh, you military men,' she said. 'You know, not everything is do or die.'

Chapter 12

DODGE CITY was closed for the night, shutter firmly locked down. Outside in the lot was Ginny's Audi. Earlier that evening, Dodge had reassured his daughter as to his state of mind, and, with cheery waves from her and John, they had driven off in the Grand Cherokee. Whether Ginny had truly believed her father was well enough to leave on his own, Dodge wasn't so sure, but he got the impression that this time she didn't *want* to know. Her mood had been too ebullient, almost daring him to break it. In a way, it was nice to finally see a selfish side to his daughter, and if a bit of romance was on the cards then Dodge was happy to play his part as Cupid Car Rental. He liked John, and Ginny deserved a break. No one had really caught her fancy in years. She had been too busy building a career and worrying about her deranged dad.

But *deranged* did not begin to describe things today. His demons had always been there, scratching to get out like a man buried alive, but now he felt their power to devastate was overwhelming him. Today, the pressure in his head was nudging critical mass. Donnie was dead, and Dodge blamed himself. His son had flown off to South America to enter what amounted to a war against his own country, and Dodge had been oblivious. Had he stopped wallowing in his own misery for a while he might have noticed. After combat, civilian life was never easy. He of all people knew that – he belonged to a generation still reeling from the fact – yet he had failed to acknowledge that history had a knack of repeating itself. Now Donnie was nothing but a faceless corpse in the ground, and, as the boy had been interred, the demons had exhumed themselves, screaming and raging against their captor.

In Namspeak, Dodge Chester was *fugazi*. Crazy. Fucked up. It had been a very long time coming, but here it was. Something in his mind had snapped or sparked or fizzed out. He didn't know what his synapses were up to, only that they had finally given up the charade.

Inside DODGE CITY the overhead fluorescents were dark, but the range was shimmering with light. The floor was littered with popped flares, patches of blinding phosphorescence spewing smoke in billowing trails of yellow and red. It drifted through the building like a cheap special effect, shrouding the military targets Dodge had sent downrange.

He blinked, his eyes smarting, watering. He could feel the pattern of the green stripes across his face; feel where his pores had been blocked by the camo cream. The olive-drab bandanna was tight around his shaved head. As he stared at his reflection in the glass, he didn't register his store on the other side. All he saw was his own form, outlined by the psychedelic glow to his rear. Nothing more than a silhouette, like the ones lost in the smoke, but he had substance, and he looked down at himself to verify the fact. The tiger-stripe camouflage of the Special Forces covered his body, the uniform cool against his skin. In his hands was a Vietnam-era CAR-15, the shorter commando version of the M-16 – and in full auto.

Dodge kicked an empty bottle of bourbon across the floor, then spun around, hefting the weapon to his shoulder. He sighted on an indistinct silhouette through the nearest booth and squeezed off a burst of automatic fire.

He was back in-country, kicking ass and taking names.

'*Rock and roll!*' he screamed, the tears coursing down his face.

He shifted along the booths, firing at the charging soldiers. No longer paper figures, now olive-clad North Vietnamese, raking the bush with their Kalashnikovs.

Several more bursts and the CAR-15 was empty. He squatted down, dropped the spent clip and reloaded. The range was silent, but not to Dodge. He was in the midst of a firefight, and the rest of his six-man team were defending themselves against the greater enemy force.

He thrust to his feet and opened up on the swarms of imaginary NVA. Breathing heavily, laughing maniacally, he was practically delirious in his reorganization of the past. Another empty mag, another quick exchange.

The empty casings spewed from the side of his weapon as he whirled round and sprayed the acrylic glass with an arc of fire.

The bullets pierced through, impacting across the front wall of grey breezeblocks. Several hit the entrance door, shattering the glass, before the full metal jackets punched through the exterior shutter and strayed into the parking lot. Dodge pulled an M26 grenade from his jacket, bit the pin out and lobbed it through the doorway into the store. But the clear path he envisaged to his target did not exist. Barely three meters away was a free-standing display unit. The grenade struck it and dropped to the floor.

The M26 had a blast radius of ten meters, dispersing one thousand fragments with a fifty percent hit probability against anyone standing in the open.

The four-second fuse-delay expired and the grenade exploded. The remaining glass cracked out and fell and Dodge was thrown backwards by the blast, feeling his body violated by the shrapnel. There was no sense of pain, merely dull thuds like numb punches thrown by an invisible hand, but the wounds did not return him to the present, only immersed him deeper in the past, tripping memories of injuries suffered way back in late 1969.

The flares in the range were beginning to burn down, but his will did not diminish with them. He crawled to the threshold of the store, propped himself against the jamb and levelled his CAR-15. He emptied the magazine in a haphazard spray, then reached his finger forward to the weapon's second trigger. Mounted under the barrel was an M203 40mm grenade launcher. He pumped the tube and pulled the trigger, and the projectile hurtled through the shop to demolish the shutter.

When everything had settled, Dodge managed to gain his feet. White blast-smoke was merging with the yellow and red from the range flares. He staggered through it and found himself firmly back in the present, staring slack-jawed at a sight even his twisted mind could not reconcile with a Vietnamese landscape.

Parked out front, his daughter's Audi was a burning wreck in the night.

Faintness overwhelmed him, and he lowered himself to sitting. Broken glass crunched under his boots. Outside, the San Fernando Valley was still humming its incessant vehicular monotone. Through the jagged metal hole by his head, the tricolor smoke swirled out like water down a plughole, and, when it thinned, Dodge could see a crowd had gathered on the sidewalk, too wary to investigate, too curious to walk away. He could hear a siren, but it might have been destined for anywhere; his wasn't the only sadness in the city. Either way, the emergency services would be there soon.

He inspected his wounds. None felt mortal, and he experienced a sudden and profound pang of sorrow for that. It could all be fixed up or replaced. His body, Ginnie's car, the building.

All but his sanity. A lifetime of hurt and loss had caught up with him.

Chapter 13

In those first hours on the road together, their rapport stood the test of time. Conversation barely faltered. John was continually amazed by the ease of communication with his traveling companion. There seemed no effort involved, no struggle for topics. He had never known anything like it. He only hoped Virginia felt the same and was not simply one of those rare individuals who could get along with anyone, because he was baring his soul that evening. No subject was taboo between them. Answers were limited by knowledge not reticence. Questioned about it, he frankly described what it felt like to kill a man. Afterwards, he realized a weight had lifted he had not known existed, and for that alone he could have kissed her.

They ended their first leg at a motel in Hawthorne, a small town off Highway 95, western Nevada. It was gone midnight when John jumped out and paid the old guy at the desk.

Inside their chalet, the double bed made him cringe.

'I asked for two singles. I honestly asked for two singles.'

Virginia appeared to find his discomfort amusing. She gave him a subtle smile, then began to unpack her case, leaving him to consider the possible interpretations of that smile.

John took his sponge bag and went through to the bathroom.

While he undressed to shower, he thought about the situation. Ironically, their obvious connection made the next step awkward. Any move on his part could seem like taking advantage, which Virginia might resent. He popped his head round the doorway and tried to lighten the atmosphere.

'Did you bring your stun-gun?'

She looked up. 'Yeah, why?'

'Just wondering whether to make up the sofa.'

As he ducked back in the bathroom, he heard her laugh, and smirked at himself in the mirror. He didn't need to worry. There was no need to force it. They had time. There would be a moment that was right; several seconds when their eyes would lock and nothing but a kiss could follow.

He pushed the bathroom door shut and stepped into the cubicle. He opened the jets straight onto his body. The cold water shot hard against his chest and made him gasp, but he didn't reach to adjust the faucet – he had been flashed back to the Gulf.

Yanbu al-Bahr on the Red Sea, Saudi Arabia, September 1990. 2REI arrives, the first contingent of the *Daguet* Division. John is there to do a job. Hopes he won't have to, but reckons he will. The Western powers aren't shipping all this hardware and manpower halfway across the world only to bring it back unused. Life has suddenly become surreal. Death dominates his thoughts. In a ground war, he will be expected to kill. Trained for just that, it is still a concept his mind struggles to grasp. The Iraqi conscripts are just kids; they don't want to be there, much less get shot for it. The force amassing against them is frightening, even to John, and he's on the frightening side.

The Legionnaires train for months in the desert, get used to wearing their C86 NBC suits. But with body armour on top, uniform beneath, equipment all around and the Saudi sun above, no one really gets used to it. It's like life in a portable sauna. Each time John sheds the load and takes a cool shower he feels physically released, but somehow mentally worse. The water acts as a wake-up call to his senses, makes him question his purpose on this earth, in this region at this time. Will the Coalition effort fail for the lack of one man? If he kills another and soils his conscience, will the world be a better place? Because his won't. He'll never be the same again.

It's all moot. He is there, and he will be until the matter's resolved. His apprehension can be no worse than the next man's, the doubts he has no crime against his profession. He's not a machine, he's a man, and not inured to his deadly function. Of course, prolonged combat might change all that, cut him off from his emotions. And that's his greatest fear, because they'll one day return with a vengeance and he doesn't want to live his life haunted by the past.

John found himself suddenly thinking of Dodge. How many lives had he snuffed out? How many NVA? How many Vietcong? How many innocent villagers mistaken for Vietcong? On how many tours of duty over how many years?

He stopped the flow of water, dried himself, tied a towel around his middle and went through to the main room.

'Virginia, do you want to call your dad? See how he's doing?'

'I just did. I got his answerphone.' She appeared pensive more than worried.

'We can go back,' John offered.

Her smile dismissed it. 'He'll be asleep. I'll call tomorrow. How about you check out the route while I take a shower?' She pulled a night-shirt from her case and nipped into the bathroom.

John changed into a fresh T-shirt and boxers and sat on the sofa with the map. The route was simple. He traced it with his finger.

Stay on Highway 95 out of Nevada, traverse the south-east corner of Oregon into Idaho, join the I-84 north of Boise, then cut back into Oregon and straight to Baker City.

'Shit,' he said, 'I am on a mission.'

He was starting their tour near to where he had met Chuck. They had stayed in Baker City the night before his strange encounter. He put the map to one side and pulled his wallet from his jacket, extracted the photo of the girl in the Disney dress and studied it. Keeping it with him had simply been the fulfilment of a childhood promise – the girl's image sparked nothing inside him. He was only curious, as he had been at eight years old. Why had Chuck been so convinced? Then why so devastated at John's absence of understanding?

He lay back on the sofa, held the picture to his chest and closed his eyes. He listened to the shower for a moment, and to the muted sounds of a TV in the next chalet. He couldn't concentrate for long. His head was swimming with tiredness. Already his body had begun to twitch at the doorway to unconsciousness. Six hours of motoring now gave him a weird sensation of forward movement, like he was physically tumbling into sleep.

A little later, Virginia woke him with a soft touch on his wrist. The chalet was dark except for a corona of light around the bathroom door.

'Come on. Come and lie on the bed,' she said. 'You need a good night's sleep.'

She took his hand, led him across the room and turned down the sheet. He climbed in and she joined him, folding the sheet back across them. She lay further up the bed than John, opening an arm for him to lie in.

Out on the highway, an eighteen-wheeler was passing through Hawthorne. The tires rushing on the blacktop struck John as the loneliest sound; the driver miles from home, his wife in an empty bed, praying he's safe.

'Thank you,' he said, his eyelids already heavy again.

'You're more than welcome.'

Sex was not on the cards, John knew that. Yet he doubted he would ever spend a finer night with a more beautiful woman.

The chalet was filled with the wonderful aroma of fresh, rich coffee. Its smell enticed John from his slumbers and he surfaced with a huge smile. There wasn't much in the world to rival waking up on clean white sheets in a broad bar of sunlight beside a person you'd fallen in love with.

For John, it was better. He had found a place where he felt at home. Whether that was in the United States or merely in the presence of this woman, he couldn't yet be sure, but something inside him had settled. He had to fight the temptation to roll over and kiss his bedmate. He turned his head, but Virginia was not lying next to him. Puzzled, he sat up in bed. On the cabinet beside him was a large Styrofoam cup, black liquid steaming away inside.

'John!' came a voice from the bathroom. 'Rise and shine! Coffee!'

'I'm up,' he groaned. 'Thanks.'

Virginia emerged in her night-shirt, which made him really confused. He watched her pad round the bed and jump in.

'Uh ... Virginia, have you just been out for this coffee?'

She nodded and switched on the radio in the console between their heads, releasing a country and western tune. Feet swaying like metronomes, she picked up her drink and took a sip. Not wishing to be presumptuous, John decided not to pursue his query.

'Why don't you grab a shower?' she said. 'Wake yourself up. Long drive today.'

'I showered last night.'

'Have another.'

He gave her a bemused look. 'Uh … okay.'

Inside the bathroom, one thought kept crossing his mind. One image: Virginia stepping into the shower with him. Was this all a ploy? It seemed odd she should have gone out for coffee and then put her night-shirt back on. He stripped off hopefully and stepped in the shower.

'Nice and hot now!' Virginia called through to him.

He did as he was told and took a long, hot shower, giving her plenty of time to join him. Why not? It always happened that way in the movies, and she was a movie person, after all.

Ten minutes later he decided it wasn't going to happen. He shut the faucet and stepped out into a room thick with steam. He grabbed a towel from the rail, then noticed it. The condensation on the mirror had revealed a formerly invisible message, written by a wet fingertip.

Sergeant Frears, come through and stand to attention.

A grin spread across his dripping face. He went through naked. Virginia was lying on top of the covers, similarly naked, her shirt now discarded on the floor. She was a vision, more stunning unclothed than he had ever imagined.

'Well,' she said with a wicked smile, 'you did say you needed a written invitation.'

He smiled back. 'And here I am to RSVP.'

Virginia eyed him up and down and lingered on his penis.

'Guess there's no point my asking you to stand easy.'

Chapter 14

The briefing room was filling up and still no sign of DeCecco. Lieutenant Möhler was standing in front of a whiteboard, waiting for the last of his officers to come through from the locker room for roll-call. A computer file page was being projected onto the whiteboard, ready to be opened.

Larry checked his watch. Where was the fucking rookie? Probably in Gilchrist's office, doing what Larry had expected him to do yesterday. In five minutes he'd no doubt get a call upstairs; pass DeCecco coming down.

'Okay, listen up!' Möhler began.

But Larry had trouble paying attention. He was wondering whether to follow through with the threats he'd made. He had always promised himself: one day, people would take him seriously. Why not start today? Make a stand. If DeCecco had thrown down the gauntlet, shouldn't Larry do him the courtesy of picking it up?

'You're screwed, DeCecco,' he said under his breath.

'Officer Roth!'

Larry gathered from Möhler's tone that he'd been addressed once already but hadn't heard. His heart began to speed up.

'Sir?'

'You'll be riding with Mallory today; DeCecco called in sick.'

Larry had to hand it to his absent partner: he'd been smart. He was staying out of trouble. He had opted for box number three when Larry had thought there were only two choices: play ball or snitch.

'Hey, Lar, any idea what's wrong with Joey tonight?'

Larry ignored Mallory and kept on driving, eyes straight ahead.

'Lar?'

'Kevin, I have a full Christian name, not just some fucking note Mary Poppins sang in *The Sound of Music*.'

'Julie Andrews. Mary Poppins was a character she played in a movie of the same name.'

'Kevin ... I don't care. Call me Larry or don't fucking speak to me.'

Mallory huffed. 'Okay, *Larry* ... Jesus, I only asked what was wrong with Joey.'

'Yellow belly,' Larry muttered.

'What?'

Larry didn't expand. He was thinking about DeCecco again. Oddly, his malice towards him had pretty much disappeared. DeCecco had taken the out that was least damaging to all. In spite of serious provocation he had opted not to retaliate. His attitude stank, of course, but at least he hadn't broken the cop code of brotherhood.

But if DeCecco thought his absence would wreck Larry's plans for the evening, he had naïvely misjudged. Mallory might have been DeCecco a few years from now and even less inclined to go for a maverick bust, but that problem was easily overcome: Larry simply wouldn't mention it. If DeCecco was smart, Larry was smarter. More to the point, Larry was driving.

21:20 hours. Six Adam Nine was nearing the end of their shift, patrolling the streets of Little Armenia along the perimeter between the Hollywood and Northeast Divisions. Suddenly, Larry slammed his foot on the brake.

'What is it?' Mallory asked.

Larry reversed the Charger and stopped adjacent to a service road that led to the entrance to a construction site.

'Put some light down there, will you, Kevin?'

Mallory obediently directed the car's spotlight into the shadows. The site was fenced off by green netting. Beyond the fence was an old hotel that was due to be renovated. And parked almost out of sight at the end of the service road were a black Suburban and a black Mercedes. Until that moment, Larry had been unsure whether tonight was the real deal, or merely Eddie spinning a yarn to sound more important than the low-life he was.

'I don't know, maybe I got a suspicious nature ...' Larry said. 'Would you leave expensive vehicles like that parked there?'

Mallory switched off the spotlight. 'Let's check it out.'

Larry pulled the Charger off the street and unbuckled his seatbelt. He liked the way Mallory was taking the lead. It would look good if it came to an enquiry – providing they were both alive to give evidence.

As Mallory climbed out and shone his Maglite down the service road, Larry unlocked the shotgun from the dash. He wasn't going in with just a sidearm, not against Armenians with automatic weapons. He needed instant stopping power. The model in his hands was a 12-gauge Remington 870 with 20-inch barrel. Eight shells of double-o buck, each the equivalent of nine .32 caliber slugs – trauma you didn't get up from.

The building had no electricity, so the crack of light along the first-floor hallway made Larry halt in his tracks. The glow beneath the door was an intense white, the sort made by fluorescent tubes. Larry guessed the hoods had brought a couple of portable lanterns. He could faintly hear a clandestine exchange, and soundlessly indicated that they should get closer, but Mallory grabbed his arm and pulled him into a doorway.

'Listen, Larry, let's sit tight and call for back-up. Meantime, anything develops, we can play it by ear.'

Larry's brain was racing like a man on PCP. If Mallory put a call through to the station and reinforcements showed up, Larry would be relegated to the same role his wife always assumed in her career: uncredited bit-part player, peripheral to the action.

'We're going in,' he whispered.

'Into what? We don't know. We got no idea who's inside, how many, what they're doing, if they're armed. Shit, they could be Armenian Power. Those guys have all the latest hardware. And so far all we got's a couple of vehicles parked outside.'

'Sounds like probable cause to me,' Larry said, and broke away down the hallway, padding quickly and softly on the threadbare carpet.

'*Roth!*' A coarse and desperate whisper.

Larry raised the shotgun and jammed the stock hard against his shoulder. His system was gripped by fierce shakes of adrenaline that made his lower back pound painfully.

'*Roth!*' Mallory tried again. '*Fuck!*'

Larry kicked the door open, planting his foot back down and canting his body forward to counteract the imminent recoil that could knock a man on his ass. He spotted a Mac-10 machine pistol and pulled the trigger, turning the nearest Armenian into a bloody, backward-leaping rag doll. In the surreal fluorescent glow, he took in the fact of five more figures, plus a table piled high with kilo bags of white powder.

The hoods reacted; Larry saw a host of muzzles arcing round at him, among them a mini-Uzi held by a boy no older than sixteen, standing behind the table. Larry sent the second blast his way. It ripped through the top load of narcotics and caught the youngster full in the chest. Larry screamed for Mallory to lend some firepower as the terminal kid released a spray of nine mils and the room became an expensive snowstorm.

His third shot took both lanterns and another perp but it was no longer one-way traffic. As the lights went out, muzzle flashes lit the room. Dodging into the bathroom doorway, Larry expected to feel each one drill his flesh, but he remained miraculously unscathed.

The smell of cordite, the taste of cocaine – Larry felt he was in the middle of a nightmare as he pumped shells four through eight at targets obscured by a misty-white darkness. Still yelling for his partner to come to his aid, he pulled his Glock and emptied the clip willy-nilly into the murk.

Only when the weapon was spent did he realize he had been the only one shooting.

The whole thing had taken less than ten seconds.

After shoving a fresh clip into the Glock, Larry pulled the neck of his white undershirt up over his nose so he didn't OD on the atmosphere, then held his breath and listened. The pulse thudding in his ears made it difficult to tell, but he reckoned he was the only one left alive. Juddering uncontrollably, he allowed himself a smile. A coke deal foiled, the bad guys dead. He was a hero.

Or not.

'Ah, fuck.'

Someone was rather conspicuous by their silence. Larry unhooked the Maglite from his utility belt and hurried into the hallway.

Mallory was motionless on the floor. Closer inspection revealed he had been hit by several shots through the plasterboard wall. His undershirt body-armor had stopped some, but the bullets had traced up from his stomach and the last three had entered his neck and head. Larry didn't need to check his carotid to know the guy was a stiff.

A sudden jolt to his senses told him this was no longer a defining moment in the history of law enforcement, this was a monumental fuck-up. When DeCecco heard about this ...

He had to claw some good from it all. His flashlight swung back into the room, its beam catching a black holdall on the floor beside the table. The other half of the deal: the money. If his cop days were over, he would gratefully accept a golden handshake from the criminal community. And if they weren't ... what the hell, a little extra cash never hurt anyone.

He entered the room again and quickly counted the kilo bags left intact on the table. Sixteen. Plus what looked like four destroyed, their contents still swirling and settling like fallout. Twenty kees in total. Depending on purity, wholesale value around $500,000.

So, take the remaining sixteen kees to sell, and four-fifths of the folding, make it appear the deal was for only four. Before he got on the radio, he would stash the haul in another room and sneak back for it the next day.

He holstered his weapon, set his Maglite on a wall shelf and worked in its coke-hazed beam. With his hands in the surgical gloves from his belt kit, he transferred the cash out of the holdall and divided it five ways. All the time he was tittering to himself, and wondered if he wasn't thoroughly stoned despite his makeshift mask. He returned four piles of cash to the holdall and added the sixteen bags of C to a large suitcase, then, still cackling like a dope fiend, he closed them both.

With the cash and the coke, he was just about to clock off on an $800,000 shift.

But the amusement caught in his throat as a voice came from the hallway.

'Freeze. You fucking *psycho*.'

For a moment, Larry thought Mallory had risen from the dead and was about to chew him out for leading them into this. Then he recognized the voice, but kept his back to the source.

'DeCecco? That you?'

'Put your hands where I can see them.'

Larry dithered, his right hand wavering close to his holstered Glock.

'Touch the gun, you're dead; I won't hesitate.'

Sensibly, Larry clasped his gloved hands behind his head, then waggled his jaw to make the undershirt drop from his mouth.

'You all better, Joey?' he said.

'I'm perfectly well and you know it. I was home watching TV when I realized: you're insane, you'll do this with or without me.'

'Shit, and I hate to be predictable.'

'Face me. Real slow.'

Thinking all the time how to kill the rookie, Larry turned round on the spot. DeCecco was dressed all in black – sweatshirt, jeans and sneakers, beanie hat and gloved hands. Even through the gloom Larry could recognize the gun that was levelled at him. A Heckler and Koch M1 Benelli Super 90. A semi-automatic shotgun capable of emptying all five slugs through the barrel before the first ejected shell even hit the floor.

'You know your weapons, Joey, I'll give you that.'

'Left hand, Larry, thumb and forefinger. Slowly hook out your weapon, set it on the floor and kick it towards me. And I know this is a real challenge for you, but don't do anything stupid.'

Larry obliged, right hand still planted on the back of his head. DeCecco felt with his foot for the gun and sent it scurrying out of sight along the corridor. Larry replaced his left hand on top of his right.

'Can I go now?' he asked sarcastically.

'You made a big mistake tonight, Larry. If Mallory was still breathing, perhaps you could swing it; come out of this a hero. But a dead cop changes everything.'

'Changes a lot for Mallory, not for me.'

'You figure?'

'Why not? We saw suspicious activity, didn't have a chance to call it in before the whole thing turned to shit.'

'So you think you'll be back in work tomorrow.'

'Maybe not tomorrow; I may be asked one or two questions first. But I did nothing wrong. I was doing my job. It's a dangerous job. People get killed.'

'So explain the contents of that case and that holdall.'

'Drugs and drug money,' Larry said facetiously. 'Didn't they teach you nothing at the Academy?'

'Funny. And why are they going with you?'

'I'm thinking of retiring. Figure I deserve more than a gold watch.' He slowly lowered his hands from his head, folding his arms across his chest. 'Joey, this is all so fucking irrelevant. What are you gonna do? Tell Gilchrist the truth? That you withheld vital information because you were too scared to piss me off? Because that's the real reason Mallory died tonight and you know it. If you'd told Gilchrist what Eddie said, he'd have deployed a SWAT team and this wouldn't have happened. If you'd been here yourself, with all your kick-ass Marine skills, this wouldn't have happened. So, don't preach to me, Joey. And don't pretend you're better than me. And *please* don't make out you'll go upstairs with this because that's career over for the both of us, and what are you gonna do then, huh? Security guard for ten bucks an hour, sitting on your ass in some warehouse watching TV all fucking night? That's not you any more than it is me. You need this job, Joey. It may not be MARSOC, but it's a shitload better than the alternatives.'

DeCecco stared at Larry for a moment then nodded.

'You're right, Larry. Can't argue with any of it. But you still ain't walking out with those. I won't allow you to profit from the death of a fellow police officer. I draw the line at that. And I will take it to IA if you test me on this, regardless of the consequences.'

'I can cut you in,' Larry said hopefully. 'There must be four hundred large here. Not to mention the sixteen kees which I could turn green by this time tomorrow.'

'You're not listening.'

'Gee. Marines must have given you *some* fucking pension.'

'I got everything I need.'

'Yeah, right, I forgot,' Larry said with a sneer. 'The little woman with her arms full of shitty diapers. What more could a man want?'

'I warned you, Larry: I get real nervous when you mention my wife. You want me to end it here and now? I could use that Tec-Nine on the floor over there. You'd be just another cop killed in the line of duty.'

'You'd shoot me in cold blood?' Larry said smiling. 'Nah. You're not the type. You're a good guy, Joey. Sure, Uncle Sam may have trained you to kill, and maybe you've ended a few lives in your time, but … you're not a murderer. You're too noble, too full of ideals. You shoot me, you destroy yourself – the person you think you are.'

'Well, that's all very deep, Larry, but you *still* ain't taking that shit. Now call it in.'

'No.'

The Benelli's barrel came up level with Larry's face as DeCecco screeched like a madman, his instant loss of calm making Larry take a step back.

'*Put the call through or I swear to God I'll blow your fucking head off!*'

Larry immediately got on the radio and didn't need to act to sound distraught.

'This is Six Adam Nine! Shots fired! Shots fired! Officer needs help!'

'What is your location, Six Adam Nine?'

Larry gave the address and listened to the operator announce a Code Three to all units. Afterwards he experienced an explosion of despair deep within him that made him physically gasp, and displaced any buzz he thought he might have had from the floating coke. DeCecco had lowered his weapon and appeared fully in control once again, and Larry wondered whether he hadn't been tricked by some fake, maniacal outburst designed purely to secure his obedience.

'Good boy,' DeCecco said.

'And you're good, too, Joey. Shit, you know, for a moment there, you really had me believing you'd pull the trigger.'

DeCecco smiled. 'Your trouble is, you don't know *what* to believe about me.'

Larry fumed at the truth of it. 'Fucking rookie.'

'Okay, Larry, you told me four hundred grand in cash so

that tells me how much coke there is, so don't let me find out tomorrow that the evidence is short because you know what I'll do if it is.'

'Yeah, you'll tell on me like the pussy you are. But maybe I won't care, because maybe this time tomorrow, *soy en Mehico, con mi plata y cocaína*.'

'What?'

'You need to leave before they get here, Joey. And maybe fifteen seconds after you're gone, I pick these up and disappear into the night.'

'You'd just run?'

Larry craned his neck towards the hallway, listening. DeCecco obviously heard it, too, because he began shifting nervously on his feet.

'Sirens,' Larry said, picking up the holdall. 'And close. You better go. I can explain being here. You can't.'

'What about your wife, Larry? You'd just leave her?'

Larry grabbed the suitcase. 'She won't miss me. Jesus, probably be glad to see the back of me.'

'I can't let you take it,' DeCecco said.

The sirens were growing louder, which made Larry smirk.

'I'm pretty good at gauging these things, Joey, and by the sound of those sirens I figure you got about sixty seconds to clear this building. Me? I'm leaving right now. So shoot me or step aside.'

Finally opting to test DeCecco's grit, Larry started towards the door and DeCecco made his decision.

Unfortunately for Larry, once again it wasn't one of the two on offer.

DeCecco deftly swung the Benelli's stock to catch Larry square under the chin with a knockout uppercut.

Chapter 15

John and Virginia made it to Baker City by nightfall and checked into the Geiser Grand Hotel in the historic downtown district, an area dominated by the Victorian architecture of the city's heyday as the hub of the eastern Oregon gold rush.

John could not recall which hotel he had stayed in as a child, but he knew he would have remembered a place like this, resplendently restored to its original 1880s grandeur. But the town itself brought back a flood of memories, many of which were unexpectedly fond, centering on the rare display of parental emotion that followed his fateful meeting with Chuck.

Despite their late arrival, they were up early the next morning. They had to buy provisions for the trip, some cold-weather gear, and snow chains for the tires; although the sky was now spotless, they had traveled into true winter the previous evening, a thing unknown in southern California.

Once correctly attired, they drove out of town to explore. John was behind the wheel with no map reference as a destination, simply following his nose. There were quite a number of ghost towns marked in the area, but John discounted them all as the one he'd stumbled upon back in '78. Virginia was quietly amused by his grim fascination.

'You're frowning, stop it,' she said.

'Am I? Right.'

'Are we just gonna drive around till we run out of gas?'

'Might happen,' John admitted with a half-smile.

'Why don't we try the places marked?' She peered at the map open on her lap. 'I've circled a few likely candidates … Bourne, Sumpter, Galena, Granite, Cornucopia, Tollgate to the north. And there are others.'

'I don't know. It wasn't on a map; that's why we got lost. And there weren't any other tourists about.'

'Maybe it just wasn't on the map you had, or maybe it's only been added recently.'

'I don't know,' John said again.

'Pull over for a minute, let's think about this.'

John steered the Grand Cherokee off the road and cut the ignition. For a couple of minutes they didn't speak as though by psychic agreement. They stared through the windows at a landscape that made the jaw drop. They were traveling the I-84 north, the Old Oregon Trail Highway, through a valley twenty miles wide, flanked by forested mountains, draped in snow, ultra-whitened by the sun.

'Wow,' John said.

'Did you know that the Oregon Trail was known as The Longest Graveyard because of all the people who died along the way?'

'Thanks. I was having a pleasant little moment 'til you said that.'

Virginia set the map against the steering wheel in front of him and planted a kiss on his cheek.

'Okay,' she said, 'are we at least heading in the right direction? Can you remember?'

'I think so. We started the holiday in Portland and did an anti-clockwise route round Oregon. So we should have left Baker City that day heading north, up to the Columbia River Gorge and back along the Washington border.'

'So north seems reasonable,' Virginia said.

'Yes, but my father wasn't. He might have chosen a different route just to spite my mother who had the map.'

'Typical man. Anyway, what time did you leave town that morning?'

John gave a shrug. 'Not sure.'

'You see, if we knew what time you left Baker City and what time you found the ghost town, we could pretty much work out a limit to your radius of travel.'

'Hey, that's not bad for a girlie.'

She knuckled him playfully in the ribs. 'Is there anything at all that sticks in your memory about the journey that day?'

John closed his eyes. Images flashed in his mind. After a minute he still hadn't spoken. Suddenly, something splattered the windshield and his eyes snapped open. A big rig had rumbled past, loaded with lumber, its multiple tires throwing up sprays of brown slush. They had seen plenty the night before on the drive in, but this one lit a bulb in John's head. He hit the wipers and cleared the glass.

'There must have been a logging depot nearby. I remember the stream of trucks. My father got pissed off with them always on his bumper. That's why he got off the main roads, to avoid them.'

She took the map from the steering wheel and scrutinized it. After a few moments, John gave a laugh.

'We're never going to find it, are we?' he said.

'As long as you want to keep looking, it's okay by me.'

'But this is meant to be a touring holiday. It's meant to be a break. You're recently bereaved. I can't keep you in the same area for a whole week looking for a dead man.'

Virginia did a double-take and John remembered he had kept that part of the story to himself. He made an awkward face. Virginia set the map on the dash.

'Ah. I can't be certain,' he said, 'but there was a gunshot, so I'm fairly sure he killed himself after I left.'

Virginia studied him for a moment. 'God, you must have been a really depressing child.'

'Oh, ha ha. Oh, shit.'

A gold Chevy Tahoe had pulled over in front of them, its roof-bar strobing blue.

The lettering on the driver's door read: SHERIFF - UNION COUNTY. The officer climbed out, adjusted his campaign hat and strolled towards them. John lowered his window and the cold air rushed in.

'Sir, ma'am,' the deputy said, 'everything okay? You lost?'

'Not really,' John replied. 'We were just deciding where to go today.'

The deputy's eyes lit up. 'Oh, okay, you're from England. Let me guess ... honeymoon, am I right?'

Virginia answered in a faultless English accent. 'That's right, officer. How very intuitive.'

The deputy smiled modestly. 'So, you folks need any help?'

John was about to decline when Virginia spoke.

'Well, actually, we are trying to find somewhere specific. A ghost town. My husband found it as a child on a family vacation and would like to find it again. Unfortunately, it wasn't on a map, certainly not back in nineteen seventy-eight.'

The deputy was captivated by Virginia's alien tones, if not her beauty. He almost had to shake himself to respond, and then only with a noise.

'Hmmm ...'

He circled round on the spot, surveying the surrounding landscape as though he might point it out to them. When he turned back, John noticed his eye contact was solely with Virginia.

'There are some,' the deputy said, then spotted the marked map on the dash. 'Oh, there you go, you got them. Wouldn't recommend you go looking, though, not this time of year. Roads ain't so good further up, and they can get worse. Looks nice now, but weather fronts can roll in real quick.'

'Better forget it, then, darling,' Virginia said to John, then smiled back at the deputy. 'Just out of interest, if we came back in the summer, where might we look? My husband thinks there could have been a logging operation nearby.'

Not wanting to disappoint, the deputy lowered his brow and thought hard.

'Well, there's been logging all over this area for years, but, uh ... hmmm, a ghost town not on a map, you say.' He tipped the brim of his hat back on his head. 'Only place I can think of would be, uh ... the locals call it Fortuna. It's kept off of the guide maps as it's pretty inaccessible. We don't want the tourons getting into any trouble.'

'Tourons?' John asked.

'Cross a tourist with a moron, sir.'

John and Virginia both cackled.

'Sorry, I probably shouldn't call them that, but ... some of them are.'

'And where exactly would Fortuna be?' Virginia asked.

The deputy pointed across the valley to their right. 'Those peaks in the distance are the Wallowa Mountains, and beyond you got the Wallowa-Whitman National Forest. Fortuna's over in that direction.'

'And you think that could be the place?' she asked, half-lapsing into her own accent.

The deputy smiled queerly. 'You been here long, ma'am? You're starting to sound like one of us.'

Virginia laughed and corrected her voice. 'We'll take your advice: just stick to the main roads. Out of interest, what would be the best route?'

'Ma'am, are you gonna head up there against my advice?'

Virginia answered with a long, flirting smile, which seemed to work.

'Well, if you were a touron, you'd carry on up to La Grande, then take the eighty-two north. Beyond that, you'd have to ask. That's Wallowa County – out of my jurisdiction.'

'No problem,' Virginia said. 'Thank you.'

'Thanks for stopping,' John said, starting the engine.

'Sure. Real nice meeting you, ma'am, sir. Take care now. Enjoy the rest of your honeymoon. And don't get lost.' He touched the brim of his hat, swaggered back to his vehicle, killed the roof lights and drove off.

'Creep,' John said.

'Who? Him or me?'

'Both. And where did you learn to do an accent like that?'

'I'm in the business, remember?'

'Then you're on the wrong side of the camera. Most Hollywood *actors* can't do an English accent that well. Mind you, we do tend to say *holiday* rather than *vacation*. Bit of a give-away, that.'

'Oh, aren't I a silly arse,' she said, reverting to perfectly clipped tones.

He laid a hand on her thigh. 'No, you're wonderful, and I'm completely in love.'

Virginia smiled but didn't reply and John hoped he hadn't spoken prematurely. But he didn't regret saying it. His emotions had been under wraps for too long and releasing them felt too good.

Chapter 16

Waking up without Larry beside her was a relief. Hayley moaned as she stretched out in bed, her head still muzzy from last night's sleeping pills. She didn't like relying on chemicals to relax, but it seemed better policy than burning incense and risking her husband's displeasure.

After a moment she began to wonder where he might be. It was ten after nine; his shift had ended more than eleven hours ago. She nodded to herself. Of course: he was slammed at a colleague's house. She would have received a phone call if there'd been an incident. Or maybe he was having an affair, but she found it difficult to worry on that score. He wasn't the same man she'd married. Losing him to another woman would be a blessing.

When the bedside phone rang she prayed it would be her agent at the other end. She picked up, dreading the pathetic, hung-over tones of her husband, making excuses.

'Hello?'

'*Way to go, Hayley!*' yelled the woman down the line. '*You got it!*'

She knew the voice, and although she had imagined hearing those joyful words a thousand times, they sounded somehow incongruous. Other actresses might receive such news, but not Hayley Roth.

'Amanda?'

'Who else? Did you hear what I just said?'

'I got the part?' Hayley said, heart thumping.

'*Malibu Mischief,* yeah, you got it!'

Hayley's world view changed in that second. Light and hope flooded in. She leapt out of bed.

'So it's mine?'

Amanda laughed. 'Yes, it's yours. Initial contract period a year. I made a tentative acceptance on your behalf –'

'*Tentative?*' she almost screamed. 'Tell them *yes!*'

'Don't you want to know the terms?'

'No! *Yes!* Yes, tell me. Is the money good?'

'Very generous indeed,' said her agent, still laughing. 'Okay, I'll call them now to confirm, then get back to you with the details. Listen, well done, sweetheart, I am so pleased for you. And Hayley?'

'What?'

'Make the most of your anonymity, you start shooting next week.'

Hayley replaced the receiver and couldn't believe how different she felt inside. One phone call and her life had changed. She finally *had* a life. No longer simply a cop's wife, she was Hayley Roth, soap star. People would stare at her in the street, ask for her autograph. She could trade in her old Beetle for something new. Larry could leave the department, work for himself or not work at all; she would be earning enough for the both of them.

In the midst of her excitement she remembered something and calmed down. She sat on the bed and closed her eyes. Silent thanks were due. In the cemetery on the day of the interview, it seemed someone had been listening.

Joey was sitting in his bathrobe at the kitchen table. He was on his umpteenth cup of coffee, which was playing havoc with his empty stomach, already sickened by the events of the previous night and a subsequent lack of sleep. The fear he harbored now for his wife's safety was a fear unrivaled by any he had known as a soldier, and Joey realized how stupid he had been to turn up at the drugs bust like some avenging angel. What had he achieved? He had failed to save Mallory, and had wilfully and violently prevented Roth from escaping with the booty, which may have seen him flee south and across the border, totally removing him from the equation – and wouldn't that have been the ultimate in desired results? Instead, Roth now had to be livid with him and hell-bent on revenge.

He suddenly looked up at the ceiling and knew from the sound of footfalls that his son had just woken his wife. Having recently taken maternity leave from the Beverly Hills school where she taught elementary, Laura now had no reason to get up early and this particular morning had managed to sleep in. It didn't always work that way. It was Junior who decided his mom's sleep pattern, and when he became active in the morning Laura had little option but to do the same.

Now she was up and Joey was facing possibly the worst day of their married life. When Laura entered the kitchen in her ridiculously swollen nightshirt he was so ashamed he couldn't even look at her.

'Hey, Hon,' she said, ruffling his hair, before heading for the percolator.

'Hey,' he said quietly.

'What time did you get back last night?' she asked, pouring a cup.

It wasn't a loaded question; she knew nothing of his exploits.

He had left the house on the pretext of picking up some breakfast provisions from the local store. Had she been awake on his return, he would have confessed there and then, but she'd fallen asleep and looked so serene in her slumbers that he couldn't bring himself to wake her. Instead, he'd gone back downstairs to make the first in a long line of coffees, and to regret ever more with each passing minute his decision to leave the house in the first place.

Laura sat opposite with her cup of coffee and noticed the sleepless, haunted expression on her husband's face.

'You look like crap,' she said. 'Didn't you sleep well?'

'I didn't come to bed,' he said, still not able to meet her eyes.

'Why not?'

'Things went badly wrong last night,' he said quietly. 'Roth shot dead six drug dealers.'

Her jaw fell open. '*What?* Roth went ahead with it?'

'Yeah. And good riddance to the dealers, that's not the problem. We lost one of our own. Kevin Mallory. Poor bastard was partnered with Roth, who obviously didn't bother to clue him in on his plans for the evening.'

Laura was ashen. 'Who told you? Did someone call? Did *Roth* call?'

Joey shook his head. 'No, Babe. I was there.'

Laura made a shocked little noise in her throat, and Joey continued, despite the fact of his wife now staring at him like he was a complete imbecile.

'I didn't go to the store last night, I went to try and stop Roth. I knew he was gonna do it, and I knew he wasn't about to tell whoever he was partnered with what they'd be walking into. But I got there too late. Roth was the only one left alive. He wanted to take the money and drugs and disappear but I wouldn't let him. I knocked him out. He'll have spent the night with Internal Affairs.'

Laura was aghast. 'Jesus, why didn't you just let the bastard take what he wanted? You don't think he'll be after your blood now? And what if he tells them you knew about it? You'll be out of a job.'

'I know, I know ... I was stupid.'

'Joey ...'

'It didn't seem right,' he explained feebly.

'And this is? Having him coming after you because you screwed him over, then refused him an out?'

'Babe, don't worry. Revenge is big in the movies, not so much in real life.'

'Well, pardon me if I'm not reassured,' Laura said.

'Meantime, we get away from here. I'll take some paternity leave. Square it with the captain. No problem.'

Laura was shaking her head. 'No. No. After years of uncertainty, never knowing where you were, when you'd be home, if you'd even be coming home, finally we've got some stability and I like it. We're not running away, Joey. I won't let him have that power over us.'

'It's too dangerous to stay, Laura, you don't understand.'

Joey was nearing the heart of the problem now, but still stopped short. For that reason, Laura couldn't understand, and even smiled.

'Are you telling me you can't handle someone like Larry Roth? With all your training, everything you've been through? You've been up against some of the worst people on the planet and you've never failed to come out on top. So what is it about Larry Roth that's got you so freaked?'

Joey met and held her gaze for the longest time. Now was the moment to restore that perfect honesty to their relationship.

'Because I'm not the one he threatened – you are.'

Laura froze.

'I'm sorry, Babe, I should have told you. Roth said if I didn't help out last night, he may try and frame you as a drug dealer.'

Laura's belated reaction was somewhere between horrified and hysterically amused. 'A *drug dealer? Me?*'

'I should have told you,' he repeated quietly.

'Yes, you should, Joey. That's rather a pertinent piece of information, wouldn't you say?'

'Sorry. Truly. But you know the person I am. I always try and do the right thing. This time it didn't work out. Doesn't mean I didn't try. I'd never knowingly do anything to place you in harm's way. You're everything to me. You're my whole life. But that's why we need to leave town, at least for a while.'

Laura thought about it, then her face took on a set that Joey found most unnerving. It was the sort of kick-ass expression that would not have been out of place on a young Marine prior to his first mission. A fear-fuelled aggression that reeked of threat. Before he could ask her what was behind it, she stood up and left the room and could be heard climbing the stairs in that ponderous way of hers. Joey wondered if she might be back down with a bag of clothes and toiletries packed for him to leave the house with.

She descended a few minutes later with a black leather fanny pack which she placed on the kitchen table before sitting down.

'I don't need it, Babe,' he said. 'I carry the Browning off-duty. You know that.'

Laura unzipped the bag and removed their home-defense handgun, a smaller model Sig-Sauer with laser sighting. She dropped the clip to check it was full, then zipped it back in the bag. She extended the strap as far as it would go and clipped it around her distended waist.

'You're kidding me. My pregnant wife is *packing*?'

'What car does he drive?'

'Silver Corvette, an older one. Why?'

'So I'll know if it's him.'

Joey looked at his wife like she was *loca*.

'Quit it, Joey. What d'you expect? I spend my life with a military man; you don't think certain things rub off? I need to know I can launch a pre-emptive strike.'

'That's settled it,' Joey said. 'We are leaving town.'

'You wanna go, go,' she said.

Joey knew her well enough to know she wasn't about to budge. Her heels were dug in hard. He tried a different tack.

'So where's your Concealed Carry Weapon license for that thing?'

She gave him a twisted smile, and the finger. 'Screw you.'

It was all too ludicrous. His pregnant schoolmarm wife had turned into The Terminator. Joey started to titter.

'You know,' he said, 'if Junior grows up wanting to be a soldier, I'm blaming you. Poor kid's got a gun strapped to him and he's still in the womb.'

They smiled at each other. They were still a team, strong and bound by love. The smiles faded in unison.

'You really don't want to leave?' Joey checked, one last time.

'No. I'm making a stand. You did it for years for Uncle Sam. Now I'm doing it for us.'

Joey nodded but knew she didn't need his approval. Her mind was made up.

'Roth won't come,' he said. 'I know he won't.'

Laura looked at him. 'But if he does, I won't ask why. He has no business being near me. I'll just red-dot the son-of-a-bitch and pull the trigger.'

'That's easier said than done – taking someone's life.'

'Watch me.'

The telephone rang.

Her husband's Corvette was in its regular spot when Hayley returned from the store. She stopped dead for a few seconds on the street and the breath held in her throat. Larry would have called it bullshit but she was picking up some really horrible vibes. After her career news that morning she would have considered her good mood to be impenetrable, but something nasty had just broken through, unexpected and deeply unpleasant, like a knife through a Kevlar vest.

She looked up at the apartment window and considered walking on by. Instead, she went into the courtyard, past the communal pool, up the steps onto the walkway and along to the front door. It was home – where else could she go? She let herself in with the groceries and stopped dead for a second time.

Larry was perched on the sofa with his head hung, having ignored her arrival. His Bianchi holster was empty on the glass coffee table, the .45 was in his hands, and he appeared to be caressing it.

'Hey,' she said gently, not really wanting to be heard. 'What's wrong?'

No answer, no movement. She didn't feel like offering sugary endearments but fear could re-write the script.

'Honey?'

'I fucked up,' he said through teeth that barely moved to allow the words out.

'Are you hurt?' she asked softly. 'You're talking like a ventriloquist.'

'I got hit on the jaw.'

Hayley closed her eyes. Sympathy was completely absent inside her. This was meant to be a day of rejoicing and he had ruined it.

If that was selfish, she didn't care. She clutched the brown grocery bag tightly.

'Put the gun away, Larry. Let's talk.'

'Why?' he said miserably.

'Because, whatever it is, we can make it better.'

She didn't believe this. There was plenty in the world beyond salvation. Perhaps this latest blow would seal their fate as a married couple. Her reluctance to simply cross the living room and embrace her husband showed up the damage to date. And she was still afraid of him; she wanted to stay by the door.

Larry was chortling at her last comment, but Hayley gathered he was mocking himself more than her.

'It can't be made better,' he said. 'Unless you got some special incense that can raise the dead.'

Hayley felt her heart sink further. She didn't want to ask and didn't really need to. He looked up at her for the first time, his smile pathetic, full of self-pity, but without malice. He seemed genuinely pleased to see her, and Hayley experienced a spark of hope. Whatever had happened, perhaps it would prove a blessing; what her favorite UCLA drama teacher would have termed a "breakthrough". Perhaps Larry's hard-nut shell had cracked open and the boy inside would need all her nurturing love.

'I killed six people last night,' he announced.

Hayley swallowed hard.

'Drugs bust. Seven if you include my partner.'

'You mean he's dead, uh ... DeCecco, is it?'

Larry snorted like he'd heard the unfunny punch-line to a sick joke. He shook his head. 'Kevin Mallory.'

'But I thought –'

'DeCecco cried off.'

'Cried off?'

'Called in sick.'

Hayley nodded, but was curious as to why Larry had phrased it so. To her, crying off and being ill were two different things. She avoided his gaze and stared into the top of her grocery sack. All the ingredients of a celebratory meal were in there.

'Are you gonna stand there all day?' he asked suddenly, and Hayley jumped. Her mind had been visiting a parallel universe in which the Roths were popping a bottle of Champagne and her mom wasn't terminal.

'Larry, you don't need the gun.'

To her relief, he put it down, and the chromed steel clacked on the glass surface of the table. He leaned back on the sofa and let his head loll. She put the groceries on the sideboard and crossed the living room and simply stood there. Before the episode with the tin of beer she would not have hesitated; she would have sat down, pulled him close and held him tight. Now, she felt like a teenager on a first date, unsure how to breach the divide. Larry looked up, his eyes questioning, and she was obliged to take a seat. After a few seconds, he rested his head on her shoulder, which Hayley found equally touching and terrifying.

'Do you want to tell me what happened?' she asked.

'Not now. I've been talking all night. Fucking IA.'

'Oh. Okay. You're not in any trouble, though, are you?'

He lifted his head and gave her a withering look.

'No, the mayor gave me a fucking medal – of course I'm in trouble.'

'But you were only doing your job.'

'My job was to wait for back-up. I was glory-seeking. IA knows it. But there's a shitload they don't know and they *know* they don't know. And until they do know, they got my badge and my gun. And if they ever do know, I sure as shit won't be getting them back.'

Meanwhile, I'm suspended from duty.'

Hayley didn't quite follow all of that but thought it best not to ask. Larry stood up and went into the kitchen and she knew he'd be back with a beer. She was surprised when he returned with two, and handed one to her.

'I know it's early but here,' he said. 'Peace offering. I don't want us to fight. We need to be strong.'

She accepted the tin with a hugely appreciative smile as he sat back down and took a gulp. Hayley didn't know what to say, so took a slurp of beer.

'Do you still love me, Hayley?' he asked suddenly.

'Of course.' In the circumstances, it was the only sensible response.

'Then we'll make it,' he said stoically. 'Whatever happens. Even if they fire me. I'll get a job, meet the payments. We won't lose the apartment. You won't suffer. I'll take care of you, don't worry.'

But Hayley saw he was worrying, and so now seemed the perfect time to tell him.

'Larry, you remember I had a second interview for *Malibu Mischief*?'

From his expression, it was clear he didn't. 'Uh …'

'Well … I got it.'

His attempt at enthusiasm was smothered by his blatant disinterest.

'Oh, that's great. Whatcha got? Coupla days?'

'Three hundred and sixty-five, actually. To start with.' She was fighting the giggles. 'My God, Larry, the money. I can't believe they want to give me all that money. You're worried about losing this place? I'm gonna be buying us a place in the hills! We can have a pool, everything!'

Hayley had a weird thought as she watched her husband's expression: she must have been speaking Mandarin and he had gotten the translation all wrong. Instead of being pleased, his face was distorting with anger.

'Did you hear?' she said.

'And this is meant to make me feel better, is it, Hayley? I kill six people, lose a partner, I may lose my job, and you fucking *laugh*?'

Hayley experienced an awful trepidation, a sinking sickness in her stomach. This was a moment she knew would transform for ever the tenor of her marriage, and she knew it had not yet developed its full potential. She began to protest but his sudden move to standing cut her short. She cowered into the cushions, the chilled aluminum in her hand speeding the shivers through her body.

Shaking with emotion, crushing and spilling his own tin, Larry glared down at her.

'You think I want to be *kept* by you, is that it? Stay home while you go earn the big bucks and laugh with your acting buddies about the dumb schmuck who's got a fucking apron round his waist instead of a gun?'

'Larry –'

He lashed out, kicking wildly at the underside of the coffee table. The circular glass top shattered and leapt in the air, all shards and jags. Hayley gawked in terror at this prolog to fury. She watched the .45 jump with the force and land on the glassy carpet, then she was grabbed by the wrist and yanked to her feet, Larry twisting her arm so viciously she felt her ulna snap. But her shriek was interrupted by a fist, which splattered her lips and broke her front teeth and sprawled her back on the sofa.

'*I'm* the fucking provider round here, not you!' he yelled, and hurled the mangled tin at her head.

Despite her hurt and horror, Hayley managed to duck and the missile went astray. She scrambled for the apartment door, moaning and tasting blood, but Larry clawed her hair and foiled her escape. Then she was flying, and beneath her was the coffee table, an empty hoop of wood.

She landed dead center. The table collapsed and she crunched down heavily on a carpet of glass slivers, screaming at the insult of multiple lacerations.

She didn't need a mirror to gauge her injuries; they were reflected in her husband. His rage had fled, gone in an instant, and in its place there was only shock. He was wide-eyed as he surveyed his handiwork.

Hayley was on her stomach looking back at him. Her left arm was burning with pain, the impact having further damaged the broken bone. She pushed her tongue through the gap where her upper teeth had snapped off. Her lips felt ten times their normal size, and now the cuts to her palms and forearms and face were coming alive, beginning to leak blood furiously. There were so many levels of physical hurt, but they paled beside the emotional trauma.

'Oh, shit, no,' Larry said, welling up. 'I didn't mean ... I'm sorry ... I love you ...'

There was a lump under Hayley's thigh, which her brain identified with crazy glee. She lifted her leg and delved down with her good arm. Larry's .45 was a real handful, but she thought nothing had felt so sweet in her grasp, although her grasp was darkly red and slimy. She thrust the gun towards him, cocked it and pulled the trigger – pure gut reaction, no thought for the consequences.

Hearing the hammer strike the firing pin, Larry yelped, but there was no bullet in the chamber and he moved quickly to claim his weapon.

Hayley had seen him work the slide when cleaning it, but she needed two hands and her broken arm wasn't up to the job. The gun was snatched from her and she thought it was all over, that he'd use it on her. Instead, he retreated behind the sofa, and Hayley understood she didn't need the gun; the picture she presented was killing him. He wasn't drunk like last time; he was stone cold sober, barely a swallow of beer inside him, nothing to cloud the image of his beaten wife. He began sobbing lustily. His life was in ruin. Career, now marriage.

'*Fuck you!*' Hayley screamed, the words distorted by her new dental arrangement, but the message crystal clear. She climbed unsteadily to her feet, screeching glassy shards against each other. 'You *bastard!* You *fucking cunt!* What are you crying for? You made it all go wrong, not me! What did I do? What did I do, huh? Now look at me. I'm meant to start filming next week. How? With a face like this? I got no teeth! I'm cut to fucking ribbons! You broke my arm! I didn't even sign the contract yet! You think they'll wait for me? They'll give the part to someone else!'

Larry was bawling.

'Why am I even talking?' Hayley said. 'We're finished.'

She wobbled to the door, her left arm held protectively to her stomach, each footstep turning the carpet a haphazard crimson. Dipping her right hand into the groceries on the sideboard she produced her door keys and meaningfully left them on one side. Then she lifted out a bottle of Champagne and placed it beside them. Where she had held it, blood ran down the gold foil.

Chapter 17

Three of the office walls were decorated with citations, plaques, photographs, and police badges in cloth and metal. As Joey entered, Captain Gilchrist dropped the blind on the fourth wall, a window that gave onto the corridor. Joey assessed his superior to be barely in control of a foul temper. On his uniformed chest, his shield was crossed by a black mourning band.

'Sit down, DeCecco.'

'Sir, I'd rather stand, sir.'

'Cut the crap and sit down,' Gilchrist said, and claimed his own seat behind the desk.

'Sir, yes, sir.'

'And quit the double sirs, you're not in the Marines now.'

Joey settled himself stiffly on the chair. Gilchrist was staring hard at his subordinate. Suddenly he picked up a report, let his eyes light on it for all of three seconds, then placed it back down.

'You seem fully recovered,' he said.

'Yes, sir.'

'Do you know why I called this morning? What you're doing here?'

Joey nodded solemnly.

'Kevin Mallory was killed last night.'

'I know.'

'And Larry Roth has been suspended pending an investigation by Internal Affairs.'

'So I gather.'

Gilchrist eyed him suspiciously. After several seconds, Gilchrist broke the moment by taking a mouthful of coffee from a mug bearing the image of an LAPD captain's shield.

'Right now, DeCecco, IA has a few questions need answering, questions that Roth seems unwilling or unable to answer.'

Joey said nothing, and felt sick to his stomach that he was effectively in cahoots with a dangerous lunatic. Gilchrist picked up the report again and read from it.

'"Then some guy with a shotgun showed up. Black clothes, black hat. Looked like a pro, something military. Moved quick, stealthy." Any ideas, DeCecco? Because I can assure you that IA is formulating one or two of their own.'

Sitting there in his black sweatshirt and black Levis, Joey only just managed to maintain his poker-face. He shook his head.

'That your mourning outfit, then?'

'I like black, sir. My wife says it suits me.'

'Uh-huh.' Gilchrist looked Joey up and down, appeared to reread a small section of the report, then looked Joey up and down again.

'Wait a minute,' Joey said, 'You're not suggesting that was me last night?'

'Not in those clothes, no. Your clothes from last night would have been covered in narcotics, so I imagine they've been disposed of already. But have you been so thorough with the vehicle you were driving? You couldn't have gone on your bike, not with a shotgun. Which means, however well you think you cleaned it, your car will be contaminated, and that's something CSI would have no trouble proving – if I decide to point them in your direction.'

Joey pleaded The Fifth with his silence. Gilchrist pushed himself backwards and the castors rolled him to the window. He stood up and looked out, speaking to the glass.

'Aren't you at all curious as to who made the statement I just read to you?'

'No, sir, why should I be?'

Gilchrist turned round. 'A vagrant. He was in a doorway near where you entered the building. You obviously didn't see him.' Gilchrist allowed himself a smile. 'Which is pretty lamentable for someone trained in the art of reconnaissance, wouldn't you say?'

'Well, I can't see a whole lot from my living room, sir, not with the curtains drawn.'

'Really? So how would you feel about a line-up? See if our witness picks you out.'

Joey shrugged. 'Night-time, dark hotel. It would be easy to mistake a person. Especially for a witness who was probably drinking.'

'How do you know it was a hotel? I didn't say where it happened.'

Joey went blank. Perhaps only for a second, but it was such a panic-filled second that it felt like a lifetime. Then he had his simple answer.

'The guys downstairs.'

It wasn't the truth, of course, but it was plausible enough. Cops talked to each other at shift-change, and Joey realized he had nearly been caught out by an extremely facile challenge. Gilchrist seemed to know it, too, because he smiled and nodded.

'Okay, Joey ...' he said, '... okay, here's what I think: I think you were there. I know *someone* was there, someone with enough skills to put Larry Roth out cold. And it wasn't any of the perps because they died where they stood. Plus, they had automatic weapons. If they'd been able, they'd have done the same to Roth as they did to

Mallory. But all Roth suffered was a near-busted jaw.'

'What's Roth saying about it?'

'Says he slipped and knocked himself out. Which is possible – there was a lot of blood and narcotics on the floor – but I don't believe it happened that way.' Gilchrist resumed his seat. 'You and he had some sort of a spat in the parking lot the other day. Someone witnessed a weapon drawn. You want to tell me about that?'

'Roth was just showing me his forty-five. A Tanfoglio. Expensive. He's very proud of it.'

'That's strange,' Gilchrist said.

'What is?'

'You keep calling him Roth. Why not Larry? You've been partners a while now. Certainly long enough to get on first-name terms.'

'I don't like him,' Joey said.

'Well, that's probably the first truthful thing you've said to me. So what's he done to piss you off?'

'I don't like his manner, sir,' Joey said. 'We have very different styles of law enforcement.'

'Meaning?'

Joey experienced an acute what-the-hell moment, and spoke his mind.

'Larry Roth is a complete liability as a police officer. There's no saying what he's capable of. I believe he came unglued when Frank Dista died and he's now hurting so bad he doesn't give a fuck if everyone else around him gets hurt. Or killed. Sir.'

'So, for Christ's sake, Joey,' Gilchrist said desperately, 'help me take him off the street.'

'I can't.'

'Have you forgotten that an officer died last night?'

'No, sir, I haven't. That's something I won't ever forget. But I repeat: I have nothing further to say on this matter.'

'Joey, if you're worried about your own position, I promise I'll do everything I can to help.'

Joey merely shook his head and Gilchrist gave up.

'I'm not impressed, DeCecco. Your military record says you were an outstanding Marine. But things obviously change because, in my opinion, you don't deserve to wear the uniform of the LAPD.'

'But as long as I am wearing it, sir, I'm at least a day away from becoming some low-paid rent-a-cop patrolling a warehouse full of electrical goods.'

'So you're saying your involvement would see you out of a job. That's very interesting.'

'I'm saying … I'm saying this is a job I know I can excel at, and I damn well intend to continue doing it.'

'Well, that may not be your decision. Not if I speak to IA.'

Joey paused to regain the proper humility of a chastised subordinate. 'Sir, I can be a real asset to this department and I believe you know that, but you've got to allow me to handle the situation my way.'

Gilchrist leaned back in his chair and hoisted his feet onto the desk. He looked like he was past caring, but Joey couldn't be sure, and posed a dangerous question.

'Sir, will you be impounding my vehicle?'

Gilchrist pursed his lips, narrowed his eyes. 'No. Though I can't stop IA formulating their own opinions as and when certain facts come to light. So if you are going to *handle* this situation, Officer DeCecco, I suggest you set about doing so pretty smartish.'

Joey nodded. 'Absolutely. Thank you, sir.'

'And I'd also suggest you have your car professionally detailed. Or that you take it somewhere remote and set fire to it. And that is not a suggestion I made because this entire conversation did not take place.'

'Sir.'

'And you can work tomorrow and Friday, DeCecco. Make up for yesterday. Plus, we're a little shorthanded right now.'

'Sir.'

Gilchrist gave a dismissive wave in the direction of the door. Joey was almost out of the office when Gilchrist produced a Columbo-style afterthought.

'Oh, did I mention? I received a call earlier from a West LA officer. One of their patrols picked up Roth's wife this morning. She was wandering the streets. She's now in hospital. Someone had given her a severe beating. But it looks like she's as dumb as you are, DeCecco, because she won't point the finger, either. So it seems that man can do pretty much anything he likes and get away with it. I'm just glad you're okay with that situation, because I'd hate to think how guilty you'd feel if he *really* lost control.'

Chapter 18

It had been tough going. Without the snow chains it would have been impossible. The Jeep had struggled through the drifts, maintaining forward momentum but snaking left and right. There had been more than a few hairy moments. During their climb, the sky had turned from blue to a laden grey. The deputy's advice had been sound: the roads higher up were not impassable, but only the foolhardy would have ventured on. His hunch about the unmapped ghost town had also proved correct. Along the 82, in the valley between the Mountains and the National Forest, they had stopped in the town of Wallowa and had enquired. An old guy in a hardware store had – with a glint in his eye that said he was glad to be sending tourons to their doom – given directions that eventually brought them to the primary trail that led up to Fortuna.

At this point, Virginia had taken over behind the wheel. John wanted to be a passenger again, as he had been at eight years old. In the end, his faded memories had not helped. Success had come from exhausting all possible routes. Where they found evidence of previous vehicular access, they realized they were simply covering old ground and the tracks belonged to their own Jeep.

Eventually, Fortuna had given itself up to them, like Brigadoon, tired of evading their search. They had rounded a bend and there it was. But for its stark whiteness, the scene had not changed. A clearing in the forest, gently sloping, undulating. Sagging grey wood structures, rusty, defunct mining machinery, and log cabins on the periphery, all loaded high with snow. Virginia switched off the engine.

'Is this it?' she asked.

John's silence answered for him. He felt overwhelmed. He had thought about his unexplained childhood encounter so many times over the intervening years and had often mused whether he might one day return, but he had never believed he would. Occasionally, he had dreamed about it, and that was how it felt now: like a surreal imagining made solid. The bright winter stillness of the place only added to his sense of awe.

'Would you like to get out?' Virginia asked.

'Not here. There's a path beyond the trees over there. I don't know whether this leads onto it. Can we try?'

She restarted the Jeep and crept forward. Heavy snow could disguise some dangerous ground, level the terrain, and it was hard to tell where it was safe to drive, but Virginia persevered. John secretly watched her out of the corner of his eye. Her features were pinched with concentration, her focus just ahead of the Jeep's hood. His heart full of flutters, he marveled at the way she could act on faith, risking her neck to satisfy his silly whim.

They reached the tree line and Virginia stopped; there was no obviously beaten path through the firs.

'Where now?' she asked.

'Somehow, the other side of these trees.'

'You know, if we get stuck we could be in real trouble. That sky's threatening some serious weather. Also, it's gonna be getting dark in a couple of hours and we don't have any survival gear to speak of.'

From her tone, John gathered she was only acting as Devil's advocate. She seemed almost as keen as him to complete their quest.

'We can go back,' he said.

She gave a slight shake of her head, shifted into first and entered the forest. The Jeep weaved through the firs, its submerged tires seeking traction, but the snow had not settled so deeply beneath the canopy and their progress was slow but assured.

They emerged a minute later, but even in those sixty seconds the world had greyed. The sky was hoarding, bulking up on its wintry cargo. The deputy's warning was playing in John's head: *Weather fronts can roll in real quick.*

'Left,' he said. 'Up the hill.'

Virginia turned the Jeep and applied some gas. Although whited-out, the route was obvious now. It hugged the edge of a mountain valley, one side trees, the other side death. A middle course seemed appropriate.

'Was it far from here? Do you remember?' she asked.

'Five minutes maybe.' He shrugged. 'Maybe. I don't know. It was so many years ago.'

'Could you see the cabin from the track?'

'No, it was some way into the forest.'

'Well, let's time five minutes from now, then stop and take a look around.'

As John checked the clock in the dash, the first flakes of snow began to blot the windshield.

It took them over two hours to find the cabin. John had misjudged at five minutes. Assuming it was more rather than less, they had ventured further up the mountain, stopping the Jeep every ten seconds or so to search into the forest. They had stayed together, knowing it would take longer, but preferring that option to one or both of them getting lost.

It was the V8 pick-up that first caught their eye, still parked where Chuck had left it that fateful day. Against a backdrop of tree trunks, its rusting hulk was easier to spot than the log cabin.

It had been a timely discovery; driving had become impossible. The snow was now a descending white wall, obscuring everything. The forest provided some respite, but the firs stood apart sufficiently that the snow had no trouble finding the ground.

John ran back to the Jeep to bring it off the track. He weaved it through the trees, pulled alongside the pick-up and cut the engine. Virginia waited for him to get out. After fifteen seconds he was still sitting behind the wheel, so she climbed in next to him and closed the door.

'You okay?' she said.

He smiled crookedly and put the wipers to intermittent. The wintry deposit was swished from view.

'This is eerie,' John said. 'I think we're the first people to see this place in thirty-five years.'

'We'll soon find out.'

He looked at her quizzically as the wipers struck again.

'The body,' she explained. 'If it's still inside, then we are the first. Do you hope it is?'

'Yes. Not because I'm morbid. I just want everything to be as it was. If the body's been removed, I imagine the cabin will have been cleared as well.'

'Would they have left the truck?'

'Well, no one's bothered shifting all that junk down in Fortuna. That's probably been there for a century.'

She acknowledged with a nod. 'Ready, then?'

'Ladies first.'

'Yeah, right.'

The condition of Chuck's skull testified to the manner of his suicide. The small, neat hole in the right temple; the jagged, fist-sized outshoot above his left ear. He had killed himself sitting at the table but had fallen out of his chair. The body had long since rotted down to bones, and the collapsed skeleton looked vaguely comical inside its jeans and check shirt.

The atmosphere in the cabin was musty and gloomy, but through its one window the snow outside lent a subtle glow. John couldn't remember whether the summer sun had provided any better light. He immediately zoomed in on the pistol still lying in Chuck's skeletal fingers. Made of blacked stainless steel, it still looked almost new.

'Smith and Wesson, Model Thirty-Nine,' Virginia said.

'You'd think. It's actually a Mark Twenty-Two, Model O.' He picked it off the floorboards and handed it to her. 'Careful.'

She read the markings on the slide. 'Smartass.'

'I know my guns. You see the hammer's down? The Thirty-Nine would have self-loaded, cocking the hammer. The slide on this can be locked to keep the mechanism closed and silent. It's also got a threaded barrel to take a suppressor, raised sights to account for that, and it fires specially-made subsonic rounds to eliminate the sonic crack. Developed for the Navy SEALs in Vietnam. Known as the Hush Puppy; for killing guard dogs – among other things.'

Virginia put the gun on the table. 'So why did Chuck have it?'

'This guy,' John said, pointing to a framed snapshot propped against a transistor radio on the table. A young soldier in tiger-stripe camouflage, standing on the skid of a helicopter.

'This photo was on the wall when I left. Chuck must have wanted it to be the last thing he saw. I assume it's his son, and it does look like he served in Vietnam. That's a Huey he's leaning against.'

'So Chuck's son was a Navy SEAL?'

'Looks that way.'

John pored over the image. Ludicrously, after more than three decades, he still half-expected to feel *kinda strange*, as Chuck had hoped he would. But all he saw was a soldier from a previous generation. He set the picture down and wandered over to the camp bed. On it was the empty frame from which Chuck had extracted his granddaughter's picture. Only one photograph remained on the wall: the black-and-white shot of Chuck on his wedding day. Alongside was the calendar, *Beautiful Oregon - 1978*, stuck at August, with Chuck's strange countdown ending on the 14th.

Virginia joined him. 'What's that all about?'

'Don't know. Have a look. He'd been up here for months, crossing off the days.'

'Waiting for you,' she said, taking the calendar off its nail. '*The one.*'

'Waiting for something,' John said skeptically.

Virginia flipped back through the months, shaking her head, then suddenly stopped and peered beyond the calendar. John noticed her eye-line. At the pillow-end of the bed, beneath the blanket, was a lump. Slowly, she reached down and revealed the cause of it.

'GI Joe!' John said with a surprised laugh.

'You know this little guy?' she said, handing the Action Man to John.

'Yeah, I left him for Chuck.' He shook his head. 'You know ... all the things I saw with the Legion, this is the strangest day I've ever known. It's like I just stepped out of a time machine.'

'I bet.' Virginia replaced the calendar. So doing, her toe kicked something under the bed. She squatted down and pulled out an old suitcase, then lifted it onto the bed. They both stared at it for a moment. Rigid and brown, its leather surface dull and worn.

'Are we wrong to look inside?' John asked.

'Why else did we drive all this way?'

John released one latch, Virginia the other.

Chapter 19

Before her interview for *Malibu Mischief*, Hayley had been naturally apprehensive, understandably excited, but fundamentally pessimistic. She had got too used to failure, or at least to extremely limited success. Now, she would have willingly accepted a lifetime's fear of what might go wrong in exchange for the fact of what had.

Amanda was in tears at her bedside. The doctor had just left after imparting some information, while the LAPD had earlier taken some away; the same patrolman who had picked Hayley off the street and driven her to the UCLA Medical Center. On hearing the name Roth, he had instantly known who her husband was. They weren't in the same division but the grapevine was in working order and it was common knowledge that Internal Affairs was grilling Larry Roth, and was not overly impressed with his explanation of events.

Hayley had decided not to press charges or to even identify the guilty party. She wanted no further contact with her husband. She didn't want to see his face ever again, not even in court. Under sedation, she honestly didn't care if she lived or died.

'You'll be as good as new,' Amanda assured, trying not to sob and undermine herself. 'You heard the doctor. They'll operate this evening and re-set your arm –'

'My face,' Hayley whispered.

'It's … it looks worse than it is. It's mostly superficial. A few cuts. They'll heal. And your lips will be kissable again in no time, and I know a great dentist, does all the big stars. He'll give you back your smile, Hayley, and I'll pay for it myself. Believe me, sweetheart, I looked ten times worse than you when I had my facelift, and that was voluntary.'

The corners of Hayley's mouth lifted minutely. 'But I've lost *Malibu Mischief*, haven't I?'

Amanda appeared to be on the verge of a buoyant lie, but checked it, and nodded. 'Sorry, sweetheart. I talked to them. They can't wait for you. They can't reschedule to that extent. It screws up weeks of planned storylines.'

'Fuck.'

'But they will remember you. They really like you. Something else suitable comes along, it's as good as yours. And you're a great actress. I remember the first time I saw you at the Freud Playhouse on campus. You were mesmeric. Talent will out, sweetheart, it will.'

Hayley graced her agent's optimism with a dopey, gappy grin.

'That's no lie, Hayley. And I'll do my part. Put you up for everything.'

Smiling faintly, Hayley closed her eyes. 'Thank you. I want to sleep now.'

'Can I call anyone?' Amanda asked.

More than anything in the world, even a deferred part in *Malibu Mischief*, Hayley wanted her mom by her side.

'No,' she said. 'No one.'

After Hayley left the apartment, Larry didn't move from his living room for over an hour. He didn't move at all. He stood in the same spot, stunned, the .45 he had grabbed from her still in his hand, dangling limply by his side. He felt no compulsion to turn it on himself; his confusion was too disabling. Life had fallen apart on him and so damned quick. His new reality had to sink in before he could make any decisions and that process of acceptance would hurt. He would have to numb the pain for a few days, the only way he knew how.

After more than sixty minutes of inactivity, animating himself was a strange sensation. He felt drugged, his movement slurred. He needed to lose the .45 – at least for the time being. He was about to indulge in a bender to end them all. Where he might wander, whom he might meet along the way, he didn't know, and when it was over he probably wouldn't remember. But he was about to mix copious booze with intense regret, and that was volatile enough. Stir in some obnoxious asshole in a bar, and Larry reckoned his loaded .45 would not stay loaded for long.

So he hid his weapon down the side of the sofa, slid his back down the wall beside the spirits trolley, and grabbed the nearest bottle to start him off.

Chapter 20

There were clothes in the suitcase. Shirts, jeans, socks, underwear, winter woollens. Virginia placed them on the bed, item by item, while John looked on with growing disappointment. He didn't know what he'd expected, but certainly more than this. At the base was another calendar.

'Beautiful Oregon, nineteen seventy-seven,' John read. '*Quelle surprise.*'

He took it out and began turning over the months. At April he stopped. The twenty-fifth was circled. Next to it, DR had been scrawled and scribbled out, replaced by the word *VISION*. It didn't elicit any comment from either of them, but John's brain was working overtime. He turned over April and May, then stopped again at June. From the fifth onwards the days were crossed off – the countdown had begun, and went right through to December thirty-first, at which point he and Virginia simultaneously looked to the wall, at *Beautiful Oregon - 1978*.

'Unreal,' Virginia said. 'He was waiting up here for over a year.'

'What do you make of this?' John said, returning to the month of April.

'Well, we understand *VISION*, don't we? From what you said, he thought God had spoken to him, told him to get his ass up this mountain.'

'Yeah, and I don't think *Dee Arr* means he had a doctor's appointment that day. I think he was going to write *dream*, but decided it wasn't the right word; he wanted something stronger, more … biblical.'

Virginia nodded. 'You know what I think? I think old Chuck here was nuts. Regular basket case. The guy has a dream and next thing you know he's built himself a log cabin in the wilderness?'

'And now you think I'm nuts,' John said, dropping the calendar back in the case.

'Why would I?'

'For doing what he asked. For carrying his granddaughter's picture around with me all these years. For risking our lives coming up here in this weather.'

'John, I'd defy anyone to forget an experience like you had. I'm just sorry there don't seem to be any answers here.'

Despite her reassurances, John felt intensely angry with himself. Through the window he could see the blizzard had not let up. Their predicament was potentially lethal. He spun away from her and kicked over an upturned crate. The alarm clock on it went flying. He immediately faced her again and apologized, but Virginia was staring at the floor behind him. John checked over his shoulder and saw a shoe box, previously hidden by Chuck's makeshift bedside cabinet. He looked back at Virginia.

'You know, if I look in there and find a pair of shoes, I'm going to be really pissed off.'

'Hey, welcome back to the world, bro.'

Hefting open his drugged eyelids, Dodge tried to focus on the person beside his bed. It looked like an ageing, emaciated Jesus, but Dodge knew he wasn't dead and reckoned he was still sane enough to know the difference.

'How you feeling?'

'I've been better,' Dodge whispered.

'Yeah, but you been worse too, right?'

Dodge pushed himself more upright in bed, grimacing at his injuries, and saw the hospital name on the bed linen: *VA West Los Angeles Medical Center.*

'How long have I been here?' he asked.

'They brought you in two nights ago.'

'Shit, what happened to yesterday?'

'*All your troubles seemed so far away,*' the Jesus-man crooned, and laughed. 'I guess you were drugged up. So, I hear you been busting a few caps. Little stress release, huh?'

Dodge managed a smile, then noticed that the Jesus-man was in a wheelchair.

'Pleiku, seventy-one,' said the Jesus-man, reading his expression. 'Got downed flying a Cobra. Awesome bird, bro.' He extended his arm. 'Friends call me Hawg.'

'Dodge.' They shook.

'So what's your story?' Hawg asked.

'I just lost it for a while, no big deal.'

Hawg didn't reply straight away, and Dodge felt himself under scrutiny.

'You're keeping too much in,' Hawg finally told him.

'Yeah? You a shrink?'

'Don't need to be; I was there, man.'

'Not where I was. Doing what I was doing.'

'You telling me you were at My Lai in sixty-eight?'

Dodge snarled. 'Screw you. I never massacred no unarmed civilians. I'd have shot that asshole Calley.'

'So if you weren't a part of Charlie Company that day, believe me, Dodge, you got nothing to say would shock another vet. It's all variations on a theme. We all got dehumanized over there. Then we took the big swoop back to the world and our own people made it worse, spitting on us, calling us babykiller, if they even acknowledged us. And we've been carrying the guilt ever since. But I've learned, bro – we don't have to. We did nothing wrong. Our country called, we answered. Any other war we'd have been fucking heroes.'

'So how come, if you learned so much, you're in here talking to me? What d'you do?'

'Nothing. Wheeled my ass through the door. Simple as. I know the signs. I know when my finger's reaching for the self-destruct. This is just a little R 'n' R.'

Dodge closed his eyes. R & R sounded good.

'Well, I'll tell you,' Hawg said, 'you better show willing for our revered head-doctor.'

'What are you talking about?'

'I'm talking about Penal Code one eight seven one zero, possession of a destructive device.'

'What are you, a lawyer?'

'I sure am. And a fucking good one.'

'You're shitting me?'

'What, I can't be an attorney cos I got long hair and I'm sitting in this thing?'

'No, I meant ...'

'Fuck you, Dodge.'

Dodge didn't respond; he felt drained. The last person he wanted to quarrel with was a fellow veteran. And he already felt he'd lost the argument. He did need to share his burden, Hawg was right. Hawg may have been crippled physically, but he seemed mentally in far better shape.

'What did you mean about the doctor?' Dodge asked quietly.

'Doc Quealy? He's the only one gonna keep the cops off your case. They listen to him. He says you're making progress, talking some, they may butt out, least for a while. But you tell the *bac si* to *didi-mao*, then you, my friend, are in big trouble.'

'What am I looking at?'

'One eight seven one zero's what we call a wobbler. Could go either way. Misdemeanor or felony. Misdemeanor, you're looking at up to a year in county plus maybe a fine of a thousand bucks. Felony, up to three years in the state pen and ten thou. You got a criminal record?'

'No.'

'Then, given you're a vet and if you claim diminished capacity at the time, I doubt they'd lock you up just for the possession.'

Dodge peered at him. 'What d'you mean, *just for the possession*?'

'Well, what I hear, you sent a missile onto the street. Now, personally, not speaking as an attorney, I think that's pretty fucking cool, but that opens you up to Penal Code one eight seven one *five* instead. Possession of an explosive device recklessly or maliciously in a public place ordinarily passed by human beings.'

'Shit.'

'Yeah. Shit is the word. That carries up to six years.'

'Then I guess I'll have to go AWOL.'

Dodge threw back his sheet and began to ease himself off the bed, wincing at his wounds.

'Ain't worth the pain, Dodge. May as well stay on your rack. We're in a lock-down and you got a VA cop on the main door. You ain't just walking out of here.'

Dodge thought about it for a moment, then settled back on his pillows.

'But, hey –' Hawg smiled and patted the wheels of his chair '– me neither.'

Even with the lid still on, John knew it wasn't shoes from the uneven distribution of weight inside. He took it to the table. Outside, heavy flurries were spattering the glass.

'I feel like a child on Christmas morning,' he said.

'Are you excited?'

'No, I feel an anti-climax coming on.' He lifted off the cardboard lid and surveyed the contents.

'This is more like it,' Virginia said, and picked out the first article, a well-worn floppy bush hat in tiger-stripe camouflage. She looked inside the brim for some ID but, apart from the DSA stamp, it was unmarked.

'Continuing the theme of Special Forces,' John commented. 'Regular grunts wore steel-pot helmets, not boonie hats.'

He took some dog-tags from the box and examined them, then handed them to Virginia.

'Harold T Olsen,' she read from the metal, then tapped the picture of the soldier. 'This guy.'

'Must be. So ... Chuck Olsen. Strange to finally know his surname.'

He put the tags next to the hat and dipped in again.

'Well, this goes with that,' he said, and placed a black silencer next to the Hush Puppy.

Suddenly struck by a revelation, he gasped and looked at Virginia.

'What is it, John?'

A smile crept onto his face, a smile of understanding thirty-five years too late.

'Harold T Olsen,' he said. 'Harold. *Harry*. Now it makes sense. Chuck was annoyed because I was so clueless, and he said, "Jesus H

Christ", which I'd never heard before; not with the aitch. And I asked him if it was Harry, meaning did the middle aitch stand for Harry.'

'Right. And he thought you were talking about his son.'

'Just for a moment. I've never seen someone's mood change so quickly.'

Virginia took more military items from the shoebox, placing a double handful of medals on the table.

'Quite a collection,' she said. 'Harry was a hero.'

'But not a SEAL,' John said, spreading the medals out. 'These are Army. We've got an Army Achievement Medal, Silver Stars, Vietnam Service Medals, Bronze Stars, Army Distinguished Service Medal, Army Good Conduct Medals, two Purple Hearts, Presidential Unit Citation, Vietnam Gallantry Cross, and … *wow* … see this one here? Congressional Medal of Honor. Not many of these knocking about.'

She regarded him curiously. 'How do you know all the names?'

'In the Legion you have to know your heritage. The Americans aren't the only people to get their arses kicked in Indochina. The French were sent packing in fifty-four after Dien Bien Phu. I just carried on the history lesson – read up on Vietnam. It's become a bit of a passion.'

Virginia nodded but was more intent on what remained in the box. She reached in and removed two letters.

'Think this is any of our business?' she asked.

'Chuck made it my business. I can read both if you like.'

She wavered, but gave him just one. She went over to the camp bed, sat down and pulled the letter from its envelope. John sat at the table with his, and they both began to read to themselves.

'Hayley, you have another visitor.'

The nurse's voice infiltrated a groggy slumber, mercifully blank.

It brought Hayley to the borderland – not awake, not asleep. Her eyelids were leaden but she didn't want them to open. If she did, she knew she would see Larry leaning over her, flowers in his hand, nothing in his heart.

'Hayley, wake up, dear, your mom's come to see you.'

Her mom? How could her mom be here? No, it had to be Larry in disguise. No, that was silly. Perhaps a dream. Drug-induced wish-fulfilment, her crazed brain delivering what reality could not.

'Darling, it's me.'

A different voice. Familiar. God, this was a shitty dream; so cruel.

'Thank you, nurse.' That sweet voice again.

'You're welcome.' A door closing.

'Hayley, please open your eyes.' The words now full of tears.

She had to investigate. Her consciousness clawed upwards through the medication and prised her eyelids apart.

'Oh, Mom ...'

'That bastard,' Marie said. 'Look what he's done to my baby now.'

'I'm okay. I will be,' Hayley said, and joined in sobbing.

'I'll kill him for this.'

'I did try.'

'I mean it. Why not? I wouldn't live to see the trial.'

'Don't, Mom. Don't talk that way. He's not worth it. It's over between us.'

'But look at you.'

'I'll heal. Don't spend your last months in hatred, Mom, please. You and I need to make the most of each other. It's been so long.'

Marie tried to calm herself. 'Well, at least he's in jail now.'

Hayley looked away.

'*What?* He's still out there?'

'Mom, please leave it.'

The younger generation made no sense, and Marie shook her head. There followed a lull in which their tears dried.

'I brought you some flowers. The nurse has them, she's finding a vase.'

'Thank you. I saw you'd been to Dad's grave. The roses were beautiful.'

'I go when I can.'

'So how did you know I was here?'

'Amanda. We knew each other in the old days. She called me, told me what had happened.'

The smallness of the world made Hayley smile. 'Amanda used to be your agent?'

'No, when she was an actress. Why didn't you have someone call me?'

'Look at me, Mom ...'

'I understand. Listen, darling, Amanda and I talked, and we agreed you should stay with her for a few days when you get out. I'd love to have you with me, but, if Larry wants to find you, mine's the first place he'll look.'

'And if he does come, you'll be on your own. I don't want that.'

'I'm not afraid,' Marie said simply, and Hayley understood.

'Mom ... did Amanda tell you about *Malibu Mischief*?'

Marie nodded. 'You'll make it, don't you worry. It'll all come to you, Hayley. Success, happiness, love with a new man, a good man.'

'Feels a long way off.'

'You've had a rough ride.'

The nurse knocked and entered, carrying a vase exploding with mixed carnations. She set them beside the TV and they were left alone again.

'I wish I could hold your hands,' Marie said sadly, staring at her daughter's bandaged palms.

'I know,' Hayley said. 'Me too.'

A battalion of emotions was trooping through John's head. He felt faint with the onslaught. Having seen active service, there was nothing new under the sun. In civilian life, if his heart suffered, if his head ached, it could never rival the affront of war. But the sheer improbability of what he now held in his hands put him into a mental frenzy that was totally unprecedented.

'*John!*'

'Mmm?' The only sound he could manage, his eyes still glued to the words.

'What's the matter?' she asked.

He blew a long sigh through his lips.

'What does it say? I've asked twice.'

He snapped himself out of it and looked at her. 'You first. This is ... worth waiting for.' He placed the letter face down on his thigh.

Virginia smiled dubiously. 'Okay. Well, this was mailed to an address in Haines; we passed through it after we left Baker City this morning. Chuck's home before this place. It's from his daughter-in-law, Harry's wife, Marie, dated February nineteen seventy-seven. The gist of it is she's breaking all contact. She's met someone new and wants a fresh start. She doesn't want Chuck muddying Hayley's head with talk of the past. Hayley's her daughter, the girl in the photo you've got, and that photo was actually sent with this letter as a final keepsake for Chuck. It's all pretty sad stuff. Really makes you feel for the guy.'

'Hayley ...' he said fondly. 'Is there a sender's address?'

'Venice Beach. But Marie says they won't be there if he comes looking. Says they're moving upstate. Won't say where.'

'So Chuck receives this letter, two months later he has a dream, and a month after that he's living here. Smacks of wishful thinking to me. Daughter-in-law craps on him in a letter so he chooses to believe God's smiled on him in a dream. I suppose that has a warped kind of logic, but where did he think I came into the equation?'

Virginia shook her head. 'So what's in yours?'

'Uh, might be best if I just read it word for word. It's not long.'

He turned the sheet over and began, and he could feel his heart thudding in his voice.

'It's dated November sixty-nine. Sent from the Wadsworth Hospital, Veterans Administration, Westwood, Los Angeles. "Dear Mr Olsen, you'll have been notified by now that Harry was KIA. I'm very sorry. I knew your son. We were close. I know he was soon to become a father. Please pass on my sympathies to his wife, and when the kid's old enough please let him or her know how Harry died. I know you won't have been told the details. He died saving my life. I took a round, that's why I'm back in the world. Wasn't for your son, I'd be dead. Maybe you wish I was. That's okay. Shrinks here say I got survivor's guilt. I don't know. I just want to get back there. I will too. I'm on the mend. Won't make no difference. We're going to lose this war. Kennedy knew how to use Special Forces. LBJ and Nixon don't know shit. Wrong targets, wrong weapons, wrong times. Charlie's dying in droves but that won't stop him. The American people don't have the same stomach. Sometime soon they'll say enough. Maybe then we can meet, talk about Harry. But I reckon not. The Nam's in my blood and the Nam's thirsty for blood. I reckon it'll take mine same way it took your boy's. Be proud, Mr Olsen. As we say over here: Sergeant Harry was Number One. The best!"'

Virginia absorbed it for a moment, then asked an obvious question: 'Who wrote it?'

'How do you feel about coincidences?'

'Why?'

'Because it's signed, "Spec Four, Dodge L Chester".'

'Let me see that.'

It wasn't a request. Virginia launched off the camp bed and snatched the letter from his hand. She read it standing up, and John could tell from her face she knew it was the genuine article. How much did handwriting change over the years? Not enough, it seemed. She appeared to review the letter several times before turning her eyes to him. Her stare was a mixture of confusion and accusation.

'Who are you, John? What the *fuck* is going on here? You say a coincidence? You believe that?'

'What else?'

She didn't have an answer, but John could sympathize with her doubts. To term their discovery a coincidence seemed pitifully inadequate. The odds against such a conspiracy of circumstance made winning a lottery jackpot look like an evens bet.

'Virginia, what else?'

She rested against the table. 'I don't know ... what if Chuck was right, and as a kid you were unwittingly involved in some ... psychic occurrence?'

'To what end?' John asked.

'Finding all this stuff,' she said.

'Again, to what end?'

'Oh, John, how should I know?' Virginia said, plainly irritated. 'Maybe this will somehow help my dad. Aren't you open to that?'

He nodded. 'Perfectly. I'd be happy if it did. Doesn't mean I think it's anything supernatural. I don't believe in the occult. When you've seen charred and dismembered corpses spread out across the desert, it tends to negate your more fanciful thoughts on life and the universe. One corpse leaves a lot of people in mourning. Multiply that one corpse by a thousand, or ten thousand, or a hundred thousand, and how many lives get destroyed as a result? Because I don't care how religious or higher-minded you think you are, or how much you believe in life beyond the grave, if you lose someone close you're going to get screwed up. If you want to believe in an unseen dimension, go ahead, but I happen to think it's just mumbo-jumbo for people with too much time on their hands and space in their heads.'

'You mean stupid people. You're saying I'm stupid.'

John realized how badly his mouth had run away on him. 'No, I ... I'm not, I just ... shit.'

'A hundred years ago, a rocket to the moon must have sounded pretty stupid.'

She went back to the camp bed, sat down and pulled the blanket up around her shoulders.

'Sorry,' he said lamely.

'Your problem is you're too closed, you lack imagination. And don't preach to me about loss, John. I've lost a mother, a brother, and every day I wonder is this the day my dad blows his brains out.'

John wasn't about to argue and make it worse. The snow was not letting up and the light was already dying out of the sky. If they were going to spend the night on that mountain together, they would need each other.

'Forgive me,' he said. 'Whatever I might say, I've been knocked sideways by this. We're conditioned by experience, and mine hasn't given me any point of reference for what's happening here. I call it a coincidence because I can't make sense of it any other way. That's just me. I'm sorry. And I don't think you're stupid. I think you have both intelligence and beauty to spare.'

It took a few seconds for Virginia to reply. 'Are you cold?' she asked softly.

'Getting.'

She gently smiled forgiveness and opened the blanket off one shoulder.

Chapter 21

After his third night in the VA Medical Center, Dodge awoke with an inexplicable feeling of hope. Inexplicable and unprecedented. His bedtime knockout pill had sent him deep. Beneath his dreams was a place without image and sound, the land of a sixth sensation. Dodge felt he'd been swirling in circles all night, as though caught in the revolving violence of a hurricane. But he'd never felt in any danger and had always felt close to a perfect tranquillity within the vortex, like falling into the eye of a storm and finding respite there. All this he took as a kind of parable: he didn't have to escape the maelstrom his life had become since Vietnam. Perhaps he never could. But it didn't matter because there was still peace to be had if he only knew how to accept it.

Hawg seemed to know, and Dodge was suddenly fascinated by the man. The pilot of a gunship, Hawg must have rained some serious lead down on the villes of Pleiku. That had to weigh on a man. Yet if he had not quite made peace with his demons, he was at least on speaking terms with them. He seemed to accept them as a permanent fixture in his psyche, and could anticipate the worst of their fury. Instead of running from the looming storm, he stopped in a safe place until it blew itself out. In this hospital he was understood, and knowing that was perhaps a cure in itself.

Since Hawg's visit the day before, Dodge had been thinking a lot. He realized he was still battling vainly for possession of a soul he had lost decades ago. His unwillingness to talk throughout the years had only fed the guilt, which was sustenance enough for the gnawing malevolence inside. Dodge wanted to understand Hawg, how he coped, how he talked to himself. Having always avoided fellow veterans, Dodge suspected this was now the perfect time for that long-feared communion. He had to prise off the lid. Emotionally, something had to release, or next time it might not be just inanimate objects he destroyed. And, unless things changed, there would be a next time – he didn't doubt that for one second.

He left his room and walked down the corridor, checking through the open doors. Nearing the secure exit, Dodge found him.

Hawg was at his wire-mesh window, one wheel flush to the wall, head turned, staring out. His hair hung in a ponytail over the back of the chair almost to the base of his ruined spine.

'Hey, bro,' Hawg said quietly, without looking round.

Dodge realized Hawg must have been blankly de-focused to have caught his arrival in the glass. He wondered where his mind had been, and for how long. He entered the room.

'See anything interesting out there?'

'Nah,' Hawg replied, nose to the mesh. 'Not for years. How about you?'

Dodge came and stood next to him. Down below were the extensive grounds of the US Veterans Administration, dissected by a busy Wilshire Boulevard. Across the 405 he could see the Los Angeles National Cemetery, Westwood village, the UCLA campus, and the long climb up to his home in Beverly Glen. It was a beautiful day, and Dodge felt even more strangely inspired.

'I see life,' he said.

'Is that what you see? Life? You think that's life? That's not life, that's bullshit,' Hawg said, and wheeled himself away to show his disgust.

'What's bullshit about it?'

Hawg spun his chair around. 'I can't speak for you, Dodge, but I ain't been alive since the war. In Vietnam, I had a life. I loved the fucking Nam. When you got death breathing down your neck, that's when you feel truly alive. You can't have one without the other.' He nodded to the window. 'People out there, all they do is fucking exist. There's no life out there.'

Dodge had got it wrong: there was nothing to learn from Hawg. He was no less screwed up, he just had different regrets. Dodge was beginning to feel quite fortunate, and not simply because of his physical state compared.

'What are you saying, Hawg? If you're not ducking rounds, there's no point living? Sounds a lot like jealousy to me.'

'You mean ignorance is bliss? Fuckin'-A it is.'

'Hawg … you can't hate people for not knowing.'

'I don't hate people.'

'Sure you do. You don't see that?'

'Ah, fuck you, blood. And get the fuck out of my room.'

'Shit,' Dodge said with a smile, 'have I just gone from being your bro to being a plain old *blood*? Why not just call me nigger and have done with it?'

'Okay, nigger, get the fuck out of my room.'

Despite asking for it, Dodge was stunned. In Vietnam, racial harmony was no abstract concept. With Charlie on the warpath the only color that mattered was olive drab. Even forty years on, how could a veteran disrespect that?

'Wanna know something, *Lieutenant Peckerwood*? It was probably a nigger like me saved your sorry ass in Pleiku after you got shot down. Chances are, you got picked up by some recon unit full of us blue boys. We got all the shitty jobs.'

'Are you leaving?'

'No.'

'Then you stay and I'll go.'

Hawg rolled himself quickly into the corridor and picked up speed.

'Come on, *bro*,' Dodge mocked, following and keeping pace. 'Let's parley – like you wanted. You came to me, remember? Into my room yesterday, spouting your paraplegic wisdom, putting me down 'cause I won't talk about it, and now you don't want to hear a few home truths yourself? Why not?'

'Leave me alone, I don't have to talk to no fucking niggers!' Hawg shouted, palming his wheels faster.

Up ahead, a cleaner had stopped soaping the floor, and was watching the trouble coming his way. Passing him, Dodge grabbed his mop and thrust it through the spokes of Hawg's wheelchair, spilling him out of his seat to sprawl on the wet linoleum. Hawg immediately starting to drag himself along, his useless legs pulling out a shiny trail like a slug.

Even as Dodge stepped on Hawg's ankle, he was dimly aware how abominable his actions were, but Hawg's insult had soiled the only decent memory he still had of Vietnam: the kinship of battle, and the ultimate sacrifice, regardless of color or creed.

'Get the fuck off of my leg!' Hawg demanded.

'You fucking redneck. I got problems because I was there; you're fucked up because you had to *leave*. I have nightmares 'cause of the people I killed; I reckon you lie awake thinking of all the people you didn't get to kill 'cause they broke your back.'

'*Fuck you!*'

'You know something, Hawg, you've really been a help to me.

I don't need a shrink. You've made me see it could be a whole lot worse. At least the only person I hate is me. You, you twisted son-of-a-bitch, you hate everyone.'

'*Get some help!*' Hawg told the cleaner, who belatedly slapped a nearby wall button, activating the alarm.

Dodge sneered. 'The only thing you love is that chair.'

'I *beg* your fucking pardon?' Hawg said indignantly.

'Sure, it makes you feel what you did was okay because you got dealt some payback. You think it evens the score, makes it okay for you to go on wishing you were back there.'

Four orderlies in white tunics appeared at the top of the corridor and came running, followed by the VA cop. Dodge released Hawg's leg and stepped away, but discovered that the orderlies were happier to play it safe rather than go on trust. Dodge was charged to the ground and restrained, and pretty soon a doctor appeared, and then a needle.

By first light, John and Virginia were once again the best of lovers. In the name of survival they had combined during the night to boost their body heat. Although John had covered Chuck's skeleton first out of respect, he still doubted the morality of sex in the midst of death, even when that death was thirty-five years old.

The snow had relented the previous evening around dusk, but they had decided against a moonlit trip down the mountain. It had been a tough call debating which choice was sanest: wait until daylight and hope they didn't wake to even more inches, or take advantage of the break in the weather and make a precarious journey in the dark.

The gamble had paid off. The sky had been kind. No more snow, now a cloudless blue. They left the cabin and trekked under the laden canopy to the Jeep. John was carrying Chuck's suitcase, containing all the parts of the puzzle: the letters, the calendars, the Hush Puppy and silencer, the bush hat, dog-tags and medals, the photo of Harry, and his Action Man. He set the case in the snow, cleared the windows all round with a sweeping arm of his anorak, then put the case in the back. They both climbed in, John behind the wheel.

'Maybe we can make this a regular thing,' he said. 'Stay longer next time.'

'Imagination *and* sense of humor, John.'

He started the engine, reversed past Chuck's rusting pick-up and turned around.

'We should call someone about Chuck,' Virginia said. 'It's not right he's left up here.'

John nodded. 'Okay. But once we've put some distance behind us. Remember he's got a hole in his skull and I was the last person to see him alive, even if I was only eight at the time.'

Chapter 22

Keen to share their discoveries with Dodge, John and Virginia drove fast, only stopping to swap seats and fill up with gas. Fourteen hours after leaving Chuck's Oregon hideaway, they inevitably wound up in the office of Doc Quealy at the Veterans Administration West Los Angeles Medical Center, formerly the Wadsworth Hospital.

Quealy was a dour individual in his late sixties. The skin of his face was practically unlined, as though it had been rarely creased by either pole of emotion. His full head of silver hair was in a military brushtop.

'How is my father?' Virginia asked, entering the spartan office.

'Take a seat, Miss Chester, Mr Frears.'

Quealy sat behind his desk and waited for his visitors to settle.

'Please, Doctor, is he okay?' Virginia said again.

'Dodge was transferred to us from Reseda Urgent Care three nights ago. He'd been patched up in their ER, but having found his Armed Forces card, and given the circumstances in which he'd received his injuries, the doctors over there decided he needed more specialist treatment, so they called us. We kept him heavily sedated the first day to allow him a little rest, but his physical condition really isn't the problem; your father is gifted with remarkable powers of recovery, not to mention incredible luck. You don't normally survive a frag grenade that close.'

'Maybe that's what he wanted,' Virginia said sadly. 'To die.'

'Perhaps. That's something we've yet to establish. But let's talk basics. How much do you know about what happened? What did you learn from the police?'

'Nothing we didn't already know from the state of the gun range,' Virginia said. 'When we found my dad wasn't home, we drove down to Reseda. We didn't know where else he might be. I could see the main shutter had been replaced so I called the cops.'

'I see. And what did they tell you?' Quealy asked.

'Just that there'd been an incident, my dad was here and that I should talk to you.'

'Good – no amateur psychology. Their job is to pick up the pieces, not to postulate on why something fell apart in the first place.'

'Excuse me?' Virginia said. 'Some*thing*? That *thing* happens to be my father.'

'Accepted. Forgive my talking in abstract terms, Miss Chester, but to a certain extent, a broken mind can be likened to a broken machine. When a machine breaks down, nothing works any more. However, there is usually only one component that has caused the failure. Find it, replace it, the machine starts working again. So it is with the human mind, except for one difference: even if you locate the problem, you can't actually replace any of the parts, all you can do is patch it up and hope it holds. Now, your father has been doing a pretty good job the past forty-odd years of holding himself together. There's no record of him having sought any professional help in all that time. I think at some level in his mind he's always known what's broken and why it broke, he just didn't know how to fix it. But, as with everything, eventually the strain becomes too great and there's a breakdown. Our goal now is to find out what exactly caused that stress fracture back in Vietnam, and why it finally gave way three nights ago.'

'Can I interrupt?' said John.

Quealy nodded.

'With all due respect, I think you're oversimplifying things. You talk as though just one event traumatized Dodge in Vietnam, and if we uncover that we solve the problem. I disagree. I saw combat in the First Gulf War, and elsewhere, and of course some days were worse than others, but it's the whole experience that screws you up. If you focus on just one element, that's like extracting a rotten tooth from a cancerous mouth; it doesn't address the real problem: that no human being should ever be in that situation, forced to take another life. However we rationalize it, something fundamental inside us balks and always will. That's what your machine analogy fails to take into account. We're not mechanical objects, we're creatures driven by emotion.'

Quealy was silent for a moment. 'Well, that came from the heart. And I concur. I was in Vietnam myself, and, like many other veterans of that war, I suffered Post-Traumatic Stress Disorder for years. I became a psychiatrist to help myself first and foremost – physician heal thyself. And I did. You're correct, you can't erase a whole experience by targeting one event, but humans do tend to encapsulate a term of prolonged, heightened emotion in specific memories. Think of your childhood. Whether it was happy or sad, if asked, you'll have one or two stories you always tell to prove your point. The rest is pretty murky, all merged in. Now, over time, those stories acquire a power of their own simply through the repeated telling of them. So what do you do? If you can't erase your childhood, you try and blunt the worst of the pain associated with it. It's like taking the biggest humps of a rollercoaster ride and trying to level them. The ride's still there, but not so scary. And, Miss Chester, in your father's case I have good reason for believing that one event did indeed cause more trouble than any other.'

Having read Dodge's letter, mailed from that very location more than forty years before, John had to agree it was a possibility. But it wasn't for him to say.

'Why?' Virginia asked, not giving any hint herself of their discoveries.

'Because of how the police found him. Did they say?'

'Just that he was in a bad way from shrapnel wounds.'

'Miss Chester, your father was found in full combat uniform, his face painted with camo cream. There were burned-out flares in the range, and it wasn't only the targets that were riddled with bullets. It was the entire building. He'd emptied several clips from a fully automatic CAR-Fifteen, released a frag grenade – accounting for his injuries – and then sent an RPG through the front door.'

'Holy shit,' she muttered.

'Indeed. Thus I would hazard that he was acting out some war game, much like a child, fantasising; only his imagination got somewhat out of his control.'

Virginia sat motionless for a moment, then quickly glanced at John. It was a look he understood – she was also thinking of the letter.

Quietly, she asked: 'Will he get better?'

Quealy sighed. 'Most spontaneous recoveries from Post-Traumatic Stress Disorder occur in the first two to three years. PTSD lasting more than five years usually becomes chronic, possibly lifelong, and often involves a major depressive disorder. His refusal to seek help in the past means his road back is going to be a long one.'

She nodded. 'I see. Doctor, you wanted to know why he snapped. I can help you with that. His son died recently. My brother Donnie. An extremely violent and … shameful death. That's why he snapped.'

'Right. I didn't know; Dodge isn't talking to me yet.'

'And he couldn't talk to me because I was a thousand miles away,' she added bitterly.

John reached to hold her hand, but she pulled it away.

'Miss Chester, this would have happened with or without you. It's clear that your father planned what happened the other night. Not the final outcome perhaps, but certainly to be on his own. Had you been there, he would have sent you away with some very plausible excuse.'

'Really,' she said, unconvinced.

'Yes, really. So-called crazy people can exhibit incredible clarity of thought. The end result might be insane but the means to that end can be extremely logically considered.'

'If you say so.'

'I do. And if you want to help your father you'll believe me. In most cases like this, guilt is a major component of the illness, whether or not it's deserved. If he sees you feeling guilty for leaving him, he'll feel even worse about what he's done. So, no guilt, please, Miss Chester. You have to be strong, you have to be patient, and you have to be understanding. Nothing negative or he'll feed off it like he did this morning.'

John looked at Virginia, who mirrored his puzzlement.

'This morning?' she asked.

'I'm afraid I've jumped ahead of myself,' Quealy said. 'I should have told you at the outset. Your father was involved in an incident this morning with another patient. Quite an ugly scene.'

'Was he hurt?' Virginia asked.

'No, but we had to sedate him again.'

'Oh, God.'

'What happened?' John asked.

'I'm still not in possession of the full facts. One of our sanitation workers caught the end of it. Apparently your father was reacting to an insult of a racial nature, although that may well have been merely the culmination of a more complex disagreement.'

'My dad wouldn't rise to petty name-calling. He has more dignity than that.'

'Your father has suffered a breakdown, Miss Chester, so there's no saying what he may or may not do. And if his illness continues to manifest itself in violence, I'm afraid my hands will be tied. For violent patients, our secure unit is not a long-term solution. Obviously there are other institutions that deal with such offenders, but if Dodge winds up in one, he might be there a lot longer than it takes to effect a cure. What occurred the other night was clearly a police matter, and the LAPD's interest in your father is far from over, especially considering some of the prohibited military hardware he had in his possession. I won't insult you by asking if you knew about that.'

'You just did,' Virginia said. 'And, no, I had no idea.'

Quealy nodded. 'The good news is we have a little time to work on some plan of action. The LAPD have been cooperative and, as long as I have your father under lock and key and the Veterans Affairs Police are standing guard, they are willing to hold off on any charges until I can make my report. So how do we handle this?' he asked rhetorically. 'I've made a start. I managed to pull your father's military record, and it makes for some very interesting reading. He had rather a colorful career.'

He opened a file in front of him and read from some notes.

'Drafted September sixty-eight, eighteen years old. Volunteers for airborne infantry. Basic and advanced individual training, Fort Gordon; jump school, Fort Benning. Assigned to the Hundred and First Airborne Division, the "Screaming Eagles". Applies for special operations duty with the Fifty-Eighth Infantry, Long Range Patrol – the LuRPs – re-designated Seventy-Fifth Infantry Rangers in January sixty-nine. In-country June of that year under Mac-Vee SOG: Military Assistance Command, Vietnam, Studies and Observation Group. Attends Mac-Vee Recondo School at Nha Trang, three week reconnaissance-commando course under the Fifth Special Forces Group. Then sent to Phu Bai, Central Vietnam. Highly decorated, including one Purple Heart, November sixty-nine. Recovered from his wounds right here on these very grounds in the old Wadsworth Hospital. Back in-country two months later. June seventy he rotates out, but extends for another tour. October, back in-country. One year later, he rotates out again and re-enlists again, and this time stays for two years. But not as a Ranger; as a case officer for the CIA, under contract to Plans and Ops at Langley. Initially based at Pakse on the Mekong River, southern Laos, heading up a thirty-man patrol of the Royal Lao Army, part of a CIA Special Guerrilla Unit, Ground Mobile. Aim: disrupt the Ho Chi Minh Trail in southern Laos, thus tie down NVA divisions and keep them out of South Vietnam. Returns to the States for good in March seventy-three.'

Quealy closed the file and looked up. 'I don't know how much of this is news to you.'

'All of it,' Virginia said.

'I thought so; you look pretty shell-shocked. The problem we have is that Dodge was in-country four years, so *if* we're searching for one particular incident, there's a lot to go at. And his first two years under MacSOG would have been extremely harrowing. MacSOG was involved in most of the major campaigns of the war, and although *Studies and Observation Group* sounds quite academic, their approach to warfare was anything but. It was a covert, unconventional, multi-service unit. We're talking sterile ops where dog-tags and insignia were removed, non-US uniforms, boots and weaponry used. Deniable ops, black ops, call them what you will – at times these people were used as little more than government assassins.'

Both men waited for Virginia to absorb the details.

'Can we see him?' she said.

'He's sleeping now, and I'd prefer it if he wasn't disturbed. I'm sure you understand.' Quealy stood up and opened the door, clearly broaching no dissent. 'By all means come by first thing tomorrow.'

Descending in the elevator, John felt awkward. Sitting in Quealy's office, seeing Virginia grow more distressed by it all, so his own guilt had mounted accordingly. He should not have asked her to come away. She should have declined, but he should not have given her the option. The invitation had been crassly timed.

'I don't blame you,' she said quietly, watching the numbers count down above the door.

'You read my mind.'

She turned and smiled at him, a resolute set to her face, like she was taking Quealy's advice and leaving the past behind.

'I have to believe he's right,' she said. 'That this would have happened whatever I did. And it may all turn out for the best. If we hadn't gone away we wouldn't now have those items from the mountain, which may be the only ammunition we have to trigger some sort of release in my dad.'

'I hope you're right.'

They reached the ground floor and headed for the parking lot.

'Why didn't you tell Quealy what we'd found?' John asked as they walked across the floodlit concrete.

'I want my dad to see it before anyone else. In his state of mind he might consider it some kind of betrayal if we go to Quealy with it first.'

They reached the Jeep and climbed in.

'My dad might *have* to talk to Quealy before they let him out, but he might want to start with someone he knows he can trust. He might not even want you in the room beyond explaining how you first met Chuck when you were a kid.'

'That's okay; I'm nothing to your father.'

Virginia took his hands. 'Yes you are, because you're something to me. But the fact remains he may not want you there, and I won't ask him to let you stay. It may be too personal. Something even my mom didn't know.'

'I get it, it's fine. So what exactly will you show him tomorrow?'

'Just the letters. I can tell him about the rest.'

She started the engine and set off home, leaving the Medical Center behind, and John wondered whether she was thinking the same as him: over forty years earlier, her father had spent time recovering there from his physical injuries. Tomorrow, they would have to take him back in time to find some answers, or his current mental wounds might see him incarcerated for the rest of his life.

Chapter 23

Coming round with a thumping head and acute DTs, Larry's first instinct was to cure it with a shot of something strong – continue what he'd started two days before. But he couldn't place himself and thoughts of booze subsided. He wasn't in his own bed, which didn't surprise him, but neither was he on a park bench, and that was odd. He did recognize the room; he just couldn't associate it with anyone he knew. After a heavy binge it always took a moment for the here and now to establish itself.

Then it dawned. It wasn't anyone he knew, and it had nothing to do with the here and now. It was someone he had *known*, from what had fast become the halcyon days of his botched marriage. This was Frank Dista's spare bedroom, and Larry felt like crying.

He had to get out. He wasn't alone in that room. He was crowded in with a bunch of memories that recently hurt like hell. Four happy people partying together, drinking into the small hours, putting a sick world to rights with their laughter. Lying down in there with Hayley, their heads buzzing, still giggling at jokes cracked hours before, hearing Frank's wife, Connie, playfully fending off his drunken advances in the next bedroom. Now four was two and happy was sad. Frank was dead, and although Hayley wasn't, he couldn't count her in his life any more.

Larry left the room and shut the door behind him.

Connie was drinking coffee on the small covered porch out back. Unchecked vines dripped through the wooden rafters. Across her face, the restricted sun laid bright patches that made her look distinctly alien. She didn't smile when she saw him. He guessed she was still in mourning, unable to summon a smile even for the closest of friends.

'Afternoon, Larry. How did you sleep?'

'Like the dead,' he said, sitting down. 'Is there any aspirin in the cupboard?'

'And coffee in the pot.'

Used to Connie being the perfect hostess, he waited for her to fetch them.

'You know where the kitchen is,' she said.

He paused, then got up and went back inside. Connie's apathy was out of character, but he supposed he didn't know her character since she'd become a widow. He hadn't seen her since the funeral. The truth was he had been avoiding her. Hayley had been round several times but he wouldn't go with her. He didn't want to be reminded, have his grief compounded. Connie without Frank – it wasn't right. What made it worse, she was still an attractive woman. If she wanted, in a couple of years, she could easily make a life again with someone new. But she wouldn't. She and Frank had been soul-mates, a connection he had never known with Hayley. Mere love wasn't the same, it didn't go as deep. Frank would never have beaten his wife, and Larry was ashamed of how different he was to the man he had most admired in life.

He brought his coffee back outside and sat down again. He was aware of Connie looking at him with a faint squint, as though trying to work him out, and he was struck by a horrible thought: in his drunken stupor he had opened up to her and revealed everything. The drugs bust, the business with DeCecco, attacking Hayley. Connie knew it all. He didn't recall any such confession but that meant nothing. Beyond the opening hour of his bender there wasn't much that he did remember.

'Connie, did we ... talk last night?'

'Yes.'

'And did I mention I may have done something, uh ... regrettable?'

'You mean something that's not been in the newspapers already?'

'Yeah.'

'Why, have you, Larry?'

Larry still couldn't tell if her being offhand was simply a remnant of grief or if she was playing games with him. 'Please, Connie, tell me. Did I?'

'And if you didn't, would you have the guts to tell me now? Now that you're sober?'

She was taunting; he wasn't stupid. She knew. 'Connie, we go back a long way. If you think I'm an asshole, just tell me.'

'If what you told me last night was the truth, Larry, you are a crown prince among assholes.'

He wasn't going to argue. How could he? He stood up. 'Thanks for the bed, Connie. Sorry I imposed.'

'Larry, sit down. If you didn't want to have this out with someone, why did you come here?'

'Evidently, I was drunk.'

'Yes, and now you're sober you want to bury it all again and hope I'll do the same?'

Larry's heart missed a beat. 'What are you saying, Connie?'

She easily read his fear, and her disgust for him was evident. 'God's sake, Larry, sit down. I have no interest in the legal implications of your stupidity. If you don't care that you got Kevin Mallory killed, that's a matter for your own conscience. I'm not about to call Gilchrist, if that's what you're thinking. My concern is Hayley. She's my friend.'

'And what am I?' Larry asked. 'I thought we were all friends.'

'And I thought you were a good husband to Hayley. Clearly a lot's happened since Frank died.'

'But I want to put things right, Connie. Doesn't that count for anything?'

'Not in my book,' she said. 'You know, when Frank used to tell me about his day, there was always one type of incident I hated hearing about above all others. I never told Frank because I knew he needed to let it out, because he hated them as well. You see, I could never understand the mentality of these people. Drug dealers, bank robbers, muggers, they're all despicable, but they have a reason for what they do. They do it for the money. Even rapists – it's a power thing. It makes them feel in control of their pathetic little lives. It's a reason – if a warped one. But wife-beaters I could never fathom. It was always beyond me. Not the violence *per se*, but the fact that they do it to the people they're meant to love most in the world, and then expect love and forgiveness in return, time and time again. Bank robbers don't return to the bank the next day in tears asking to be forgiven. They know they're assholes who don't deserve a break. So why don't you, Larry? Why aren't you that self-loathing?'

'I am,' Larry moaned. 'But I have to try. I love her so much.'

Connie shook her head. 'Love and violence are mutually exclusive. Whatever you feel for Hayley, it's not love.'

'But, Connie, it will never happen again.'

'Sure, until the next time it happens. No, you keep away from Hayley. She deserves better.'

'Come on, in all the time we've known each other, have you ever thought I might be violent?'

'No.'

'So?'

'But Frank did.'

It hurt John seeing Virginia's face when they entered her father's hospital room. It looked like she had been suddenly bereaved, though Dodge wasn't dead, wasn't even unconscious. John took it badly himself, a proud man like Dodge strapped to his bed, the side rails up like a baby's crib. Dodge smiled at his daughter, but it was Quealy who spoke first.

'Good morning, Dodge. Will I be okay to take the restraints off now?'

'Hey, knock yourself out.'

Quealy raised one eyebrow impatiently. Virginia went to the bed, kissed her father on the forehead, then turned to scowl at Quealy.

'You mean will the crazy man attack his own daughter?' Dodge asked. 'No, and John's safe, too. I don't reckon either of them's gonna call me a nigger, do you?'

Quealy bowed to the pressure of six staring eyes and released his patient.

'Hit the wall buzzer if you need anyone,' he told the visitors, then finally accepted he really wasn't welcome in the room and bowed out, leaving John to close the door he had left open.

'How was Oregon?' Dodge asked cheerily, rubbing his wrists.

Virginia was not impressed by such glibness. She tutted, dropped one of the guard rails and sat on the bed. Dodge took her hands and adopted a more sincere attitude.

'Ginny, I'm okay. Sore in a couple of spots but I'll live.'

'And that might be some comfort to me if this was a regular hospital and you were in here because of a straightforward accident.'

Dodge didn't reply to her. 'How was Oregon, John?'

'Interesting.'

'Dad, you will hear all about our trip to Oregon, believe me. First things first, though. Very simple question: do you want to get out of here, yes or no?'

Dodge was wearing a quizzical smile like he didn't know what the problem was. He added a clueless shrug to complete the façade. Virginia released his hands and stood up.

'Dad, open your eyes! You're in a bughouse, and if you don't fess up to someone real quick you're gonna wind up in the State Pen! I mean, what the hell were you thinking keeping an automatic weapon and frigging grenades?'

Dodge shrugged, and Virginia spun around to face the meshed window. Dodge glanced sheepishly at John, who felt compelled to speak.

'I don't think Virginia intended the conversation to run quite this way, Mr Chester. I think she's annoyed because she's so worried about you, and ... well, she hoped you might be a little more ... co-operative? Tell me if I'm speaking out of turn.'

John waited to be told just that, but Dodge had been cowed by his daughter's outburst and shook his head. Hearing no objection, Virginia turned round.

'Dad, you are in serious trouble and the only possible way out for you is to talk. Tell me what happened. *Why* it happened.'

'If my being here is the problem, Mr Chester, I can leave,' John said.

'It's not. And call me Dodge, for Christ's sake. Virginia, Donnie died. Period. Isn't that enough?'

Virginia bowed her head briefly. 'Dad, he was my brother as well as your son.'

'Meaning?'

'I didn't go off the deep end over his death.'

'No, you went on vacation.'

It was a cheap shot but her head bowed once more, and this time stayed down. John felt his arbitration services were required again.

'Mr Chester – Dodge – you can't make Virginia feel any worse about leaving you than she already does. She shouldn't have gone. That's my fault. I shouldn't have asked her. And I think you understand exactly the point she's making about going off the deep end; why you did and she didn't.'

'I take it you two had sex on your travels,' Dodge said.

John was struck dumb, while Virginia looked up.

'Good for you,' Dodge said. 'I'm pleased. You make a nice couple.'

The lovers exchanged glances.

Dodge winked at John. 'I've never seen my daughter let anyone speak for her like that. She must think a lot of you.'

'Nice sentiments, Dad,' Virginia said. 'And I do. But quit changing the subject. You being in here is not just down to Donnie. This has been building for years. So now it's time to offload a little.'

'I got nothing to say, Ginny. You want me to describe every day I spent in Vietnam? All the moral insults that ate away at me, bit by bit? The process of dehumanisation, seeing things no human being should see, doing things only an animal would do.'

'No. I just want that one day from your nightmares. The one that encapsulates the whole four years.'

'No such day.'

Then the extent of her knowledge registered. He got out of bed and put his back to them at the window.

'Four years …' he whispered. 'Son-of-a-bitch read you my file.'

'Dad, you have to accept: your past has caught up, and not just with you. Don't you think I'm affected by all this? Dad, turn around, look at me.'

He wouldn't.

'I've grown up with it. My whole life, watching that distant look come over you and knowing you've gone someplace I can't reach you, can't help you. Hearing you shout out in your sleep. Even now, have you noticed how few nights I spend at my own apartment?'

'I've never asked you to stay,' Dodge said coldly.

John saw Virginia welling up, went over and put his arm around her.

'Dad, I do it because I want to, because I love you. And I never asked for anything in return. Until now. Just talk to me.'

'Ginny, I … I can't.'

Virginia turned her face to John, who had been waiting for a signal. He could see in her teary eyes it was now. Her words had failed to work the oracle; it was time to confront Dodge with his own words, written over four decades before. John slipped a hand inside his jacket to retrieve the letters, but Virginia pre-empted the handover.

'Dad, Harry had a daughter.'

Larry was reeling, winded, as though from a gut punch. Connie had to be lying. Why would his trusted partner have been badmouthing him on the quiet? As far as he was aware, he had never used unnecessary force in front of Frank. If anyone had a hand problem, it was Frank himself.

'That's not true, Connie. You must have misunderstood what Frank meant.'

'He didn't say you *had* been violent, he said he thought you could be.'

Larry felt the niceties depart. 'Connie, you can fucking well explain that or take it back.'

She maintained her composure. 'Frank said he occasionally caught a glimpse of someone inside you he hoped he'd never meet. Now, only you know what that might mean, or if it has any meaning at all.'

'But you think, in light of recent events, it must be true. Jesus, Connie, thanks for the vote of confidence.'

She made a falsely apologetic face before standing up and clearing the table. While she was in the kitchen, Larry arrived at a way of stopping her subtle onslaught. He would shift the focus; draw a few storm clouds over what he assumed must be her sunny memories of her husband. Connie returned but didn't sit down.

'I have groceries to get,' she said, a plain invitation for him to leave, but Larry only slouched more comfortably in his chair.

'I know what this is about, Connie. All of this. Your … righteous indignation. It's not about Hayley, or Kevin Mallory, or that asshole DeCecco. It's about you. Because the things I've done … they're not the greatest testament to Frank's memory, are they? If I'm a bad cop, Frank's character may also be called into question because we were like two peas in a pod, me and Frank. And that reflects on you. How well did you know your husband? If you knew he was bad, you were colluding; if you didn't, you were blind.'

'I have to go to the store,' Connie said, and disappeared inside.

'And let me tell you something, Connie!' Larry shouted, getting up and following her to the bedroom door. 'You *have* been blind,' he finished smugly.

Connie emerged with her purse. 'You think?' she said.

He nodded. 'Everything I know, I learned from Frank.'

To his surprise, she began to laugh.

'What the fuck is so hilarious?' Larry said. 'You think I'm shitting you?'

'No, Larry, not at all. I just think it's funny you thought that might be news to me. Was that supposed to rip into me, tear my heart out or something? Do you think I don't know the man I was married to for thirty-two years? That I thought he was some kind of a saint? Frank was a bent cop from day one. As a law enforcement official he was seriously flawed. But I loved him in spite of that, because as a man, as a husband and a father, he was the best. Kind, gentle, loving, *protective*.'

Her emphasis was not lost on Larry, who was buckling beneath the truth again. She went to the rear of the house to lock the French windows, then came back. She opened the front door and he obediently stepped outside.

'You, Larry,' she said, closing the door behind them, 'you don't make the grade on any level. To call you simply a bent cop would be an insult to bent cops the world over. You've joined the other side. You're up there with America's Most Wanted. And as a man, and a husband to that sweet and lovely girl you married ...'

She showed a look of disdain and Larry got the message. She set off briskly for her car, leaving him to ponder where exactly he might turn next.

At the mention of Harry's name, John saw Dodge jolt minutely, his spine stiffen. Virginia waited for her father to turn round, but Dodge was keeping his face to the window and keeping his counsel.

'Marie named their daughter Hayley,' Virginia said. 'Marie is Harry's wife, if you didn't know. We came across a letter to Harry's father.'

'I don't appreciate you digging in my past, girl.'

'We weren't. Dad, this is something to do with Harry Olsen, isn't it? Sergeant Olsen? He died saving your life, right?'

When Dodge finally graced them with eye contact, his emotions appeared fully in check.

'I take it you're expecting some kind of breakdown right about now, like Rambo at the end of *First Blood*? Oh, you got the right wound, I'll give you that. But it's not the wound, it's the infection that got *in* through the wound.'

'I don't understand,' Virginia said.

'And I won't enlighten you.'

'Then I hope you like this place. In fact, no. You won't get to stay here. You'll go to jail.'

Another impasse for John to referee. If he had known how many ghosts he would have to lay to rest apart from Donnie's, he would never have left England.

'Dodge, wouldn't you like to meet Hayley? Find out if she's okay. Maybe tell her about her father. You're the only one who can do that.'

'John, I don't feel guilty because some kid grew up without her pop. Many times I could have died hauling someone else's ass out of trouble. It went with the territory. In those four years I saw a lot of kids made fatherless, wives made widows, on both sides. Harry knew the risks; we all did. He made a sacrifice, but nothing I wouldn't have done for him. I don't lose sleep over it.'

Virginia blew a fuse. 'Then what the fuck *do* you lose sleep over, Dad? Because something in your head sure as hell keeps me awake nights.'

When Dodge didn't answer, she grabbed the letters from John, threw them at her father, and left the room.

For a long while, Dodge stared guiltily at a blank wall. John felt privileged that he wasn't asked to leave, and hoped that might be Dodge leaving a door open back into the past.

Finally breaking his gaze, Dodge rubbed a big hand across his bald dome and looked at the floor. Then his eyes narrowed and John knew why. He stooped and picked up the envelope bearing his own handwriting, slowly extracted the letter, and began to read. John watched his eyes slowly track line by line to the foot of the page and stop there, and stay there.

'Must be odd seeing that again,' John said, to snap him from his reverie.

'Explain something, John. If Quealy only just showed you my file, how the hell did you know *four days ago* to go all the way to Oregon to track down Harry's old man?'

'We didn't.'

'You're asking me to believe you found him by accident?'

'No, we were looking for him.'

Baffled, Dodge said, 'John, is it me, or is this conversation going in circles?'

'We were looking for him, but not in relation to you.'

'Son, either you're talking a bunch of crap or I must be more screwed up than I thought, because I can't make sense of a word you're saying.'

John pulled out his wallet and took Hayley's photo from its slot, then bent and scooped Marie's letter from the floor.

'Actually, the story's very simple,' he said, and handed both items to Dodge.

Dodge looked at the photo. 'This is Hayley, right? Harry's kid?'

'Yes, and it came with that letter. If you read it, you'll see Marie sent that picture as a final keepsake before she cut all contact.'

'Why did she do that?'

'It's all in there. The thing is, I didn't get that photo out of that envelope.'

Dodge scowled. 'John, I should tell you at this point, I'm becoming mightily pissed off with these riddles of yours.'

John held up his hands to indicate they were at an end. 'I've had Hayley's picture in my possession since nineteen seventy-eight.'

Not surprisingly, Dodge maintained his disgruntled expression.

John smiled. 'You might not want to tell us anything, Dodge, but I've got one hell of a story for you.'

Larry's eyes burned as he imagined a neat hole in Connie's brow and the back of her skull blown out. The image lasted two seconds. The fire in his eyes was quickly extinguished by unexpected tears, and the wickedness in his head was washed away.

He was wishing ill on Frank Dista's wife. Frank, the man he had always secretly regarded as a belated replacement for a father who had skipped town when he was still in diapers. Which made Connie his honorary mom.

As he walked the streets of Rancho Park, Larry examined the root cause of his anger and hoped it might attach to someone else – Hayley, DeCecco, Marie Olsen, Connie, even Frank for dying in the first place – but it kept swerving at their doorsteps and coming back to roost on his own. He had made foolish decisions and people had reacted naturally, closing him out to safeguard themselves and their loved ones. No one had been vindictive towards him. He had screwed up. He had nobody to blame but himself.

Larry slowly came to a standstill as though his batteries had run down. The realization had literally stopped him in his tracks. It was a breakthrough moment, like standing up at a first AA meeting and announcing his weakness to the group. The problem was him. Jesus, this was freeing. Life wasn't out to get him. People didn't have it in for him. He didn't need to hold any grudges. It was all down to him.

Knowing this, the anger seemed to drain out of him, taking the threat of further violence with it. Which meant Connie was wrong. He *could* ask for forgiveness from Hayley, because he would never need to request it again. He had seen enough domestic incidents to know it took a lot more than two beatings to make a good and loyal wife give up on her man. Some women withstood years of abuse before calling it a day. Was his Hayley any less resilient? She suffered figurative knocks from her career every day the phone didn't ring.

With hope creeping tentatively but inexorably though every capillary, Larry Roth – the new, improved version – resolved a fresh start for himself. He guessed Hayley had been taken to the UCLA Medical Center, but as much as he wanted to heal his rift with her straight away, he realized she needed time to recover, space to heal on her own; allow some distance between the crime and the plea for absolution.

In the meantime, there were other hurt parties to placate.

'Shit, son, you wanna throw a flying saucer in there for good measure?'

'How do you mean?' John asked.

'You don't think there's perhaps something strange in what you've just told me?' Dodge said.

'Coincidences are always strange. Especially ones this big.'

'Coincidence? You're happy with that label, are you, John?'

'You as well, eh?' John said. 'Your daughter started on about the supernatural back in Oregon. I'm afraid I gave her very short shrift.'

'Depends on how you interpret supernatural. To me, just means there's stuff we can't explain. As a race we're pretty screwed up in that department. It's the ultimate human conceit: thinking we know it all. Only God does.'

'You believe in God?'

'I believe we're not the whole story. I don't want to believe we're the whole story. We're as good as it gets? That's terrifying.'

John shrugged, quite willing to leave it at that, but Dodge had more to say.

'You know how many ways a man could die in Vietnam? You got a cherry fresh off the plane at Phu Bai and within a week he's being loaded back into the hold in a box. I spent four years over there, in the thick of it. I only took a bullet once and I was back in-country inside two months. After a while you get to thinking maybe you're not meant to die, that somebody up there likes you.'

'You think you were spared for a reason?'

Dodge looked suddenly exhausted, as though such talk had drained him.

'Well, if I was, then I've let a lot of people down in the time since.'

John decided not to prompt; Dodge had a faraway look that promised more.

'All the guys who died over there, I owed it to them to live a good life when I got back to the world. But I couldn't. After Harry died, I had a death-wish. I went back to Vietnam because I wanted to die there. The shrinks call it survivor's guilt. But the bullets just kept missing me. So when I came home for good I had ... shit, I don't know, death-wish guilt, I guess. While I was trying to get zapped, I had two kids growing up Stateside, and a wife who couldn't figure out why I wouldn't stay home. You know how shitty that made me feel after the event, to think I knew what I was doing to them and still didn't care?'

John risked a quiet reply. 'That's what you meant about the infection that set in after Harry died.'

Dodge nodded gravely, then looked rather startled. It appeared his brain had caught up with his words. He stared John straight in the eye.

'I just broke my silence, didn't I?'

'You did. How do you feel?'

'Too early to say. John?'

'What?'

Dodge paused before asking, 'Do you suppose we *could* find Hayley Olsen?'

'We could certainly try,' John said. 'But I'm not sure about the *we* part. You mean you as well?'

'Can you talk to Quealy? Explain all this to him? Get me out of here?'

John shrugged. 'I don't know. I'll do my best, but … he'll want to hear all this from you. I know you don't like the man, but could you tell him what you just told me?'

Dodge considered for a moment. 'Sure. Sure, I can do that.'

Chapter 24

When John pulled open the driver's door, Virginia, slumped in the passenger seat, awoke with a start. She looked shattered.

'Sorry,' he said. 'Out like a light, eh?'

'The instant I sat down. How'd it go?'

'See for yourself.' He pointed past her.

Virginia turned to her right and yelped with delight. '*Dad!*'

Dodge and Quealy were standing side by side. While Quealy was immaculate in a dark suit of razor-sharp creases, Dodge was attired in an old shirt and jeans courtesy of the hospital's left property. Their expressions were also in sharp contrast. Whereas her father looked happy, Quealy looked, if not sad, then at least woefully concerned.

Dodge leaned in through the lowered window and pecked his daughter on the lips.

'But ... how?' Virginia asked. 'Doctor Quealy ...?'

'Mr Frears will explain the situation, I'm sure. And I confess it's not one I'm at all comfortable with. This is certainly a gross breach of protocol, but I seem to have had my words cleverly manipulated against me. So I'm releasing your father into your and Mr Frears' care for a period of no longer than forty-eight hours. Mr Frears knows what plan of action we've decided upon, and I *do not* want your father left alone for one single minute, is that understood? Any concerns, you are to call me immediately. *Not* the police, unless you want to see me locked up alongside your father. Mr Frears has my card. Any time. Day or night.'

Virginia nodded. 'We will.'

Quealy turned to Dodge and offered his hand, which was grasped firmly and pumped several times.

'Now, Dodge, you know the risk I'm taking with this. I'm putting what's left of my career on the line for you. But I was a man of action before I became a physician – a veteran of Vietnam just like you – and action is what's needed now, not talk. The fact remains, though, that I am potentially endangering the public by letting you out. So, *please*, do not let me down.'

'I won't,' Dodge said humbly. 'And thank you.'

'Two days, Dodge. Then you need to come back and face the music. I wish you the best of luck.'

Quealy gave Dodge a military salute, about-faced and headed back towards the hospital. They all watched him go, all three of them perfectly silent as though they expected he would turn around any second with a change of mind.

With Quealy safely inside the building, Dodge climbed in the rear of the Cherokee and shifted across behind the driver's seat to get an easier eye-line with his daughter. John got behind the wheel, started the engine and drove them off the Veterans Administration grounds onto Wilshire Boulevard.

'Dad, are you sure you're fit to be leaving hospital?' Virginia asked. 'I mean physically?'

'Sure, don't worry. Surface scratches. Like I said to John: someone up there likes me. I'm damn near indestructible.'

Virginia didn't smile. 'I don't get it.'

'In about a mile,' Dodge said, clapping a fatherly hand on John's shoulder, 'take a left onto South Beverly Glen Boulevard. What don't you get, Ginny?'

'I still don't understand how you got out.'

John answered: 'Like Quealy said: I used his words against him. Remember what he said about the machine breaking down and how we had to find the one broken part? Well, when I told him we'd found that part but we couldn't fix it with Dodge locked away, he was obliged to let your father out or look like a prick who didn't believe in his own theory.'

'What, he just accepted your word that you *had* pinpointed the problem? I didn't figure him to be that gullible.'

This wasn't something that John wanted to explain. He looked to Dodge, forcing the baton into his hand.

Dodge sighed. 'John told me all about Oregon and I ... well, I returned the favor concerning my time in Vietnam.'

'Oh ... okay,' she said, and faced front.

John gave her a subtle sideways look. He could see her feelings had been deeply hurt, but her response showed she was more concerned with her father's state of mind than with revealing her own. Dodge had to be kept on an even keel, and upsetting his only beloved daughter would not have been conducive.

'Girl, don't be upset,' Dodge said, sensing if not seeing her expression. 'It was my letter, the one I wrote back in sixty-nine. You'd gone before I could read it. It just got me talking. I wasn't even aware until I'd finished exactly what I'd said – John'll tell you. And you didn't miss much, honestly. I didn't go into detail.'

Virginia looked round and smiled at her father. 'It's okay, really. Let's get you home. I need to pick up my car. I've got a production meeting coming up and I left some preliminary sketches in the trunk.'

It went very quiet in the back. Then there was one word: 'Shit.'

'What? Dad, what's that face for?'

'Do you have your vehicle insurance documents up at the house?'

'No, they're at my apartment. Why?'

Another telling silence. John reckoned he maybe knew the punchline already.

Virginia's tone dropped. '*Dad* ...'

'Uh, yeah. You might want to check the small print, the exclusions. See if there's not something about *accidental targeting by lunatic with grenade launcher*.'

John had never known a more pregnant pause.

'Dad, tell me this is a joke.'

'I can't. I blew your car to pieces.'

Another ghastly pause.

'Sorry,' Dodge added.

'Assuming – only assuming – this is true, then when you say you blew it to pieces, you don't mean that, do you? What you really mean is it got hit by shrapnel, right?'

John didn't have to turn round to know Dodge was shaking his head. Perversely, he could sense an outbreak of the giggles threatening.

'Pieces,' Virginia repeated carefully, as though the word itself was liable to explode. 'And just how big were these pieces, Dad?'

'Small. *Real* small.'

John erupted, and the word *giggles* did not do justice to what emerged. Too much stress had built in the past few days for it not to find a release. Virginia was giving him the evil eye but he couldn't stop laughing. He hoped she would find it infectious, because this was the sort of thing that could kill a relationship stone dead.

'Sorry,' he spluttered.

For some reason, this set Dodge off, but his support was more damaging than helpful. On recent evidence, he was already cruising happily along Batshit Boulevard; he *would* find it funny.

'That scorch mark on the concrete, right?' John managed to ask.

'Yeah,' Dodge said, and howled.

'You total assholes,' Virginia said amiably; a great relief to John.

They drove in amused silence for a while, briefly taking Sunset Boulevard before joining North Beverly Glen.

'Sorry about the sketches,' Dodge said quietly. 'Can you remember what they were?'

'I keep copies, don't worry. Guess I'll have to drive a rental until the insurance pays out.'

'You won't have to wait that long. I made a call from the hospital. Old buddy of mine in the trade. You'll have a replacement by tomorrow. Exactly the same, even down to the talking alarm.'

'Thanks, Dad.' She reached back to squeeze her father's hand.

'How's the range looking?' John asked.

'It'll be closed for a while. And, Ginny, I'm transferring ownership to you. Even if I manage to stay out of jail, they won't let a basket-case like me keep on running the place.'

She smiled. 'Looks like I've come out of this pretty well.'

They arrived back at Angelo Drive. While Dodge went upstairs to change, Virginia and John carried their mountain mementos through to the living room and waited in silence. A few minutes later, Dodge entered the room, looking far more at ease now in his own clothes in his own home.

'Let me see the suitcase,' he said.

'Uh ... sure,' Virginia said, but that momentary hesitation had betrayed her reluctance, which John assumed was down to Harry's Hush Puppy.

'John, my daughter will feel happier if you take the gun out first and keep a hold of it. Although I don't know why. She knows I have other weapons in the house. If I was looking to shoot the place up, I wouldn't need an antique Smith to do it.'

John laid the case open on the coffee table in front of him. Inside, the items were all jumbled about, and Dodge simply pored over them for a minute. When he began handling them, he did so with great reverence, as though they belonged to pre-history and might crumble to dust. This he did in silence, his expression unreadable. With the militaria inspected and placed to one side, he checked the calendars. Any thoughts he might have had, he kept to himself. Gently, he returned everything to the case and closed it. He looked up, his expression perfectly mellow. From those articles of war, Dodge had drawn a kind of personal peace.

'If we do find Hayley,' he said, 'this belongs to her.'

John nodded, but Virginia had her reservations, and put them to her father as carefully as she could.

'That's fine, Dad, but you do know that's a pretty big if. That Venice Beach address is way out of date. Marie said in her letter: she was moving away with a new husband.'

Dodge sagged a little at this reality check.

'Sorry, Dad, I don't mean to rain on your parade, I just don't want you hoping for too much and getting disappointed.'

Dodge smiled at her. 'I know, Ginny. I know you're worried about me. And if I can't find her then, yes, I will be disappointed. But I have to take that risk. Just like Quealy. If he didn't think there was a chance of some healing, he wouldn't have let me out. Maybe just the act of searching will make me feel better. I think it has already. It's a focus. I need that.'

She shrugged. 'Yeah, it ... it just seems such a long shot.'

John touched her arm. 'Hey, what do we have to lose? You

never know, maybe a neighbor might have an address, or still be in contact. Would that be any stranger than us unearthing a letter from your dad in a log cabin a thousand miles away?'

'I guess not. But I still worry.' She looked back at Dodge. 'What happens if you do find her?'

'I'll see if she's doing okay, ask if she needs anything, and let her know what kind of a man her father was.'

'What if she's not interested?' Virginia asked. 'Are you prepared for that?'

Dodge leaned back in his chair with a weary sigh that turned into an angry growl.

'Ginny, I don't know, okay? You're asking what's in my head. If this happens, how will I react, if Hayley says get lost, what will I do. I have no idea. I haven't known what's been going on for over forty years; why should it be any different now?'

'Dad, I'm just saying she may want the past to be left where it is. I just want you to be ready for that.'

Dodge pressed his palms against his ears and squeezed his eyes tight shut, as though he couldn't allow the words and pictures outside his head to soil those on the inside, and John realized that Dodge was lying. Since learning about Hayley, he had clearly let his imagination create the most perfect meeting between the two of them, a piece of wish-fulfilment that could prove every bit as damaging as his warped mental projections at the range a few nights ago.

'I don't know,' Dodge said, opening his eyes. 'You tell me, Ginny: if things had worked out differently, and I was the one who hadn't come home, would you want Harry knocking on your door to fill in some of the blanks?'

Virginia nodded. But she wasn't Hayley so it meant nothing. Her father *had* come home and she couldn't imagine it any different.

Still, it was an end to the discussion, and Dodge closed his eyes again and didn't wake up for a further two hours.

Chapter 25

The Beverly Center stood eight stories high across seven acres of land, an imposing mall at the edge of Beverly Hills and West Hollywood. A good place to kill time, become faceless.

Laura DeCecco turned off South San Vicente Boulevard into the entrance to the parking and found a spot on the second level, positioning the Honda Civic nose out for a quick getaway. She stayed in the car for several minutes, checking the vehicles arriving behind her, the Sig-Sauer in her lap.

Whether it was wise to have left the safety of her home, Laura wasn't sure, but she quietly suspected she was being a bit too ballsy for her own good. Her bravado with Joey had seemed genuine enough at the time, but now it felt like a sham. She had always believed she had been borrowing drop by drop from her husband's pool of courage over the years, making herself a stronger, braver individual by dint of his deeds. It certainly took considerable strength of character to let the love of her life fly away to unfriendly lands for covert missions the rest of America was oblivious to.

But this was different. This was *her* potentially facing mortal danger. This wasn't some peril she was experiencing vicariously through her husband; this was Laura DeCecco in the line of fire – perhaps literally since events had moved on from Roth's threat to frame her. That particular threat had been to secure her husband's skills in the drugs bust, but Joey had not only failed to provide the back-up requested – a passive betrayal through neutrality – he had then positively declared war on the man. So how much more vicious would Roth be now in his retribution? Considering he had one of the most heinous *curriculum vitae* of any cop in the country, would there be anything he'd find anathema? She doubted it. He had beaten his own wife half to death, so why would he have any qualms about killing someone else's? And she didn't at all believe her being pregnant made her untouchable, rather more of a delicious target; two dead for the price of one bullet.

So why was she out in the open? Where was the sense in that?

No sense. She was stubborn, always had been. She had never let anyone push her around, and, whatever her fears, she wasn't about to now. Had there been a waiting game to play, she might have felt differently. If Roth had been destined for jail, she may have stayed in the shadows until he was locked away. But Roth wasn't going to jail. Internal Affairs didn't have the evidence and his wife didn't have the guts or the inclination. Larry Roth was out there. And if revenge really was a dish best served cold, there might never be a time Laura would feel completely safe.

The only option was to face the situation. If it was going to happen, then bring it on. Get it over with.

Satisfied there was no silver Corvette on her tail, she zipped the Sig back inside the fanny pack and got out of the Civic.

Riding the elevator to the stores on level six, she was physically alone but accompanied by a floating seasonal melody that issued from the ceiling. Carol singers celebrating the birth of the baby Jesus on Christmas day in Bethlehem long ago.

Unconsciously circling her palm around her swollen belly, Laura began to cry.

Watching DeCecco's wife hurry to the bank of elevators, Larry's worst fears were realized. Her movements were all wrong, completely at odds with her condition. He had never seen a pregnant woman move but slowly, ponderously. Equally, he had seen too many nervous individuals in his job not to recognize the signs in her. She looked shit-scared; trying to hide it, but, to the eyes of a seasoned cop, failing.

Larry had not been able to check on her state any earlier. Despite waiting up the road from the DeCecco family home, he hadn't managed to get a good look at her because she'd driven straight out of the garage in the Civic. So he'd followed her to the Beverly Center. Staying two cars behind, he was aware how sinister it must have looked. Had she noticed the tail he would have been branded a stalker and no words from him could have persuaded otherwise. But if she was checking at all, it would have been for a silver Corvette, and circumstances had put him behind the wheel of Hayley's Beetle. Time wasn't all he had lost while bar-hopping; somewhere along the way he had also managed to lose his precious car keys.

No, there was no question – DeCecco had made his wife aware of the situation. So she probably also knew about the Armenians, Kevin Mallory, and what Larry had done to his own wife. Which meant she now had to fear far more from him than simply being framed for a crime she had not committed.

He couldn't just drive away. If he was going to become that better person, it was imperative he set the record straight with her, restore to her that mythical, maternal glow, because the shame he now felt for stealing it literally shivered through him, leaving gooseflesh in its wake. How could he have threatened a pregnant woman, even via a third party? Whatever the gripe with his partner, he had no right to involve anyone else. He had to apologize.

The problem was how. How to get close enough to say the words? The moment she saw him she would scream and run away, or, worse, grab the nearest mall cop. So Larry stayed in the Beetle and just watched as she stepped into the elevator and rose into the mall. She would have to come back down sometime.

By then he might have figured out how to say hello and not scare the poor woman half to death.

For more than an hour, Laura wandered aimlessly around Bloomingdales and Macy's and a bunch of smaller boutiques whose names she didn't even register. In and out of the stores she ambled, under the bright lights of the consumer heaven, bedecked with the added tinsel and sounds of the season. Trying to find interest in material objects she might ordinarily have craved, but that now appeared as so much empty aspiration. Even the baby sections – *especially* the baby sections – left her feeling emotionally hollow, as though she no longer dared to presume a future in which such items might be of use to her.

She was exhausted. She needed to sit and eat something. She went down to the California Pizza Kitchen at street level, but the food only made her more tired, her energy further depleted by the process of digestion.

There was no option. Home. She wanted her bed, regardless of what dreams or nightmares lay coiled in its springs. The security system could be armed downstairs while she slept upstairs, the gun within easy reach. She put another call through to Joey to update him, then returned to the elevator and pressed for level two. This time she was joined by a party of shoppers. Folk either side of her held onto carrier bags bulging with garish parcels, and

Laura felt her heart suddenly and wonderfully soar. In a year from now this horror would be behind them, and she and Joey would be buying gifts for their son. He wouldn't understand the fuss, but they'd still squat down by his buggy and point it all out to him: the decorations, the *à cappella* singers, the bearded man in the red suit, cloned in every mall across the country.

Laura smiled. When the door slid open she headed out towards her car, and Larry Roth already seemed to her like the ghost of Christmas past.

Someone had stuck a flyer on her windshield, no doubt advertising some whacko weight-loss regime. Laura didn't bother to check. She snatched it from under the wiper blade, balled it and dropped it.

Then she noticed. The windshield next to hers was clear. Down her row and opposite, there was not a single flyer. In fact, nowhere could she see another leafleted vehicle.

Her eyes were drawn to the crumpled paper by her feet, and her heart sank with her focus. Other eyes were on her, she was sure of it. She was being watched, and knew her paranoia was not to blame for what she felt.

Holding the Honda's wing mirror, she lowered herself to squatting and took out the Sig. She smoothed out the note and checked the signature first to confirm what she already knew. Staying low, she read what Larry Roth had written.

Dear Mrs DeCecco, don't be alarmed, I come in peace! I didn't know how else to do this. I wanted to say sorry. I didn't mean what I said to Joey. You have to believe my threats were empty. I wish neither of you any harm. I admit I was annoyed with your husband but I can let that go as well. I've made mistakes and hurt people but I'm not a bad person. I want to explain over a coffee. We can chat. I think I need to talk – that may be the whole problem. I'm watching you now and will come over when you put this note down. Please don't be scared. Please. Sincerely, Larry Roth.

Fuck that, Laura thought. Trust Larry Roth? The man who had deceived Kevin Mallory, leading him into a lethal hail of bullets; who had threatened to kill an informant; threatened her; threatened Joey; beaten his own wife; wiped out a gang of drug dealers like some dark avenging angel from a Marvel comic. Now, practically overnight, he was a reformed character? He seriously expected her to believe that?

Around her were the footfalls of her fellow Angelenos, coming and going, laughing and talking. Door slams, short tire squeals, engines starting up, cutting out, growing or fading on the ramp. None of that worried her. It was what she *couldn't* hear that bothered her, the silent figure sitting in his parked car watching her. How on earth had she failed to spot him?

If she ran he might shoot her or find her someplace else, perhaps without warning next time – no bullshit note on her car.

She wanted this to be over. Activating the laser sight beneath the barrel, she crawled away to another vehicle. Joey had often talked about his recon training – the element of surprise. She could gain it now. Larry would be expecting a quivering, sobbing wreck beside the car, begging for mercy.

He wouldn't find it. Instead, her red dot would find his heart.

With her own heart thrashing, adrenaline surging, her whole body shook like she was lying naked on ice. Inside her, the little one was already reacting to his mother's state and kicking like crazy.

Shit, where'd she gone? Had she fainted? Was she hiding? Larry waited vainly for her to pop up into view again. One minute.

Two minutes. Fuck. This was bad. He had to speak to her. Had to. The wording of the note meant nothing unless he could get close enough to *prove* he meant no harm.

He punched the dash and swore, got out of the Beetle and quickly picked a route through the vehicles, an apology running on a loop in his head.

The concrete between the Civic and the car alongside was bare. She hadn't fainted. So where the hell was she?

'Mrs DeCecco?'

He squatted down and checked under both cars, then stood up again.

'I've got a gun, Larry. Don't make any sudden movements. Believe me, I am extremely liable to shoot you.'

She was behind him and he had no reason to doubt her. Her voice was jittering with nerves, but the words were spun around a sinew of steel.

'Should I put my hands up?' he asked.

'Yes. *No!* No, just keep them away from your body. Don't draw attention. I don't want anyone calling security.'

Larry didn't like the sound of that. 'Why not?'

'Shut up, I'm thinking.'

'I'm not armed,' he said, which was true if he ignored the Tactical One-Hander down his sock.

'Shut up!'

Several seconds passed and she didn't speak. For Larry, the silence was ominous. He ventured a question. It seemed fair under the circumstances.

'*Are* you going to shoot me?'

'I want to. I should.'

'But you're not going to.'

'Turn around.'

Larry did so, slowly, and swallowed past a lump in his throat. Her aim was low, and he was joined to her gun by a line of red light. It jiggled around his belly button like some weird umbilical cord. If she pulled the trigger he'd be gut-shot, and he knew from his years on the street what a shitty wound that was.

'Jeez,' he said humbly, 'that's some serious hardware. Joey give you that?'

'My God, I want to kill you. Does that sound bad? When I've got a new life growing inside of me, to be thinking of killing someone?'

Larry tried to make his shrug not appear dismissive. She was livid, a product of intense fear. There was a real chance he might get shot today.

'I'm sorry,' he said.

'How *dare* you put me in this position. How *dare* you. What gives you the right to fuck with people's lives?'

'I'm sorry. That note, it's the truth, I didn't want you to be scared any more. I thought – ... Mrs DeCecco, are you okay?'

Her face screwed up again. Suddenly, she looked more fearful than ever. Eyes like marbles, her mouth fell open as she drew in a hoarse breath.

'Mrs DeCecco?'

She staggered a little, and Larry was no longer her focus. The two-handed grip on the gun changed to one and the barrel dipped to the concrete. She screamed and her free arm wrapped across her stomach like she was trying to keep something in.

Horrified, Larry realized she was.

Chapter 26

Dodge was nervous as he stood on the stoop, waiting for his knock to be answered. He looked back over his shoulder, requesting encouragement. From the Jeep, Ginny smiled and her boyfriend gave a thumbs-up, but Dodge was already feeling the wind die in his sails. He was chasing ghosts and didn't even know where the graveyard was. The trail would begin and end on the doorstep of this Venice bungalow, and what would that do to his head?

His first impression of the woman who opened the door was that she was sick. Her color was bad. Seeing the suitcase, she made an understandable assumption.

'I'm not buying,' she said, and shut the door.

He turned back to the Jeep and shrugged.

'Try again!' Ginny shouted.

With a lackluster fist, Dodge rapped on the wood. Shortly, the woman reappeared and stared at him through the glass, her arms folded, a symbolic bar against his intrusion.

'I'm not selling,' he told her. 'I'm looking for someone who used to live here.'

'You must have the wrong address; I've been here for ever.'

Dodge smiled; perhaps it did feel that long to her.

'I'm going back a few years,' he said. 'Nineteen seventy-seven. February.'

She paused slightly before telling him: 'Kindly get off my property, I'm tired.'

Dodge watched with a frown as she retreated into a back room. This was certainly the address on Marie's old letter, and Marie had certainly stated her intention to move away.

But what if she hadn't?

'Mrs Olsen?' he called. 'Marie Olsen?'

After a moment, she moved into view, framed by a doorway down the hall.

'Who are you?' she asked.

'My name's Dodge. Harry may have mentioned me in letters home. Spec Four Dodge L Chester, Seventy-Fifth Infantry Rangers. You are Marie Olsen, aren't you?'

She barely acknowledged her own name. She had been instantly transported, and Dodge knew how easily that could happen. As though in a trance, she approached, her expression one of bitter-sweet memories, nostalgia battling truth. She unlocked the door, pulled it wide and went into the front room. Dodge accepted this silent invitation. He nodded to Ginny and John and took his case inside.

Marie was already seated. It appeared she needed the support. Close up, he reckoned his earlier assessment had been kind. She was more than just ill; she was dying. In the war he had seen the life ebb from countless individuals, but once or twice he believed he could have pointed to the fighting fit who were all set to piggy-back the Grim Reaper into battle. Sometimes death could taint a person long before the bacteria worked their stench into the flesh.

'Please, sit down,' she said. 'You must forgive my rudeness a moment ago. I'm not too receptive to visitors. It's been a gruelling week, one way or another.'

'We can postpone this to a better day,' Dodge said sympathetically, but desperately hoped she wouldn't want to.

'There won't be a better day,' she said, strangely balancing her doom-laden pronouncement with a hearty smile. 'Now, I want to know: why should a friend of Harry's be knocking on my door after all these years?'

'Well, for one thing, I didn't know where you were until today.'

'I'm intrigued.'

Dodge gave a lopsided grin. 'To be honest, it's not you I'm looking for. Well, not just you. It's your daughter Hayley.'

A brief cloud, dark and troubled, dulled what little light remained in her eyes.

'I see,' she said curtly. 'Do you have war stories for her? Because she doesn't need them right now.'

'Just one. Perhaps if you hear it first you can decide whether or not she hears it. Do you have the time?'

Marie smiled inscrutably. 'Enough to hear what you have to say.'

'Thank you,' he said. 'Actually, it's in two parts, the story. One of which it's best you hear from my daughter and her friend. They're outside. Would it be okay if I brought them inside?'

'Why not?' Marie said. 'Let's have a party.'

The Cedars-Sinai Medical Center was thankfully less than a block away. Larry paced the corridor outside the delivery suite like an expectant father, but his worries were tenfold. He wasn't just concerned for the wellbeing of mother and baby; he now truly feared for his own life. Having narrowly avoided the 9mm wrath of Mrs DeCecco, he still looked destined to die at the hands of her hubby. When DeCecco learned what had befallen his wife, Larry's noble motives would count for zilch.

He stopped pacing for a moment and tried to resign himself.

Events had overtaken him and stolen the lead. Until certain people acted on those events and brought him up to date, he was in limbo. DeCecco was one, Hayley another, and then there were the suits from Internal Affairs. He guessed it was apt payback. How must DeCecco's wife have been feeling, packing a gun, awaiting his ambush, wondering how her happy days of pregnancy had vanished in a stranger's threat, pondering when that stranger would allow her normal life to resume?

Behind him, the swing doors flapped back together, and Larry turned to see Doctor Haslam, the obstetrician who had received them. Garbed in green gown and cap, his mask was pulled down off his face, revealing a cautious smile.

'Congratulations, you have a son. They're both doing fine, but we did have to perform an emergency C-section. The baby was becoming tachycardic and I didn't feel it wise to wait.'

'Oh. But it's okay now?'

'Absolutely. Don't worry.'

Larry nodded. 'Is she awake?'

'Yes. Laura opted for a spinal. Better for the baby.'

Laura. He hadn't even known her name.

'And how is she … in herself?' Larry asked.

'Really very distraught. But that's not unusual for a woman who's been looking forward to natural childbirth at term, then finds herself undergoing a major op, suddenly and prematurely. You'll need to keep a close eye on her in the next few months; this sort of thing can be a contributing factor in the onset of post-natal depression.'

'Fuck, really?'

Haslam's expression showed he didn't quite understand Larry's need to curse. 'I'm afraid so,' he said.

Physically carved up and emotionally screwed up. That was the wife Larry was handing back to DeCecco. He swore again.

'However, let's not worry too much about that now,' said Haslam. 'This should be a happy time for you both. Please, go through, say hello to your son.'

'Uh ... no, I'm not the father. I told the nurse at the desk. I'm a ... family friend.'

'Ah. I see. Well, would you have .... have we met before?'

Larry recognized the doc's facial set: thinking eyes and a vague smile that wasn't sure of its ground. He'd seen the same look maybe a hundred times since his own face had been plastered across the TV news following the disastrous drugs bust; a niggling familiarity some people just couldn't pin down. Was he an old buddy? A minor celebrity?

'I don't think so,' Larry said. 'What were you about to ask?'

'Uh ...' Haslam had to mentally backtrack. 'Oh, yes. Would you have a contact number for Mr DeCecco?'

'He's a cop. Works Hollywood. You'd need to call the station.'

'Okay.' That look again. 'Are you an actor?'

Larry found Haslam's question bitterly amusing. His laugh was more of a yelp.

'I wish I was. I wish you were. I could ask for a fucking rewrite.'

After the introductions had been made, John recounted his tale of 1978. Marie stared at the carpet the whole time and John wasn't sure if any of it was getting through. He gave Dodge a worried glance.

'Marie?' Dodge said.

'I'm listening, carry on.'

So John jumped to 1990 and the Gulf and how he met Donnie who linked him to current events. Then Virginia shared the telling of their trip to Oregon and the items they'd discovered that bound them all together.

Marie finally looked up, her eyes moist. 'May I see the letter I wrote, please?'

Dodge unlatched the case and gave her the letter from inside. Marie put on a pair of spectacles, took it from the envelope and opened the pages.

She quickly stopped; too quickly to have read it all. She slipped it back in the envelope and removed her glasses with a vexed sigh.

'I know what it says. Every word. I've not forgotten.'

John saw the undiminished pain in her eyes. Her anguish seeped like sweat from every pore. Suddenly, she made a face as though her pain was not just emotional.

'Marie?' Dodge said.

It passed, and her features returned to normal.

'I'm dying,' she said. 'Cancer.'

No one said anything. Marie got up and opened a sideboard to produce a large brown bottle of liquid morphine. She took a swig and sat down with her medicine.

'So what's your interest in my daughter?' she wanted to know.

Dodge didn't answer verbally. He went to the suitcase again and handed her the letter he had written to Chuck.

After reading it, she looked at him.

'So you do want to tell her war stories; how her father died. Is that for her benefit or yours?'

'You're most intuitive, Marie. Let's just say I have a vested interest.'

'No, let's say rather more than that. If you want to see my daughter, I want to hear everything.'

Reluctantly, Dodge began to detail his years of psychological torment, culminating in the episode at the range. John hoped it wouldn't queer his chances of meeting Hayley, but knew Marie had given him no choice. When Dodge finished talking, Marie studied him for several seconds.

'Well, you don't make a very good case for yourself, do you, Mr Chester? How can I be sure you won't come unhinged when you see my daughter?'

'I won't. Why would I? And please call me Dodge. Do that for me, at least.'

'All right, Dodge. Perhaps you can tell me what happened in nineteen sixty-nine. I was never told; just that Harry was killed in action.'

Suddenly nervous, Dodge put a hand to his brow, which popped instant perspiration. 'I'm not sure I can.'

'This is what concerns me,' Marie said. 'What's in you that doesn't want to come out? And will it be dangerous to my daughter?'

Dodge looked to his own daughter for reassurance.

'Dad, you can do it. Coming back from the hospital you were about to talk. Why not now?'

'This is ...' A flick of his eyes towards Marie said the rest: *different.*

'Whatever you tell me, Dodge, I won't blame you,' Marie said gently. 'If Harry died saving your life, then my only feeling is pride in his actions. I don't hate you for sitting here now instead of him.'

Dodge smiled gratefully. He blinked, and spilled two wet tracks down his cheeks. He wiped them away and there were no more tears. He calmed himself with a deep breath, and began.

'We were a six-man team, one of many being inserted along the edge of the mountain range from Leech Island north to Camp Evans. Harry was Team Leader; I was ATL and forward observer; Randy Moraga was radio operator; Greg Bloch, Dan Schroeder and James Benedict were the riflemen. Benedict was a cherry, his first time out, at least with us.

'We were tasked with monitoring NVA infiltration from the Roung-Roung and A Shau Valleys towards the coastal plain, chiefly Hue and the military bases around Phu Bai. If we encountered a significant force we were to call in a fire mission on their co-ordinates. As it was a free-fire zone, if we came across any smaller units it was left to the discretion of the TL as to whether we engaged; higher-ranking NVA sometimes carried sensitive documents.

'Early afternoon we boarded our slick and lifted off with two Cobra gunships as escort. I remember it was a Tuesday. Extraction was set for oh-nine-hundred Friday, unless we were compromised before that time. When we got near the LZ, our pilot did a couple of feints to confuse any spotters, then we all un-assed onto the ridge. The chopper went off into a wide orbit a couple of klicks away in case we needed immediate extraction, and the team laid dog for fifteen minutes.'

'Dad?' Virginia interrupted. 'Laid dog?'

'Sorry, Namspeak. Finding cover to listen for enemy presence. Thankfully our LZ wasn't hot. I shot an azimuth to check we were in the right place, then we called in a sitrep and moved out to find a good NDP – that's a night defense position. We had to be secure before dark. We descended the ridge towards the valley floor, moving slowly to minimize noise. The jungle below was dense double-canopy, but as we dropped down through it we saw a narrow trail at the base of the ridge. Twenty meters above it Harry signalled for us to stop. He wanted to set up an OP for a while – an observation post. An unused trail grows back pretty quick; this one was trampled bare. No vegetation. A lot of foot traffic had been through, and recently. Harry didn't like staying so close to our drop-off point – neither did I – but he reckoned the trail was worth monitoring. We found cover and stayed there for a couple of hours, but saw no movement on the trail so carefully edged down and crossed it one by one, disappearing into heavy brush on the other side. We'd all seen the tracks in the dirt.

Couldn't have been more than thirty-six hours old. We called in our observations and a little later the relay team radioed back to say our Six – our company commander – wanted us to stay there for the next twenty-four hours. So we set up a perimeter of five Claymores and concealed ourselves ten meters back from the trail. We organized security for the night, a rotating two-man watch every two hours, and waited for dark.

'The night passed without incident. I remember it was pitch black – no moon. You could hardly tell if your eyes were open or shut. Morning came and we took turns to eat chow, then began trail-watching. You've no idea how boring that is, you almost yearn for some contact to break the tedium.

'There was nothing the whole day. With dusk approaching, Harry gave the order to ruck up and move out. We pulled in the Claymores and policed up our patch, leaving it the way we'd found it. We'd stay off the trail but flank it; see if it forked someplace further along. If not, we'd set up another NDP and keep another blind watch through the night. If there was still nothing by the next morning, we'd use our remaining time to check out the rest of the valley. That second night was uneventful. Until shortly before dawn.'

Dodge appeared to catch his breath.

'Dad?'

'With hindsight, we should have kept a closer eye on the cherry. Turned out Benedict had popped too many Dexedrine trying to stay awake, and too many Dex tabs had a habit of making people crazy. Hallucinations, wild behavior ...'

Dodge paused again, long enough this time for John to prompt.

'What happened that morning, Dodge?'

'We had thirty unfriendlies appear on the trail right in front of us. Maybe Benedict was so wired he found himself looking at a bunch of winged demons. I don't know. What I do know is they sure weren't searching for us because they were way too noisy. Had we kept our heads down they would have passed us and we could have brought some arty down on them further along the trail.

'But Benedict lost it. He clacked one of the Claymores and opened up on them. We had to follow suit. Hit hard and fast, then E and E. We blew the other Claymores and let rip with everything we had. Those we didn't kill ran off down the trail, but as the Fifth NVA Regiment was rumored to be in the area, we didn't wait around to see how many came back. We radioed for immediate extraction from our original insertion point where we'd signal with a mirror. It was safer than having to pop smoke and alert the enemy to our position.

'The climb back up the ridge was tough and the cherry kept dragging ass, having completely flaked by then. Harry and I had to physically haul him up the hill. Then we came under attack. The rest of the team gave covering fire and we finally got Benedict onto the ridge. Miraculously, we hadn't taken any hits, but we still had to wait for our extraction ship to show. By that time we'd been told the inbound Huey was only five minutes out, but with no Snakes riding shotgun because it wasn't our official bird. Some pilot returning from delivering a consignment of Coca-Cola to one of the camps had heard our distress call and figured he was closer than anyone else. That's what you call a hero. He didn't need to respond. He was piloting a supply ship; he was totally vulnerable. If he got downed, we'd still have an extraction, we'd just have to wait. But he must have figured we didn't have that luxury so he risked his life coming in for us.

'Anyway, we found some cover, a hollow in the ground, and waited. Well, those five minutes felt like a lifetime, and the enemy arrived before our ride home. The NVA crested the ridge and opened up on our position. Only four of our team returned fire. Moraga had his hands full keeping the cherry from standing up and getting his head blown off. The NVA continued to close in, and I swear it looked like an entire regiment was swarming towards us.

'When we heard the rotor blades we decided to pop smoke; there was nothing left of the mission to compromise. The slick flared above us and dropped down. We were on-loading when I got hit, then Benedict. I knew the kid had bought it but I didn't want to let go of him. Not realizing what had happened, the pilot pulled pitch. The skids lifted off but we were still standing on them, and when he dipped the Huey's nose to gain speed, we both fell off.

'I'd have understood if Harry had gotten the rest of the team to a safe distance, waited for the Cobras to arrive, then come back for us. The alternative was to risk the lives of everyone on board that Huey by getting the pilot to set it back down. But Harry chose a third option. He jumped off – from a good twenty feet in the air. The ship was taking serious hits so he waved it away. He dragged us to a safe spot, then single-handedly engaged the enemy, keeping them back for just long enough.'

Dodge stopped talking. The story wasn't finished, but any one of them in that room could have brought it to its conclusion. Fittingly perhaps, it was Marie who did so.

'The Cobras got there but Harry was already dead.'

Dodge nodded. 'He got hit by possibly the last round the NVA fired before the gunships cut them to pieces.'

Hiding in the men's washroom did not fit with Larry's long-standing image of himself, but it had also finally dawned that the man inside didn't always match the one the world saw strutting like a Storm Trooper. Having kept a watch on the hospital parking lot, Larry had seen DeCecco arrive in a black-and-white, tires screeching, roof-bar strobing. In fact, he had heard the siren long before the car appeared, and DeCecco wasn't alone. Another car was following, a black unmarked Caprice, with a red strobe flashing frantically just inside the windshield. Out of this second car stepped Captain Gilchrist, and, even from several floors up, the little *contretemps* between he and DeCecco was easy to read. The body language was plain. Gilchrist was trying to get his officer to calm down. Which left Larry in no doubt that Doctor Haslam hadn't called the station, Laura had. A post-op, pissed-off Laura.

The washroom was only a temporary sanctuary. Larry had decided it would not be policy to greet DeCecco before he had checked his wife and kid were okay. He didn't relish saying hello at all, but he had to face the music at some point. He still harbored hopes of rectifying matters with as many hurt parties as possible.

He opened the door a crack and spied DeCecco and Gilchrist emerging from the elevator. They weren't talking. DeCecco went to enquire at the desk while Gilchrist took a seat. One of the nurses produced a calming smile and showed the concerned father through a set of swing doors.

Watching this, a profound sadness struck at Larry's heart and made him feel sick with regret that he and Hayley were still childless. That, like everything else, was his fault. He had never really wanted kids, and he guessed he had brainwashed his wife into thinking she should do without them herself. Or maybe he had just silenced the words she always wanted to say to him by constantly using her career against her. *What if Hollywood calls and you're six months gone?* Thus the time had passed until their relationship reached a point where their feelings for each other could no longer support the idea of parenthood. And now Hayley's age made even trying a doubtful and risky proposition, and, anyway, who was he kidding? The leap of imagination required to take him from cowering in a crapper, friendless and hated, to making love with his estranged wife was too mammoth even for his warped mind.

He closed the door, leaned against it, closed his eyes. He felt faint. His stomach was empty and the smell of the room was only adding to his nausea; harsh chemical cleaners that did not quite banish the reason for their use.

Then the door hammered against his back – someone trying to get in. He stepped to the row of basins and pretended to adjust his hair. The door opened and Larry found himself staring at the reflection of his superior officer, who did a faintly amused double-take at the sight of his subordinate.

'Ah, the infamous Larry Roth,' said Captain Gilchrist, and shook his head. 'Shit, you must be even dumber than I thought. If I were you, right now I'd be a million miles away from Joey DeCecco. He's after your blood and he's not listening to me.'

Larry was strangely touched, which said a lot about just how friendless he felt.

'You don't want him to hurt me?' he asked.

'Well, there is that. But mostly I don't want another messy crime scene to clean up – not after the other night.'

Larry opened a faucet, bent down and splashed water on his face. Gilchrist waited until he straightened up.

'Roth, what the fuck were you doing following Laura DeCecco?'

Larry pulled some tissue from a dispenser and dried himself and turned round.

'Ask your star rookie. Or let me guess: you did that already and he's given you jack shit.'

'I know there's something going on between you two.'

'Yeah, we're lovers.'

Gilchrist peered at him. 'You're pretty cocky for a dead man.'

'I beg your pardon?'

'When Laura called Joey and said she was okay but she was in the hospital and you were there ... Christ, you should have seen him, he went ballistic. You know, I don't think you're in his good books. In fact, I think I might be all that's standing between you and a round from his Glock.'

'That's kind. I accept your sacrifice.'

'Oh, I'd duck, believe me. But tell me: how have you gotten Laura DeCecco so scared she'll go into premature labor at the sight of you?'

'Who says it's my fault?'

'DeCecco. He's in no doubt.'

Larry decided to throw Gilchrist a morsel in the hope he might back off a little.

'I was just trying to clear up a misunderstanding, okay? It's not police business. It's personal.'

'Bullshit. I think it's to do with your Armenian slaughterfest. It was DeCecco knocked you out cold, wasn't it.'

'I slipped.'

'Internal Affairs don't believe a word you've told them.'

'Well, it's my story and I'm sticking to it.'

Oddly, Gilchrist smiled. 'You know, I like Joey – a lot more than I ever liked you – but I'm at that stage where I just don't give a crap any more. You can both go your own sweet way. Six months, I'll be gone. Nice fat pension, sell up and move to Wyoming. Mountains, rivers, fresh air. Good riddance, LA. No more sleaze, drugs, smog, homicide or assholes like you. It'll all be a distant memory.'

'You watch, you'll wind up as bear shit. They can smell city folk a mile off.'

Gilchrist laughed. 'You ought to consider somewhere like

Wyoming. Not that I want you as a neighbor, but it might be a good place to hide out. I really think DeCecco means to kill you.'

'He can get in line,' Larry said quietly.

Gilchrist shook his head, went to the urinal and relieved himself, which Larry took as a non-verbal comment on the situation. Gilchrist zipped up, washed his hands and headed for the door.

'Sir?'

Gilchrist stopped and turned, surprised by the respectful address. 'What?'

'When DeCecco's done with his wife, could you bring him in here, please?'

'You want to die in a shithouse?'

'If you could take his sidearm from him, I'd be grateful.'

'You think he needs a gun to kill you?'

Larry lost his temper. 'Will you fucking do it or won't you?'

Gilchrist stared hard at him, then smirked. 'Oh, it'll be my pleasure.'

No one spoke. John felt he was the one person who *couldn't* break the silence. Although he had made their meeting possible, he had the least stake in it all. Speaking prematurely might seem insensitive, belittling. He glanced furtively around the room but caught nobody's eye. The other three appeared temporarily traumatized, their focus down at the carpet, a blank convergence, as though they could see something he couldn't.

'I'm sorry your husband died saving my life,' Dodge said, not looking up. 'I didn't know how guilty I felt until now. I told John that it didn't bother me, that it went with the territory and I'd have done the same for Harry, which is all true. But that's the logic by which I've kept a deeper truth buried for over forty years. I did feel guilty. I have done ever since. When I returned to the States after my first tour, I hoped seeing my baby boy might make me want to stay. But it just made things worse. It brought home to me how I had what Harry never got a chance to see. A life he'd created, his own flesh and blood. So I extended. And even when Ginny here was born eight months into my second tour, I knew I'd still go back again for a third, and a fourth. I had to prove to myself that I was willing to make the same sacrifice Harry had made. Maybe if I died so someone else could live to see their kids grow up, I'd have repaid the debt.'

'It was a noble intention,' Marie said.

'Was it? When it hurt my family? All I achieved was an extra burden of guilt; how I wasn't there for them and didn't care if I never was. Maybe Donnie would be alive today if I'd just ...'

He tailed off, more angry than tearful, which John considered a bad sign, the sluice gate opening on yet more self-recrimination. Virginia went and knelt beside her father and held his hands. John smiled at Marie because she was looking at him, but she did not respond in kind. Her eyes were pinched small with puzzlement, as though she had only just noticed his presence in the room and didn't wholly approve. John tried another unreciprocated smile, then turned his attention to Virginia. He assumed Marie was trying to figure his part in the affair, beyond the obvious; someone else sifting through a collection of whacko theories on his behalf. As he listened to Virginia try and comfort Dodge, John was constantly aware of Marie's unnerving scrutiny.

'Dad, I never felt we lacked love, not once. I can't even really remember that you *were* away. We were both too young.'

'But Donnie joined the Army because of me.'

'Yes, because he loved you, he was proud of you, wanted to be like you. You don't follow in a person's footsteps unless you think they're something special.'

John was studying Dodge and could tell her words weren't helping. Still aware of Marie's probing stare, he snapped his eyes towards her, this time using a hard frown rather than a smile to dislodge her gaze. It didn't work, but Marie's expression had also changed. For a woman with terminal cancer she now looked strangely content, as though she had decided exactly which whacko theory made the most sense.

'Ginny, that's my point,' Dodge countered his daughter. 'Your brother died because of the example I set for him. I could have been out of Vietnam in a year, but I went back. Same with Donnie, except Desert Storm was over so he had to find some other conflict. He needed to carry on fighting, even when it wasn't his war. Just like his dad.'

'But he didn't know what happened to you in Vietnam, how long you were there, or why.'

Dodge shifted his eyes back to the carpet.

'Dad?'

'Maybe it's not the kind of story you tell a daughter. Not if you want her to keep on being Daddy's Girl.'

The newsflash broke their hand contact.

John had seen Virginia's expression before: up in Oregon, when he told her who had authored the letter he had just read out: the shock of an unwilling belief.

'You're saying Donnie knew your history?' she asked.

'Just that I went back,' Dodge said. 'But he didn't know why. And I couldn't tell him.'

'But he knew what you were? That you were Special Forces? A Ranger? He knew where you went? What kind of assignments you carried out? You could tell him all that but you couldn't tell me?'

'I'm sorry,' Dodge whispered. 'I didn't know how you'd feel about me if I told you. I knew Donnie would understand.'

Virginia shook her head at her father. *It seems he did*, she thought. *Far too well.*

The way DeCecco came through the washroom door, Larry knew he had made a big mistake thinking there might be some meaningful dialog between them. He suspected Gilchrist, on the other hand, had not made a mistake, but had wilfully neglected to disarm his subordinate. DeCecco had the heel of his palm on the butt of his pistol, with the hammer restraint unsnapped. His eyes were as cold and hard as the steel in his holster. He shouldered a pay-and-weigh machine in front of the door, then stood in front of it.

'Now, Joey ...'

'Make a move, Larry.'

'What?'

'Your wounds have to look right.'

'What?'

'For the medical examiner. Come for me, arms out like you mean to grab my throat. They can tell a lot by entry and exit wounds, trajectory, how the body falls, all that shit. You have to come for me, Larry. Help me out. Make it look like self-defense.'

'I'm not armed,' Larry said feebly. 'I wasn't when I talked to your wife; she must have told you. Jesus, I brought her here, didn't I? Doesn't that mean something?'

'Yeah, that you're a fucking moron. I warned you to stay away from her. Didn't I say that? Didn't I tell you to stay the fuck away from my wife?'

Larry nodded, and noticed the steel in DeCecco's eyes turn molten.

'Then my conscience is clear,' DeCecco said, and pulled his weapon.

'You can't,' Larry said quickly. 'You want your son growing up with his father behind bars? You can't get away with it. It's murder. I'm defenseless.'

'With a Jennings twenty-two in your hand?'

'Huh?'

'Okay, actually it's in my ankle holster at the moment, but it'll be in your hand five seconds after I put a forty caliber slug in your brain.'

'Joey, I fucked up, but I was trying to put things right, I swear. Come on, your wife's okay, isn't she? If I'd wanted to hurt her she'd be on a slab by now.'

DeCecco looked like he'd tasted something bad and needed to spit it out.

'The mood I'm in, Larry, you really don't want to put an image like that in my mind. And I don't regard my wife being cut open or my son's heart rate going crazy as *okay*. Anyway, it was my wife who got the jump on *you*; you're lucky to be alive, you fucking amateur. But that's easily rectified. Get on your knees.'

Someone in the corridor pushed the door once, twice, then gave up. As Larry lowered himself he nearly called for help, but realized it would be futile. A bullet could cross the washroom quicker than DeCecco could be overpowered, especially with the door so heavily blocked. He wanted to say something profound about the love he had for his own wife, but doubted she would believe it even if DeCecco passed it on.

Instead, he asked, 'Where's Gilchrist?'

'Waiting in his car.'

While he still had a brain to think, Larry pondered on the extent of Gilchrist's complicity. Was the bastard really turning a blind eye to murder? Was the LAPD just going to execute him in cold blood? He could feel the Tactical One-Hander against his ankle bone. It wouldn't help. DeCecco was keeping his distance; he knew the score. A muzzle pressed to the forehead was fine for the movies, all very menacing, but it was utter folly to get that close in real life. It was too easy to be disarmed and shot by your own weapon. Even with hand-to-hand combat skills, which DeCecco no doubt possessed in abundance, he was still not willing to take the risk.

The Glock came up horizontal and Larry stared into the black hole that could issue his death warrant. All he could do now was try not to look so scared, a last gesture of defiance to appease his dwindling machismo.

'You don't have to do this,' he said.

'Oh, but I do. I can't take any more risks with you. I gave you a chance and you blew it. I don't trust you. It's that simple.'

'Please,' Larry whimpered, failing dismally in the butch department. 'I'll go away ... Wyoming, anywhere.'

'*Sssshhhh*. You are going away, Larry. Right now.'

Larry watched DeCecco's trigger finger as it curled tighter. If DeCecco was bluffing, he was playing a dangerous game. Larry could see the pressure being exerted and knew the trigger had little resistance left to offer. At least he wouldn't hear the fatal shot. Before the sound reached his ears, the round would be in his head, his brain a mush, his hearing deactivated.

A millimeter more and the bullet would fly.

It happened. The finger snapped back as the trigger gave. It was the last thing Larry saw.

There was a final piece to the puzzle. It was not directly relevant to Dodge, but if today was a time for exposing skeletons, there was another closet still to empty. Marie seemed to accept this, because instead of showing them the door, she went to the kitchen to make some tea.

It was her turn to talk.

When she called, John carried the tray through for her. He resisted the temptation to ask why she'd been ogling him; it would doubtless not elicit what he considered a sane response.

After pouring the tea, Marie picked up her old letter again and made a troubled face as she mentally read the address on the envelope.

'I hurt Chuck very badly with this, didn't I.' she said.

No one answered what was obviously a rhetorical question.

'I can still remember sitting at the kitchen table writing it. I didn't want to. They weren't even my words. They were dictated to me. I still missed Harry, still loved him, but he'd been dead eight years and I was tired of being alone. I'd brought up Hayley on my own, trying to keep her father's memory alive, telling her everything I could about him. I made him as real as I could, so she'd have more than a few photographs, she'd have some memories, even if they weren't hers. Maybe that sounds stupid. We went to his grave together to lay flowers. We kept in touch with Chuck, another source of memories for Hayley. When we could, we visited, or he came to us. On those occasions it almost felt like we were a family. It wasn't the same, though. I was in the prime of my life, but I was a widow. But it wasn't too late for me to find someone else, and I thought I deserved some happiness. Harry and I had hardly been married more than five minutes when he went to Vietnam. He was my first love, my first boyfriend, but eight years is a long time to be on your own. Provided I could find a good man, someone to love us and take care of us, I believed Harry would have understood. He wouldn't have wanted me to be alone the rest of my days.'

She took a sip of tea, chased it down with a swallow of morphine, then a sip more tea.

'I was working in a local store at the time. The manager liked me. Terence. He'd asked me out several times. One day I surprised him and said yes. He took me to a restaurant in Westwood on our first date. I felt a bit funny knowing Harry was buried only a couple of blocks away, but Terence didn't know and I didn't mention it, not then. The date went well. Terence was the perfect gentleman.'

It sounded like the sort of reminiscence that should make a person smile, but her face was stony.

'We started seeing each other on a regular basis. If I went out in the evening, my neighbor looked after Hayley. Pretty soon I thought it would be okay for her to meet the new man in my life. He came for dinner and we all got along fine. I was reluctant to let him stay over in case it affected Hayley. I didn't want her getting used to a father figure if it might not work out. But the weeks passed and it all seemed very cosy. He started staying nights, and after a couple of months we decided he should move in here as his apartment was only rented. A month later we got married. Finally, we were a family. A happy family.'

The words were still at odds with her expression. John guessed perhaps Terence had begun beating her, or cheating on her.

'Very quickly after we were married, Hayley started having trouble at school. Her behavior went downhill, her work suffered. At home she became withdrawn, moody, prone to tears. She couldn't stand any physical contact. I thought perhaps she was being bullied, but she didn't have any bruises that I could see. It carried on for weeks. I wondered whether it might not be a delayed reaction to having Terence around. She'd been so used to it just being the two of us, I thought she might be starting to resent having to share me with someone. I'm ashamed to say I wasn't very understanding. One night when Terence was working at the store, we had a big argument. She became hysterical. I said it was too late her reacting this way now we were married. If she'd wanted to object she should have done so sooner. I called her selfish and told her to get used to it – Terence was a good man, a good husband to me, and could be a good father to her if she'd only let him get close. Well, that did it. She screamed at me. She said, "He *does* get close".

Marie took a drink, and John noticed her hand was shaking. The years had barely dulled the emotional hurt.

'Maybe if I hadn't phrased it exactly so, she might not have been able to say it. I asked her to explain herself and she went very quiet. To be honest, I already knew what she meant. That's not to say I had reason to suspect it was the truth. In fact, I thought she was lying. I didn't know where she'd got the idea from – talk at school perhaps – but I didn't believe it. I thought she was just being nasty, trying anything to make me turn against him. I didn't help matters; I didn't try to coax it out of her, I yelled at her. But it didn't work, she'd clammed up. So I spoke more softly and tried again. And I kept trying until eventually she came out with the inevitable. In a whisper, she said that Terence was touching her, coming into her room whenever I wasn't there, or sometimes in the middle of the night. I didn't attempt to qualify her accusation, ask her exactly what she meant by … *touching*. A wall had come up. I didn't want to hear another word. Suddenly, she wasn't my daughter any more; the daughter I knew would never speak such filthy lies. I told her I had the right to a life of my own and she wasn't going to wreck that now because she was selfish and wanted me all to herself. Terence was a good man and he was staying and that was the end of it.'

Marie paused, practically out of breath.

'But it wasn't the end of it. Of course it wasn't.'

'Did you confront Terence?' Dodge asked.

'Not when Hayley first said it, no. In the weeks following, her attitude altered, but it didn't improve. Instead of open anger, she had a distant air about her, like she'd gone inside herself to find a place she could hide, and all I was seeing was a shell. It was the sort of look I'd expected Harry would return with from Vietnam. Whenever I asked Terence what he thought might be wrong with her, he always managed to put my mind at ease. He'd say I shouldn't worry, it was probably just a phase, a reaction to his being in the house. It sounded plausible because I was telling myself the same thing. And how could I believe Hayley was telling the truth? How? My God, that would mean I'd married a paedophile.'

'Had you?' John asked straight, earning a frown from Virginia.

Marie looked at him. 'Yes.'

'How did you find out?'

'I had a dream.'

John very nearly groaned.

'I dreamed I was with Hayley on Venice Beach. She was walking in the surf, but with her head down, not having any fun like she used to. No one else was on the sand. Suddenly I knew someone was behind me. I turned and there was Harry in his jungle uniform. I burst into tears and hugged him like I've never hugged anyone; I was so happy. Then I remembered I'd remarried, and I felt I'd betrayed Harry in not waiting longer for him to come back. My heart broke all over again. But Harry calmed me down and kissed my forehead and told me it was okay, he understood. He pointed to Hayley, and I told him she was the daughter he'd never seen. He said he knew, he knew everything. So I asked him how I could make her smile again, and he said one simple thing: "Believe her."

'When I woke up I didn't mention the dream, but I did tell Terence what Hayley had said weeks before. It didn't faze him at all. As usual, he applied some amateur psychology and dismissed it; said Hayley naturally resented him and was trying to get rid of him. She'd come round sooner or later. To my eternal shame, I took the coward's way out and tried to forget what Harry had said.'

John felt the need to speak. 'But, Marie ... it was just a dream. Surely that wasn't the first time you'd dreamt about Harry.'

'No, I dreamed about Harry a lot. I still do. But it was so vivid. It had a quality I'd never known before. Or since, come to that. I can't explain it.'

John was grateful for small mercies, but Virginia had something she wanted to show Marie. From the case she took the calendar of *Beautiful Oregon - 1977*, flipped it to April and handed it over. Marie studied the circled date and the writing beside it: *DR* scribbled out, and, underneath, the word *VISION*.

'We reckoned that meant Chuck had a dream,' Virginia said, 'then decided it was more like a vision, and that's what prompted his move to the mountain.'

Marie either wasn't listening or had nothing to offer. She put the calendar down. Dodge returned them to the original point.

'Marie ... the letter. How did Terence get you to write it?'

'He convinced me I should cut all ties with the past. He reasoned that as long as Hayley kept seeing her grandpa, hearing stories about her real father, she would never accept his place in her life.'

'Did they ever meet?' Dodge asked. 'Chuck and Terence?'

'No. I think Terence feared if they did, Chuck might see through him. Either that or, face to face, Hayley might break down and tell her grandpa what she'd told me, only Chuck wouldn't be so disbelieving.'

'So how did it come to a head?' John asked. 'It obviously did.'

'Yes, but it took another month, and when I tried to re-establish contact with Chuck he was long gone. If you hadn't shown up today, I'd have gone to my grave not knowing what happened to him.'

John wasn't certain that meant she was pleased.

'Sounds like I'm the one who's most responsible for his death,' she added.

'Don't you dare!' Dodge said vehemently. 'Marie, you need to forgive yourself, not take on even more guilt. If the man believed he'd had a vision, I don't think anyone could have kept him from going up that mountain.'

Marie merely smiled her thanks for his effort.

'Do you want to hear what happened with Hayley?' she said. 'How I found out? I'd like to tell you. I've never felt able to speak about it before.'

Dodge nodded; he knew about the healing power of first confessions.

'My bladder woke me up one night around three a.m. Terence wasn't in bed and I felt an instant sickness in my stomach. I knew something was wrong. I crept out of the bedroom and along to Hayley's, and … there he was. When he saw me, he had the shock of his life. I should have been shocked, too, but at that moment I realized I'd always known Hayley wasn't lying, I'd just refused to accept it. I'd been so desperate to have a man in my life that I'd blocked out the damage he was causing to Hayley's.'

'What did you do?' Virginia asked.

'I beat the shit out of him, went completely berserk. I could have killed him, I wanted to kill him. He didn't fight back, he just started crying like a child. By that stage, Hayley was beyond tears. She just watched … eyes empty, soulless. There was no relief in her expression, but … I guess I hadn't really saved her from anything.' Marie smiled bravely at her guests. 'It destroyed our relationship. We only made up a few days ago. Can you believe that? At last we can talk and I'm about to die – we don't have any time.'

Delicately, Virginia asked, 'Is that what prompted you to make up?'

Marie shook her head. 'She needed me. She's been having a rough time lately and she wanted her mom.'

'Rough how?' Dodge asked.

Marie responded with a bitter smile.

'Put it this way, Dodge: we Olsen women don't have much luck with husbands.'

The last thing Larry saw before he squeezed his eyes shut was DeCecco's finger snap back inside the trigger guard. There should have been nothing else, not sight, sound, smell, touch or taste.

There was a click. It was a mistake Larry would not have expected from a man so highly trained. There was no round in the chamber. DeCecco had neglected to work the slide and load the first one up from the magazine. It took a split second for Larry to think this, and he did not expect he would have more than a further two seconds before the oversight was corrected.

'Larry.'

Hearing a human voice, even DeCecco's, made him want to cry. He opened his eyes and the tears were already formed. Released, they fell down his cheeks.

DeCecco did now work a bullet into the chamber, but then lowered his weapon.

'Remember what this felt like, Larry: the fear, the expectation of death. That's what my wife's been feeling; what you made her feel. So listen good. If anything like this ever happens again, you're dead. And in case you're thinking of killing me, you should know that I told my old team about you and the deal is this: anything happens to me or mine, they'll come after you and they won't make it quick. You'll suffer first. But you leave us alone, they'll leave you alone. Now, is that message plain enough for you? Does that pea-brain of yours understand the seriousness of your situation?'

Larry nodded. DeCecco backed to the pay-and-weigh and barged it aside.

'No more warnings, Larry. That's it.'

Chapter 27

It was an afternoon without visitors, which Hayley spent watching TV and pushing her tongue through the gap in her front teeth. Amanda had been in that morning, and Marie had been scheduled to drop by later. The phone call to say she wasn't coming should have been a disappointment, but for the other information it had conveyed. Her mom had just said goodbye to some visitors of her own, including an old Army buddy of her father's with a few interesting tales to tell. She would not elucidate, except to say it had been an emotional meeting that had left her drained, hence the canceled trip to her daughter's bedside. Hayley had pestered for details but Marie could not be swayed. After she was discharged tomorrow, she would hear all about it, first-hand from the man himself.

Considering the course of recent history, not to mention the history of her younger years, Hayley felt in amazingly good spirits. She didn't want to test this with a look in the mirror, but there was a distinct sense of a corner turned. She was facing a brand new horizon, and although the sun was perhaps a long way off cresting, she knew it was there, the promise of warmth and comfort, light and life. Out of all the bad she could suddenly see the good, and that was no abstract theory she had read in a book on positive thinking; it was truly how she felt. Although she was in a poor state physically, her body would heal or be healed by outside forces; although her mom was dying and their time together was short, any time was better than none at all after so long apart; although her marriage was over, she felt more like a widow than an estranged wife – the man she had married had effectively died the same day as Frank Dista; although she had never known her father, she was finally to hear the story of his last days – a lifelong wish come true; and although *Malibu Mischief* had gone, at least it had proved something: there were people out there who thought she was worthy of the big bucks. She was a star-in-waiting. Her day would come.

If he had not exactly prayed following DeCecco's departure from the washroom, Larry had certainly stayed on his knees for several minutes, fully aware of the significance of his position. Mortality had never been so clearly defined. Larry Roth was going to die. His day would come. It could happen next week or in another fifty years, but he had never been more dazzlingly aware of the finite nature of his tenure on this earth. He had checked in forty-two years ago with no say in the matter, and he would check out just the same way. The killing of others had not brought it home to him; quite the opposite. For him, offing six drug dealers was life-enhancing. He had derived a buzz from his power to order a bulk check-out. Even the profound effect of Frank's death had failed to tap this scam in him. After Frank, he had become concerned with achievement and career goals; building an impressive résumé with which to increase the column inches of his own distant obituary.

But DeCecco pulling that trigger, Larry believing one hundred percent that his time was up ... that made a person think. Really stop and think. If his death could be that easy, he needed a purpose to what remained of his life, a purpose beyond rank, respect, or even an Armenian pay-day. And the more he thought about it, the more he realized he knew exactly where to look for it.

Hayley. Once upon a time, she had loved him. An unconditional love, unrelated to the size of his pay packet or the color of the shield he wore or the pension he was building for later life. In many ways, it had endured in spite of these, cutting through his trivial fixations to find the heart of the man, and provided there was love in that heart for her, she was happy. Year after year she had endured the setbacks of her career with remarkable fortitude, and he had never understood how. Now it made sense. Success had not been the most important thing in her life, merely the icing on the cake. The tragedy was, his recent behavior had probably *made* it the most important thing in her life.

He understood DeCecco a lot better now as well. For all his mockery of the white-picket-fence scenario, from Larry's present enlightened viewpoint it looked just about perfect.

While Virginia went back to her Santa Monica apartment to reconstitute her costume design portfolio, John stayed with Dodge up at Beverly Glen.

Since leaving Venice Beach, Dodge had become disturbingly quiet, and the childhood abuse of Harry's daughter was not the cause of it. In the end, Hayley had overcome. Having set her heart on an acting career, she had studied at the UCLA and then married a police officer. Countless bit parts had finally culminated in a plum role in *Malibu Mischief*. All this had made Dodge beam proudly like Hayley was his own flesh and blood, although John guessed his feelings may have amounted to something even stronger than that.

Then the bombshell: where Hayley was at that very moment, and why. Dodge had looked ill, worse even than at Donnie's funeral. Studying a newspaper report of the screwed drug bust, he had stared so hard at Larry's picture that John had thought the page would ignite. Leaving them alone, Virginia had entrusted John with quite a job: he had to get her father talking.

'Will you have a beer with me?' he asked as a start.

Dodge nodded, so John went to the kitchen and brought two cold ones back to the living room.

'How do you feel about tomorrow?' John asked, settling.

'I don't know how I'll react seeing her all beat up like that.'

'Bet you'd like to kill her husband, eh?'

'Wouldn't you? This is the girl whose photo you've carried since you were a kid. I know you saw *my* face when Marie told us what had happened, but I was looking at you, too, remember? If he'd walked through the door that second, you'd have ripped his throat out.'

John shook his head.

'Sure you would,' Dodge insisted.

'No, I'd have taken Harry's pistol and put one through his eye.'

Dodge gave a big grin. 'I'll drink to that.' And they both did.

'About the pistol ...' John said, '... it's a SEAL weapon. How did Harry get hold of it?'

'He picked it up the year before I got in-country. He told me the story. He was down at the Recondo School at Nha Trang, his three weeks nearly up. A couple of SEALs had been getting some R 'n' R at nearby Cam Ranh Bay and were heading back to their camp on the Bassac at Long Phu. Five minutes in, their helo has engine trouble and goes down in Charlie's back yard. Harry volunteered to join one of the LuRP teams heading for the crash site. Long story short, the SEALs were extracted just as the VC closed in on their position. Harry struck up a rapport with one of the SEALs who gave him the Hush Puppy as a thank you. It became a treasured possession, and useful on many occasions.'

'Who brought it back to the States?'

'I did. I was gonna keep it for myself – and one or two other bits and pieces. After a while, I didn't want them, couldn't even look at them. I thought Harry's father might appreciate them. I knew the military would have taken care of Marie with the medals, the dog-tags, things like that.'

'So how did Chuck end up with *all* of it?'

'I expect that bastard Terence found it hidden away and mailed it to him without Marie's knowledge. But … could have been worse, he could have put it all in the trash.' Dodge drank, swore softly and shook his head. 'Harry's death changed everything. I sometimes think it's the ones who died in Vietnam who got off easy. Their suffering ended with their last breath. What about the living? Marie lost a husband, Hayley a father. Then Hayley got a stepfather who stole what was left of her childhood, which led to mother and daughter not speaking for years. All because one man died. But you know what's really sick? I came back alive and *still* managed to screw up the people I love. You heard Ginny at the hospital.'

'Hey, Virginia's doing fine. And she loves you. If you'd really caused her any damage, she wouldn't have looked after you this long. She wouldn't have been able to.'

Miserably, Dodge said, 'Okay, but what about Donnie?'

'Dodge, people join the military for different reasons. I joined the Legion to spite my parents. Your son joined the Army to emulate you. If you can't be proud of him, at least accept that he was proud of you. Whatever Donnie went on to do after Desert Storm was not your fault.'

'And my wife?'

'I can't answer that one. But she didn't leave you, did she?'

'I'll never know why not.'

'Because she loved you?'

'I wrecked her life,' Dodge said, and drained his beer.

'Did she love you?'

'Yes.'

'Then how could you have wrecked her life?' John asked. 'If you love a person, you don't regret meeting them no matter what happens afterwards. You may wish the path had been smoother, but if you can look back and wish you'd never met, that's not love. You probably made her feel more alive than anyone.'

'And how d'you figure that?' Dodge said gruffly.

'Because she had to struggle. She knew she had something worth fighting for. Some people never know that passion their whole lives. They're the ones I feel sorry for.'

Suddenly Dodge was smiling, as though at some private memory. He snapped out of it, gave John a long, scrutinising look, and spoke.

'It is not the critic who counts, not the one who points out how the strong man stumbled or how the doer of deeds might have done them better. The credit belongs to the man who is actually in the arena, whose face is marred with sweat and dust and blood; who strives valiantly; who errs and comes short again and again; who knows the great enthusiasms, the great devotions, and spends himself in a worthy cause; who, if he wins, knows the triumph of high achievement; and who, if he fails, at least fails while daring greatly, so that his place shall never be with those cold and timid souls who know neither victory nor defeat.'

'I like that,' John said. 'Where's it from?'

'It's called *The Man in the Arena*. From a speech by Theodore

Roosevelt. I knew it from school, but it was Harry made me memorize it. He told me one day it would make sense, but the only thing puzzling me was why he thought I didn't understand it already; seemed pretty straightforward to me. But what you just said, about people who never experience passion ... that gives it a whole new slant. It's not just about soldiers fighting wars. It's about passion in whatever you do. What makes a life worth living, that's also what makes it okay to die.'

John merely smiled. Dodge was finally battling his demons with the one force they could not resist: reason. He was using reason to justify his own passion for war, and the passing of a wife who had loved him despite the mental wounds that passion had inflicted upon him.

'John, do you think that's what Harry meant? I do. Shit, all this time I've been my own worst critic, looking back on the person I was – the man in the arena – pointing out how I'd stumbled in life, never giving myself any credit, always thinking I wasn't worthy of love. But my wife gave me credit, didn't she? Every day she loved me. We were two of a kind. I faced death so many times in Vietnam and I never ran. And when she knew the tumor had gotten hold of her, she wasn't afraid either, because she'd known the great enthusiasms, the great devotions.'

Dodge grinned to himself.

'*Yeah*,' he said, and the tears began rolling freely down his face.

Joey was already seated in his black-and-white when Larry emerged from the hospital into the sunlight, where he stopped briefly, as though dazed, as though seeing the sun for the first time. Or as though he believed five minutes ago he would never see it again.

Larry gathered himself and headed over to a white Beetle, got in and drove off. Joey eased the Charger out of the lot and slipped in behind to follow, not holding back in the traffic to hide his presence. Rather, he stuck close to Larry's rear bumper, and noticed his eyes return again and again to the rear-view mirror until he indicated and pulled into the curb, and Joey followed suit.

Larry got out of the Beetle and walked back to the Charger, a reversal of the normal traffic-stop procedure. Joey thought he looked frustrated more than angry; certainly in no mood for an argument.

'What are you doing, Joey?' Larry asked.

'Watching you.'

'Why? You don't believe your message hit home? I got the message, Joey, loud and clear. I believe you. I fuck with you or yours, I'm dead.'

'Correct. Where are you headed now?'

'*Home*,' Larry said, his tone almost pleading to be left alone. 'Where I'm going to open a bottle of Jack Daniels and drink myself unconscious. I've had a shitty day. You may have noticed.'

'No more so than my wife.'

'Accepted. But what do you want me to do, Joey? I can't turn the clock back.'

Joey shrugged. 'I don't want you to do anything. You carry on. I didn't indicate for you to pull over. I have lights and a siren for that.'

Larry closed his eyes, shook his head, let out a deep sigh. 'I take it,' he said, 'that you're coming all the way to my apartment.'

'Yep.'

'For how long?'

'Can't say.'

'Well, I can show you a parking spot where you can get a good view of my front door and my fire escape, both at the same time. That way you'll know once I'm inside, I can't leave without you seeing. Thing is, Joey, you're gonna have to return the cruiser at some point and go back to the hospital to see your family.'

'Is that a threat?'

Larry snorted. 'No, Joey. It's a simple fact. You can't watch me all the time, so why watch me at all? You've got to trust me. I'm done ruining people's lives. So you get on with yours and I'll get on with mine. And, by the way, thank you for allowing me to do so.'

Joey couldn't tell whether Larry was employing any sarcasm, but offered a little of his own, just in case.

'Move along,' he told him, 'you're in a no-stopping zone.'

Another impotent shake of his head and Larry returned to the Beetle. Joey watched him climb in and drive away, and moved off himself, accelerating up to the Beetle's bumper again.

When they pulled up outside Larry's apartment block, Joey was pointed to the appropriate spot on the street, as promised, where he parked the Charger and cut the engine. Larry made an arms-out, palms-up gesture of bewilderment at Joey's paranoid behavior, then entered the communal courtyard that led to the steps up to his home.

Joey waited two hours before making a move. The sun had gone down. He went up to Larry's apartment and peered in through the walkway window. Larry was out cold on the sofa, his .45 and an empty bottle of JD beside him. Joey stared at the comatose form for several minutes, profoundly troubled by what he saw. He didn't like the combination of excess alcohol and firearms, especially not given Larry's state of mind. He didn't know a lot about these things – psychoanalysing the enemy had not been a part of his military remit – but he had always worked on the assumption that if an enemy looked dangerous, they probably were, and required shooting dead to eradicate all doubt. The reason for their mind-set was irrelevant.

So, was Larry to be treated any differently? They might have worn the same uniform but Larry was certainly an enemy, and a demonstrably dangerous one. Could he really trust that Larry had suddenly gotten all sane? One thing Joey did know: if this had been a military environment, and the decision had been his, Larry's file could have been marked in only one way: *Terminate with Extreme Prejudice.* The fact that he was still breathing was down to simple expedience; Joey could not have got away with murder in a hospital washroom.

In the next sixty seconds, however, he could be in and out, having put a round from Larry's own gun into his head, silently through a pillow. It was an attractive proposition. Scrub out the threat for good.

But he was too exposed. The very thing that allowed him to blend into the darkness also made him vulnerable to identification: his uniform. For all he knew, he had been spotted already; some elderly neighbor, not alerted by any sound, simply peeking through the curtains out of a lack of anything else to do.

Joey returned to the street and drove back to Cedars-Sinai.

Chapter 28

It was time to leave and the replacement Audi had not arrived. As Virginia's connection to Hayley was the most tenuous, she stayed home to take delivery while John and Dodge went off together.

Inside the Jeep the mood was somber, talk absent. Despite yesterday's healing tears, John suspected his silent companion was still hoarding too much, but every time he thought to speak, the words he had planned seemed suddenly redundant. Until they met Hayley it would all be so much conjecture.

As they pulled off Gayley Avenue and drove up to the entrance to the UCLA Medical Center, Marie was getting out of a yellow cab. Dodge had offered to pick her up but she had turned him down, Venice Beach being so far out of their way. Insisting had not worked, Marie stating that the next free ride she accepted would be in a hearse. While she was still breathing, she would get around on her own, thank you very much.

Dodge parked and they both went over. There was an awkward moment before Dodge decided a hug was probably in order. Marie reciprocated, then smiled at John and hugged him as well.

'I think you should stay here,' she told them inside the foyer. 'I'll go up and fetch her down.'

They both nodded and found a couple of seats. It was a minute before either of them spoke.

'I feel sick,' Dodge said quietly, staring at the floor.

The butterflies weren't exactly calm inside John. He couldn't believe he was about to meet the girl in the photograph. The girl in the Disney dress – now a woman. He wondered if he'd recognize her, then realized of course he would. She would be the one with the cut face, swollen lips, missing teeth and broken arm.

When sufficient time had elapsed, they both turned their attention to the elevators. Each set of opening doors pulled their eyes like a magnet. John felt madly eager, like a child playing *Snap!*

Eventually, Marie emerged arm in arm with the saddest sight John had ever seen. He hated to think what turmoil Dodge was in at that moment. They simultaneously rose to their feet. Marie indicated the two men to her daughter, whose responsive smile instantly brightened John's mood.

'Hayley, sweetheart, this is Dodge.'

'Hello, Dodge.'

'Hello, Hayley. You don't know what it means to me to finally meet Harry's little girl.'

Hayley's smile widened to reveal the gaps. Marie made the other introduction.

'And this is John. He's the reason we're all together today.'

'I don't understand,' Hayley said.

'I knew your grandfather.'

'Grandpa Chuck? How?'

'I met him when I was a kid,' John said. 'I was on holiday.'

'And do you know where he is now? We haven't seen him for years.'

John glanced at Marie but reckoned he was the best person to tell her; he knew the details better than anyone.

'I'm sorry,' he said. 'Chuck died a long time ago. Shortly after I met him.'

Immediately after, more like, but he could keep that for later.

Hayley bowed her head in a brief moment of private mourning, before looking up.

'So how is this little gathering down to you, John?'

'That's something we need to sit down for,' he said. 'There's a lot you have to hear.'

Marie stroked her daughter's hair. 'He's right, sweetheart, all in good time.'

'Okay,' Hayley said, then noticed something amiss. 'Where's Amanda? I thought I was staying at her place.'

'We thought it best you stay with Dodge,' Marie said. 'I called Amanda to let her know. It's safer this way. Larry's a cop, remember? He knows how to find people. He could trace you to Amanda's by a process of elimination. But you have no obvious connection to Dodge here. There's no way Larry could find you.'

'And don't I have a say in this?' Hayley asked.

'Yes,' Dodge answered, smiling. 'But if you don't come with me, I can't tell you about your father, and John can't tell you about your grandfather.'

Hayley nodded. 'Then I guess I'd like to stay with you, Dodge. Mom, you're coming with us?'

'No, dear. We'll see each other tomorrow, and I'll call tonight – to hear your thoughts on what these gentlemen have told you.'

'I don't suppose you'd accept a lift,' Dodge said to Marie.

'Thank you, no. I think I'll ask the cab driver to drop me at the beach. I fancy some ice cream. Maybe get my feet wet.'

Looking at her, John thought he could see the mythical last bloom of the terminally ill. Her skin had lost the sick hue it had yesterday. As she kissed them all goodbye, he got the strangest feeling that none of them would see her alive again.

Joey had been back at the target address since 8.30 a.m. after staying the night with his wife and new-born at Cedars-Sinai. None of them had slept much. Laura was suffering post-operative pain and the constant feeding demands of Junior DeCecco, both of which would have kept Joey awake even in the best of circumstances.

His mind was in turmoil, considering the pros and cons of murdering Larry Roth. An irritating voice in his head that sounded remarkably like Laura's had kept telling him he wasn't above the law any more than Roth, but didn't the plain unpredictability of the man give him *carte blanche* to launch a lethal pre-emptive strike? His moral dilemma had been like a headache that wouldn't go away.

What swung it, steeling him to act, was holding his son in his arms that morning while watching his wife snooze, and knowing he would be more able to square his conscience with Roth's death in years to come than cope with the possible loss of his family because he'd been too damn precious about his own morality.

The decision made, Joey had begun preparations. Using one of his shadier ex-military contacts, he had secured two items of kit: an innocuous-looking camper van with false plates and a muddy history of ownership, and an unregistered and silenced 7.62 caliber Remington 700 sniper rifle.

And when the moment was right, he fully intended sliding the door open a crack on the former, and pulling the trigger on the latter.

Hayley was up to speed on John's involvement even before they reached Angelo Drive. Uncertain where to start, he had let the photograph speak for him. She could vaguely remember the picture being taken by her mom, but didn't know it had been sent to her grandpa. Everything flowed from there. John's possession of it begged too many questions and she would have been less than human not to indulge them. She heard practically his entire life story, the minutiae of which were skipped only in deference to his desire to give an overview that would make her quickly rapt. He feared if their connection was not sincerely established by the time Dodge cut the ignition, the impetus would be lost. Judging by Hayley's joy at meeting the older man, John gathered she had been as keen to meet Dodge as John was to meet her. The prospect of his relegation to nothing more than a catalyst made him feel desperate. He craved her attention almost like a jealous lover.

When Dodge pulled off the road and parked up beside a gleaming red Audi, John knew he no longer had to worry. He could now happily let her sit for the next few hours listening to war stories of her father. She was hooked. He felt he could have flown back to England and she would have followed. The final party had been drawn into a thirty-five-year-old mystery.

Virginia was waiting at the kitchen window. John saw her and smiled, and realized that for the last half hour or so he hadn't thought of his new girlfriend once. He jumped out, went around and helped Hayley onto the driveway. Virginia opened the front door of the house.

'I know you may feel scared and alone,' Dodge said gently to his guest. 'But you got us now, and we won't be strangers for long. Now let's get inside. Hayley, this is my daughter Virginia.'

Virginia spoke to her father first. 'Dad, thanks for the car, it's beautiful.'

'No problem.'

Then the women politely shook hands on the doorstep.

'I feel I know you already,' Hayley said.

'How's that?' Virginia asked.

'Your trip to Oregon. John told me about it.'

Hayley entered the house and Dodge closed the door behind them.

'Really?' Virginia smiled at John. 'You don't waste time, do you?'

'Sorry,' he said, feeling he had stolen thunder that should have been shared. 'It sort of spewed out; it's been a long time building.'

'Hayley, can I fix you something to eat?' Dodge said.

'That's okay.'

'Don't be polite, girl. Can I fix you something to eat?'

She conceded with a gappy smile. 'I am a little hungry, but ... soup's about all I can manage.'

'Soup it is. Ginny, show Hayley through to the living room, see what she wants to drink.'

'Dodge ...'

He halted at the kitchen threshold and turned.

'Thank you,' Hayley said. 'All of you.'

'Hey, you're Harry's girl, you're as good as family. And don't worry, you're safe now. No one's gonna hurt you again. I promised your mother, and I'm promising you. You got a Legionnaire and a Ranger to take care of you. Ain't no one getting past us.'

The hangover was barely troubling, which meant Larry had probably slept late. He checked the time. Nearly one p.m. He would be glad when he could make up with Hayley and no longer need the booze at night. Good sex always made him sleep well.

He swigged some orange juice from the refrigerator and sat down at the kitchen table. He truly felt like shit. There wasn't a single aspect of his life he could be proud of. Not only was he a wife-beater, he was a disgraced cop who'd been on the take for years, and he was under investigation by Internal Affairs because they clearly suspected what he knew: that he was also a vigilante cop and a failed coke thief. The vagrant implicating an unidentified person had swung the spotlight to DeCecco, and his stonewalling had knocked it glaring double-strength back at Larry. There were a lot of unanswered questions. If the mystery man *was* DeCecco, why had he let Mallory ride along in his place only to show up later in civvies? And what had Larry done that required the cop code of brotherhood to protect him? All these questions had been fired at him, and would be again, because something stank and it didn't take a seasoned suit from IA to know it.

Larry rasped a hand round his stubbled chin and cursed as he remembered his keyless Corvette parked on the street. Damn, if Hayley was going to tell him to get lost, he wouldn't even be able to drive away in style.

He padded into the bedroom and got dressed, grabbed the Tactical One-Hander off the bedside cabinet and tucked it down his sock, then went into the living room for the Tanfoglio .45, which he vaguely remembered cuddling the night before along with his bottle of Jack Daniels. He slipped the weapon under the concealing hang of his shirt at the back and into his jeans. Nothing more than habit – no malice intended towards anyone.

The cold touch of the steel against his skin felt good, except it made him think of all the times Hayley had nagged him to take the damn thing off around the apartment. Women didn't understand. Folk weren't safe even in their own locked home, and unless a weapon was immediately to hand there was no point owning one. Better to have and not need than need and not have.

A guilty stab in his heart made him realize he was wrong. Hayley was one woman who certainly did understand that the home was not the safest environment. He had proved that to her himself.

Larry drank a cup of strong coffee, then decided he'd go to the store and buy some flowers for the apartment – women seemed to appreciate crap like that. If Hayley wasn't home by the time he got back, he would call the local emergency rooms. Failing that, Marie would know where her daughter was, and this time he wouldn't accept the old broad's Alzheimer's act.

Hayley now knew how her father had died. Dodge had added extra details to this second telling as though they could hurt him less and less. She had then requested a more detailed version of John's story from start to finish, including Virginia's viewpoint from the moment of her initial involvement. In the coming days, John reckoned Hayley would become *au fait* with a great deal more. Having lifted the restricted access off his memory files on Vietnam, Dodge would no doubt recollect anecdotes about Harry he thought he'd long forgotten. John hoped he would be there to hear them all, but realized his overt interest in Hayley was already causing considerable pique in his girlfriend.

When Virginia excused herself to go to the bathroom, John followed and grabbed her waist outside the door.

'Give me a kiss,' he whispered.

She obliged with a platonic peck.

'That's it?' he said.

She offered the smile of one who had accepted defeat. 'She's a sweet girl.'

'I don't fancy her.'

'I can't compete. I've had a few days with you; she's been in your heart for years.'

'Virginia, there's no competition. Of course I have feelings for her, but they could be nothing more than pity for the physical state she's in and everything she's been through.'

'I think it's more than that.'

'Maybe, but I do know my feelings for her aren't romantic.'

'Not yet. But feelings like that can creep up on you.'

'Well, they didn't creep up on me with you, they hit me like an express train and I'm still recovering. I'm the one who's more likely to get hurt in this relationship. I've been more upfront than you. I've told you exactly how I feel. I've fallen madly in love with you. I'm so worried I'm going to scare you off with talk like that but I can't stop myself; I need you to know.'

She took his hands but still looked like she was ready to bow out gracefully.

'John, you have a connection with her. A blind man could see that. And it'll only get stronger.'

'Virginia, this is ridiculous. If we're not careful, we're going to lose each other because we're scared of the same thing: losing each other. How stupid would that be?'

Her façade crumbled and she gave in to her emotions. She hugged him, and he could feel her tears spring against his cheek.

'I love you, too' she said softly. 'Head over heels. It's crazy.'

'Hallelujah,' he said, and kissed her.

'You would let me know, wouldn't you?'

'I won't need to,' John assured her. 'What I feel for Hayley is ... I don't know ... what a brother might feel for a long-lost sister.'

Their embrace was interrupted by Dodge calling for John as he came out of the living room. Virginia disappeared into the bathroom to hide her tear-tracked face, and John turned to see Dodge wearing an intense grin, which for some reason gave him a trepidation he hadn't known since active service with the Legion.

'Lock and load, sergeant; we got a warning order for a mission this afternoon.'

The cross-hairs awaited the arrival of Larry's head. The side door was open two inches, and Joey was sitting back inside the van where he couldn't be seen, the supressed barrel of the Remington resting steady on a seat. Carrying out the hit at the apartment had not been ideal. There weren't enough comings-and-goings on the street to conceal his getaway. False plates wouldn't help if he found his fellow cops in hot pursuit before he could dump the vehicle and dispose of the weapon.

After half a mile, Larry had stopped at a supermarket, parking on the fringe of the lot, and Joey had quickly spotted his perch, heading to the roof parking of a store on the adjacent street. By the time he had pulled into a spot overlooking the supermarket, his target had disappeared inside, and he had taken the opportunity to set himself up. He would let Larry get back in the Beetle, then clip him through the open window as he sat behind the wheel. Someone would eventually glance over and notice the Beetle's gaudily redecorated interior, but by that time Joey would be long gone.

He lifted his eye from the scope and frowned hard. A couple of bottles of Jack Daniels and a six-pack – that was the kind of shopping Joey had expected to see Larry emerge with. But *flowers*?

Yet again, his resolve began to flake. Who were they destined for? He needed to know. If they were *en route* to Cedars-Sinai to be left at the front desk for Laura, his pulling that trigger in the next five seconds would put him on a par with Larry the night he wiped out the Armenians – choosing the bloodiest option not because he had exhausted all peaceful solutions, but because it suited him.

But what if it was a bluff; the flowers a decoy, a ploy to get him back into maternity? Larry didn't look exactly jolly. In fact he looked positively pissed off, not at all like he was about to right wrongs.

Joey sighted again, laying the cross-hairs over Larry's head, scoping him across the lot. He reached his Beetle and got in, oblivious to the lethal attention thirty meters away. Joey's finger curled tighter on the trigger, but it would not pull through. Shit. Where was that killer instinct he had thought was second nature? Larry started the engine, reversed from his spot and nosed onto the street.

Too late to act, Joey laid his weapon down. It seemed, in the battle for his soul, Laura and the babe had brought his better nature to the fore, relegating second nature to second place. He had been wrong to suppose he could square his conscience with cold-blooded murder; not when there was another way out. If he wasn't prepared to risk criminal proceedings by telling Gilchrist what he knew, he reckoned he had denied himself the right to enforce a vigilante justice on Larry.

Joey closed the side door and scrambled into the driver's seat. From the direction in which Larry had gone, he could have been heading back home or through to join Santa Monica Boulevard all the way to Cedars Sinai. As Joey screeched down the ramp and out onto the street in belated pursuit, he prayed his reluctance to fire had been justified; that he would find the Beetle parked once again outside Larry's apartment building.

If so, it was over for him. He would re-join his family at Cedars, and there he would remain night and day, standing guard, until Laura was well enough to leave. Then screw stubborn pride – his and hers – and *adios* LA.

Chapter 29

The section of street was lined with apartment blocks. Virginia edged the Jeep into the curb a little way down the road. Dodge was sitting beside her, John and Hayley behind them, and John had noticed Virginia's eyes go to the rear-view mirror rather too frequently to be simply a part of her road-craft.

'He's home,' said a disappointed Hayley. 'That's his car, the silver Corvette.'

'Least that saves us breaking the door down,' Dodge said.

'Dad, I'm not happy about this.'

'Ginny, don't worry.'

'What if there's trouble and the cops come? They'll find you carrying, won't they? What have you got, the Walther?'

Dodge nodded. 'And the carry license to go with it, so what's the problem?'

'And what's Quealy gonna say? He thought he could trust you.'

'Ah, Quealy can kiss my ass. I'm more concerned that Hayley can trust me to take care of her.'

'I don't want to cause a problem,' Hayley said.

Virginia twisted in her seat to face John, ignoring Hayley. 'And I suppose you're packing as well?'

'This fellah's killed six people already,' John said by way of admission.

'Don't remind me. Hayley, no offense, but these two men mean the world to me. What exactly have you left behind that's so important you want to risk their lives for it?'

'Ginny!' Dodge barked, glaring at her.

Hayley didn't rise to the taunt. She appeared utterly tranquil, as though she simply didn't have the energy.

'I left my life behind. But you're right; it's not worth the trouble. I'll go on my own. I'll ask him for what's mine: financial bits and pieces, things like that. A few clothes. He can keep the rest. I'll be in and out in five minutes. He won't hit me again looking like this. He's more likely to start bawling.'

'And will you go back to him if he does?' John said.

'No.'

'Which won't please him,' Dodge said. 'So it's best he doesn't get the chance to ask. Ginny, I'm sorry, we have to go with her. If you were in Hayley's position you'd want someone to help out, wouldn't you?'

'Wait a minute,' Hayley said. 'My car's gone.'

In the rear-view mirror, John saw his girlfriend roll her eyes before she spoke.

'You mean he's not in, after all?'

'He doesn't normally drive my car, but ... unless it's been stolen, I guess he must have taken it.'

Virginia impatiently snatched her father's cell phone off the dash.

'Hayley, what's your landline number?' she asked, then tapped it in as Hayley dictated. Unanswered after fifteen seconds, she cut the connection. 'No-one home. What car do you drive, Hayley?'

'White Beetle convertible. Old shape.'

'Right,' Virginia said. 'So I'll know if he shows.'

'You'll sound the horn?' John asked.

'Don't worry,' she said, and beckoned him closer. He leaned between the seats to receive a kiss, as much a statement of ownership for Hayley's sake as a sign of her love. 'Do this quick,' she said. 'There's been enough upset in this family.'

No one afforded him the slightest respect. Larry knew he had earned precious little of that commodity in uniform, but at least the fear he had instilled in people had *looked* like respect. Now, even his impressive body count served only as a source of amusement. The check-out girl at the store had riled him badly. Po-faced bitch, asking whether he didn't require more flowers considering he had six graves to visit. He wanted Internal Affairs off his case. He wanted to get back to work. The effect of his police shield was out of all proportion to its size. It protected him, sanctioned his actions. The thug he really was could hide behind it like a school bully escaping punishment in the shadow of his headmaster father. When he hit someone, who could they complain to? The way things were now, he was the one fending off the blows, and he had lost the impunity of retaliation.

He purposely overcooked the turn onto his street, screeching the rear of the Beetle in a skid. Correcting it, he accelerated hard and quickly had to hit the brakes to swerve into the curb outside the apartment. He grabbed the flowers from the passenger seat and jumped out. He jogged round the pool, took the steps in twos, and abruptly halted at the top – his apartment door had been kicked in.

His peace offering was laid gently on the walkway and out came his gun. He felt much happier swapping flowers for a .45. It made him feel vaguely inhuman again. Hugging the wall, he slid along to just short of the doorway, thumbed the safety to off, and tried to calm his breathing. He listened. Two male voices. Not in the living room; too faint. Kitchen? More like the bedroom. Questions about what should be taken.

Unbelievable. On top of everything else, he was presently being burglarized. Well, they'd picked the wrong place on the wrong day. He was in no mood to make a citizen's arrest and reckoned he'd never get a better opportunity to legitimately waste another couple of scumbags.

As he prepared to enter the apartment, he jumped as a familiar face popped out of the doorway, perhaps attracted by his tire-squealing arrival. Then he peered at the face and realized it wasn't quite as he remembered. His once-gorgeous wife was a mess.

Hayley froze, her eyes wide with horror – not the look you gave a person just prior to kissing and making up. It was the wrong thing to do but he grabbed her good arm. If he could have a minute to explain how he'd seen the light, she might give him another chance. Once the friends who were helping her pack entered the equation, they'd try and take her away. He made a soothing noise like she was a baby about to cry, but Hayley had glimpsed the drawn weapon and her shout was out. Still holding his wife, Larry moved quickly into the doorway, ready to assure her pals that she was in no danger. If they were actors they'd probably become hysterical and wet themselves when they saw a real-life firearm.

When the guns appeared from the bedroom, Larry's first instinct was to put something between him and them. That something was Hayley. He yanked her to his chest and held her there, ducked his head behind hers and pointed the Tanfoglio towards the threat, which split in response. The white guy with the .357 stayed close to the bedroom door while the older black guy with the chunky Walther moved into the living room. Both were in combat stance.

Larry flicked his eyes from one to the other. They didn't behave much like actors; he'd seen veteran cops show more nerves than these two. These guys looked like pros, and it crossed his mind that Hayley had hired a couple of bodyguards, or even hitmen. His .45 wavered between the two.

'I just want to talk to my wife,' he said.

'With a gun?' said the white guy.

'I thought you'd broken in.'

'We did,' said the black guy. 'You wanna talk? Prove it. Lose the cannon.'

'Oh, sure. Or maybe I should just blow my own brains out.'

'Works for me,' said the white guy.

Larry shot him a stare – a poor substitute for a slug from his .45 – and noticed something less than professional in his eyes: emotion. The white guy was pouring hatred towards him.

'Who are you?' Larry asked suspiciously. 'What's my wife to you?'

'You wouldn't understand,' was the reply, loaded with meaning.

'Honey, are you fucking this Limey?' Larry said pleasantly in his wife's ear. He withdrew his muzzle to rest against her temple.

'You'd love it if I was, wouldn't you? Means you wouldn't feel so bad about nearly killing me. But no, Larry, I'm not. I came to get my belongings, and they came to make sure I was safe. They're friends.'

'I didn't know you moved in such circles.'

'Lose the gun, Larry,' said the black guy. 'You want to talk to your wife, okay. But not with the piece. And we're staying right here.'

'What are you? Marriage guidance? How do I know you won't kill me?'

'I won't.'

'And what about him?' Larry nodded at the other guy. 'He'd sure like to. I can see it in his eyes.'

'You're not going to shoot this man, are you?' Dodge said to John.

Larry didn't like the telling pause before John shook his head, so re-acquired him as a target.

'How about you two disarm first?' Larry asked, little expecting a positive response.

Both men refused by keeping perfectly still.

'Then looks like we got us a real fucking problem,' Larry said. 'Either of you two see *Reservoir Dogs?*'

A nightmare was unfolding. The likelihood of one or more firearms being discharged was extremely high. John couldn't believe how this situation had arisen. Hayley had only left the bedroom for a matter of seconds. He guessed she had gone to check on the screeching tires outside, which he'd also heard but had ignored because a warning honk from Virginia hadn't followed. What was his girlfriend doing down there? Sleeping? In his mind's eye, he saw himself attending his second funeral in a week, reading the inscription off the brass coffin-plate: *Hayley Olsen. May she rest in peace, because she sure as hell didn't live in any.*

Idiot, not keeping his mouth shut. His words had only antagonized. Dodge was the one trying to calm things down, and John felt like an amateur alongside him, a rash youth. Now, they had a Mexican stand-off. Trust had gone out of the window. It would not be resolved without blood spilled.

They had to keep talking. Someone had to say something. John knew from experience that when diplomacy failed it wasn't long before the bullets started to fly. He could see the panic building in Larry's expression, a sort of gleeful terror. There was only so much craziness a person could keep inside.

If a voice didn't break the silence soon, a gunshot would.

Suddenly, Larry made a move.

It wasn't his business. Joey kept telling himself this as he monitored events up on the walkway – Larry grabbing his wife at the door, then the ensuing confrontation, only half of which he could see, but obviously with someone inside the apartment.

It wasn't his business. He had a wife and child who needed him alive and well.

'That's crap,' he said to himself. True, but crap; an excuse. If it wasn't for his selfish silence, Larry would have been in custody right now and this wouldn't be happening.

One last chance to act like a cop. With his shield on the belt of his jeans, he pulled the Browning from his shoulder rig, slid open the side door and jumped out. He ran across the street, but stopped short of entering the courtyard.

His presence was no longer required. The situation had been resolved without him.

The move Larry made was to collapse on the floor. John gawked as it happened, half-suspecting it was some bizarre bluff to lower their defenses. Neither he nor Dodge lowered their weapons. Not just yet.

Not until Virginia's voice was heard on the walkway.

'Don't shoot,' she said, and stepped into view, grinning and holding her stun-gun like she was in a TV commercial.

'Why didn't you honk the horn?' Dodge said angrily.

Virginia lost her smile. 'Because this way no one got killed, did they?'

'Girl, we could have all been dead before you even got here.'

'Thanks, Virginia,' Hayley said, looking down at Larry who was groaning, totally immobilized. 'But why didn't I feel anything?'

John was thinking the same thing and wondered if Virginia had been secretly hoping Hayley *would* be shocked.

'The current doesn't pass, even if you're touching the assailant. Listen, we should get out of here. He won't be like that for ever. Is everything packed?'

'I've got what I need,' Hayley said, eyes still on Larry's prostrate form. 'Is he going to be all right?'

'Providing he doesn't have a pacemaker fitted,' Virginia said.

John put his gun in his belt and waited for Dodge to holster his own, but the semi-automatic was wavering impatiently at his side as though Dodge felt it needed to lose the weight of at least one round. He was staring at Larry.

'Dodge ...' John said.

He snapped his head up, like waking from a trance, disappeared into the bedroom and returned with a holdall.

'Take his gun, John. Hayley, any others in the apartment?'

'Not to my knowledge.' She looked at Larry again. 'What exactly's wrong with him?'

'He's a complete arsehole,' John said, bending to pick up the .45.

'No, I mean –'

Virginia interrupted to explain as they all cleared out of the apartment.

'The shock interrupts the neuro-muscular system. The pulse frequency tells the muscles to work very hard very fast, which instantly turns the blood sugar to lactic acid so the muscles have no energy and fail. He'll come round feeling like he's fallen out of a third story window onto the sidewalk. Here.' She offered Hayley the stun-gun. 'A gift. Your need is greater than mine.'

Hayley shook her head. They reached the Jeep and climbed in. Virginia started the engine, then turned in the driver's seat and again extended the stun-gun towards Hayley.

'I don't want it,' Hayley said. 'Thank you.'

'Ginny, leave her alone.'

'Dad, we can't protect her for ever.'

'I can,' Dodge said.

'Well, you didn't make a very good start, did you?'

'If you'd hit the frigging horn like you said you would –'

'You'd have shot the guy and wound up in jail.'

'*And Hayley would have been safe!*'

Virginia was furious with his response. 'And what about me, Dad? She is *not* your daughter! *I am!*'

The conversation curtailed, Virginia squealed the Jeep out from the curb. No one said another word the entire journey back to Beverly Glen.

After jotting down the Jeep's license plate, Joey decided not to adopt yet another change of plan. Joining his family was still his best bet. Further surveillance would tell him nothing he didn't already know: that Larry would come round in the foulest mood imaginable. He had seen the stun-gun in the woman's hand as they returned to their vehicle. There was no doubt Larry deserved a zap, and there had been considerable pleasure in watching it happen, but it did Joey's peace of mind no favors whatsoever.

In fact, he feared it might prove akin to the final jolt that brought Frankenstein's monster to life.

Chapter 30

'John, let her go.'

'Virginia!' John shouted again, watching her storm off along Angelo Drive. He was still coming down from his adrenaline high and found it very easy to yell.

Dodge placed a hand on his shoulder. 'She'll be okay, John. I know my daughter. She just needs some time alone.'

'But where's she going?'

'Just to the end of the street. There's a view over the city. She goes there to think sometimes. Don't worry.'

'This is my fault,' Hayley said. 'You're falling out because of me. I'll call a cab and go stay with my agent.'

'No, you won't,' Dodge said. 'You're not to blame for what happened back there. We should have been more careful, we slipped up. But you're safe now and there's no reason to go changing that.' He removed the keys from the ignition where Virginia had left them dangling, and locked up.

John stared off at the shrinking figure of his girlfriend, then at the road surface outside the Chester driveway – the tire marks left by Virginia's wild swerve off the street. He shook his head.

'She'll be fine, John, don't worry. Come on.'

Inside the house, Dodge gave Hayley a fatherly look over. 'Girl, you're beat.'

She smiled at the irony.

'Sorry, what I meant is, you look tired. Why don't you go lie down upstairs while we decide what to do?'

Hayley nodded, so Dodge showed her up to the spare room and saw her settled. Back downstairs, he joined John in the living room and closed the door for privacy.

'We got a problem,' he announced straightaway, and took a seat.

'Big one,' John agreed.

'Someone could have died today, and if Larry gets his way I think someone will.'

'What do you propose? Virginia's right: Hayley can't stay here for ever. Do you think we can persuade her to press charges for the other day?'

'Maybe. It's not a long-term solution, though, is it?'

John could only think of one truly long-term solution, but was loath to share it with Dodge; not through any reluctance to put the idea in his head but because he was certain it was already there. The silence between them was a sham, their pensive expressions a façade.

Eventually, Dodge quietly broached the subject: 'In Vietnam, we called it a wet job.'

'Assassination. I know.'

'So I'm not crazy to think it.'

'No more so than me. It's whether you'd do it.'

Dodge fell quiet.

'Is she worth it?' John asked.

'Her father died for me. If I don't do something, she could die, too. I couldn't handle that.'

'What about Virginia? What happens to her if you end up in prison?'

Dodge laughed. 'John, I'm heading there no matter what. They could give me six years for that shit at the range.'

'Really?'

'Oh, yeah. Anyway, without me to look after, I imagine she'd get a new lease of life.'

'You don't believe that. You're the only family she has left.'

'Then I'd have to make damn sure I didn't get caught. Wouldn't be too difficult.'

John held up a hand. 'This is purely hypothetical, right? You're not seriously going to murder this guy. For one thing, Hayley might not thank you for it. In spite of everything, she still cares about him. You could see that after Virginia stunned him.'

'John, the guy's a fucking loser. And Harry *would* thank me for it. That's his little girl. I owe him. If you're worried about my conscience, don't be. This is one death I would not lose any sleep over.'

The living-room door burst open, and from the naked fear in Hayley's eyes John thought Larry must have climbed in through her bedroom window. He reached for the .357.

'*My mom!*' she screamed. 'She lied to protect me. He knows that. I told him. He'll think I'm there!'

'Hey, calm down,' John said.

'*Larry!* He'll go to Venice Beach! Why didn't I think?'

Dodge stood up and made Hayley sit down.

'Listen to me,' he said. 'Your husband is probably not even fully functioning yet. Virginia gave him a good long jolt. Even if he's up and about, he will not be thinking straight. I can get there before him.'

'Dodge, I'll go,' John said quickly.

'There's a phone in the kitchen,' Dodge said to Hayley. 'Give your mom a call, tell her I'm on my way, not to let anyone in. If she sees Larry, to dial 911. And, Hayley … calm down.'

She ignored his advice and ran from the room.

John rose to his feet. 'Dodge, I'll go.'

'You'll stay with Hayley. All I'm gonna do is collect Marie and bring her back here.'

'Then why shouldn't I go?' John asked reasonably.

Dodge lowered his voice to a whisper. 'Because if Larry does show up, I'm best equipped to handle him.'

'Come off it, you'd shoot the guy.'

'Exactly. How many men you waste, John?'

'Oh, this is a great time for one-upmanship.'

'How many?'

'Enough.'

'Yeah. Meaning you're not ready to waste any more.'

'I'll do what I have to do.'

Dodge grabbed him firmly by the shoulders for emphasis. His iron grip was persuasion in itself.

'I lost count, John, that's what I'm saying. I can end this asshole in a heartbeat. I got no fucking qualms. Can you say the same? Because if you can't, going there is likely to get both you and Marie killed.'

Hayley barged back in. 'She's not answering! Oh, Jesus …'

Dodge dropped his hands from John and switched to his soothing voice again.

'You tried her cell?'

'I don't know her number. I don't even know if she has one.'

'Calm down. He could not have got there and done something in this time. Remember what your mom said at the hospital? She might take a walk on the sand? That's where she is. She's eating ice cream on the beach. Just go back in the kitchen and keep trying.

And remember: as long as you can't reach her, she's out of the house which means she's safe.'

Hayley looked to John for confirmation, who nodded in spite of his doubts. Marginally less panicked, she returned to the phone.

'And what do I tell Virginia when she gets back?' John asked desperately.

'Nothing,' Dodge said, taking Chuck's suitcase from the corner of the room. 'You say you went to the bathroom and when you came out I'd gone.'

'Sure. And she'll think you've gone to Larry's apartment to finish the job and she'll follow you there. Only you won't be there but Larry might be, and he'll get to meet the girl who put a million volts up his backside. Good thinking.'

'Then tell her I've gone to the store,' Dodge said. He opened the case and removed the Smith & Wesson, screwed in the suppressor, and slipped it inside a folded copy of the *Los Angeles Times*, concealing the whole length of the weapon.

John had joked about it earlier, but he could see Dodge was serious.

'Oh, talk about a grudge. You're taking a dead man's forty-year-old service pistol to use on his daughter's husband. That's what you meant about it not being difficult, is it? Dodge, I think you're confusing difficult with noisy. You should go and see Quealy right now.'

'That's it! You say Quealy called and asked me to drop by and give him an update. Square it with Hayley. Make sure she knows the story.'

'Shit, you are really dropping me in it with your daughter, you know that? When you get back here with Marie, she'll know I was lying and that's us finished. You might as well tell her I screwed Hayley while she was out.'

Dodge came face to face with John, who didn't much like the reckless glint in his eye.

'I'm going now, John. All you gotta do is plead ignorance. When I get back, be just as pissed off with me as Ginny. You didn't know, okay? I lied to you, yes? She loves you, she'll believe you.'

John watched helplessly as Dodge left the room and headed for the front door with his holstered Walther and his even deadlier *LA Times*. Belatedly, John hurried outside and caught him reversing off the driveway.

'Dodge ...'

'You can't stop me, John.'

'I know. Just take care.'

'Always do, sergeant.'

'I mean it. You stopped being a Ranger a long time ago.'

'Son ...' Dodge said, and smiled, '... you never stop being a Ranger.'

As John walked up Angelo Drive towards the green space at the end, he was torn. Keen to show Virginia that at least one of the two men in her life had not forgotten about her, he was equally reluctant to leave Hayley alone in her present state.

Virginia had won out due to ulterior motives, and John felt bad. Even with Hayley's connivance, for the lie to ring true he had to prevent his girlfriend from returning to the house while Hayley was still frantically holding the phone to her ear. Virginia wasn't stupid. She would realize exactly where Dodge had gone, and why.

The concrete stopped and the parched grass began. He could see Virginia sitting beneath a tree, just shy of where the ground fell away, the city in the distance, silver buildings soaring out of the brown smog towards a blue sky as though reaching for clearer air. She was hunched up, arms circling her knees to her chest. John had never known his heart to ache with so much yearning for someone. He was paranoid about losing her, and seeing her like this he almost resented Hayley, which he knew was unfair considering how eager he'd been to meet her for so many years, but he was beginning to understand that his feelings for the two women were not the same. Hayley belonged to the past; Virginia was his future.

'Hi, gorgeous,' he said.

She turned her head to show him a weary smile. 'Hey.'

John sat beside her. 'Sorry,' he said quietly.

'For what?'

'You want someone to blame. Well, here I am.'

She shook her head.

'Yes. It's not Hayley; she didn't force Dodge to do anything. And it's not Dodge; in a way, he's being driven by forces beyond his control. He's trying to put the past to rights. I'm the one who started all this by taking you to Oregon. I'm the one you should be shouting at.'

Virginia stared into the distance. 'I'm worried, John, that's all. I don't mean to blame anyone. I'm scared. Under different circumstances I'm sure I could get along fine with Hayley.'

'So you *don't* like her.'

'I don't like her being here. She's making my dad crazy.'

John raised his eyebrows and gave her a look.

'Okay, crazi*er*,' she said.

'Exactly,' John said. 'Think where we picked him up from this morning. Hayley might be the one person who can pull your father round. He's got a purpose now.'

'But how can a stranger mean more to him than his own family?'

'She doesn't, not really. It's what she signifies. She's a chance for him to draw a line under the past.'

'But he'll draw a line under everything if he's not careful. Did

288   VETERAN AVENUE

you catch the look in his eye immediately after I stunned Larry? If he'd been alone, I swear he'd have put a bullet in the guy's head.'

John didn't say anything, which was answer enough.

'Where's it going to end, John? *How's* it going to end? As long as Larry's out there, my dad won't relax. There's only one way he's ever likely to feel Hayley's safe ...'

It was a re-run of his conversation with Dodge, and John felt the truth ready to blurt out of him. If he didn't speak now with Virginia so close to the facts, his deceit would seem tenfold to her later on, because he was under no illusion he could kid her on this. Anyone else perhaps; not her. Either what he felt for her would steal his conviction, or the lie maintained would irreparably taint his feelings towards her.

'Virginia ...'

She waited, then prompted. 'What?'

'Your dad's gone. He wanted me to tell you he's seeing Quealy but he's not. He's gone off to get Marie.'

Virginia groaned lightly, suggesting she was no more than disappointed at the prospect of another stranger in the house. John's heavy brow made her re-assess.

'Shit,' she said, realizing. 'He thinks that's where Larry's headed.'

'I couldn't stop him.'

She climbed to her feet and John rose with her. 'How long ago?' she asked.

'Not long.'

She peered at him. 'John, tell me this isn't as bad as I think it is.'

He held her hands firmly to prevent her bolting. 'He's taken Harry's pistol.'

Her tug away was half-hearted, more a token than a serious attempt to escape his grasp. She wilted on her feet and stared at the ground.

'Sorry, Virginia, I really couldn't stop him. He has to do this, you know that. Hopefully he'll just get there, pick her up and bring her back.'

'But if Larry's there he'll kill him.'

John paused before replying. 'If he has to.'

'No, if Larry's there he will kill him.'

John shrugged. 'I think he sees it as part of the healing; the only way he can properly make amends for the past.'

'But he has nothing to make amends *for*.'

'That's irrelevant, it's how he feels, how he's felt for over forty years. In his eyes, it's his only chance for peace.'

Virginia looked out over the hazy vista of Los Angeles, as though trying to psychically track her father's progress towards Venice Beach.

'I can't believe we're letting him do this,' she said in a voice as distant as her focus.

John squeezed her hands. 'He'll be back, don't worry.'

'Then what?'

He wanted to echo his reassurance, but he couldn't; if he'd wanted to lie he would have stuck to the story about Dodge visiting Quealy.

'Come on,' he said, 'let's wait back at the house.'

Chapter 31

After what had felt like a brief connection to the national grid, Larry had regained full physical control, but could not be as confident about his mental faculties. He thought perhaps the shock had caused an important fuse in his head to blow. The part of his brain that housed his temper felt like a hot-wired engine he couldn't shut down. He kept telling himself that Hayley was not having an affair with the English guy, but it wouldn't kill the ignition. He had uncovered a conspiracy, stumbled on relationships he didn't know existed but reckoned he understood. What else but sex could put such venomous passion in a man's eyes as he had seen in the Limey's?

Larry decided he had better leave the Beetle on an adjoining street. It seemed he was genuinely starting to think like a criminal – if he hadn't done so all along. He had chosen clothes from his closet he rarely wore and had donned a Raiders cap and dark glasses. A measure of his blind fury, he was only vaguely aware of the significance of adopting a disguise: that he might need to flee unrecognized. Only at the very back of his mind did the fact lurk that he was leading a charmed life in his so-far-successful avoidance of prosecution; his continued liberty had taken second place to the punishment of others.

He turned off the sidewalk and went round the back of the bungalow into a small grassed yard where he wasn't overlooked. Providing no one had seen him arrive and thought it conspicuous, he would gain entry undetected. He put his ear to the screen door and heard a phone ringing somewhere inside. After a while it stopped, but he heard no one speak so assumed it had simply rung off.

Marie was out. Not the best result, but not a dead loss. He would just have to prove his investigative credentials. Find a name, an address, something to lead him to Hayley and her protectors. He tried the handle and found the door wasn't locked. Larry pulled his weapon, removed his sunglasses and slipped into the kitchen.

He jumped as the phone rang again. He waited, not moving. Perhaps Marie had been sound asleep and this time she would wake. Eventually the warbling tones ceased, but they had continued for long enough that Larry suspected it was the automatic disconnect that had silenced them, rather than the caller who had given up. He smiled. It wasn't hard to guess who might be so desperate to get through – warn *Mom* that trouble could be heading her way. But why had Hayley's henchmen not already collected Marie?

It wasn't important. What mattered was finding his wife, and then if he was so inclined he could ask her face to face.

He took a quick look around the kitchen, then moved into the bedroom. He couldn't see anything obvious and was about to rifle some drawers when a bottle on the bedside cabinet caught his eye. A brown glass medicine bottle. He picked it up and read the label. Marie was in pain. He didn't know from what exactly, but was happy knowing it was severe enough to warrant liquid morphine. He set it down and was reaching to open the cupboard beneath when he heard someone come in the front door.

Her home felt all wrong. *Violated* was the word she would have used. Marie stopped in the hallway and listened. Nothing. She gently closed the door behind her and strained her ears again. No, nothing. She dismissed it. It wasn't in the bungalow, it was inside her head. She had never been more tuned into the reality of death. Her death. She had spent a blissful time on the beach – miraculously thoughtless. Then her return to the tomblike silence of the place where she knew she would breathe her last. Perhaps she had subconsciously *wanted* someone to be waiting for her. Anyone. Even Larry. Talking, arguing, communication of any kind – it would all erode the remaining hours, leaving less time for morbid contemplation. She had so many regrets, and too few happy recollections to dilute the pain of them.

The phone rang, the sudden noise making her heart bang in her chest. She answered it in the living room and the voice made her grin, and how good that felt on her face.

'Hello, sweetheart,' she said.

Hayley's panic flooded down the line and Marie's smile faded. She listened to her daughter recount the incident with Larry and her resulting paranoia. At the end of the call, Marie was smiling again. It sounded like a dangerous confrontation, but when she pictured Larry's comeuppance she couldn't stop her cheeks from twitching.

'Say thank you to Virginia from me. That bastard deserved every last volt. Listen, I'm home safe and sound, and I'll lock up and wait for Dodge and call nine-one-one if I see Larry, okay? Now sit tight. I love you and I'll be with you soon.'

Hayley echoed the sentiment and ended the call. Marie took a shallow breath, which was as deep as it would go. The day had overtired her. It would have done had she been well – the emotional strain alone. She went into the kitchen and found some morphine to swig, sat down at the table and laid her head on her forearms. Her eyes closed instantly as exhaustion pounced. She was never sure whether this drifting was the onset of sleep or death, but each time she awoke she was saddened by her resumption of life.

This time she knew it was death had crept up on her.

'Hey, *Mom*.'

Marie's head snapped upright to see Larry smiling down on her, although not with any affection, and with his hands menacingly behind his back.

'Long time no see. Remember me? Gary? I think that's my name. I can't recall. Someone shoved a cattle prod up my ass, but you know that already.'

Once the initial surprise had passed, she was actually glad to see him. If he was here in Venice Beach, he wasn't in Beverly Glen, and obviously didn't know that his wife *was*. And why *should* she be afraid? If he killed her, what would he be taking from her? Days. Nothing more.

'Larry,' she whispered, the equal of his unflinching stare.

'*Larry*, of course,' he said. 'It's all coming back to me now. Yeah. Everything *is* coming back to me. Including my wife. So where is she?'

'Safe.'

'That's not what I asked.'

Marie shrugged. Her breath was short. Even long, it would have been wasted on him. She hated Larry for abusing her daughter. Having allowed a man to do that once before, now it would be over her dead body.

'Who were those people with her?' Larry asked. 'I heard you mention Virginia? Who's Virginia?'

'You mean where – where's Virginia. It's a state on the east coast.'

Larry produced a pistol from behind his back. 'Now, Mother, we can do this the easy way or the hard way.'

'Either way, you can fuck off.'

'My, that's a foul mouth for an old lady.'

'Well, *Gary*, you must bring out the worst in me.'

Larry thrust the muzzle between her eyes. 'I'm gonna count to three ...'

'That something you just learned?'

His eyes blazed and his lips puckered tensely. His lack of effect was making him mad, and Marie experienced a buzz unrivalled even in perfect health. This was the best she had ever done for her daughter, and when it mattered the most. In another hundred years she could not redress the balance, but she had tipped it as far back level as it would go. She closed her eyes as Larry counted slowly through one, two, and three.

'*Shit!*' he shouted. '*Where's my fucking wife?*'

Marie looked at him, feeling her serene acceptance of death glowing in her skin. He had stepped back, the gun lowered, pleading tears in his eyes.

'She's safe, Larry, and I hope you don't see her again as long as you live. I hope she finds someone else, settles down with them and lives the rest of her days in perfect bliss. She will, you know. You never deserved someone like her. She is going to start afresh with another man while you drink yourself to death in some seedy Hollywood bar. But before you peg out you're going to look up at the television in the corner of that bar and see your ex-wife there, a successful actress, and you're going to think of the life you could have had with her if you'd only stopped being such a *pathetic loser* for one minute.'

The muzzle of Larry's gun was wavering around her forehead again as furious tears spilled down his cheeks. One more inflammatory comment and he'd shoot her. She had to make it count.

'Hayley always said you had no balls.'

His eyes flared wide and Marie thought she'd succeeded. Then his expression altered like he was surfacing from a hypnotic spell. He gave a quizzical look that seamlessly turned to a smile, before he retreated a pace and lowered his aim.

'Hayley always said that, did she?'

Marie nodded, but realized her mistake.

'That was when exactly, considering you two haven't spoken in years?' He snorted his disdain. 'I know your game, Marie. I see the morphine on the counter there. I saw it in your bedroom. What is it? You dying? That why you and Hayley made up? You got cancer or something?'

She didn't mean to, but she must have reacted because Larry's smile broadened.

'Oo, the Big C, that's tough. You want flowers or a donation to charity?'

'I want you buried next to me, before I get there.'

'Or behind bars. You'd like that, wouldn't you? That's why the taunts. I kill you, you don't care, you're dead anyway. In fact, I save you some pain. But your daughter's free of me. You'd sacrifice yourself to save her. Shit, you must have hurt her real bad when she was a kid.'

'I did,' Marie said through gritted teeth.

'So we're not so different, you and I. She forgave you; she can do the same for me. I do love her.'

Marie was disgusted by him and let it show. 'Larry, we're worlds apart. What I did, I never meant. Yet when I knew what I'd done I loved her so much I couldn't face her. But you? You want to jump straight back in her life like nothing's happened. You don't love her. You wouldn't be here now if you did, you'd be lying on a shrink's couch getting some help.'

Larry affected a bored expression. 'Yada yada, you done? Because I'm done with you. You know, Marie … I'm gonna let you live. Rather, I'm gonna let nature take its course, let you die slowly, painfully. I'll find Hayley, don't think I won't. If you won't tell me where she is, some clue in this place will. And if that fails, just remember I'm a cop. I'll track her down. She can't stay hidden for ever. She won't want to – she's an actress, for Christ's sake.'

Marie watched him exit the kitchen and she felt defeated. He was right: sooner or later Hayley would reveal herself. Fame and fortune had been tantalisingly close. Once recovered, she would not be able to stop herself.

The bungalow was small. Larry reckoned he could tip the place upside down before Marie could bring a black-and-white to the curb. If there was an address book, he would find it. Thinking about it, the black guy at the apartment was Marie's age. Maybe he was wrong about the Limey. Maybe Hayley wasn't connected to either of them. Maybe it was Marie.

In the living room he slipped his gun in the back pocket of his jeans and opened a bureau next to the telephone table. His fingers searched quickly through the shelves and drawers inside, sifting and discarding.

Then he smiled and ceased rooting for a moment. He had come across a photograph of Hayley as a young girl, standing in the ocean's surf, holding an ice cream. Her dress was billowing in the breeze, a dress patterned with Mickey and Minnie Mouse inside love hearts. He recognized the material as the same she tied in her hair on occasion. He had never known its history and had never bothered to ask, which now struck him as very sad. Given his time again, he would extract every last trivial piece of nonsense from her. Because none of it was nonsense. Without all the bits of her past, how could he hope to know the woman she was today? Would she be estranged from him today if he had made the effort to question what made her tick? Maybe he hadn't nagged enough so she was never convinced he really wanted to know the thoughts that haunted her, or made her laugh. Captivated by regret, he couldn't tear his eyes away from her image.

Something stroked his butt and he whirled round to find Marie pointing his gun straight back at him, hammer cocked. For the second time in twenty-four hours he was staring into the business end of Laura DeCecco's nine mil Sig Sauer, which he'd taken from her and left in the Beetle overnight.

He couldn't speak. The absolute certainty of death had struck him dumb. A loaded nine mil held by a woman who wanted him dead, who had nothing to lose by killing him, and in her view everything to gain for her daughter. What a thoroughly crappy end to his life. At least yesterday he might have been killed by a badass Marine. Now he was going to die at the hands of a skinny-assed Marie. It was just plain fucking embarrassing.

Marie held out her free hand. 'Photo. Give it to me. I don't want your filthy paws on my baby; not even her picture.'

Larry did what he was told, then Marie stepped back to put a safe gap between them.

'God, you have no idea how badly I want to pull this trigger. It would solve everything. And I wouldn't have to live with the guilt for very long – that's if I felt any at all.'

She was talking. Good. While she had something to say, he had to be alive to listen.

'What I really want, though, is for you to go to jail. They'd love you in there, a famous police officer like yourself. Especially the

Armenian fraternity. I think you'd have a lot of fun in the shower. You'd be the resident soap picker-upper.' She chortled at the image in her mind. 'You see, I want you to suffer for what you did to Hayley. I want you to know what it's like to be scared, to be bullied.'

Marie paused for so long that Larry felt compelled to speak, and suspected he was meant to, kind of cueing in a punch-line.

'Why would I go to jail?' he asked carefully. 'You mean if Hayley pressed charges? Me threatening you? What?'

'Where exactly would you serve life without parole, Larry? I want you to talk about it, make it real in your own mind. Where would they send you, Larry?'

Although he couldn't discern any logic in the question, he thought it prudent to indulge her. 'Uh ... the state prison's at Lancaster ... probably there.'

'And where for Death Row?'

'Death Row? San Quentin. Why?'

'And can you picture yourself there, Larry, waiting ten years for all your appeals to fail before you're strapped to the gurney and the toxic chemicals enter your bloodstream?'

He shrugged helplessly. 'Well ... not really. I mean ... I'd have to murder someone in cold blood.'

'You did.'

Marie swung the muzzle back at herself, put a shot past her head to the right, past her head to the left, and then stuck one straight between her eyes.

Dodge had been fortunate not to pick up a speeding ticket. He had been even luckier avoiding a felony arrest for packing a silenced handgun. Had he dropped by Quealy to explain his intentions he would have been locked up again, and not released for a very long time. It appeared that his thought processes had started operating with the same skewed rationale that had led to the destruction of DODGE CITY. But Dodge knew this was different. His face was not painted, he was not dressed in camo gear, he was not shooting at a phantom enemy to save a long-dead comrade because he was mourning his son. He was trying to protect living, breathing people from flesh and blood malevolence, and he believed he would have done so regardless of history.

He roared up the street and stopped outside the bungalow.

His dash through the city from hill to coast had been in vain. The wide-open front door, the neighbors out on their stoops, the approaching sirens – Dodge didn't need X-ray vision to know that Marie was lying on the floor inside. The only question was whether Larry had pre-empted that cellular mutiny in her body with something less insidious but equally fatal. He wanted to see for himself, help her if it wasn't too late, but he couldn't risk being detained by the cops at the scene. Apart from any awkward questions, Larry already had the jump on him if Hayley's whereabouts had been discovered. He called through his window to the nearest neighbor.

'You see the guy?'

The elderly man in the Panama hat shook his head. It may have been the truth or a reluctance to get involved.

'What happened?' Dodge asked.

'Gunshots. Three of them.'

'How long ago?'

'No more than two minutes. You a cop?'

'Was he driving a Bug? Corvette? What?'

'On foot.'

Dodge scowled. 'And you didn't see him, huh?'

The man tipped his head to hide his face behind the Panama's brim, and Dodge screeched away. But before he could reach the end of the street, a white Beetle streaked across the intersection.

Chapter 32

Confessing to Virginia had been a wise decision. Had John chosen to pursue the deceit about her father seeing Quealy, it would not have worked. The moment they walked in the front door a buoyant Hayley greeted them with her news. Her mother had answered the phone at last. A second call ten minutes later had received no reply, which meant Dodge had safely picked her up. They were on their way, and Hayley could rest easy.

Only after she had finished did her brain catch up with her careless words. She offered John a squirming, apologetic look, and was relieved to hear that it wasn't necessary. Then the momentary eye contact with Virginia restored her dismay. Her willingness to participate in the lie had not endeared her any.

John was therefore amazed when Virginia suggested he spend time with Hayley while she worked on some sketches upstairs. He escorted her up to the bedroom for a whispered exchange.

'Why?' he asked.

'You're a free agent.'

He groaned – did his reassurances count for nothing?

'No, John, listen. What I'm saying is, I trust you. If you truly see her as some kind of sister figure, you must have so much you want to ask her. If I tried to stop that you'd only resent me. When you come back to me, I don't want you still thinking of her. Satisfy whatever curiosity you have, get it out of your system, and when you're done, I'll be here. Now, go away, I have to work.' She playfully pushed him out of the room, winked and closed the door.

Downstairs, he found Hayley sitting at a kitchen counter, looking out over the street. He sat on the stool next to her. They smiled at each other but neither said a word. As the seconds passed, John realized this was the antithesis of the comfortable silence he enjoyed with Virginia. He had no idea what to say to her. To make him feel slightly less awkward he angled himself away to lose her from his peripheral vision. It was true: Hayley did feel like a long-lost sister, there was a whole life to catch up on, but what right did he really have to hear any of it? Though he had carried her photograph since childhood, she was no more connected to him than a random face cut from a *National Geographic*.

After several agonizing minutes he was ready to open the only topic of conversation he could think of. He didn't relish asking why she thought Chuck had given him her picture – so far, no one seemed willing to simply accept it might all be an amazing coincidence worthy of a slot on the appropriate TV documentary – but the prospect of their not communicating for another five minutes was infinitely worse.

Drawing a breath to speak, he turned to her ... and said nothing. Hayley was staring at him, eyes wide and rapt, a curious smile on her face, and John reckoned his reluctance to speak had been justified. She looked all set to impart some great theory with which he would not be terribly impressed.

'What?' he said warily. 'Have I got food in my teeth?'

'How do you feel about the States, John?'

'I told you this morning.'

'Tell me again.'

'Very at home. Why?'

She shook her head but appeared strangely content.

'Hayley, I've seen that look before. From your mum. I didn't like it then.'

'Why not?'

'Well, you tell me: what's the thinking behind it? I haven't been sent across time to save you. That's a Schwarzenegger movie.'

She laughed.

'Really. Chuck did not know what he was doing when he gave me your picture. He'd been on his own for months, literally waiting for some dream to come true, waiting for *the one*. He was desperate, probably crazy. If I hadn't come along, I expect he'd have given your photo to a passing elk. Besides which, it wasn't me who saved you today, it was Virginia.'

'But without you, Virginia wouldn't have known me *to* protect me.'

'I give up,' he said, holding his hands in surrender mode. 'I admit: I am from a distant galaxy and you are the mother of the unborn savior of our universe. Okay?'

She smiled, a glint in her eyes again.

'Hayley, why are you looking at me like that?'

'It feels nice being with you,' she said candidly.

John was glad Virginia couldn't hear this, or see his reaction. His skin had flushed red; he could feel the warmth. Before he knew it he had kissed her.

'What was that for?' she asked softly.

Blood boiling in his cheeks, utter confusion in his mind, John apologized. Had the impulse been platonic, pseudo-brotherly, or had his girlfriend been right?

'Don't be sorry,' Hayley said. 'I know why you did it even if you don't. You think you know me. It seemed natural. I feel I know you, too, John, almost as though I've had *your* photograph with *me*. There's something about you. I didn't sense it when we first met but I feel it very strongly now.'

John could hear the heavy footfalls of the Mumbo-Jumbo approaching. He faked a pensive expression before turning back to the window, but Hayley tapped his arm.

'You think I'm crazy, don't you?'

He looked at her. 'I think you've had a raw deal.'

'I *know* I have, but what I'm saying is not down to some knock on the head. Nor am I on the rebound, trying to cling to the first guy I meet who's my age. Virginia has nothing to fear from me. She may not believe that, but it's the truth. I like that you kissed me, but not for the reasons you're thinking.'

Hayley had him all wrong. She thought he was afraid of a romantic interest on her part, but he could handle a mere crush. It was equally ominous that she had not interpreted *his* intentions as sexual.

'When Dodge gets back with my mom, I'd like to show you something. Will you come?'

John nodded. How could he refuse? He had made this happen. He had waited a lifetime to meet Chuck's granddaughter. It was too late for denial.

At Santa Monica, Larry joined the Pacific Coast Highway heading north. Until he could work out the probable conclusions of the official detective assigned to the case, his best option was to get out of the city. His eyes moved between the rear-view mirror, the road ahead, and the speedometer. There were no cops on his ass and he wanted to keep it that way.

'Fucking bitch,' he muttered. 'Sly fucking bitch.'

His mental autopilot took over driving; the windscreen was replaying the death of his mother-in-law. First shot into the wall behind to her right, second shattering the glass of a picture frame to her left, and the third into her forehead, the hairy piece of skull flying off the back, punched out in a bloody spray by fragments of bone and lumps of brain.

The vindictive bitch had tried to frame him, but had she? Did the facts prove his innocence or conspire cruelly against him?

The weapon used. He had left it behind in his rush to get out, but it wasn't his, it was Laura DeCecco's. Unfortunately, it would not be hard to ID the middle-man who had transported it from the Beverly Center to Venice Beach.

The two shots prior to the fatal bullet. Those could screw his defense, as Marie had clearly intended they should. How many suicides missed their own head at point-blank range? With wrist-slashing, there were often hesitation wounds before the deep cuts, but no jury would accept those first two shots as being in the same category. By definition, hesitating took a certain amount of time, and Marie had fired three rounds in quick succession. It would have sounded to the neighbors exactly like it was meant to sound: an assailant trying to nail a moving target.

Forensics. This could well incriminate him. Ironically, the lack of gunpowder residue on his hands would not prove him blameless of pulling the trigger, because another test would find matching submicroscopic particles of metal in his skin, proving he had held the Sig very recently. A prosecuting attorney would then simply accuse him of thoroughly washing his hands after the murder, which could sometimes remove gunpowder but was highly unlikely to shift trace metal. The fact that both tests would show positive results with Marie meant little. A frail women, he might have clamped her hand round the butt of the pistol before turning it towards her, a scenario that would explain her prints on the weapon, powder burns around the in-shoot, and two shots going astray as she desperately struggled to keep the muzzle away from her head.

Of course, if he could avoid the law for a couple of days neither test would work on him, but running would in itself be an indicator of guilt, especially when Marie's death did not fit the mould of a classic female suicide. A woman often left a note, typically lay down to kill herself, and would normally choose drugs, poison or hanging before picking up a gun. Even then, she would rarely put a bullet into her own face.

Recent history. This was damning. It was more than just circumstantial evidence, it was practically mitigating circumstances. He could imagine his attorney telling him to plead diminished capacity rather than maintain his innocence. It all started with Frank Dista dropping dead. Larry's there, sees it, begins to crack; falls out with his new partner; takes Mallory to a bust where six bad guys and Mallory wind up dead; investigated by Internal Affairs; beats his wife who leaves him; held at gunpoint by DeCecco for causing the premature birth of his son; dropped by a stun-gun during an armed confrontation with Hayley and persons unknown. Then he goes to Marie's house to find Hayley, but Marie won't talk so he kills her. It sounded like the most natural progression in the world. With all that, would a jury have enough reasonable doubt to acquit? No. Not when the points in his favor were so negligible: if Marie were terminal, her committing suicide was not so improbable … and that was about it.

Larry abruptly pulled the car off the highway onto the hard shoulder and cut the engine. His route up Highway One had flanked the ocean. To his left stretched the Will Rogers State Beach; on his right the hills of Pacific Palisades rose up, hiding the homes of the rich and famous. He looked sadly from one to the other. Marie was right. This could have been his life. Hayley had been all set to earn the big bucks in *Malibu Mischief*, filming just along the coast from there. After a couple of years in the show she might have broken into the movies.

His stupid temper and worthless pride had ruined it, destroyed their future. Not only had he hurt the woman he loved, Hayley had been the hand that would feed him, and he had done more than just bite it, he had literally nearly snapped it off.

A sudden panic attack made him gag for air. He got out of the car but the sunshine and ocean breeze only reinforced his tragedy. Such simple pleasures. Why had he asked for more? Why had he not embraced the life and love that was freely available?

'Because I'm a fucking asshole, always have been,' he said to himself, and decided it had gone far enough. He hadn't killed Marie and he wasn't going to run as though he had. He would find a good defense counsel and take his chances.

He checked both ways but could not see any Highway Patrol vehicles. What the hell; he would take a leisurely drive up to Malibu Beach, stop at a bar, have a few beers, a little tequila, ogle the women, and when he was thoroughly smashed he would call the cops to come pick him up. He nodded to himself, unfastened the Beetle's soft-top, folded it back and climbed in. He started the engine, waited for a gap in the fast-moving traffic and re-joined the carriageway.

Communication had barely improved. Each time he heard an engine looming along Angelo Drive, John prayed it belong to the Jeep. Not just because he wanted to see Dodge and Marie back safely, but because their arrival would end the awkwardness he felt being alone with Hayley. He had never wanted to be somewhere else as much as now, not even during the worst times of his military service. Whenever he looked at her she was always looking at him, wearing that persistent smile that so unsettled him. He could sense how utterly contented she was just to be sitting beside him.

He was amazed he felt this way. His disappointment was colossal. He was like a little kid worshipping a supermodel for years, and when he finally meets her he discovers she has pimples, halitosis, BO, and is long overdue a depilatory session on her top lip. He was ashamed to admit it considering the sorry physical state she was in, but he wanted to say something to wipe the smile off her face. She was making him deeply anxious. He'd thought only airline personnel could maintain such fixed grins for so long. This was more frightening; this was genuine.

Eventually he couldn't stand it any longer. It was undoubtedly a harsh way to curtail her bliss but it was all that came to mind.

'I hope nothing's happened to them,' he said.

Her happiness was strangely undiminished. 'I know where they'll be,' she said.

'Oh?'

'Same place I'll be taking you.'

'And where's that?'

'You'll see.'

'So you think they're okay?' John asked.

'Oh, yes. More than okay. They've gone to the place of new beginnings.'

John didn't even try to look like he understood, but Hayley's mysterious optimism was undaunted. If he had been asked to label it, he would have called it something akin to religious fervor.

'I need the loo,' he said, and left the room.

Larry may have murdered the mother, but at least he didn't know where the daughter was. He was running blind, that was obvious. If Marie had revealed where Hayley was hiding out, then why was Larry taking the PCH north?

Dodge was in control. He did not have to relinquish the element of surprise, overtake Larry and stop his progress. Larry was going nowhere near Hayley. He could take his time and enjoy it, the easiest of hits on a target unaware he was marked for termination. One last wet job, and one that made perfect sense. He wasn't obeying orders, hunting a quarry because someone said he should. He was not killing for a dubious political ideology. He wasn't fighting a war he didn't really believe in but was too gung-ho, then *fugazi*, to opt out of. He was stalking a demonstrably bad person whose demise would release others from fear, and, unlike all those times past, he was suddenly very aware that he wanted to live through it. His death-wish was over. This would be the ultimate healing, the exquisite paradox. For, once it was done, Dodge fully expected to spend the rest of his days in perfect mental health, all debts repaid.

Up ahead, the white Beetle was still stopped on the hard shoulder. Dodge kept his engine running. He wondered whether he should pull alongside Larry and finish it, then cursed at a potential oversight. He guessed it was actually quite amusing. His entire adult life had been spent with firearms, and yet he had not considered whether his chosen weapon was up to the job. He thought it would be – its stainless steel construction pretty much ensured its longevity, and Harry had always obeyed the golden rule: take care of your weapon and it'll take care of you – but supposition got people killed. Dodge could not risk a misfire at the crucial moment.

Keeping an eye on the stationary Bug, he lifted his newspaper off the passenger seat onto his lap. He opened it out, popped the clip from the butt of the Smith and Wesson and unscrewed the silencer. He didn't need to look as his experienced hands worked swiftly to dismantle the semi-automatic. In pieces, he gave it a quick visual once-over. All it required was a little lubrication. He reached beneath his seat and produced a can of WD-40, liberally sprayed the parts, then reassembled the weapon by feel alone. He worked the action three times, re-attached the silencer but did not reinsert the clip. The gun was sound, but there was still an unknown quantity: the old ammunition. Although it would reduce his firepower by half, he decided to dump it. The nine mils in his other gun were compatible, so he thumbed the rounds from the top of the Hush Puppy's clip, dropped them in the door compartment, and loaded from the Walther's.

Up ahead, Larry had put the Beetle's roof down and was now looking up and down the highway. Dodge couldn't figure him out. Maybe he was debating between Mexico and Canada like the draft-dodgers during Vietnam. While he waited for Larry to do something, Dodge decided to test-fire the Hush Puppy to make sure. He worked a round into the chamber and locked the slide shut. He opened the passenger door a few inches and poked the extended barrel towards the verge. Back at the range he had apparatus that would do this remotely and less hazardously. He looked back down the highway. A big semi-trailer truck was approaching. He needed its noise to drown the shot. These rounds weren't subsonic like the originals. Even with the silencer, they would sound. The big rig rumbled past and Dodge squeezed the trigger. The shot discharged safely, if a little noisily for his liking. It was a problem, but one he could see his way around. He would keep the slide locked and press the muzzle firm against Larry's skin so the bullet would effectively not get into flight, preventing its sonic crack and alerting no one to what had taken place, thus allowing Dodge the time to E & E.

Larry's left blinker was flashing to re-join the highway. Dodge manually ejected the spent shell, closed the door and slipped the gun back into the lubricant-stained pages of the *LA Times*. When Larry left the hard shoulder, Dodge accelerated away to continue his clandestine pursuit.

Chapter 33

Virginia was sitting in an easy chair by the window, a sketch pad on her lap, a smug smile on her face. 'Don't you think you should go back down?' she asked.

John was leaning his back against the bedroom door as though he expected Hayley to charge through. He shook his head.

'You're enjoying this, aren't you?' he said.

'And you're not? I thought there was some kind of family reunion going on downstairs.'

'Come down with me. Please. I can't talk to her.'

'I'm working.'

'That's good! Talk to her about work. Acting. That's common ground. Bring her back down to earth.'

Virginia laughed and set her pad on the bed. 'You think I can bring her back down to earth with talk of Hollywood? Jeez, she must have her head *way* up in the clouds.'

'Please. She's saying some really strange things. And giving me some very weird looks. She said she wants to take me somewhere.'

'Well, don't forget your parachute.'

He went and sat on the arm of her chair. '*Please*,' he said.

'Poor John. She's really freaked you out, hasn't she?'

'Tell her about the jobs you've had, the stars you've worked with. Give her some hope. Or make her jealous, I'm really not bothered. Just get her off my back. I'm sure she won't talk the same way if you're there.'

She held his hand, a girlfriend again, not a tease. There was no gloating when she asked: 'Do you wish you hadn't met her now?'

'Oh, Ginny, I don't know.' He laid his cheek against her hair.

'I like that,' she said softly.

'What?'

'Calling me Ginny. I'm surprised. I've never liked anyone but my dad calling me that.'

John kissed her hair, and properly noticed the page in her lap she was working on. Around the costume ideas and notes were doodles that made him smile. Schoolgirl love hearts pierced by arrows, her name on one side, his on the other. And in tiny letters he had to squint to make out, a combination of their names: Virginia Frears. He was shocked by how unperturbed he felt. Not so long ago he would have been lacing up his running shoes after seeing that. But perhaps it wasn't a matter of time, not in the sense of him having reached a certain level of maturity. He suspected it was rather simpler: at last he had met someone he didn't ever want to lose. He put a finger under her chin and tilted her face up to his.

'Don't leave me,' he said. 'Ever.'

'I won't. Now where did I put my air-traffic-controller's hat?'

'Pardon?'

'Let's see if I can't talk Hayley down.'

Somewhere beyond Malibu, Larry had turned off the PCH and driven down to a beachfront bar. It was a watering-hole for rich beach bums and poor surf dudes. The mix of vehicles outside testified to that. The building was transparent; plate glass windows on both the road side and facing the ocean; a bar along the left wall, washrooms on the right. Steely Dan was playing loudly on the sound system, drifting out across the lot. Several patrons were seated on a balcony over the beach. Ten or twelve were inside, among them Larry, presently buying himself a beer and a chaser like he didn't have a care in the world.

It was a pleasant place to die. The winter sun was warming, the ocean breeze cooling, the girls good-looking. If he had been choosing his own death scene, Dodge would not have wanted much more for himself than this. He guessed that Larry was contemplating giving himself up, and was taking mental Polaroids for when the time came that his only view would be a razor-wired high fence.

And if Dodge could have been certain that *would* be Larry's fate, he might have U-turned and driven back to LA. But odd things were known to happen in U.S. courtrooms these days. Smart lawyers regularly worked minor miracles to dump major scumbags back on the street.

Dodge couldn't take the chance.

Larry paid for his drinks, knocked back the short and downed the beer. His attention never left the pretty female bartender. For a man on the run he seemed ridiculously unconcerned with passing traffic, especially with the Beetle's license plate no doubt now the subject of an All Points. Dodge wasn't complaining. This lack of vigilance only made his job easier, and confirmed what he suspected: that Larry was enjoying the equivalent of a last cigarette before the firing squad took aim. It was truer than he would ever know.

Dodge had parked across the forecourt from the Beetle, and the Jeep's smoked glass served to soften his outline as he watched and considered whether to make his move at that particular place. He had no trouble sitting tight. Vietnam had taught him patience.

Days and nights spent in the boonies, silent and motionless, awaiting the enemy's footfalls. They would piss in their trousers rather than risk announcing the team's position by movement.

But whether in the A Shau Valley or on a Pacific beach, the principle remained the same: patience was a virtue, but the longer a mission went on the higher the risk of compromise. There was no such thing as the perfect opportunity, there was only the right time to take your best shot, and that had to happen before you got tired and careless. No matter the planning or equipment or manpower involved, once guns were drawn there were no foregone conclusions, and the sharper mind could make the mortal difference.

Larry ordered a second beer and glugged it straight down. There was a good-natured exchange across the bar, then the bartender disappeared and returned with a towel, which she handed to Larry. Dodge couldn't believe it – fucking guy was going for a swim. He watched as Larry headed for the beach-side balcony that led down to the sand. Dodge quickly opened the glove box and took out a pair of Ray-Bans and a black baseball cap bearing a legend in white: *DODGE CITY Gun Range*. He removed from his belt the empty Walther in its holster and hid it away under the seat. Getting out of the Jeep he decided to take his shirt off. If Larry had any cause to give him a second glance, recognition might dawn. The shirt was a bright yellow, and if Larry's subconscious didn't recognize the color from earlier at the apartment, the cop-fugitive in him might simply wonder what it concealed; Larry *seemed* relaxed enough, but his mind had to be in turmoil, and fired by a generous dose of paranoia. Besides, a bare chest would fit in better on the beach – better camouflage.

Dodge unbuttoned his shirt, took it off, folded it collar to hem and tucked it behind him down his waist. The blast injuries that had been left to knit on their own were healing nicely. The more serious wounds had been stitched and covered. He peeled the dressings from them and smiled at the amazing speed of his recovery. It was a miracle he hadn't died. He would be left with a bunch of scars, any one of which could have spelled the end for him. It might have made certain people entertain some pretty outlandish thoughts regarding fate and destiny, but Dodge was doing more than entertain them, he was positively embracing them. In his mind, he had been specifically spared for what he was about to do.

He donned his cap and sunglasses, reached to the passenger seat and reversed the *LA Times* around the Smith so the stains were to the inside. It was minor adjustments like these that had kept him alive in Vietnam. Larry was hardly likely to sniff out WD-40 like the North Vietnamese had been able to smell American soap and deodorant on the regular grunts, but being careful to the point of paranoia was a hard habit to break, and now certainly wasn't the time to try.

Dodge locked the Jeep and set off down the side of the bar, sauntering leisurely as any man would who wanted a quiet afternoon on the beach with his newspaper.

As arranged, John returned to the kitchen a couple of minutes before Virginia so her arrival would not look like what it was: moral support. Whether those two minutes would fool Hayley was a different matter, and a moot point anyway; John was more concerned with making sure he wasn't left alone with her again.

'Coffee?' he said, trying to fill the two minutes with activity.

Still in that dreamy way, Hayley said, 'Thank you, no.'

'I think I will,' he said, aware of the false jollity in his voice. It was difficult, but he resisted the temptation to whistle something tuneless as he poured himself a mug from the percolator. It didn't help that she had swivelled on her stool to watch his every move.

'Are they not back yet?' he asked stupidly.

She shook her head and her blissful smile never flickered – not even when Virginia appeared.

Having struggled to keep his happy mask in place, it now hung there quite naturally, his facial muscles no longer out of tune with his emotions.

'You can't have finished already,' he said to Virginia, playing his part.

'Oh, I'm not in the mood. How are you doing, Hayley?'

'Better spiritually than physically.'

'Well, I'm sure the physical side will catch up.'

Hayley turned back to the window and John got a look from Virginia that said *I see what you mean*, before she perched on the stool next to her unwanted guest. John stayed behind them, observing.

'Did John tell you we're in the same business, you and I?'

'You're having rather more success than I am, though,' Hayley said amicably.

'That'll change, don't worry. Once you've impressed people, they tend to come back to you. You'll get another break, maybe not in *Malibu Mischief*, but in something just as good. Maybe bigger, maybe a movie, who knows?'

Oozing pure serenity, which John doubted was a result of Virginia's reassurances, Hayley glanced meaningfully over her shoulder at him before making a portentous announcement.

'Life is on the up and up. I think so, too.'

John noticed his girlfriend flounder, then recognized her next comment as a desperate bid, even fib, to direct Hayley's mind away from him.

'I could make some introductions,' she said. 'I know some important people.'

'That's a very generous offer. You'd do that for me?'

'Of course.'

'No you wouldn't.'

Unseen by them, John made a cringing face. In the leaden lull, the clash of personalities had been deafening, but at least Hayley's eerie smile was finally gone. As for Virginia, she had lost all semblance of amity and was giving Hayley a cold, hard stare.

'You're right: I won't now.'

'Virginia, do you think I can't recognize blatant insincerity when I see it? Oh, I didn't for a long time, but I wised up when Larry did this to me. You don't care about me; you're just trying to keep me from talking to John.'

Virginia let out a harsh, involuntary laugh. 'You got that dead wrong, girl. I'm trying to keep you from *not* talking to him.'

'Ginny –'

'No, John, she needs to hear this. Hayley, to which scintillating conversation are you referring exactly? You don't talk; all you do is sit there staring at him. So he *can't* talk to you because he feels so goddamned awkward. If you want the truth –'

'Ginny ...'

'– you freak him out.'

'Really?' Hayley said. 'I guess that must be why he kissed me.'

At that precise moment, John wished a Scud had landed on his head back in the Gulf. He wanted to deny it. He *needed* to. But he couldn't lie to Virginia, and now several seconds had passed since the accusation, there was no point.

'Ginny ...' he said feebly.

'Virginia to you.' She got off her stool and left the room. Shortly, the front door was heard to slam, and for the second time that day John let her go. If Dodge was right, chasing her would not help matters. She needed time to calm down. Even then, he thought he shouldn't be very hopeful.

'Well, thanks a bunch for that,' he said to Hayley.

'I'm sorry but she deserved it.'

'And what about me? Did I deserve it?'

'Depends whether you told her I freaked you out. Did you?'

'Words to that effect, yes.'

Hayley looked away as tears welled.

'Oh, come on, Hayley, if you've been acting normal, I'd hate to see what odd looks like.'

'Can I help it if I'm happy to be with you?'

'But *why* are you happy to be with me? And why doesn't it *look* like happy? Why does it look like ... bloody weird?'

She responded with an enigmatic smile and John lost his temper.

'That's what I mean! What the hell is that face for? If I didn't know any different I'd think you'd just had a good seeing to.'

'Huh?'

'A fuck,' he said bluntly.

'Oh.'

He spoke again before one of their uncomfortable silences could descend. 'So, Hayley, what is it I'm picking up from you?'

The smile began to spread again until a stern look from John flattened her mouth. He raised his eyebrows at her, impatient for an answer.

'I'll tell you when we get there,' she said.

'No, tell me now.'

She shook her head and turned back to the window, indicating that the subject was closed.

'Fine,' he said.

He pushed away from the counter and left her alone. His heart wasn't in that room; it had just walked out of the house. No matter what Dodge said, John couldn't risk Virginia thinking he didn't care enough to chase after her.

Out of the sun, the sudden coolness made his flesh crawl. Dodge had stopped in the shadow of the balcony's overhang, next to one of the stilts that supported the bar. To onlookers he would simply be selecting a good spot to relax, but behind his Ray-Bans his eyes were scouting for Larry. The beach was sparsely populated and Dodge located him quickly. He had walked parallel to the road for twenty meters and had nearly finished shedding his clothes. Once down to a pair of red briefs, he appeared to adjust his crotch, then trudged laboriously through the soft sand towards the water.

'Can't wash away your sins that easy,' Dodge said to himself. 'Trust me. I know. But if it's absolution you want ...' He squeezed the paper-wrapped steel in his hand.

Larry reached the surf and waded steadily into the ocean until he had to start swimming. Pointing directly out to sea, he got into a breast stroke, and Dodge wondered momentarily if his aim was to keep going until exhaustion dragged him under. If victims of drowning really did see their lives flash before their eyes, it wasn't the way Dodge would have wanted to go. His experiences were not for repeat broadcast, even in a drastically condensed form.

Then Larry's legs flicked up as he dived under, and when he resurfaced he was facing inland, treading water. Dodge made an instant decision to move into the sun. He was more likely to attract attention standing in the shadows than showing himself. As he headed along the beach, Larry resumed swimming, and Dodge reckoned if he did look like anything out of the ordinary, he probably looked famous. A celebrity down from the hills, incognito in cap and shades, catching some rays.

He ambled diagonally along the beach. Passing Larry's clothes he couldn't see a handgun lying among them, but he wasn't inclined to believe it had been ditched. What did strike him as significant was the towel. No longer rolled up, it was now spread out ready to receive a wet body, suggesting Larry was not about to just dry himself and return to his car. He was going to lie down and sun-dry himself, and hopefully nod off.

Ten meters beyond Larry's position and five meters forward of it, Dodge halted and sat down. If Larry looked his way, Dodge thought his close proximity to a couple of beautiful women would justify his choice and make it seem wholly innocent. Putting Larry to his rear appeared to be a potentially fatal error in military terms, but Dodge was not in fact left blind by it. Any movement behind could be detected on the inside of his Ray-Bans. It wasn't the clearest of images, but it was enough.

Some distance offshore, Larry was still calming his troubled soul in Pacific waters. Dodge put the newspaper in his lap, pretended to read it for a moment, then leaned back on his hands and looked out to the horizon. After a few minutes he straightened up and tugged the shirt from his waist. He wiped his sandy palms on the yellow material and dropped it on the paper. Another apparently idle scan of the ocean, then he carefully pulled the paper from around the Smith, leaving the gun covered by the shirt. Even an FBI surveillance team would have been fooled. He held the paper as though engrossed, but his hidden eyes never left the swimming figure.

Five minutes later, Larry curved back into the shallows ten meters away from the point where he'd gone in. He swam, waded, then walked out of the surf directly in front of Dodge, and all Dodge could do was act natural; keep up the charade of reading. It was okay, though, because he hadn't been spotted and he was armed while Larry was in his underwear. He furtively slipped a hand under his shirt and grasped the butt of the Smith & Wesson. Beneath the brim of his cap, behind his sunglasses, he secretly kept an eye on Larry, who seemed totally preoccupied with the skimpy bikinis ahead of him. He settled into a slow jog through the sand as though his show of fitness might impress. The guy was a bona-fide jerk; having ruined one pretty face, he was trying to win undamaged smiles from two more. Dodge had never relished the prospect of killing someone as much as he did Larry, and once the bastard fell asleep he wouldn't wake up again this side of Hell.

Unfortunately, with the line Larry was taking, Dodge would get a face full of sand as he passed by, which raised an interesting dilemma. Should he react angrily like a normal human being and risk being recognized, or stay quiet and look suspicious?

It was not a decision he had to make. Not minding where he was going, Larry stumbled and began to fall towards him, and Dodge had a plan zap through his head. The second Larry hit the sand, he would insert a round into his head and leave him lying there. The crashing waves would probably be enough to disguise the noise.

Virginia had left the front door ajar. John was about to go through it when Hayley called to him.

'Don't bother, John!'

He stopped and seethed. Her tone was so flippant, the callous cow, like she knew the damage she had inflicted was irreparable. He yearned to yell something offensive but would not give her the satisfaction. He would not even slam the door on his way out. As he pulled the door wide open, Hayley shouted again to tell him what he could already see.

'She's back!'

Virginia was striding purposefully up the drive. There was no sign of anger in her expression – nor forgiveness. She looked more business-like than anything.

'Inside,' she said, passing him.

He shut the door and followed her into the kitchen. She was leaning arms folded against the counter opposite Hayley, who had turned on her stool to listen. John stayed by the kitchen door, closer to the stairs that led up to the holdall he anticipated he would soon be packing.

'I am not going to be forced out of my own house by a stranger,' Virginia began. 'If anyone's leaving, Hayley, you are. Okay, you're here by invitation, but not from me. My dad seems to think you're some kind of a panacea for the past. I'm not so sure. He's already nearly gotten himself killed over you, and I can't see how that helps anyone *but* you. Now, I want to know exactly what you and John feel for each other so I can know exactly where I stand, and if I'm not happy with what I hear, you can both hit the street. So who wants to start? John? You want to tell me why you kissed her?'

He looked at her hopelessly. 'I honestly don't know.'

'Not good enough. If you want to be with me, I have to know if kissing complete strangers is something you're going to be doing a lot of.'

'I'm not a complete stranger,' Hayley chipped in.

'Why, because some crazy hermit gave him your picture once upon a time? I can see how that could make John grow up curious about you, but it doesn't explain your interest in him.'

'My interest,' Hayley said defiantly, 'is why Grandpa Chuck thought he should have my picture in the first place.'

'I told you,' Virginia said. 'Cuckoo.'

'We'll see.'

Virginia looked with pleading amusement at John, then back at her rival and laughed in her face. '*How*? Are we gonna hold a séance, call up Gramps and ask him?'

'You can mock,' Hayley said, unflustered.

'I can, yeah, it's real easy. I mean, how long has insanity run in your family?'

'This isn't helping,' John said quietly.

'That's where you're wrong. I feel better already. I've just established she's as whacko as her grandfather. Which means if you want to be with her I'll know you're crazy, too, and that pretty much eliminates my sense of loss. One screwed-up war veteran I can live with – I have done all my life – but I'm not a collector.'

John tried not to smile but Virginia caught his effort.

'Did I say something funny?'

'Only to someone who loves you,' he said, and saw the most remarkable transformation take place. It was as though Virginia had suddenly realized she was not being ganged up on, but was a part of the gang.

'Truce,' Hayley said, knowing she had been suddenly side-lined. 'Virginia, I am not after your man. In fact I am not in the least bit sexually attracted to him.'

'Oh, cheers,' John said, and turned to Virginia. 'Don't listen to her; I am sex on legs and you know it.'

Virginia couldn't help but smile.

'Don't worry,' Hayley said, 'that's not as bad as it sounds. I *can't* feel that way about you, John, and before the day's out you'll understand why.'

Virginia took a deep breath as she reassessed her suspicions.

'I don't know why, Hayley ... but I believe you.' She looked at John. 'Now what about you, sergeant? What about that kiss?'

'It wasn't sexual,' Hayley answered for him.

'Thank you,' Virginia said, 'but I'd like to hear that from John.'

'I love you, Ginny,' John said. 'And I know you believe me. I don't want anyone else. I can't imagine I ever will. You are more than I ever dreamed I'd get in this life.'

Although Virginia smiled again, she sounded weary when she spoke. 'But you still can't tell me the kiss you gave her was purely platonic, can you?'

'I can tell you it wasn't romantic.'

'How? You couldn't a moment ago. Don't play games with me, John.'

'I'm not. I admit when I kissed her I was confused. I still don't know exactly why I did it. Maybe I was testing myself. But feeling what I feel now, I know beyond any doubt that Hayley is no threat to you, romantically or sexually.'

'*Touché*,' Hayley said wryly.

Virginia ignored her. 'How do I know those aren't just words?'

'Because if you ask me to walk away from her right now and never see her again, I will.'

'*No!*' Hayley squealed, nearly falling off her seat in her scramble to beg up close. 'You can't! Virginia, please don't ask him to do that.'

John wondered how magnanimous Virginia would be, and hoped he would not be disappointed by a previously-unseen cruel streak in her. With Hayley's pitiful physical condition, it would be a cruel person indeed who would rub salt in her wounds.

Having deliberated with evident relish, Virginia put a question to Hayley, couched in terms already used: 'And before the day's out I'll understand why, right?'

Hayley nodded eagerly, desperately.

'I'd better,' Virginia said. 'Or rest assured I will hide John away from you like you're hiding from Larry.'

The hammer was pulled back ready. The trigger was under mounting pressure from an itchy finger. Beneath his shirt, the silencer was shifting round to its target like some directional boner. For Dodge, the world had moved into slow-mo. It seemed an age before Larry hit the horizontal right next to him, and when he did it looked comical, like a pratfall, arms flailing like flightless wings. There was a soft thud, a spray of sand, and a glint of metal in the sun.

Dodge felt the punch to his guts and knew it wasn't simply a punch.

He gasped as he was knocked flat on his back. The gun remained in his hand but both arms flew out into a crucifixion spread so the Smith's muzzle buried itself in the sand. Larry pushed the gun out of his hand and submerged it out of sight, then shifted quickly to straddle Dodge like a dominant lover, gripping his wrists.

Lifting his head, Dodge looked down at his stomach. Blood was beginning to spill over his abdominals and run down his flanks. Several sand-coated crimson globules rolled like ball-bearings and settled on his sternum. The cause: a silver handle sticking out, its blade wholly sunk. Larry hadn't been adjusting his crotch before the swim; he'd been stashing a knife.

Dodge rested his head back and stared at the great blue sky.

Larry smiled at him, then checked both ways along the beach. When he looked down again the smile was still there, because no one knew a man was dying. The knife handle was hidden between Larry's thighs. If anyone was paying attention, it would be because they resembled a gay couple, openly romping.

'Die quiet,' Larry said gently. 'Don't shout. Don't make me kill anyone else.'

Dodge didn't think he could shout. He thought he could already feel his blood pressure dropping and guessed his insides were slowly filling with blood that should have been in his veins.

'Yeah, you'd hate that,' he whispered.

Larry leaned down like he wanted a kiss. Instead, he used his teeth to bite the Ray-Bans from Dodge's face and drop them in the sand.

'I don't know who the fuck you are, boy, but you should have known better. I got a baaaaaad reputation. I'm infamous. What d'you think? You could just sneak up on me and pop me? I saw you coming a country fucking mile away.'

'Was a time you'd have never seen me coming.'

'Or heard you, huh?' Larry said. 'That's a badass piece you got there, silencer and all. I didn't know my wife knew people like you. What are you? Some kinda hitman? Ex-CIA? What?'

'I spent time in their employ,' Dodge said weakly.

'Wanna tell me where that bitch-wife of mine is?'

Dodge minutely shook his head.

'Wanna tell me who you are?' Larry said.

'Tomorrow. Tell you tomorrow.'

Larry grinned. 'A joke. I'm impressed. You're not afraid to die.'

'It's long overdue.'

'This you?' Larry said suddenly, nodding at the baseball cap lying in the sand. 'Are you the Dodge of DODGE CITY? Sounds like a nigger's name to me.'

'No, I'm the fuck of fuck you.'

Larry used his thigh to knock the knife handle, but Dodge stubbornly swallowed on the pain inside him.

'Tough bastard,' Larry said admiringly, then inspected the pre-existing wounds on his victim's body. 'I see this ain't the first time you've been on the ground losing blood. You've been in the wars. Lot of new damage, but this one here looks old. I'm guessing a souvenir of Vietnam?'

Before his strength ebbed completely, Dodge decided to strike. He brought a knee up hard into Larry's back, but only succeeded in provoking a head-butt that practically knocked him out.

Larry kept his forehead in contact, which also connected their noses and left a mere inch between their lips.

'You're a relic, old man. However good you once were, that time has gone. You fucked up today.'

Dodge heard the words through a crack of consciousness. He knew he would not recover to be fully cognizant again. Only one thing was clear in his head. In a whisper, his speech slurred, punctuated by labored breaths, he began to share it with Larry, who immediately lifted his head away.

'It is not the critic ... who counts ... not the one who points out ... how the strong man stumbled or ... how the ... doer of deeds ... might have done them better ...'

Forcing his eyes open, Dodge thought his solitary listener appeared enthralled, but realized his focus was not as sharp as it might have been.

'The credit ... belongs to the man ... who is actually in the arena ... whose face is ... marred with ... sweat and dust and ... blood ... –'

'Fucking soldier boys.'

All things being equal, Dodge could have resisted what happened next and maybe turned the tables. Without six inches of steel in his gut and a rising lake of blood that should not have been there either, he was physically Larry's superior. As it was, Larry manhandled him with ease. Dodge was flipped over onto his front, his scream as the manoeuvre swiped the knife through his insides muffled by a face marred by nothing so poetic as sweat and dust and blood; only sand.

He couldn't breathe. The coarse particles clogged his nose and filled his mouth. The last he knew was a hand delving into his back pocket to extract his wallet. A wallet that contained his driver's license, printed with his home address.

Chapter 34

Unwilling to keep any further information from his wife, Joey proceeded to tell Laura about the washroom incident and the business at Larry's apartment. Laura was not impressed. Joey imagined that Roth himself could do little to surprise her any more; it was *his* handling of the affair that was starting to grate. The situation was now totally out of control and they both knew it. Joey staying mute about his ex-partner's actions and intent during the coke bust no longer guaranteed Larry's reasonable behavior – if it ever had done. Although Laura understood her husband threatening Larry, the emotions behind it, and was in fact amazed he had managed to stop short of murder, she thought it had most likely made matters worse. Larry's brain was not working on the same wavelength. Where such threats would make a rational man toe the line, they could nudge a deranged individual right over the edge. Add a dose of enforced temporary paralysis to the mix and there was no saying how Larry might react.

'Joey, you have to tell Captain Gilchrist about the other night.'

'We've been through this,' he said, then attempted a change of subject by beaming at the new-born, cradled in his mother's arms. 'God, he's perfect.'

'That's right. Perfect. Untouched by the sickness of this world. He's as pure as a human being can be, and we have to keep it that way as long as possible. You can help protect him, Joey. Not as a cop, as his father. I know you can only do so much – it's a drop in the ocean – but right now you can make it so there's one less psycho out there just waiting to hurt this little guy.'

As though responding to his mother's fears for his future, DeCecco Junior began to cry, and was presented with a wholesome nipple not five minutes after getting off it. Joey had never witnessed such complete dependence. If just a fraction of Laura's responsibility lay on his shoulders, then his purpose on this earth suddenly meant more than he could ever have envisaged. He had created a life, and for the first time in his own life he felt truly worthwhile. Inside him was an unprecedented sense of vulnerability that took his breath away. But Laura gave no quarter to the tears brimming in his eyes.

'This is bigger than your career, Joey. Didn't you realize that when you saw me strapping on that gun? Did you think I *wanted* to carry that thing around with me? I mean, Jesus ...'

'I'm sorry.'

'You could have got us killed,' she said, staring at the wisps of black hair on the babe's scalp.

'I'm sorry. Seeing you like this, with our son, I feel sick to my stomach to think I let things get this screwed up.'

'But you're not making it any better. Stop thinking like a cop, stop thinking like a Marine. Your chief role now is to be a father to this child, to protect him. Okay, so you're here now and you've got a gun. Terrific. What happens a week from now? A month? You can't be with us twenty-four seven, Joey. You need to start making some adult decisions.'

Joey was hurt by her unforgiving tone. 'But I thought we agreed,' he said. 'I thought you didn't want me to tell Gilchrist. Wasn't that a decision we both made?'

'No, Joey, you made it, so I tried to stand by you, but it should never have been an issue. You should have been in Gilchrist's office the minute you suspected Larry wanted to go it alone.'

'Hon, doesn't the name Serpico ring any bells with you? Because it does with Larry; he made that crystal clear.'

DeCecco Junior had fallen asleep on the nipple, so Laura woke him up and proceeded to burp him.

'Laura, talk to me.'

'Okay, Joey, you couldn't say anything before, I understand that. But after ... come on, it's not like he shook down a hooker for a couple of bucks and a blow-job. This was major league. Seven people dead, one of them a cop, and Larry all set to run with the money. Your choice was to let him go or turn him in, but you did neither.'

Junior forestalled his father's response by a loud burp which brought part of his meal back onto Laura's shoulder. Joey grabbed a wet-wipe from a dispenser and mopped up the milky mess, then put his arm around his wife and perched on the bed.

'Laura, I wanted us to be settled when he was born, not have Internal Affairs crawling up my ass while I looked for a new job. I may have to face criminal charges – withholding evidence.'

'Cut a deal,' she pleaded. 'Can't they give you immunity from prosecution or something? Maybe they'll even let you keep your job, just give you a transfer someplace else. But I don't care if you're not a cop, I don't care what you do. Long as we got each other, the three of us, we can make it.'

Joey believed her. Everything he needed was right there in that hospital room. He had always measured his self-worth by the size of the risks he was willing to take. Now, taking risks for some sense of macho pride seemed stupid. Sacrifice meant nothing without a just cause, and his wife and son were just that.

'I'll call Gilchrist,' he said.

His cell was up to his ear and back down without a single digit being input. The knock on their room door came at the wrong time, as though testing Joey's nerve, daring it to fail him. After the visitor had come and gone, would he have reconsidered? Had a bold new man emerged just a moment ago, or had he been shamed into merely peeking over the parapet to gauge the flak before ducking out of sight again? Joey could already sense doubt creeping in. Once he had been a part of the country's military élite, now he might wind up as just another of America's least wanted – disgraced, unemployed, and on trial. If he talked to Gilchrist.

'Come in!' Laura called.

The handle turned and the door opened. Laura's midwife entered briskly. She smiled hello and unhooked the blood-pressure monitor from the wall.

'Would daddy like to hold baby for a minute, please?'

Joey took his son while the midwife went about her business. The new life in his arms re-focused his priorities.

'Don't look so worried,' the midwife said to Joey, having taken the reading. 'They're both doing really well. You can take them home in a couple or three days. Now, Laura, how's his appetite?'

'I'll eat later,' Joey said, staring at his son.

After a beat, the women simultaneously burst out laughing. Joey looked at them, then grinned like a banjo-playing hillbilly.

'Oh ... this fellah.'

'Feeding fine,' Laura said to the midwife.

'Good.' She replaced the apparatus on the wall.

'Thanks,' Joey said, and returned his attention to his baby boy.

He heard the midwife leave the room and was vaguely aware she had not closed the door behind her.

'Joey,' his wife said quietly.

'Who's going to break some hearts when he's older, huh?'

'Joey ...'

'Yes, you are. Just like your dad before he met your mom.'

Laura's voice was more insistent. '*Joey.*'

'Mmm?' He looked up and felt more like a criminal than ever.

Gilchrist was standing silently in the open doorway, letting his uniform establish his authority. He was cap in hand, but only literally. There was nothing in his expression to suggest he had come to beg or cajole.

'And how are you, Laura?' he asked, instantly pleasant.

'Very well, thank you.'

'The little one looks in rude health; very bonny. Have you a name for him?'

'We're still deciding.'

'I see.' Gilchrist stepped forward and closed the door. 'May I make a suggestion?'

'By all means.'

'How about Lucky?'

Even before that comment, Joey had taken a dislike to Gilchrist's I-know-something-that-you-don't manner. He offered his superior officer a churlish stare.

'If he says *meow* or *woof* in the next few minutes, maybe we will.'

'I only say that because if he still has two parents by the end of the week, he will be *extremely* lucky.'

Joey looked at his wife and watched the color drain from her face. He experienced a burst of intense hatred towards his captain for that, but kept it inside. He guessed he had caused her far greater distress himself in recent days, and doubted Gilchrist would have made such a comment out of hand.

'May I sit?' Gilchrist asked, placing his cap and car keys on the trolley table over the foot of the bed.

Laura nodded and the captain sat stiffly on a visitor chair, body language already translating what was to come. Joey felt his guts roll with dread.

'I wouldn't ordinarily discuss police matters in front of an officer's spouse,' Gilchrist said, 'especially not under these circumstances, but what I have to say concerns the both of you. An officer from the Pacific Division has contacted me about a suicide. A woman by the name of Marie Olsen killed herself a short while ago. Put a gun to her head.'

The information was left hanging like it was supposed to mean something.

'What's that got to do with us?' Joey asked.

'They lifted some prints off the weapon used. Most were smudged but they managed to get a couple of clean ones off the mag. Yours, Joey.'

'What?'

'A Sig Sauer. Laser sighting. Ring any bells?'

Joey closed his eyes and nodded, and Laura carefully took Junior back from him.

Gilchrist continued: 'The deceased woman has a daughter named Hayley. Larry Roth is married to a woman named Hayley, whose maiden name happens to be Olsen. This is no coincidence. So let me speculate. You provided your wife with this weapon for the purpose of self-defense, specifically with Larry Roth in mind. She pulled it on him at the Beverly Center but went into labor, which put the gun in Roth's possession. He took the gun to Marie Olsen's house where she somehow managed to get it away from him.'

Joey opened his eyes and began his confession by refuting Gilchrist's assumption.

'Sir, it wasn't suicide. However it may have appeared, she didn't kill herself. He did it. Roth. Think about it: how could she have disarmed an experienced cop? He was searching for his wife, she gave him squat, and so he shot her.'

'That was certainly the impression she wanted to give; she fired twice into the wall before killing herself. But it *was* suicide.'

'I don't believe it,' Joey said.

'Neither do I,' Laura echoed, gently rocking the babe, perhaps more as a comfort to herself.

'You've heard of a cadaveric spasm?' Gilchrist said to Joey.

'Of course. Where instant death causes the hand to clutch whatever's in it.'

'Right. Marie Olsen's grip on the Sig was vice-like.'

'Isn't that rigor mortis?' Laura asked.

Joey had clicked to the implications, and explained the difference to his wife.

'Rigor mortis comes slowly to a dead body, then leaves slowly. A cadaveric spasm is both instant and permanent. What the Captain's saying is that she was definitely holding the weapon when she died.'

Laura frowned as though they were both missing a glaringly pertinent fact.

'Couldn't he have had his hand over hers?'

'Yeah, what about that?' Joey said, still keen to damn his ex-partner.

'Sounds good,' Gilchrist said, 'but for one small detail. In Marie's other hand was a photograph of her daughter. Also gripped tight. Now, if an attacker had forced a gun into your hand, attempting to aim it at your head, squeezing off shots trying to get one on target, wouldn't you want your free hand empty to defend yourself? Wouldn't you drop whatever was in it?'

There was no need to answer.

'Apparently, Marie Olsen was riddled with cancer. She must have thought she had nothing to lose by framing her son-in-law. Now, I assume in light of Roth's recent spousal battery that Marie was trying to protect her daughter from further harm. That makes sense to me.' Gilchrist fixed Joey with a glare, and did not spare Laura the same. 'So what I need to know is why you both were so convinced he had a mind to commit murder.'

Joey and Laura exchanged a look while Gilchrist kept up the pressure.

'Because it would appear that Roth is thinking much the same way as you were a minute ago – I don't think he realizes she failed to put him in the frame. Eye-witness reports have him leaving the house like a bat out of hell. He clearly believes he's now the prime suspect in a murder case, so if he feels he has any scores left to settle, why would he not indulge himself? You see how this is stacking up? See why I'm concerned for the parents of little Lucky here? Joey, you knew Roth was dangerous even before this; for God's sake, your pregnant wife has been walking around with a gun. And if you're about to tell me it wasn't because of Roth, explain your reaction yesterday at the station when you found out he was here with her.'

'Okay,' Joey said, holding a hand up. 'Okay. Believe it or not, I was about to give you a call when the midwife came in. I had the phone in my hand.'

'You can make me believe it by talking now,' Gilchrist said. 'Tell me about the Armenians. I know you were there. Tell me about them.'

'I will. I'll give you Larry Roth, but I need a few minutes alone with my wife first.'

'It can wait,' Gilchrist told him.

'It can't. Go and get a coffee. And close the door on your way out.'

Gilchrist bristled but evidently realized Joey was the third person that day who had nothing to lose. His brief career in law enforcement was over; rudeness would not make things any worse. Gilchrist stood up and left the room, closing the door behind him.

With Gilchrist out of earshot, Joey twisted to face his wife. He opened his mouth to speak but she cut him short.

'Tell me you're not having second thoughts.'

'Babe, I've had third, fourth and fifth thoughts about this, all in the last five minutes.'

'But you're still telling Gilchrist?'

'No.'

'What?'

'You are.'

'I am? Why can't you?'

'I need to do something.'

'Like what, for Christ's sake?'

'I think I can find Hayley,' he said.

'So tell Gilchrist!' she shouted.

'Keep your voice down; I don't want him back in here.'

She calmed herself with a deep sigh. 'Tell him, Joey.'

'If Hayley wants to come forward once Larry's safely locked away, that's her choice. She doesn't trust the system and I sympathize. If she did, she'd have put him through the courts for beating on her. Now, I don't know who she's with, but they've protected her once already so I'm not about to take her away from them. All I'm gonna do is warn whoever's with her that Larry's on the prowl and advise them to lie low until he's out of the picture.'

Laura looked on the verge of launching a tirade against him, then softened. 'That's it after this, Joey. Promise me.'

'I promise. And you'll be safe. Just tell Gilchrist not to leave this room until I get back. Anyway, Larry's not coming here. He wants his wife, not you. And if he's given up on that, he'll be halfway to Mexico.'

Resigned to it, Laura nodded. 'You better go, quick.'

'Tell Gilchrist what you know about Larry. He'll have enough to pick him up. He can have a written statement from me later.' Joey snatched Gilchrist's car keys from the table. 'May as well add theft to the list.'

'You're taking his car?' Laura asked incredulously.

'Just the keys. Tell him they're under his seat.'

'What do you need them for?'

'Babe, I don't have time to explain.'

Joey kissed his wife and son and popped his head into the corridor. Gilchrist wasn't there. Joey ran.

Down in the lot, Joey reached Gilchrist's black unmarked Caprice. He let himself in the driver's side, settled in the seat, put the key in the ignition but didn't start the engine. Instead he activated the onboard police computer. He took from his pocket the scrap of paper on which he'd jotted the Grand Cherokee's license plate and quickly input the information.

'Dodge Lincoln Chester,' he read from the details that flashed up. Address of Angelo Drive, Beverly Glen. He committed it to memory and switched off the machine. He left the keys under the seat and ran for his van across the lot.

Chapter 35

John was in the living room remotely scanning through the multitude of TV channels, completely disinterested. He didn't want to be with Hayley in the kitchen and didn't think Virginia wanted him upstairs with her. Until Hayley let him in on her big secret he was in limbo, his love-life on hold.

He had been there for fifteen minutes when Virginia came down to see him. She closed the door and squatted in front of him, took his hands and kissed him. John was pleasantly shocked but his smile was not returned. She looked up at him seriously and he could sense a proposition looming.

'I can't stand this,' she said. 'I love you and I can't stand this. I want you to take my car and take that woman wherever she wants to go. Find out what's going on with her.'

'She wants to wait until Dodge gets back with her mum.'

'I won't have her dictating to us, John. Not in my own home. Tell her you'll go with her now or not at all. I'm going crazy waiting. I need to know that we're together.'

'We are.'

'Okay, I need to know that *she* knows it.'

'She's really got under your skin, hasn't she?'

Virginia shook her head. 'All she's done is piss me off. I'm worried she's got under *your* skin.'

'No, I'm inquisitive, that's all.'

'But you'd still walk away? If I asked you to?'

He nodded and Virginia kissed him again. 'Then go with her. Now.'

'Okay,' John said. 'You know, she might make me feel awkward but I don't want her feeling no one cares. She's vulnerable. What a life. A dead father, a mother who turned a blind eye to an abusive stepfather, a violent husband who ruined her big acting break, then she's reunited with her mother only to find out she's dying. It's hardly surprising she's clutching at straws, looking at me and putting my presence here down to ... fate ... destiny. You did it yourself back in Oregon. You thought maybe it was all to do with healing your father.'

'I was only thinking out loud,' Virginia said defensively.

'I know, but like I said: Hayley's vulnerable, which makes it more than just an idle thought. She really believes Chuck gave me her photo so I could come back and save her from Larry. I think it's bull, but some people have these thoughts when they're down. It's like turning to religion in your hour of need.'

'And are we right to encourage her? I mean, where the hell does she want you to go?'

The door opened slowly to reveal a blandly calm expression on Hayley's face. Something in the momentary silence before she spoke announced that she had been eavesdropping.

'Thank you, Virginia, I will take you up on the kind offer of your car. There's no need to wait for our parents. I expect we'll find them in Westwood.'

'Westwood?' John said. 'Why?'

'I'll be outside.'

They watched Hayley turn in the doorway, walk down the hall

and leave the house. The front door was left ajar, waiting for John. He looked at Virginia, squatting before him. They were still holding hands, and John felt an intense reluctance to break their contact. For a man who pooh-poohed the occult, some strange fears were tickling his hackles. It was the second time that day. The first had been at the hospital as Marie left on her own in a cab. Now, he had palpitations at the thought of leaving Virginia on her own.

'I'm not going,' he decided.

'I said it's okay.'

'I know; I don't want to.'

'Why not?'

He shook his head, shrugged.

'John, go. Personally, I can't see the point. Then again, I can't see any harm.'

'Come with us,' he said.

'I wouldn't want to even if the Audi *had* a third seat.'

He laughed and felt some tension release.

'The keys are in the cutlery drawer,' she said. 'Remember the alarm.'

'The cutlery drawer's alarmed?'

She rose to her feet. 'Ah, English humor. Ho ho.'

The flippancy helped, but John couldn't shake his free-floating dread. He got up and went to the drawer, but not the one containing the cutlery. This one was in a sideboard in the dining room. The .357 he had borrowed earlier was in there, and Larry's .45. He chose the Tanfoglio. He checked the semi-auto's clip was full and that a round was chambered, then tucked it into his trousers under his shirt. He returned to the living room and handed the snub-nosed revolver to Virginia.

'You know how to use it,' he said. 'Keep it in your hand until I get back.'

She placed it on the arm of the sofa. John picked it up and gave it back to her.

'No, in your hand.'

Mildly amused, Virginia kept hold of it. 'Why? You think Larry's coming here? He doesn't know this address. How could he?'

'Call me paranoid.'

'You're paranoid.'

'Fine, now humor me and keep it in your hand while I'm gone.'

'You'll only be an hour. Westwood's only just down the hill.'

'Ginny ...'

'Okay, okay,' she said, ushering him into the kitchen where she gave him the keys.

'That didn't go off,' he said, pointing at the cutlery drawer.

'Don't make me rethink our relationship, John.'

He smiled and she kissed him.

'Drive carefully; that's a new car.'

Virginia had barely sat down with her sketch pad when she heard the Jeep arrive outside. She recognized its engine noise and was shocked by how relieved she felt; John's fears had infiltrated more than she had known. She chucked her work on the bed, on top of the .357 she had disobediently discarded, and flew down the stairs. Her face was set with a grin and when she reached the hall and heard the latch key turn, she nearly shrieked her hello.

The first thing through the door was the barrel of a silencer. Virginia stumbled to a halt. She felt the adrenaline sluice through her, leaving nausea in its wake. If a color could be felt, she thought she had turned grey.

'Larry,' she mouthed soundlessly.

He backed up against the door to close it, holding a finger to his lips.

'That's good,' he whispered. 'Keep it that volume. Now, you have me at a disadvantage ...'

With a gun pointed straight at her, Virginia doubted that.

'You obviously know me,' he said, 'but I ...'

Virginia waited for him to finish his truncated sentence.

'Or do I?' he said suspiciously.

'Where's my father?' she asked, finding a voice. 'If you've hurt him ...'

Larry nodded. 'Yeah, we've met – after a fashion. Virginia, isn't it? I heard Marie mention your name. You know, I really don't appreciate what you did to me. That was a lot of fucking volts.'

'A million. But I'd settle for two thousand AC through a chair.'

He responded by slapping her with the back of his hand so she fell against the stairs.

'Where's my wife?' he snarled.

'Where's my dad?'

'You tell me, I'll tell you.'

'Fuck you.'

'I guess that must be a Chester family motto. Your late father said the exact same thing.'

A pitiful, gasping sob escaped her and Virginia hated that she couldn't stop it; Larry would only feed off her pain. She nearly lost control and rushed him then, but was amazed when some voice inside her blocked the impulse before it could become a suicidal action. It was almost as though her father had barked a military order for a tactical retreat.

'Okay,' Larry said, 'as a goodwill gesture, I'll go first. Your father is turning the sand red up the coast because I stuck a big knife in his guts. Now where's my wife?'

She tried not to react, keeping her venomous gaze locked on him, but she could feel the skin pinch around her eyes and the heat of imminent tears come into them. She would have sold her soul to Satan to feel the .357 in her hand at that moment. Bloodlust had made her not care any more. She tried to contemplate life without her father, but the concept was too huge, too alien.

'Don't start sniveling,' he warned. 'Just tell me where Hayley is and I'll leave you alone. That's all I want.'

'And when you find her?'

'I'm the one with the gun, bitch. I don't have to explain anything to you. And what's it to you, anyhow?'

'I care about her as much as you do,' Virginia said, testing the depth of his delusion with irony.

'So help me make it up with her.'

'Why? So she can visit you on Death Row? You killed my father. You don't get to live happily ever after.'

The reality check bowed his head briefly and the gun dropped with his focus. Virginia seized the moment. She kicked him backwards, turned and scrambled away, pulled by the lure of the .357 on her bed. Halfway up, the stairs zagged back above Larry's head. If she could just get past that point, his line of fire would be obscured, and when his blind rage made him stupidly follow after her, she would be waiting with a jacketed hollow-point or two.

She gained the bend and began up the second flight. It seemed like a miracle and she squeaked with terrified glee as Larry disappeared from her peripheral vision. She imagined it was her father keeping her safe, granting her winged feet while paralyzing the bastard who'd taken his life.

Then the stair carpet began spitting fibers. It was like a surreal movie set with some special effects man detonating harmless squibs at her feet. But these tiny explosions were not staying a step behind like they always did with Jason Statham. Virginia felt her hair flick as a round skimmed her scalp and embedded itself in the ceiling. Then her trailing calf took a hit that tripped her and sprawled her flat, elbows on the very last stair. She let out a guttural scream, more in fury and shock than pain, and knew the next shot would find an easy target – a whole torso. Larry would know he had stopped her progress, and the thump above him would have drawn his aim.

She heard him climbing the stairs. Maybe he wanted to place the shot more accurately; see the fear in her eyes. It was not something she could mask. She lay still and waited. Her leg was white hot, although she didn't expect the discomfort to last for more than a few seconds. She could sense him now standing behind her. What was he doing? Prolonging her mental agony? Or was his sick mind working through the pros and cons of finishing the job?

'You'll live,' he said. 'A through-and-through, as we call them.'

She rolled to face him, then looked at the darkening denim below her right knee and experienced the first shard of pain.

'What's up there?' Larry asked.

'The upstairs part of the house.'

'Don't be fucking obtuse. You know what I mean. I saw his cap. Your father owns – sorry, *owned* – a gun range. Are you telling me there are no guns in this house?'

She said nothing, which answered his question.

'And you weren't going for one?' he asked.

She wondered which would rile him the most: an obvious lie, or a brash truth that might be taken for defiance.

'I'd shoot you this second if I could.'

He smiled and nodded. 'Good. Honesty is good. You may yet need only one stick to get around. Now, we must be alone because you'd have woken the dead screaming like that. So, I'll ask just one more time. Where ... is ... Hayley?'

'Please, let me get something to tie round my leg to stop the bleeding, then I'll tell you what I know. There's a scarf in my bedroom.'

'This had better not be some trick.'

'It's not.'

He debated for a moment. 'Okay, go ahead.'

Favoring her left leg, Virginia slowly stood up. She gripped the banister rails, turned round and made it up to the landing.

'Nice ass,' he said, following. 'Very nice. Maybe if we have a little time later ...'

She glared back over her shoulder, eyes as fiery as the hole through her calf.

'You better be into necrophilia, pal, because that's the only way you're getting into my knickers.'

'Oh, don't fucking flatter yourself. Just move.'

Virginia continued staring for a few seconds then carried on limping towards her bedroom, leaving red splatters along the carpet. A satisfied smile crept unseen onto her face; however short-lived and token, she had just empowered herself. She halted at the open door. On the bed was her sketch pad, hiding the Magnum – empowerment that made a real difference.

'Okay if I go in?' she checked.

'Hey, it's your funeral if you try anything.'

She hobbled towards a chest of drawers opposite the foot of the bed, but she had no desire to reach it.

'I'll do it,' Larry said, unwittingly answering her prayer.

Virginia stopped, wobbled, and hopped her left foot to find balance.

'Which drawer contains the gun?' he asked knowingly.

'None. See for yourself. Listen, I need to sit down, I feel faint.' She flopped back onto the bed without waiting for his permission, instantly leaning back on her hands. She estimated the gun to be inches from her grasp.

Larry never took his eyes off her as he felt for the handle of the top drawer. He pulled until it came completely out of the chest and spilled its contents on the carpet. Still holding the handle, he threw the empty drawer to one side. He did the same with the three beneath, then kicked and trod his feet through the heap of clothes; nothing weighty had hit the floor but he wasn't taking any chances. Satisfied there was no weapon among them, he stepped to the window and indicated with a nod that Virginia could now search for a tourniquet.

Her fingers were so close to the revolver that she didn't want to move, but she had no choice. It was only luck that she wasn't dead already. With no staircase between them now, Larry would not miss. Reluctantly, she pushed herself to the edge of the bed and looked at the floor. She noticed her right sneaker was drenched, and either the sight of it or the actual volume of blood lost began to make her feel genuinely faint. She sifted hastily through the clothes, digging out a silk scarf no longer a ploy.

'I see you're a costume designer,' Larry said conversationally, approaching the bed.

Virginia gasped and held her breath, realizing he had spotted the sketches. Her search became frantic. If Larry discovered the gun underneath, she guessed her leg wound would not be her worst, but if he did let her live she did not want to bleed to death for the lack of basic first aid.

'Found it,' she said, and quickly tied the ends of the scarf together. She pulled the looped silk over her foot to above the knee, grabbed a hairbrush off the floor, slipped it inside the scarf and began to twist until the silk went tight, constricting her veins.

'Of course, it's not exactly my field of expertise,' Larry said, 'but I'd say you got a real talent.' He reached to pick up the pad. 'Yeah, these are – *fuck!*'

Virginia froze then something hard cracked the crown of her skull and pitched her onto the floor with a yelp. She scrambled away to the farthest wall and looked back at him, cowering.

'*You were gonna fucking kill me!*' he shouted crazily, shaking the Magnum in his fist. '*Bitch!*'

Virginia thought his indignation was somewhat hypocritical but kept her opinion to herself as a worrying calm descended on him and he aimed the old service pistol at her head.

'Kill me now and the trail goes cold,' she said.

'What?'

'Hayley's not staying here. If you kill me, that's it. You won't find her before the cops find you.'

He narrowed his eyes. 'Which would suit you just fine, huh?'

She risked a laugh, full of irony. 'You really think I'd die for Hayley? Much like you, I don't give a flying fuck about your wife. I've lost my father because of her and taken a bullet and I really fucking resent her for that. If I could turn the clock back – give her to you and save my father – I would. Before this morning I'd never even met the woman. You want to kill your wife, that's your business.'

Larry appeared thoroughly confused. 'So tell me where she is, for fuck's sake. I'll walk out of here, leave you alone. I'm not a bad person. Your father was going to shoot me; I was only acting in self-defense. And I had nothing to do with Marie's death.'

Virginia stared at him. 'Marie? Marie's dead?'

'Fucking framed me – shot herself in the fucking head.' Suddenly drained, he wilted against the empty chest of drawers, both guns pointing harmlessly down. 'Please, just tell me where Hayley is.

Why's that so difficult if you don't even like her? Come on ...'

Because Hayley wasn't alone, and Virginia knew that John would not simply stand aside when Larry requested he do so.

'I don't *know* where they've gone.'

'They? You mean the English guy? The Limey's with her? Shit, I knew it; I knew she was fucking around.'

Without the blood loss, shock and near-concussion, she might have been more circumspect, but at least she and Larry had finally found some common ground: they were both repulsed by the thought of Hayley and John together.

'Maybe you'd feel better if she was, but she's not,' Virginia said. 'He's my boyfriend, not Hayley's. It's a long story, but I guess you could say their families have known each other for years. It's not a boy-girl thing. It's more like brother-sister.'

Larry grunted. Miserably, he said, 'Shit, why can't she talk to me? Tell me these things?' which Virginia decided was best left rhetorical. Even to a professional counselor, this was one marriage way beyond salvation. Larry probably knew it himself, but she was not under any illusion that knowledge would halt his crusade. He had caused too much irreparable damage. There was no way back. Ultimately, he would be killed or jailed so what did he have to lose? However futile his goal, it might at least provide a few extra hours in which he could satisfy the basic human need to feel purposeful. Given a choice, who *would* want to go meekly? All of which made Virginia even more acutely aware of the danger she was in. Having promised information, she had just denied any knowledge of Hayley's whereabouts.

He suddenly made a move, but not towards her. He shoved the .357 down his pants, bent down beside the chair she had been sitting in to sketch, and stood up with her bag. His crazy-face was back, like he was about to unearth the Ark of the Covenant.

He tipped its contents onto the bed, the stun-gun among them, and Virginia cursed quietly as the word *payback* came to mind. But Larry ignored it, spreading the other bits and pieces with his fingers and selecting her cellphone.

'What's his name?' he asked with a hint of triumph.

'John, and he doesn't live here; he's on vacation. He doesn't even have a cell.'

After a momentary pause, Larry growled and hurled the phone at her, which she managed to deflect with her hand.

'*Then give me the name of his fucking hotel! Now!*' Larry screamed, storming across the bedroom to loom above her, the silencer's muzzle pressed cold against her forehead.

'Westwood!' she blurted, and felt an inch gap open between skin and steel.

His temper visibly cooled. 'Which hotel?'

'No, that's where they've gone.' She felt she was betraying John by talking, but she knew her death had been only seconds away, and such pure fear could free even the best-kept secrets. Besides, it was hardly the greatest scoop for Larry. Including the UCLA campus, Westwood was no small area to scour.

'Westwood,' he whispered, thinking.

'That's all she said,' Virginia added. 'She was behaving real odd, insisting he come some place with her like it was the most important thing in the world.'

The blossoming smile on Larry's face was interrupted by a ring on the front doorbell.

Assuming she was about to shout a warning, Larry clamped a palm over her mouth so forcefully that her head cracked the wall, making her eyes squeeze shut.

It was them. He could sense it. They were back. He had to

answer the door before they became suspicious waiting, but he didn't want to silence this woman permanently because she might make a good bargaining tool. Neither could he just leave her upstairs in case she grabbed a gun from somewhere. And he was loath to deliver a knockout blow because it might not simply knock her out; such finely-weighted violence belonged only to his wife's world of TV fiction. In real life, people died.

He had an idea and needed both hands free, but thought he could rely on his superior strength and her weakened state. With one hand still maintaining her silence, he de-cocked the silenced Smith & Wesson and slid it away, then used that hand to grab her hair and yank her up and onto the bed. She seemed to realize his intent at that moment because she began to struggle, but Larry reached for the stun-gun and hooked her thigh up to its million volts.

The doorbell sounded again. Larry climbed off her limp form, retrieved his gun from the carpet and popped the clip from the butt to check how many rounds were left. Three, and one chambered. Plus six in the Magnum down his pants. He slid the magazine back in and thumbed the hammer, then made his way quietly downstairs and crept to the front door where he looked through the security peephole. The fish-eye view of Joey DeCecco was not what he expected, but at least his day would not be a complete loss if his hunch about Westwood proved incorrect.

Wearing an anticipatory door-to-door salesman smile, DeCecco did not look exactly combat-ready. He would be as surprised to see his ex-partner as Larry was to see him, and Larry suddenly understood the deal: DeCecco was somehow in league with the late Dodge Chester.

The conspiracy against him was unbelievable. Larry was incensed. His life had been wrecked by that fucking soldier-boy outside. He was tempted to just open the door and pull the trigger but decided that would be too quick. With all DeCecco had done to him, Larry wanted to see pain in those eyes – the emotional pain of realizing that parenthood would be an extremely short-lived affair; that his wife would be a widow, his son left fatherless.

Larry snatched the door wide open and simply stared, relishing the shock in DeCecco's eyes. With a gun pointed at his heart, DeCecco stayed perfectly still. After a moment, he ventured a question.

'You gonna use that?'

'Already did. Hook out your piece, Joey – careful. Left hand.'

DeCecco awkwardly delved inside his jacket under his left arm, tugging the Browning Hi-Power from his shoulder rig. He pinched it harmlessly between his thumb and forefinger.

'Lay it on the step and back away,' Larry told him.

DeCecco was in no position to argue so surrendered his weapon and moved back a few paces. Larry picked it up and put it down his waist next to the Magnum. His pants were getting very tight.

'You thought I was dead, huh, Joey?'

'Why would I think that?'

'Sure, you don't know what the fuck I'm talking about, right?'

'That is right.'

Larry shrugged at the dumb act. 'You're too late.'

'For what?'

'I canceled his contract.'

DeCecco frowned. 'Contract? What? Whose?'

'I don't need you, Joey. I know where Hayley is. Westwood. Veteran Avenue. The cemetery. I'd bet my last dime on it. You failed. All of you.'

'Larry, I have no idea what you're talking about. Just put the gun down. I talked to Gilchrist and you're not in the trouble you thin–'

Larry fired four times point-blank into DeCecco's chest. DeCecco stumbled backwards and fell into a bed of shrubs, practically disappearing among the greenery.

Larry was fascinated by his own wickedness. Killing DeCecco marked the moment where his self-image aligned with the view he reckoned the world had of him. He could claim self-defense with the Armenians; he could claim a pre-emptive strike against Dodge; and, however thoroughly she had implicated him, he was truly innocent in the death of Marie Olsen.

But this was a coldly-calculated homicide. He stepped forward into the shrubs and kicked DeCecco gratuitously in the head. It was somehow more satisfying than the actual kill.

He now had to move fast. Although the shots had been muffled, the confrontation had happened in full view of the neighbors. None had come out to remonstrate, but who with half a brain would have done? Any sensible onlooker would have dialled 911, which meant a unit might already be on its way. He raced back inside and up the stairs. He needed Virginia. If the English guy refused an exchange, she would at least be a hostage for when the cops showed. It was the only reasoning he could apply – to anything. So much had gone wrong that his mind had delegated responsibility to his autopilot. It was all that stopped him from sinking to his knees and bawling. He couldn't even anticipate his reaction if he did find Hayley. Would he apologize to her or shoot her?

Virginia Chester was still lying inert on the bed, uttering low moans. He was glad now he had let her apply the tourniquet; she was no good to him dead. He discarded the empty Smith, lifted her over his shoulder and went carefully back downstairs, feeling her blood soaking into his shirt front where he held her legs.

Outside, he wasn't able to manage even a glance in DeCecco's direction and realized he didn't feel too proud of himself. He thought of Laura and the new-born waiting for daddy to visit. They were the ones who would really pay for the events of today. Despite his remorse, Larry didn't break his stride as he headed for the Jeep. His autopilot wasn't really designed to receive emotional input, only give out physical instructions. He dumped the woman out of sight on the floor behind the front seats, then climbed in and reversed onto Angelo Drive.

Chapter 36

Hayley's final direction to John was to pull over and switch off the engine. Although their destination was no longer a mystery, John did not experience an easing of tension. The vista of white headstones beyond the railing fence made him shiver, and Hayley's incongruous beaming smile somehow made it doubly morbid.

'This isn't the Universal Studios Tour,' he said, trying to lighten his own mood and change her eerie smile into laughter. The attempt failed on both counts. Hayley merely shifted her contented gaze from him to the cemetery before getting out of the car and waiting.

'In for a penny ...' John said to himself and followed suit. Neglecting to alarm the Audi, he joined her at the entrance. Hayley looked at him and her smile widened, which he hadn't thought possible.

'I usually bring a white rose,' she said, 'but you're here now.'

If that was meant to make sense it didn't, but John nodded rather than request a premature explanation he knew he wouldn't get. Hayley heaved an expectant sigh like they were about to enter Xanadu, then took his hand and led him into the cemetery. John soon realized she was not going to let go of him.

As they walked, he read several inscriptions either side of him. It began to play on his mind how inappropriate it was to be packing a gun in the midst of deceased war veterans. He now had a pretty good idea what Hayley was doing there, but it didn't make him any less confused about his own seemingly vital presence.

'Is your father buried here?' he asked gently.

She replied with a nod and kept on walking. A quarter mile in front, the traffic on the San Diego Freeway was moving steadily, throwing up a visible pall of pollution; an endless stream of lives passing each other by, never meshing except by way of a fender-bender. And what were the odds on that contact being significant to both parties, other than for reasons of personal injury or litigation? Not for the first time did the theory of coincidence seem a little weak, even to a stalwart skeptic like John.

After thirty seconds that seemed much longer for the silence in which it passed, Hayley stopped and offered the smile John had come to think of as intensely irritating. He tried to reciprocate but felt a major component was missing – happiness. If he'd believed in a sixth sense he would have been very worried by the alarm bells it had set off in his head. As it was, he put it down to the simple discomfort of being with a woman who appeared just as self-cozened as her grandfather had been. She nodded in response to nothing he had said, then led him off the path and through the headstones, until she stopped again and stared down at one commemorated by a dying white rose and a thoroughly lifeless bunch of red ones.

John took in the information before him.

HAROLD T OLSEN
MEDAL OF HONOR
SGT
US ARMY
VIETNAM
JUNE 1944
NOV 1969

'Kneel with me,' Hayley said, squeezing his hand.

John did so. The seconds dragged as he waited for Hayley to talk, but nothing came from her. He read the words to himself again.

'So young,' he said, purely to break the silence.

'Mmm,' she went, not looking at him.

'Not as young as most in that war, though.'

'You know a lot about Vietnam?'

'I've had an interest since the Legion. My old regiment was at Dien Bien Phu in fifty-four.'

'That's why the interest?' she queried doubtfully.

John gave her a confused look, and then thought he understood. 'Oh, you mean because of the business with Chuck when I was a kid. No, it can't be that, not even subconsciously; I didn't learn of the Vietnam connection until just recently.'

Hayley turned back to the headstone, but John thought her expression suggested a superior knowledge he would never possess. Her smugness galled him sufficiently to pull his hand away and speak bluntly.

'All right, enough. Talk. What am I doing here?'

Placidly, she said, 'You don't know?'

'No, I don't; how should I? God, Hayley, you nearly wreck my relationship with Virginia, you bring me here like you're about to reveal the second coming, then you expect me to throw my hands in the air and scream *hallelujah* like it all makes sense. Well, it doesn't!'

The first trace of disquiet appeared in her eyes. 'You don't feel at all strange being here?'

John was flashed back in time to 1978 and a lonely cabin in the Oregon wilderness. Hayley's words were almost a perfect echo of Chuck's at the moment when he first began to realize his young guest might not have shared the same vision as him. He couldn't pretend to grasp the situation any better now.

'Hayley ... I feel sad that your father died so young; I feel sorry you grew up without him; I feel sorry you got screwed up as a child, fell out with your mum and married a man who hurt you; but most of all ... most of all, I feel sorry you've been reduced to this.'

'To what?' she said warily.

'Clinging to a complete stranger for comfort.'

'I'm not. You're not a stranger.'

John got to his feet. 'Yes, I am. That's exactly what I am. Okay, there's a connection, and I admit it's pretty mind-boggling, but it doesn't change the fact that you and I had never met before today.'

'You can't walk away from this, John. You can't.'

'Listen, Hayley, I'm honored you brought me here, but if I stay you'll just make me argue with you, and I have too much respect for the sanctity of this place to do that. You're obviously a lot more open-minded than I am – most people are – but I'm happy in my ignorance. If you believe Chuck was some small-time Nostradamus, fine, that's your constitutional right as an American, but I don't have to listen to it. Now, I don't want to leave you here alone so, please, come back with me. Being here is only going to upset you.'

Hayley turned back to the headstone. 'Bullshit. I'm happier here than anywhere. And if you really had respect for the dead, John, you'd sit your ass back down and grant me five minutes of your precious time. You don't have to say anything, in fact I'd prefer it if you didn't – not until I've finished. And then if you still have nothing to say, you can go with my blessing and never see me again.'

John scanned across the stones until he located the Audi on the street. Its pull was strong. He pictured himself sitting behind the wheel with no one to his right, heading back to Beverly Glen and things he understood, like love and sex and a cold bottle of Bud. Then he looked back to Hayley, still staring straight ahead, her face cut and bruised, several teeth short of a decent smile, her plastered arm in a sling, and he really couldn't see any harm in giving her what she wanted.

Thankfully, Virginia had not received payback on a par. In his haste to answer the door, Larry had delivered a mere half-second shock, around four seconds less than she had given him. She guessed maybe ten minutes had passed since then because she was still dazed and experiencing muscle spasms, but it could have been longer if her previous trauma was delaying her recovery. But even in perfect health she would have found movement difficult. She was lying cramped in the rear foot-space of a speeding, swerving vehicle, which she recognized as the Jeep. Her head was on the driver's side, and her view under the seat showed Larry's legs operating the pedals. She squinted to focus on his right ankle; there seemed to be a patch of blood on his white sock. She wondered how it could have transferred from her calf. Maybe when he picked her up to bring her downstairs. But what was the shape inside the sock? Long, thin.

She closed her eyes against the onset of tears. Even with her brain still scrambled, she thought she knew what it was: the knife that had killed her father. In a way, it was her blood.

Hatred like this had never before been a factor in her life. It belonged to the film scripts she read. She finally understood her father's illness since Vietnam; the desire to kill consumed her like a demonic possession. If she had been able, she would have ripped Larry's beating heart from his chest. A gun was too removed, too clinical. She literally wanted his blood on her hands.

She tried to order her thought processes to coincide with reality. In her current position, Larry's death happening any time before her own was a pipe dream, never mind it happening by her decree. She had been shot and stunned already. Now she was lying in a confined space, fearful of any movement that might attract his attention and warrant more of his discipline. What further use did he have for her? Was she a kind of surety? She had no doubt she was expendable.

It seemed wise to keep still, play dead. He would find a pulse if he checked for one, but, providing he didn't suspect a bluff, he would hopefully assume she was unconscious and leave her there while he went off to roam Westwood. Then she could raise the alarm and get medical help. She looked at Larry's blood-stained sock again and prayed it work out that sweetly, although hearing on the evening news how some SWAT team had finally taken the bastard out would still be second best to doing it herself. Unfortunately, the worsening pain in her leg was making it harder by the second to keep her face immobile. If he looked at her for long enough, no way would he miss the involuntary muscular tics that betrayed her true state.

She closed her eyes to begin practising, but her lids had barely touched when they opened again – wide. Something fantastic had registered. Something unbelievable. Something in the shadow beneath the driver's seat.

Her father's holstered Walther P99.

Obediently settling cross-legged to listen, John suddenly became aware of how in the midst of death he was. Not just now, in this cemetery, but ever since touching down at LAX. With the exception of Virginia, he had not encountered anyone who wasn't dead, dying, responsible for the death of others, or fearful of their own violent death. Hayley had probably brought him here to announce she thought he was the Grim Reaper incarnate, cutting a swathe through the city.

'Okay, John. Now … I don't want to hear a word until I'm done. I mean it. Don't even tut, roll your eyes or shake your head.'

'Wait a minute,' he said. He checked nobody was near, then took the concealed .45 from his waist and hid it under a knee. 'That's better, I couldn't breathe.'

'What is that for?' Hayley asked, displeased.

'Your Larry may not be the brightest bulb in the hallway, but if he knows about this place he may turn up. Does he?'

Hayley nodded. 'But he's never been here before.'

'Has he ever been this keen to find you?'

She acquiesced with a shrug.

'Okay, let's hear it,' he said.

Hayley glanced meaningfully at the headstone once more, and began.

'I'm gonna list the facts as you've told them to me, John, like a lawyer in a courtroom. First off, there's grandpa building his cabin, waiting all that time for *the one*. There's the word *vision* on the calendar, the days crossed off. Then you arrive, he gives you my picture and tells you to keep it safe, no matter what. After that, he believes he has no reason to live, which means he'd been staying alive for you, John, for your visit. As you grow up, you actually do what he says. You take my picture everywhere with you. When you think about it, that's incredible. Kids don't do that. Kids lose things, or they get torn, neglected. But you keep it safe, like a part of you knows how precious it is, and what significance it might have for the future.'

John was impressed by his willpower. How he didn't interrupt was a mystery in itself.

'You join the army. You go to the Persian Gulf and meet Donnie Chester. Years later and his death links you to Dodge. You decide to take a road trip to Oregon. Miraculously, you manage to locate the ghost town where you met Grandpa Chuck. Not only that, but you find his cabin and his personal effects, among them a letter from Dodge. I mean, *hello*, is this becoming a little bizarre or what? So you confront Dodge with the goods and he opens up to you about his past. You, a complete stranger; the first person in over forty years he talks to. Next, you track down my mom, and you told me how oddly *she* kept looking at you. Then you meet me and you wind up taking care of me, protecting me. You kiss me, you can't help it, but you don't know why. You admit to an obsession with Vietnam and to feeling at home in the States after years of *wanderlust*. John ... need I say more?'

'Yeah, you better had. I have no idea where this is leading.'

'Okay, what about the bust-up with your parents? You understand now why that had to happen?'

'Nope.'

'It was karma. You had to be released from them to follow your true path in life, to join the Foreign Legion so you could meet Donnie and the people who matter to you on a spiritual level, not a biological one.'

John found his eyes wanting to roll manically. He fixed them on a single blade of grass as a counter-measure.

'You are truly blessed, John. Most people *never* break those constraints.'

She left a long enough pause that John thought he should respond.

'Karma?' he asked.

'Yes, thank you,' Hayley said gently.

'No, I meant ... what you said. With a kay not a cee.'

'Oh.'

'I don't believe in karma.'

'You don't need to, John. It exists whether you believe in it or not.'

He took a deep breath. She was really starting to bug.

'Tell me how you feel,' she asked.

'About what?'

'Everything. Weren't you listening?'

He smiled crookedly. 'Well, none of it's news, is it? As you said, it's all stuff I told you.'

'But I bet you never put it all together; heard it in one big lump before?'

John scowled. 'Why do I get the feeling you're about to add two and two and make twenty-two?'

Hayley became instantly peeved. She blew theatrically through her gapped front teeth like a Prima Donna ignored at the stage door, and began nearly screaming.

'*God*, you are so *closed!* Can't you see it? It's as clear as day! It's staring you in the face! *Look!*' She pointed to the gravestone. '*There!*'

From Angelo Drive onto Briarwood, all the way down North Beverly Glen Boulevard onto Sunset Boulevard to skirt the northern perimeter of the UCLA campus, Larry drove in a manner befitting his mental state. He barreled along, overtaking, undertaking, and paying no attention to red lights or rich folk out for a cruise. A Ferrari leaving the grounds of the Bel-Air Country Club narrowly escaped a visit to the body shop. Larry knew his behavior was likely to attract unwanted attention, but any traffic cop who tried to cite him for a moving violation would have his own movement terminally violated. All he cared about was getting to Hayley as fast as possible.

At the north-west corner of the campus he took a screeching left onto Veteran Avenue before immediately reducing his speed. The cemetery was coming up and he didn't want to alert Hayley's English minder, who he had to assume was still armed. He gave another quick glance behind between the seats, and reckoned his hostage had not minutely altered her position. She hadn't moaned for over five minutes either. It didn't look good. Then again, what did? And so what if she was dead? Years from now, when all his appeals had failed and they finally strapped him to the gurney and hooked up the IV, what would they do? Double-dose his lethal injection?

He slowed and edged into the curb. The rows of white stones made him shiver. He couldn't spot Hayley, but perhaps she was one of the more distant figures he could see. Getting a fix on her was essential. If he didn't, they could leave from one end of the cemetery while he was still wandering around the opposite end. To make that less likely he needed to cover the widest area possible from one vantage point. He moved off and stopped the Jeep further along. He vaguely noted the brand new red Audi parked nearby, and he thought of his own treasured Corvette, a pleasure extinct to him now. It was his own stupid fault, but knowing it did not provoke any self-recrimination, it only made him want to kill someone else. There was nothing left apart from that. He looked back at the body behind him on the floor.

'Hey, bitch, wake up.'

She didn't stir so he jabbed a punch at her ribs, but there was still no reaction. He knew the effects of the stun-gun would have largely worn off by now, which meant her tourniquet hadn't worked so well. It seemed she had lost too much blood and passed out. She was in dire need of medical treatment.

'Ah, fucking bleed out,' Larry said, facing front. He put on his

Raiders cap and sunglasses and set his eyes to the task of visually sweeping the cemetery, trying to ignore the possibility that he was wrong, that Hayley and friend were in some bar in the village. He decided to give it a few minutes, then take a meandering walk among the stones. Perhaps he would stumble across them both kneeling in quiet remembrance. If not, he would have to embark upon a systematic search of Westwood's watering holes and restaurants. He removed the two handguns from where he had stashed them under his thighs for easy access in case of a police traffic stop.

Before he got out, a realization dawned. Although he couldn't remember a conscious decision, somewhere between the hills and the cemetery he had made up his mind. Of the two options open to him, apologizing to Hayley was not his preferred choice.

'Harold T Olsen,' John read out loud from the headstone. 'Medal of Honor, Sergeant, US Army, Vietnam, June nineteen forty-four to November nineteen sixty-nine.'

He screwed up his eyes, trying to appear more ponderous than he felt; after her last reprimand he didn't want to be accused of glibness. But the truth was that he found this particular inscription no more or less sad than any other. Thousands were buried here. The only difference was his knowing a little of Harry Olsen's history.

Hayley's expression was a mix of cranky and desperate. She was obviously waiting for his *eureka,* so he read it all again to himself, slowly, like a child having difficulty with a math sum.

'Well?' Hayley said.

John abandoned his false effort. 'Sorry if I'm being thick, but I don't know what on earth you want me to say.'

Her frustration had her teetering on the brink of another outburst, then she closed her eyes and seemed to employ some yogic breathing technique. After a few seconds she looked at him and smiled, but John doubted the serenity went very deep.

'Okay, John ... okay ... answer me this: in conversation today, have you mentioned how old you are?'

John thought back. He had crammed practically his entire life story into the journey from the hospital to Beverly Glen that morning, but he couldn't recall giving his age. There hadn't been any reason to.

'Don't think so,' he said.

'You haven't,' she assured him. 'So how do I know you were born in nineteen seventy? You were, weren't you?'

He nodded, then shrugged. 'Probably because I look my age.'

'Because it fits, John. It fits. It all fits.'

'Twenty-two,' John said provocatively, deliberately attempting to rile her because she was starting to piss him off with her renewed zeal.

Hayley made a face. 'Huh? Twenty-two?'

He smiled at her confusion and stood up, tucking the .45 back in his belt. He was adamant she would not persuade him to sit down a third time.

'Two plus two. It's what I knew you'd come up with. Now you either tell me why you think I'm here in the next five seconds, or I'm leaving.'

It blurted out from her like vomit.

'Young people who die violent deaths often come back quickly.'

Her explanation had to sink in. Once it had, he gave a harsh, incredulous laugh.

'You mean *reincarnation*?'

'My father died November sixty-nine,' she said, getting to her feet. 'Two months before I was born. I was his only child and he never saw me. We all go around with the same people time after time, we just don't know it. But Chuck knew it. He had a vision. He knew you were coming back to find me. Unfinished business, John, that's what this is about.'

John stared at her, uncertain whether to be amused or horrified. Hayley must have thought he was captivated by the awesome truth.

'You see, John, how it all makes sense? Doesn't it feel good after all these years to finally know why it all happened?'

'What are you saying?' John asked.

'John … I'm your daughter; Chuck was your father.'

After a split second to absorb this newsflash, John began cackling, and such hysterics were clearly mistaken for The Joy of Universal Understanding because Hayley, with tears streaming, went to hug him with her one good arm. But he stepped back, not even a mocking smile on his face now. What was she doing, involving him in her warped fantasies? She had jeopardized his relationship with Virginia for this crap?

'You, my girl, are nuttier than a bucket of squirrel shit.'

Hayley's features sagged. 'But what about Dodge? Why did he open up to you unless some part of him knew who you really were?'

'*Because he was ready!*' John said, his frustration dictating his tone of voice. 'Fuck's sake. Donnie died and he flipped his lid. He was ready to talk and he talked to me precisely because I *am* a stranger. Don't you have the Samaritans over here? It's the same principle.'

'What about my mom?' Hayley asked weakly.

'What about her?'

'The way she was looking at you.'

'No idea. Squirrel shit, I expect.'

Some impulse made her try to hug him again, and John retreated further.

'I'm not your fucking dad, Hayley! Okay? Jesus … get some help.'

He turned and walked away, and she didn't bother chasing after him.

It was a good thing Larry had told her to wake up first. Had he simply punched her without notice, Virginia thought the shock alone would have made her squeak or jolt or both. After that, she decided to keep her eyes open. If his feet moved it might indicate him turning round to punch again, and she would have a vital couple of seconds to steel herself. More than that, the sight of the nine mil under the seat gave her hope. Perhaps she could save the LAPD SWAT budget the expenditure of at least one round. In an ideal world where she wasn't lying on her arms, she might have been able to empty the clip up through his ass to blow out the top of his skull.

'Peek-a-boo, I see you,' Larry whispered, interrupting her daydream and nearly stopping her heart. She tensed, awaiting his punishment for her deception, but his feet had not shifted and Virginia guessed his focus was outside the vehicle. He had found what he came for, and she was overwhelmed by a selfish relief when he got out. The sudden absence of evil was palpable, like a malignant tumor had been excised. But if she didn't move fast, someone else would be struck down and that someone could be John. She shifted awkwardly to free her arms and immediately loosened the tourniquet, letting fresh blood flush her limb to prevent the onset of necrosis. The wound was not haemorrhaging so badly, so she let it be, leaving the silk loose. Staying low in case Larry glanced back at the Jeep, she reached under the driver's seat and grabbed the holstered Walther. She pulled it out and checked the magazine and could barely contain her tears – empty. She pulled back the slide, praying that her father had left a round in the chamber. She was an excellent shot. Carefully placed, one bullet would be enough.

'*No!*'

How much time did she have to formulate an alternative plan, if she could even think of one? She peeked over the window to see where Larry was in relation to John and Hayley and just caught the bastard stealing some flowers from a grave. She could see her own blood on his shirt and the two guns tucked down his waist, and then they vanished behind the spray of mixed blooms. Looking past him further into the cemetery she spotted his targets, who were too concerned with each other to notice Larry, now slowly walking along the main path towards them. John was standing up talking to Hayley, the cause of this whole damned mess. Even from a distance their body-language suggested some kind of disagreement. Suddenly, John threw his arms up and backed away from her and started hurriedly towards the same path Larry was on, prompting Larry to veer off and kneel at a stranger's grave.

Seeing that he was laying an ambush, Virginia became frantic. She could think of only one drastic solution. Larry had left the keys in the ignition. She would have to get behind the wheel, crash through the fence and aim the Jeep straight for him. If she missed, she would have at least alerted John to the danger. The ghastly thought of driving over graves and destroying headstones was relegated by her desire to save the man she loved. She crawled out from the back and opened the driver's door to climb in.

As she did, a metallic rattling made her halt. It was a sound she knew well, and right now she believed it was heaven-sent. Holding her breath, she looked in the door compartment and saw them: a handful of nine millimeter rounds.

Chapter 37

John would never forget this day. Walking briskly, he kept shaking his head, trying to negate what Hayley had said. Although he believed it was utter nonsense, she had not entirely failed to get through. By merely saying it she had planted a seed. He didn't expect it would germinate if he lived to be a hundred, but it would always be there.

Eager for a quick getaway from all this insanity, he took the car keys from his pocket, hooking a finger through the metal loop that connected the key to the alarm fob. Nearing the street, he passed a man in a baseball cap who was laying some flowers, but paid him no heed.

It was the woman making an ungainly dash along the sidewalk towards the gate who stopped him in his tracks.

'Virginia?' he said to himself.

She was limping badly, her right leg crimson from the knee down, a frenzied look on her face and a semi-automatic in her hand. The Grand Cherokee was parked just along the street, but there was no sign of either Dodge or Marie. Virginia pushed through the gate, gesticulating wildly and silently, and John understood the threat was immediate and close by – the man in the baseball cap.

John grabbed the .45 from his belt and began to spin round but Virginia had already screamed his name out loud and John realized he would be too late.

He was bringing the barrel up when Larry opened fire.

All Virginia's emotions bar one demanded she look to John. Her strength of love for this man was out of all proportion to the time they had known each other, and now he had taken a hit. Larry had got his shot off before John, and his aim had been true. Her boyfriend jerked with the impact, dropped his weapon and sunk to his knees. Had she taken her eye off Larry for even a second, he would have swung round and shot her before she had a chance to reacquire him.

But her hatred for Larry at that moment was greater than her love for John. She kept the bead on his heart and squeezed the trigger.

After an instant of stunned horror, Hayley began running, an agonized wail trailing from her mouth. She ran not from danger but into it. She felt possessed, all concern for her own safety gone. She believed she had just watched the man she had come to hate kill the man she had loved all her life, just yards from the spot where the bones of his old life lay buried. The pain was too intense to allow any rational thought. She only knew that Larry had to die for what he had done and she would use her bare hands to make it happen, and if a bullet from his gun meant she failed to close the gap in time then she would at least be with John in Heaven. It really didn't matter; Hell would always be waiting for Larry whoever dispatched him there.

The hammer fell, but the Walther did not kick in her hand. Heart thrashing, Virginia gasped and made to eject the dud round.

Even as she did it, she knew it was a forlorn action. She would never find out if the next round in the stack was any more potent. Her misfortune had provided Larry with the crucial advantage. In what seemed like slow motion, the slide came back and the dud flipped out.

Robert De Niro in *Taxi Driver*. That's who he was. He wasn't John Frears, he was Travis Bickle with a hole through his neck, only this was a disappointing remake in which Travis signally failed to clear the scum off the streets before getting shot himself. Larry was still upright, unhurt, and putting the good guys down.

John cried out as he watched Virginia spin through 360 degrees and hit the ground. She immediately began to writhe, clawing at her left shoulder, but that didn't mean she'd escaped with her life. If the slug itself hadn't caused mortal damage, it might have made secondary missiles out of bone fragments, the smallest of which in the wrong place could prove fatal. One thing he knew for sure: from the state of her jeans leg, she certainly couldn't afford to lose very much more blood from this new wound.

As his lamentable cry faded, John became aware of another sound of human torment. He turned to see Hayley tearing along the path, uttering a shrill outpouring of grief as other visitors to the cemetery scattered in every direction *but* the one she was taking. Then he locked eyes with Larry, who was again directing the Browning his way. Larry looked nervous, and John foolishly glanced down at the pistol lying on the ground beside his right knee.

'Shit,' he mouthed, suspecting he had just signed his own death warrant; to effectively deal with Hayley, Larry would have to eliminate all other threats, and John knew he had just declared a hostile intention by looking at the .45.

A calmness born of resignation came over him. Damn, he wouldn't even come close to reaching it. His right hand was clasped to his leaking neck, and, even had he been ambidextrous, Virginia's car keys and alarm fob were in his left hand, still slipped tightly around his finger like a wedding ring.

John saw the skin pinch around Larry's eyes, the subtle link between the brain's impulse and his trigger finger's response.

One final flash of inspiration: before Larry could squeeze the trigger, John squeezed his left hand tight shut.

'*Armed!*' said a lifelike voice from the street.

In panicked confusion, Larry's head whipped round, gun barrel scanning for the source – perhaps a SWAT commander with a loudhailer.

John took the opportunity to grab for the .45 as Hayley collided full force with her husband.

It was a bad time to lose focus. John felt his head swimming, his vision blurring, his breath beginning to labor. These were no doubt natural reactions to getting holed through the neck, but another sixty seconds without them would have been nice.

He tried to keep his gun trained on the wrestling match in front of him. They were lying on their sides like lovers in the park, but it looked like Hayley was trying to bludgeon Larry to death with her plastered arm. If they separated sufficiently, John hoped he might pick off the villain while he could still differentiate between them, but having failed to daze him with the initial contact, Hayley was soon overcome, Larry slamming the base of the Browning's butt hard against her forehead.

As she went limp, John thought about risking a shot, but Larry's sense of self-preservation was well developed. He pulled his wife close, using her as a shield. Now it was John who needed some cover, so he scrambled away towards the nearest gravestone. He felt guilty leaving Virginia out in the open and vulnerable, but knew that any attempt to drag her to safety would have made them both sitting ducks. A bullet clipped the stone as he hid behind it, proving the wisdom of his decision; Larry had clearly not finished shooting at people.

Trying to recoup his senses, John summoned all his willpower to battle the debilitating effects of his injury, then peeked out to check on things. It was dangerous, but less so than making assumptions about where Larry had got to; it would take only seconds for him to creep up and poke his gun around the stone.

Larry, however, was sticking with the hostage option. He had rolled Hayley so they were in a spoons position, her back to his front, and he was now struggling to get her onto her knees. With Larry's gun arm busy, John took up an offensive position on his belly, thrusting the .45 towards his target with two hands. Keeping as much of himself behind the stone as possible, it left Larry with little to aim at.

Managing to achieve a kneeling position for Hayley that protected his own, Larry braced her in front of him with an arm across her breasts, then turned the gun to her temple.

'I'm not fucking around here, John Boy! If you don't throw out the gun, let me leave with Hayley, I'll kill her!'

John didn't have the energy to reply. With his mind drifting further from him, he wanted desperately to close his eyes. He didn't have any answers. He shrugged to himself, mentally more than physically; if he passed out, perhaps he'd wake up in hospital with Virginia in the next room, both of them on the road to recovery.

But where did that leave Hayley? He didn't think he should mind, but he did.

'Okay, how about this?' Larry called. 'You don't back off, I shoot your girlfriend again. I don't think she can take another round, do you?'

A brief burst of siren was followed by an amplified announcement.

'You in the cemetery! Let go of the woman, lay your weapon on the ground and walk towards me, hands in the air!'

A narrow view through the stones revealed to John a single black-and-white on Veteran Avenue. One of the cops was behind the hood of the car with his Glock drawn, speaker-mike to his mouth. His partner had maneuvered to just inside the cemetery, using a trash can for cover.

'Drop your weapon! Move away from the woman!'

John gathered he had gone unnoticed, and he certainly wasn't about to reveal himself and surrender his weapon. His extra firepower might mean the difference between a quick conclusion and one more prolonged and more problematic; although Larry's bullet had passed through his neck on a miracle route, avoiding carotid arteries, trachea and larynx, John knew he was in the same boat as Virginia: without fairly swift medical attention, he would likely bleed to death.

The cop shouting orders had now abandoned the mike to take up his partner's position, since his partner had moved forward to the first row of headstones, close to where Virginia lay. He leaned out to reach her but Larry fired a warning shot to dissuade him.

John looked back down the sights, concentrating on keeping his aim steady, his mind sharp. The trauma of his wound pretty much dictated against that – the shock, the feel of his life literally draining from him, the blood cooling on his skin when it should have been warm within.

Larry spoke to him again, and his softer tone showed he might have been mad but he wasn't deluded. He knew this was the end of the line.

'Hey, John?'

Although he would give himself away to the cops by answering, John thought dialog would be more constructive than letting a lethal tension build in the continuing silence.

'What is it?'

The cop by the grave turned his head sharply to look at John. Eyes wide and anxious, he wavered for a moment but decided his weapon was still best employed covering Larry.

'*We got another wounded over here!*' the cop shouted to his partner. '*He's armed!*'

Larry had rested his brow on Hayley's shoulder and seemed now to be hugging her as a wife rather than holding her as a hostage.

'What is it, Larry?' John asked. 'What's on your mind?'

Larry looked up, and the nearest cop let out a startled curse.

'Shit, Roth. *It's Larry Roth!*'

'Fame,' Larry said bitterly to his wife. 'It's not all it's cracked up to be.'

'*Larry, put the weapon down, we can work this out!*' the cop called.

'I don't think so,' Larry responded. 'I know how this deal goes down. No point me requesting an airplane and five mill in used bills. I've been a cop too long to believe shit like that happens. I ain't leaving here except in a body bag. One minute from now, SWAT's gonna be staring at me through scopes.'

'So give up,' John said to him. 'Now, before that happens. You didn't kill anyone yet.'

Larry smiled and began laughing. 'Oh, John, you are *way* behind the times. I give up now, the state's gonna put me to sleep. So maybe I should have some fun first, whaddya think?'

'Larry, I'm Officer Reinhardt! Let's all calm down. Just –'

Larry loosed off another wild shot in Reinhardt's direction, then yelled at him.

'That was very fucking rude! I ain't talking to you, I'm talking to John here. Shut the fuck up!' He quietened down and continued his conversation. 'John, if you hadn't gotten involved, stolen Hayley away from me, I wouldn't have had to do any of this shit. This whole thing was none of your fucking business.'

By now, Hayley had come round from her pistol whipping, so Larry no longer had to support her dead weight with his left arm. He put the muzzle back to her temple and slipped his left hand between their bodies, producing the Magnum, which he pointed across at Virginia.

'Okay, John, you enjoy making decisions that affect other people's lives? Make one now. Your girl or Hayley. One dies. Your choice. You can't decide – both die.'

It was the ultimate nightmare, except John was not about to wake up from it. He looked from one pair of pleading eyes to another, from Hayley to Virginia, back to Hayley, and again to Virginia, until he couldn't take it any more and stared down at the bloody grass beneath his dripping neck.

'So,' Larry said. 'Which bitch, John? You got ten seconds.'

Ten years would not have been long enough. John could never passively sacrifice an innocent like that. In theory the choice was simple: one dead or two. But either way John knew his own existence would be forever blighted. If he chose to save Virginia, their future together was forfeit. The knowledge of the terrible price paid would undermine all potential for happiness. And if he spared Hayley, he would hate her as much as he hated himself.

But if he let them both die he would feel doubly responsible, always believing a truly courageous man would have chosen to save at least one life regardless of his own mental tortures in the years to come. Of course, that was assuming Larry wasn't bluffing, intending to kill both women whatever he said. The guy was crazy; there was no saying what he might do.

For John, it was a genuine no-win situation, the psychology of which Larry understood perfectly well. He had already said: this was his idea of fun.

Larry's countdown was nearing an end and John made a decision. He lifted his head, sighted as best he could, and fired. Larry squealed as the bullet tore through his outstretched forearm, making him drop the .357. He gritted his teeth, then bared them at John in a lunatic snarl. He removed the Browning from Hayley's temple and forced the barrel into her mouth, then placed his head directly at the back of hers.

He was going to dissolve their marriage with a single bullet, and John was helpless to prevent it.

Larry's skull exploded a second before the shot rang out. It took a moment for his muscles to register the destruction of his nervous system, then he crumpled onto the grass.

Bizarrely, Hayley was left unscathed, her mouth still wide from where the barrel had fallen out of it. Her long moan cut through the deadly lull as she opened her eyes and realized she was going to see another dawn.

John watched, not understanding for a moment. Then it began to make sense. Larry had lost the side of his skull, not the back, and the sound of the gunshot had followed its very visible effects. Someone had taken him out from a distance. A wet job. The two cops stayed down, eyes darting here and there, searching for the shooter. John looked over at Virginia and saw she wasn't moving. He left his gun on the grass, crawled over and lay down beside her. The approaching sirens meant he couldn't hear any breathing. He felt for her hand and held it tightly.

'Marry me?' he whispered, praying for a response. 'Ginny?'

'Sure.'

John grinned. If he died now, it wouldn't be so bad. He wondered idly if there were any spaces available nearby. He was a veteran, after all.

'You couldn't choose, could you?' Virginia asked, her voice soft, like she was at the border of dreamland.

'I did choose.'

'You didn't. It's okay, though. You did the right thing. It worked out.'

'I trusted he wouldn't kill his wife. I knew he'd kill you. I had to take the shot.'

She squeezed his hand, but he barely felt it. Either his senses were fading, or her strength. Probably it was both.

'You did good, *sergent*. You did.'

The winter sun on John's face was suddenly blocked.

'Hang in there,' said the silhouetted Officer Reinhardt. 'EMS is here now.'

'Who shot Larry?' Virginia asked whoever might know, but no one did.

John closed his eyes and finally gave in to unconsciousness.

TWO MONTHS LATER
EPILOG

'Who is it?'

'Hayley, for you.'

Ginny smiled knowingly, took the phone from him and sat down on the sofa.

'How's it going, girl?'

John sat opposite so he could watch her. He never tired of watching her. When he awoke in the night, he even watched her while she slept. He supposed he experienced the same joy being with her as Hayley did with him. Reincarnation wasn't the only way to come back from the dead. They had only just survived that day in the cemetery, Ginny's heart stopping on the way to the hospital before a miraculous act of resuscitation.

He stared at the diamond solitaire on her finger. It still seemed remarkable that she wanted it there. An engagement ring – from him. In a world full of people, how could she have chosen him to spend her life with? It felt like another miracle. But that was just love doing its thing.

There was no rivalry between the two women any more. Larry had bound the three of them together. It was difficult to harbor resentment after such a close call, and John could even laugh now when Hayley occasionally called him Dad. She made out it was only to wind him up, but she had never backtracked from her original beliefs. It didn't matter, though. Her views did no one any harm, and if they made her happy ...

Ginny roared with laughter. 'Good on you, girl! Go for it!'

John didn't need to know the conversation to laugh along. Love was like that. The more he learned about his fiancée, the more he found her to be an amazing individual. He admired her resilience, her unfailing support of her father over many difficult years, and her stoical acceptance of his passing. She was still mourning, but death would not screw her up as it had Dodge, and John was learning from her that he could also leave his past behind.

'Keep me posted, Hayley, take care.' She set the phone down and raised her eyebrows at him. 'That director I introduced her to? They hit it off, big time, in more ways than one.'

Hayley would have been gratified to hear John respond like a concerned father.

'It's not a case of the casting couch, is it?'

'Not this guy, he's cool. Mind you, that's not to say her career won't benefit.'

'Thanks, darling.'

'For what?'

'Helping.'

'She deserved a break.'

He was getting up for a cuddle, and whatever might follow on from that, when the doorbell rang. He diverted himself down the hallway and opened the door to a man in a brown uniform, carrying a small packet and a letter.

'Sign, please.'

John obliged, and the UPS man walked briskly back to his truck. John shut the door on a balmy Angelo Drive and returned to the living room.

'What's that?' Ginny asked.

'Don't know,' he said, and proceeded to tear open the envelope. He took out the letter and unfolded it. 'It's on headed notepaper. A Ranger station in Big Timber, Montana. It says: "Wasn't sure whether or not to send this, but thought you might like some answers. I'll keep it short. I relocated here with my wife and new-born son a month back. Before that, I was with the LAPD. I prefer it up here in bear country. Not so dangerous. Bears don't carry Uzis! The only vest I've worn since arriving is thermal against the cold. Different from LA, where Kevlar was a way of life – thank God. I'd have suffered more than a brief concussion without it".'

John paused to give Ginny a baffled look.

'Go on,' she said.

'"If this doesn't completely make sense, then what's in the box might. I had it specially engraved."'

Ginny put her hand out and John gave her the packet to open. It was small, the size of a jewellery box that might contain a bracelet or a pendant. She removed the brown wrapping. It was a jewellery box. She hinged back the lid and stared at the contents, and, gradually, a smile began to appear.

John couldn't see what it was, so she handed it back to him.

A 7.62 caliber rifle brass, highly polished, with two initials engraved on the side: *"L.R."*

'Who sent it?' Ginny asked.

'The letter's not signed.'

Her smile broadened. 'Fancy a road trip?'

'Big Timber, Montana?'

Author photograph by Jade Pepper.

By now, Mark Pepper really should be on his fourth wife and in rehab at some idyllic retreat in the foothills of the Santa Monica Mountains. Graduating from RADA in 1990, he believed he would be a Hollywood star by the time the U.S. hosted the World Cup four years later. It didn't work out that way.

His acting career was spasmodic, to say the least. There were high points: peeing on the Aidensfield Arms hearth-fire in the first-ever episode of *Heartbeat*; taking Lulu hostage in the Christmas special ten years later; acting with icons like Tom Bell and Helen Mirren; and popping up in *Coronation Street* several times. But there were vast deserts of unemployment between these little oases and Mark quickly turned to writing as an alternative source of expression.

His first novel, *The Short Cut*, was published in hardcover by Hodder & Stoughton in 1996 and in paperback by Hodder's New English Library in 1997, and his second novel, *Man on a Murder Cycle*, was released by the same publisher hardcover in 1997 and paperback in 1998.

Since then, Mark has had a host of jobs, but for the past decade has been a Client Intelligence Analyst, which he likes mostly because he can genuinely tell people he's CIA.

After spending seven years living in Murcia with his (first) wife and daughter, he recently returned to the UK as he missed the dull skies, frequent downpours, and especially road-rage.

He is delighted to have been adopted by the Urbane family, and is looking forward to his resurrected writing career.

Urbane Publications is dedicated to
developing new author voices, and publishing
fiction and non-fiction that challenges, thrills and
fascinates.

From page-turning novels to innovative
reference books, our goal is to publish what
YOU want to read.

Find out more at
urbanepublications.com